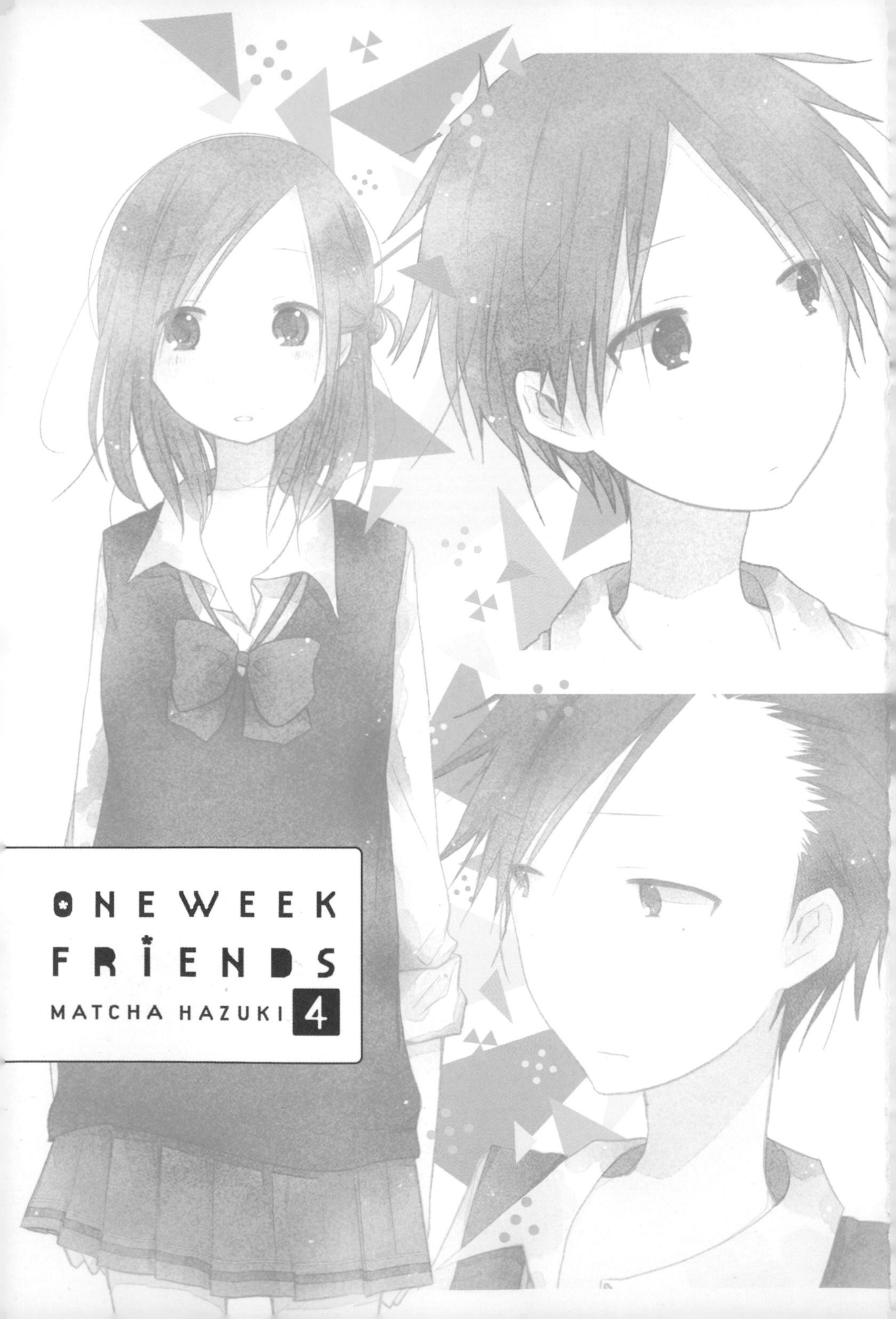
ONE WEEK
FRIENDS
MATCHA HAZUKI
4

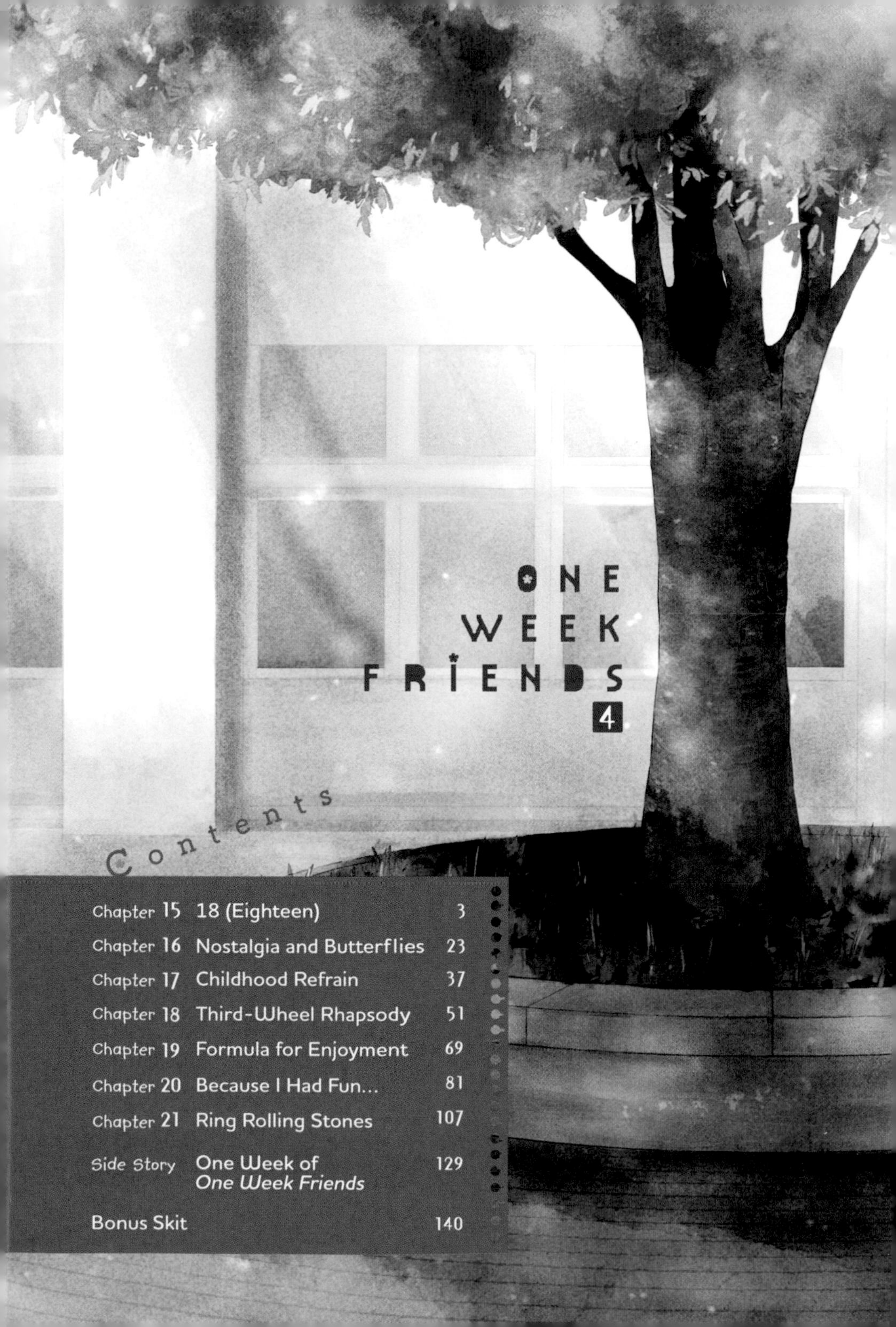

ONE WEEK FRIENDS 4

Contents

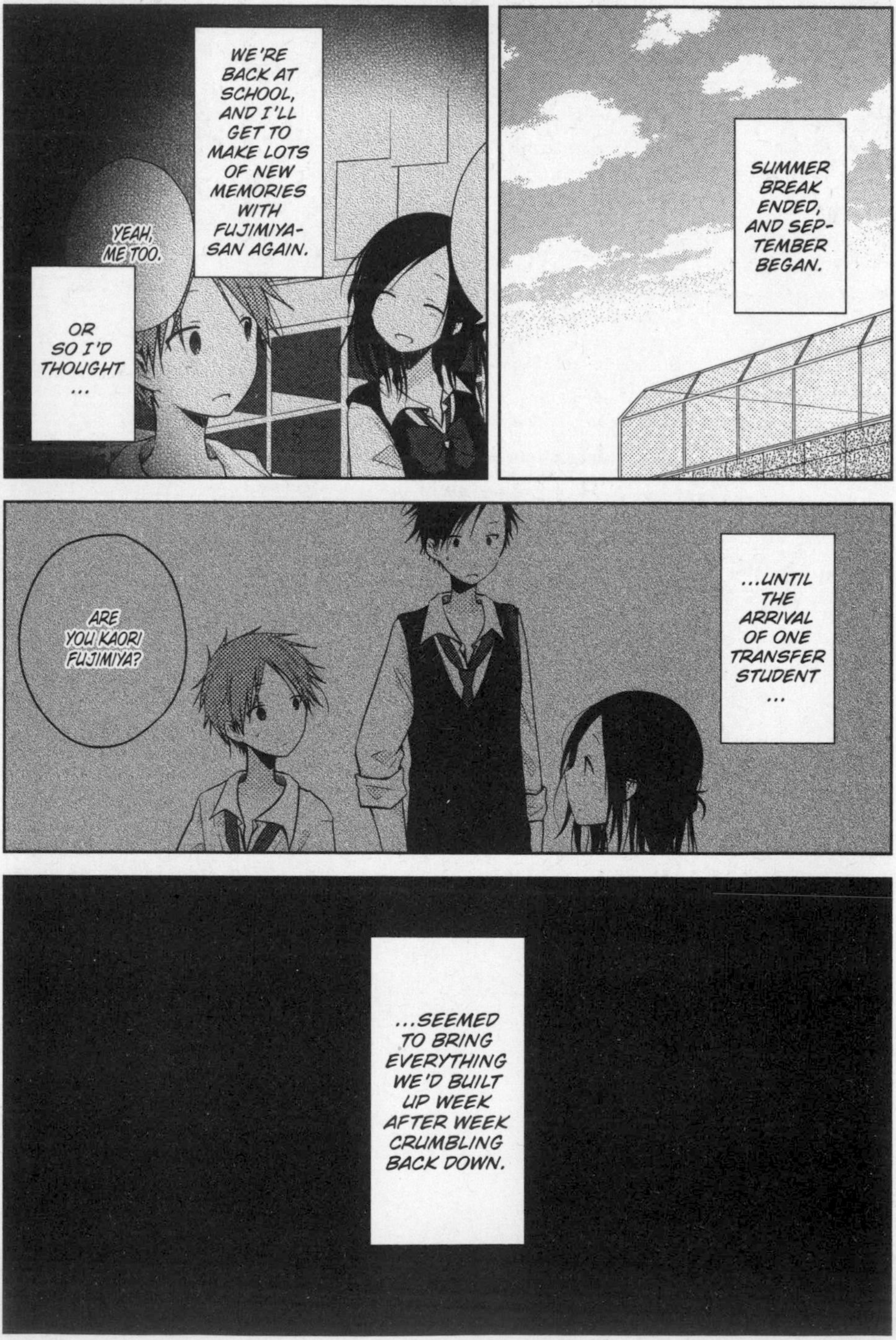
SUMMER BREAK ENDED, AND SEPTEMBER BEGAN.
WE'RE BACK AT SCHOOL, AND I'LL GET TO MAKE LOTS OF NEW MEMORIES WITH FUJIMIYA-SAN AGAIN.
YEAH, ME TOO.
OR SO I'D THOUGHT...
...UNTIL THE ARRIVAL OF ONE TRANSFER STUDENT...
ARE YOU KAORI FUJIMIYA?
...SEEMED TO BRING EVERYTHING WE'D BUILT UP WEEK AFTER WEEK CRUMBLING BACK DOWN.

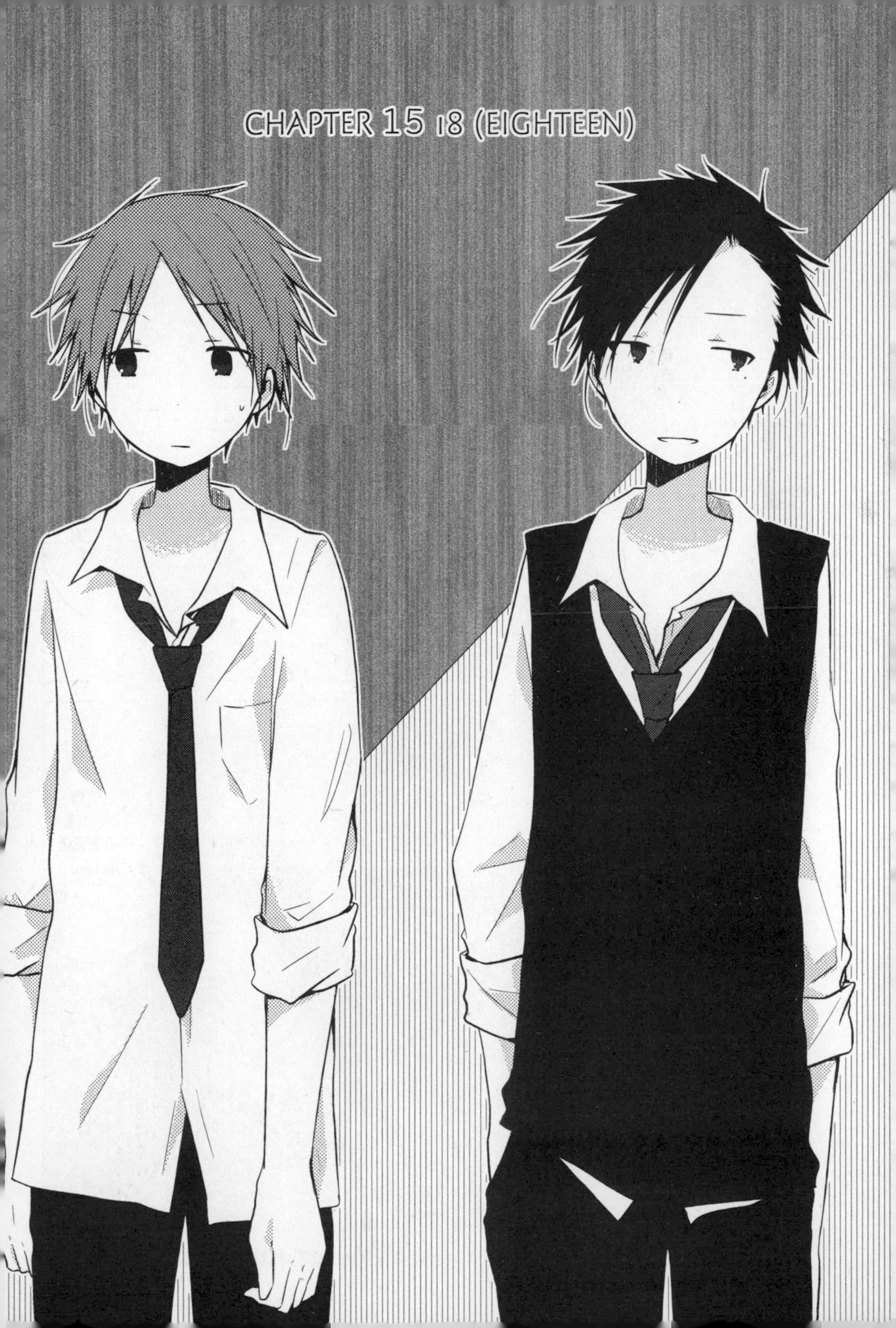
CHAPTER 15 18 (EIGHTEEN)

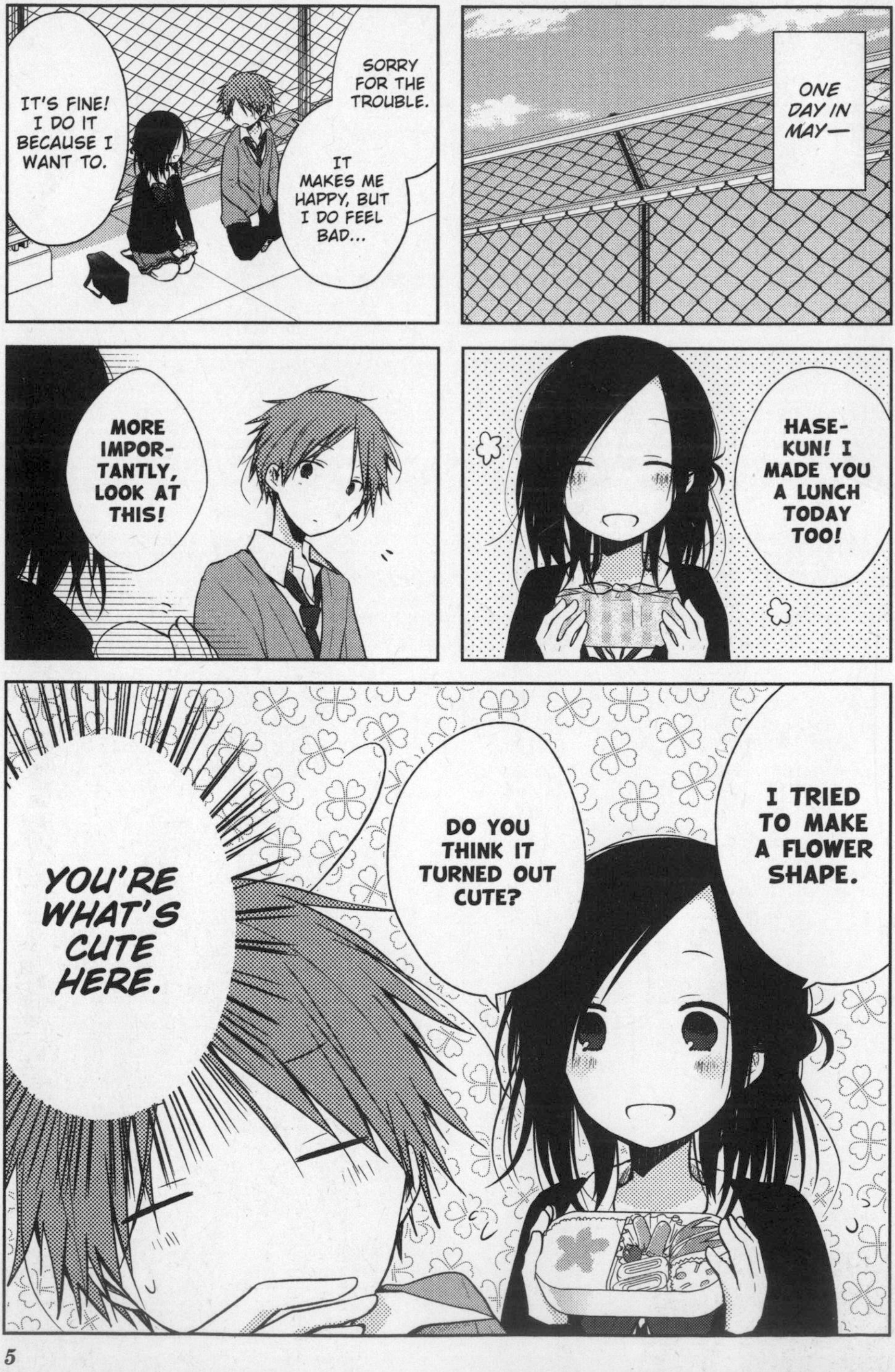
ONE DAY IN MAY—
SORRY FOR THE TROUBLE.
IT MAKES ME HAPPY, BUT I DO FEEL BAD...
IT'S FINE! I DO IT BECAUSE I WANT TO.
HASE-KUN! I MADE YOU A LUNCH TODAY TOO!
MORE IMPORTANTLY, LOOK AT THIS!
I TRIED TO MAKE A FLOWER SHAPE.
DO YOU THINK IT TURNED OUT CUTE?
YOU'RE WHAT'S CUTE HERE.

COOKING

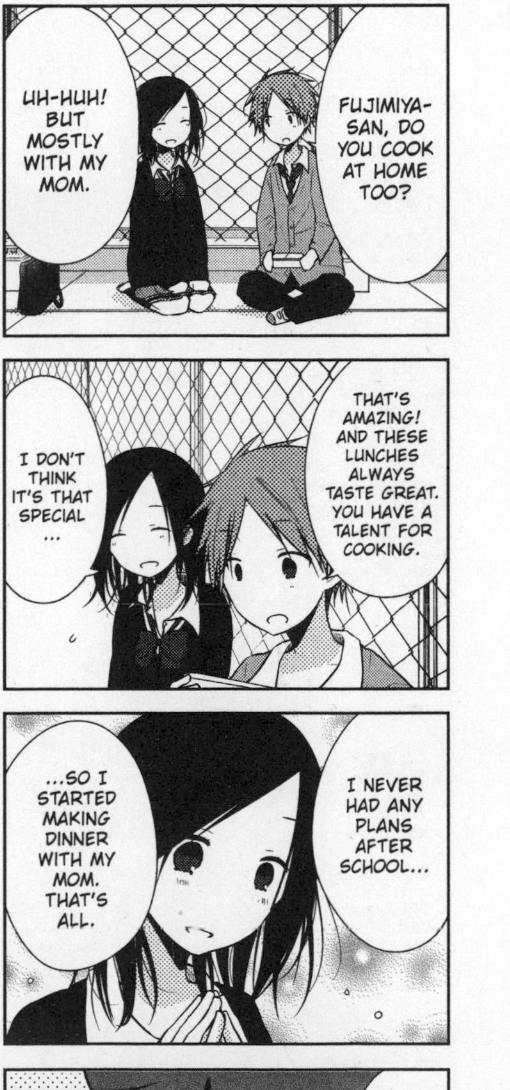
FUJIMIYA-SAN, DO YOU COOK AT HOME TOO?
UH-HUH! BUT MOSTLY WITH MY MOM.
THAT'S AMAZING! AND THESE LUNCHES ALWAYS TASTE GREAT. YOU HAVE A TALENT FOR COOKING.
I DON'T THINK IT'S THAT SPECIAL...
I NEVER HAD ANY PLANS AFTER SCHOOL...
...SO I STARTED MAKING DINNER WITH MY MOM. THAT'S ALL.
BECAUSE I HAD NOTHING BETTER TO DO...
BLOOSH
I'M SORRY!!
GYAH!

SO GLAD

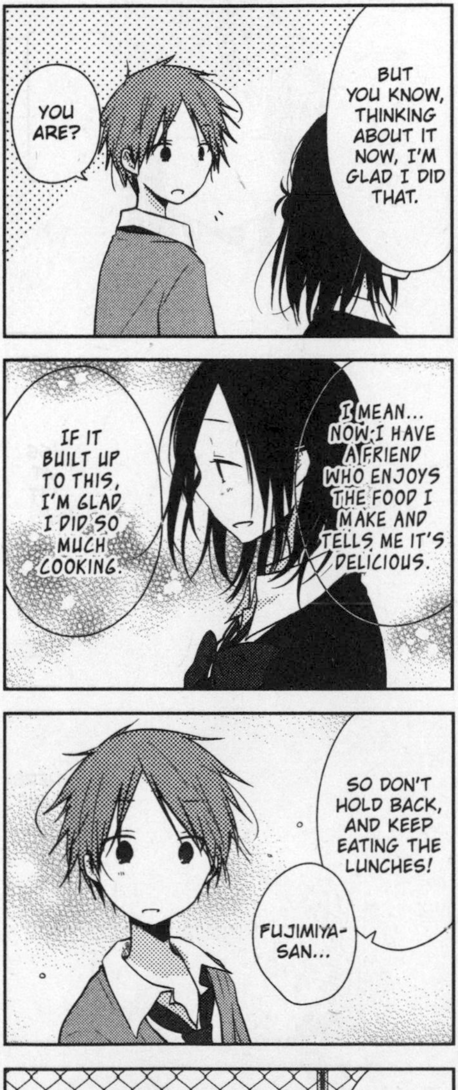
BUT YOU KNOW, THINKING ABOUT IT NOW, I'M GLAD I DID THAT.
YOU ARE?
I MEAN... NOW I HAVE A FRIEND WHO ENJOYS THE FOOD I MAKE AND TELLS ME IT'S DELICIOUS.
IF IT BUILT UP TO THIS, I'M GLAD I DID SO MUCH COOKING.
SO DON'T HOLD BACK, AND KEEP EATING THE LUNCHES!
FUJIMIYA-SAN...
SO GLAD I WORKED UP THE COURAGE TO TALK TO HER...!

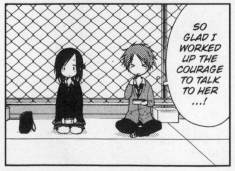

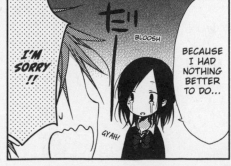

THE 18TH

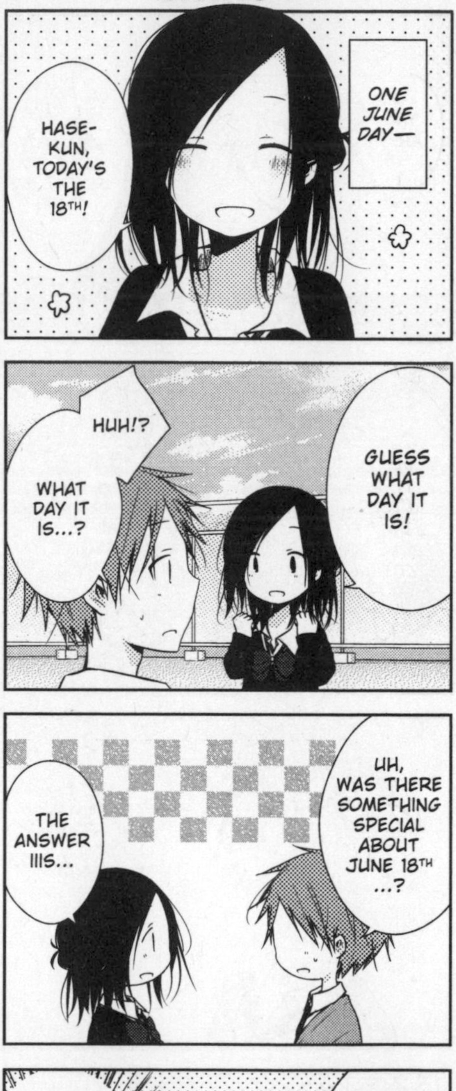
ONE JUNE DAY—
HASE-KUN, TODAY'S THE 18TH!
GUESS WHAT DAY IT IS!
HUH!?
WHAT DAY IT IS...?
UH, WAS THERE SOMETHING SPECIAL ABOUT JUNE 18TH ...?
THE ANSWER IIIS...
IT'S "DAY WITH EIGH-TEEN IN IT"!
ARRRGH, AND SHE'S LIKE THIS WITHOUT EVEN TRYING. WHAT'S A GUY TO DO?
TOO CUTE...

EXCITEMENT

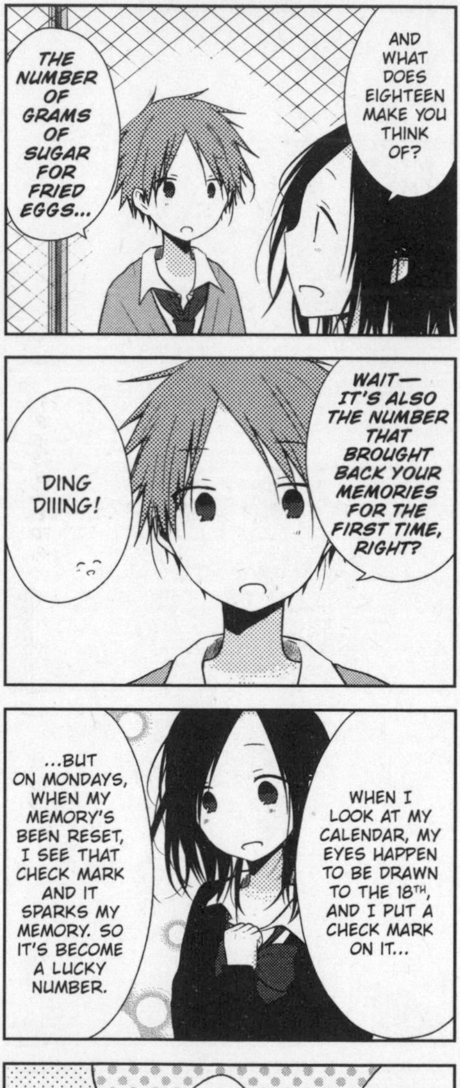
AND WHAT DOES EIGHTEEN MAKE YOU THINK OF?
THE NUMBER OF GRAMS OF SUGAR FOR FRIED EGGS...
WAIT— IT'S ALSO THE NUMBER THAT BROUGHT BACK YOUR MEMORIES FOR THE FIRST TIME, RIGHT?
DING DIIING!
WHEN I LOOK AT MY CALENDAR, MY EYES HAPPEN TO BE DRAWN TO THE 18TH, AND I PUT A CHECK MARK ON IT...
...BUT ON MONDAYS, WHEN MY MEMORY'S BEEN RESET, I SEE THAT CHECK MARK AND IT SPARKS MY MEMORY. SO IT'S BECOME A LUCKY NUMBER.
THAT'S WHY TODAY IS "DAY WITH EIGH-TEEN IN IT"!
IT'S SO EXCITING, RIGHT!?
WHEN YOU SEEM EXCITED, I GET EXCITED TOO!

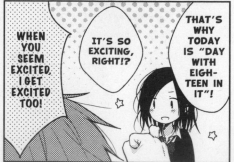

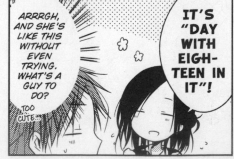

NEW MEMORIES

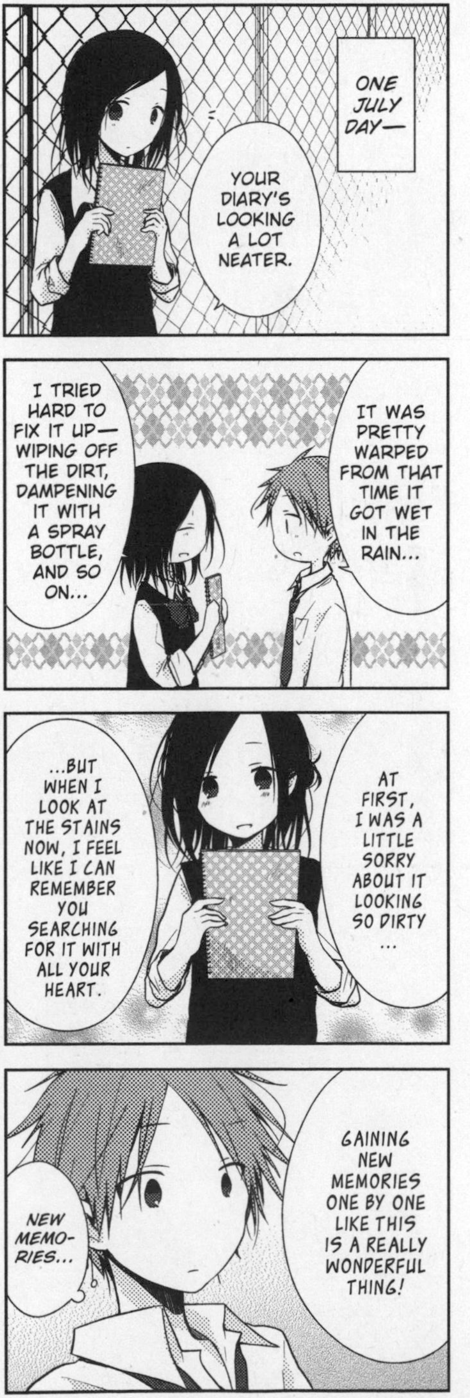

ONE JULY DAY—
YOUR DIARY'S LOOKING A LOT NEATER.
IT WAS PRETTY WARPED FROM THAT TIME IT GOT WET IN THE RAIN...
I TRIED HARD TO FIX IT UP—WIPING OFF THE DIRT, DAMPENING IT WITH A SPRAY BOTTLE, AND SO ON...
AT FIRST, I WAS A LITTLE SORRY ABOUT IT LOOKING SO DIRTY ...
...BUT WHEN I LOOK AT THE STAINS NOW, I FEEL LIKE I CAN REMEMBER YOU SEARCHING FOR IT WITH ALL YOUR HEART.
GAINING NEW MEMORIES ONE BY ONE LIKE THIS IS A REALLY WONDERFUL THING!
NEW MEMORIES...

UNFILTERED FEELINGS

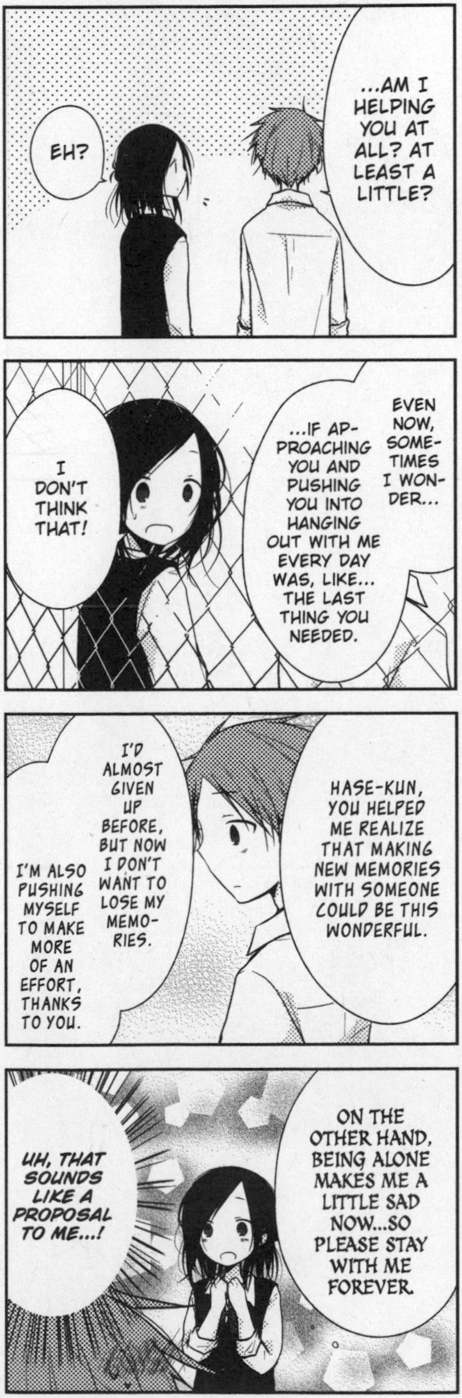

...AM I HELPING YOU AT ALL? AT LEAST A LITTLE?
EH?
EVEN NOW, SOMETIMES I WONDER...
...IF APPROACHING YOU AND PUSHING YOU INTO HANGING OUT WITH ME EVERY DAY WAS, LIKE... THE LAST THING YOU NEEDED.
I DON'T THINK THAT!
HASE-KUN, YOU HELPED ME REALIZE THAT MAKING NEW MEMORIES WITH SOMEONE COULD BE THIS WONDERFUL.
I'D ALMOST GIVEN UP BEFORE, BUT NOW I DON'T WANT TO LOSE MY MEMORIES.
I'M ALSO PUSHING MYSELF TO MAKE MORE OF AN EFFORT, THANKS TO YOU.
ON THE OTHER HAND, BEING ALONE MAKES ME A LITTLE SAD NOW...SO PLEASE STAY WITH ME FOREVER.
UH, THAT SOUNDS LIKE A PROPOSAL TO ME...!

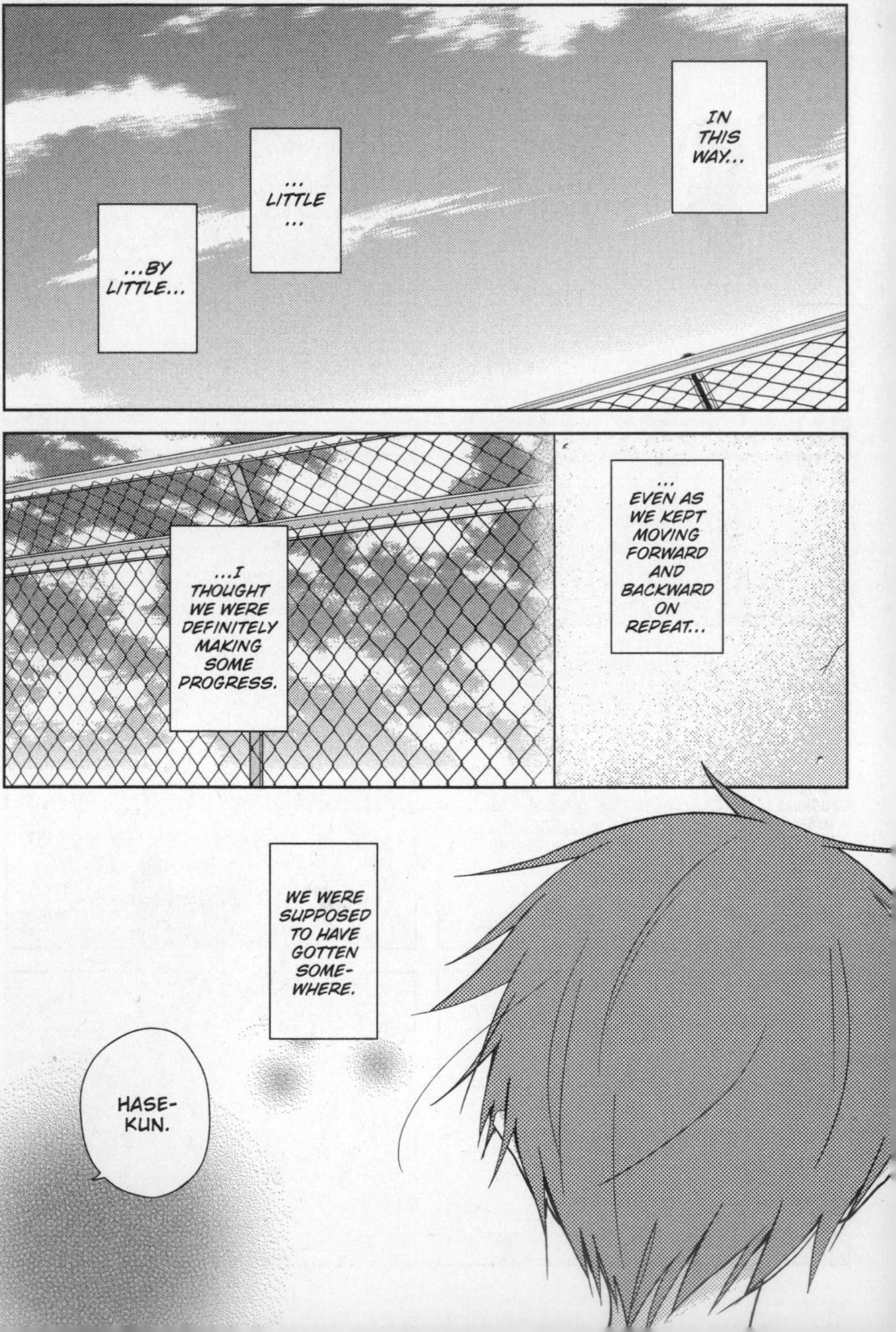
IN THIS WAY...
...LITTLE...
...BY LITTLE...
...EVEN AS WE KEPT MOVING FORWARD AND BACKWARD ON REPEAT...
...I THOUGHT WE WERE DEFINITELY MAKING SOME PROGRESS.
WE WERE SUPPOSED TO HAVE GOTTEN SOME-WHERE.
HASE-KUN.

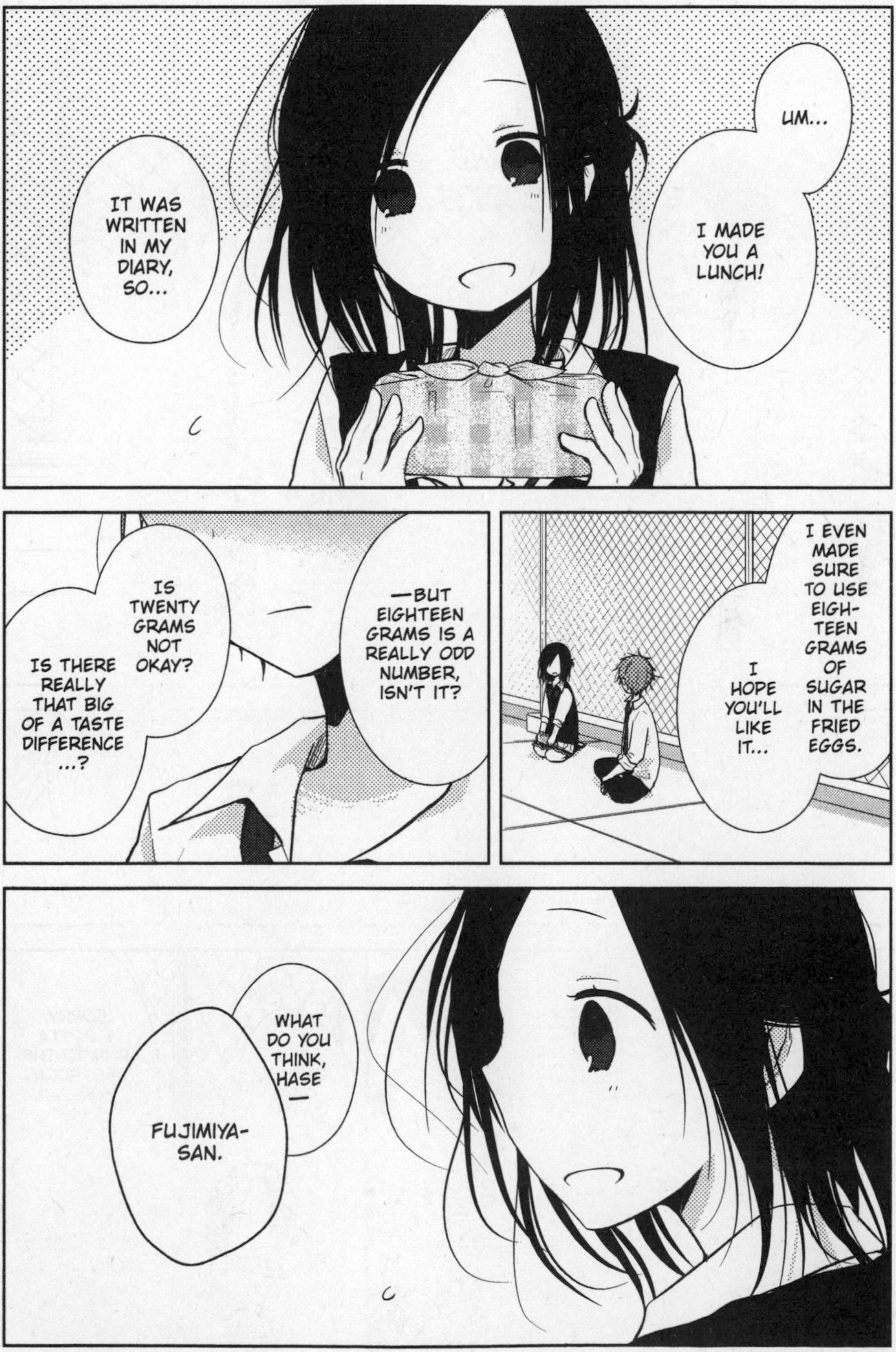
UM...
I MADE YOU A LUNCH!
IT WAS WRITTEN IN MY DIARY, SO...
I EVEN MADE SURE TO USE EIGH-TEEN GRAMS OF SUGAR IN THE FRIED EGGS.
I HOPE YOU'LL LIKE IT...
—BUT EIGHTEEN GRAMS IS A REALLY ODD NUMBER, ISN'T IT?
IS TWENTY GRAMS NOT OKAY?
IS THERE REALLY THAT BIG OF A TASTE DIFFERENCE ...?
WHAT DO YOU THINK, HASE—
FUJIMIYA-SAN.

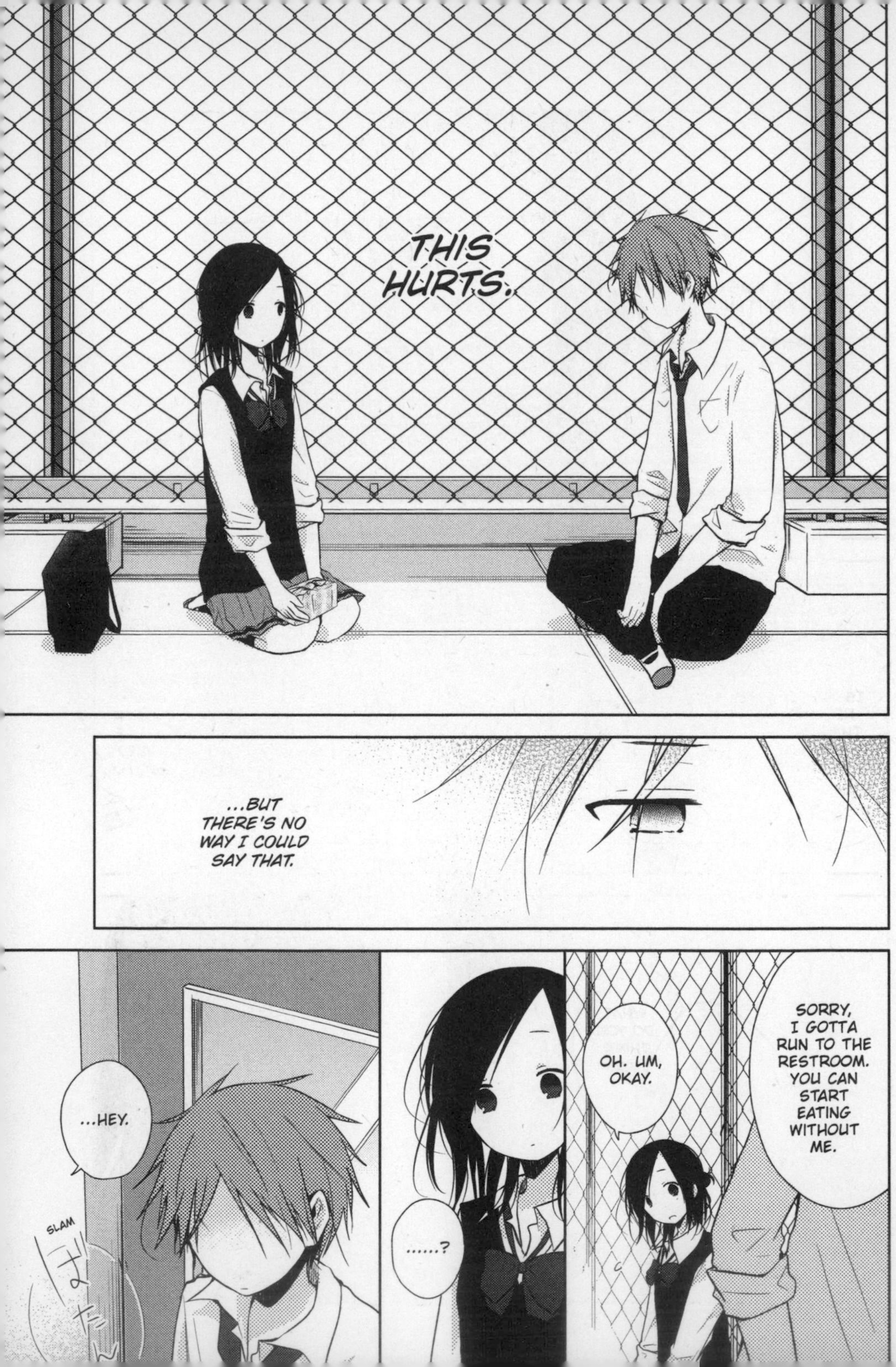
THIS HURTS.
...BUT THERE'S NO WAY I COULD SAY THAT.
SORRY, I GOTTA RUN TO THE RESTROOM. YOU CAN START EATING WITHOUT ME.
OH. UM, OKAY.
......?
...HEY.
SLAM

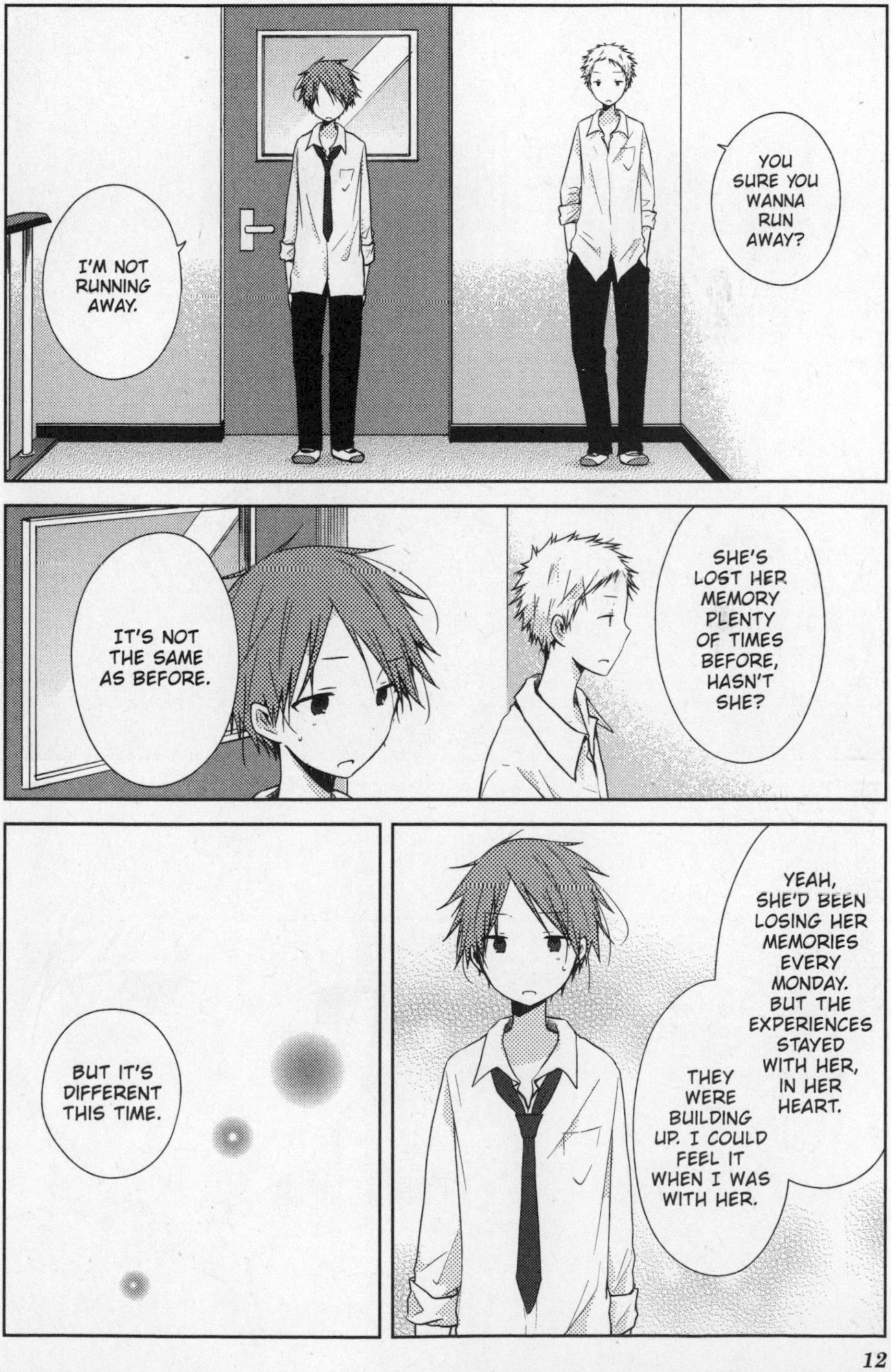
YOU SURE YOU WANNA RUN AWAY?
I'M NOT RUNNING AWAY.
SHE'S LOST HER MEMORY PLENTY OF TIMES BEFORE, HASN'T SHE?
IT'S NOT THE SAME AS BEFORE.
YEAH, SHE'D BEEN LOSING HER MEMORIES EVERY MONDAY. BUT THE EXPERIENCES STAYED WITH HER, IN HER HEART.
THEY WERE BUILDING UP. I COULD FEEL IT WHEN I WAS WITH HER.
BUT IT'S DIFFERENT THIS TIME.

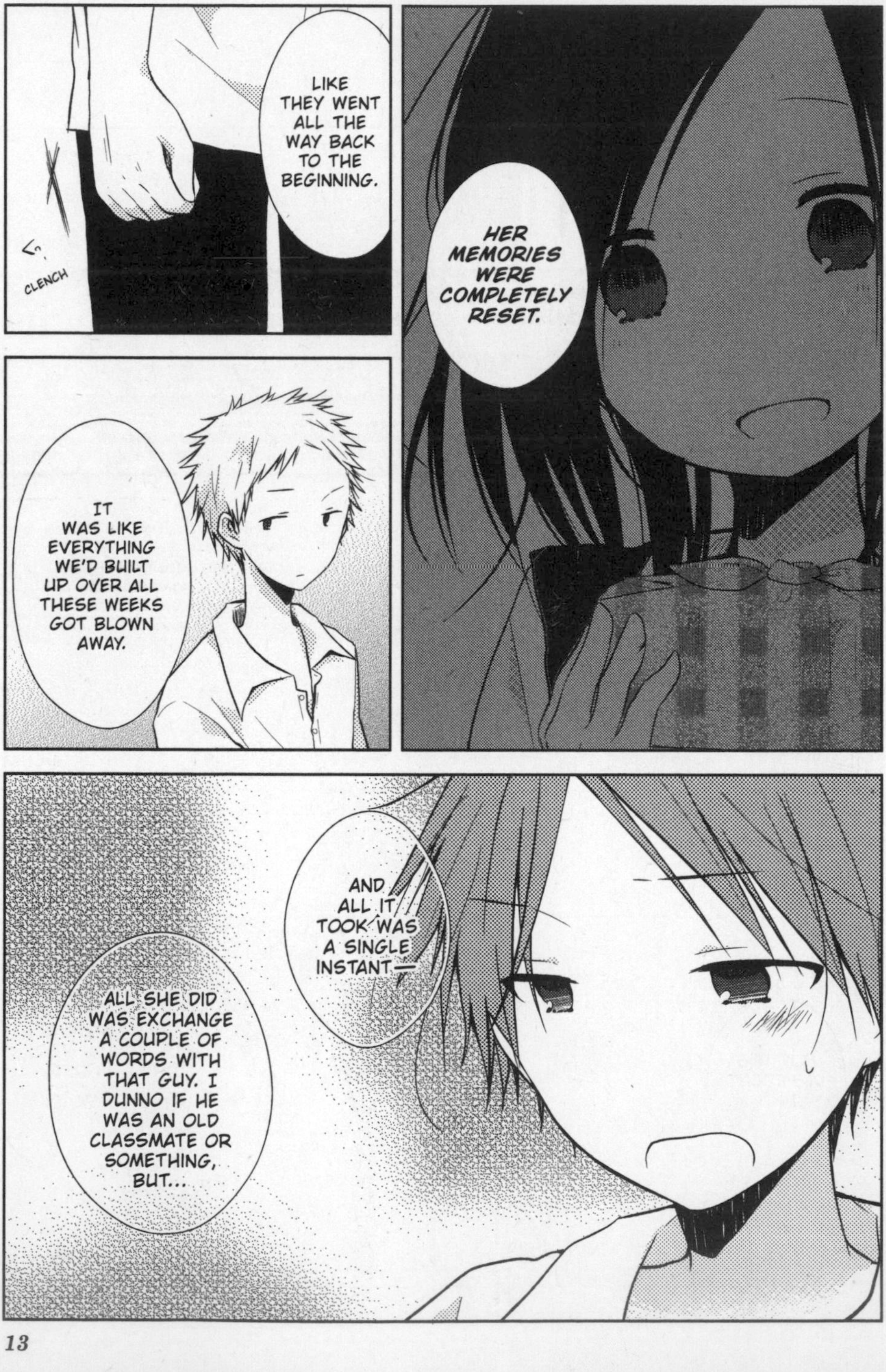
HER MEMORIES WERE COMPLETELY RESET.
LIKE THEY WENT ALL THE WAY BACK TO THE BEGINNING.
CLENCH
IT WAS LIKE EVERYTHING WE'D BUILT UP OVER ALL THESE WEEKS GOT BLOWN AWAY.
AND ALL IT TOOK WAS A SINGLE INSTANT—
ALL SHE DID WAS EXCHANGE A COUPLE OF WORDS WITH THAT GUY. I DUNNO IF HE WAS AN OLD CLASSMATE OR SOMETHING, BUT...

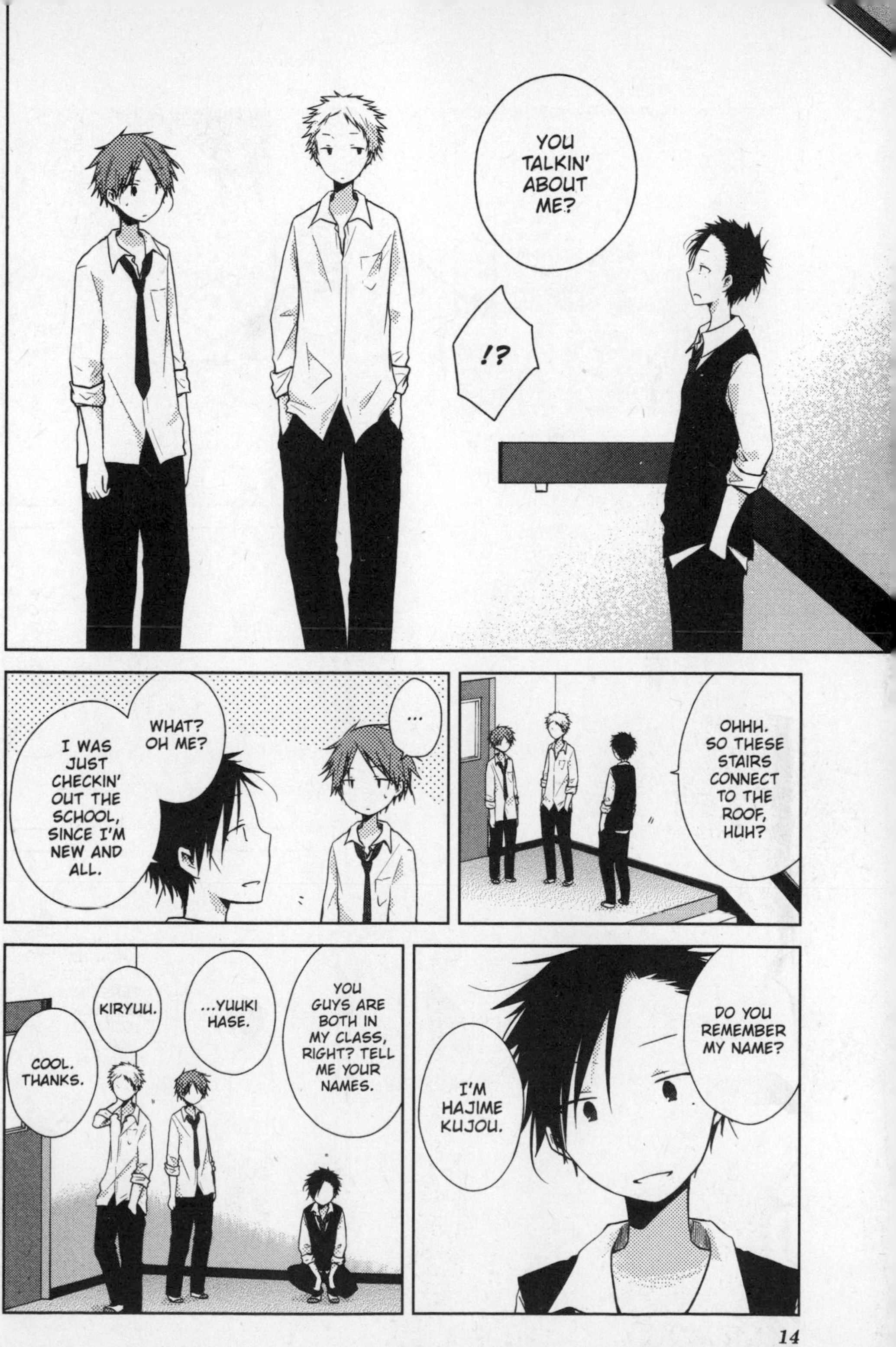
YOU TALKIN' ABOUT ME?
!?
OHHH. SO THESE STAIRS CONNECT TO THE ROOF, HUH?
...
WHAT? OH ME?
I WAS JUST CHECKIN' OUT THE SCHOOL, SINCE I'M NEW AND ALL.
DO YOU REMEMBER MY NAME?
I'M HAJIME KUJOU.
YOU GUYS ARE BOTH IN MY CLASS, RIGHT? TELL ME YOUR NAMES.
...YUUKI HASE.
KIRYUU.
COOL. THANKS.

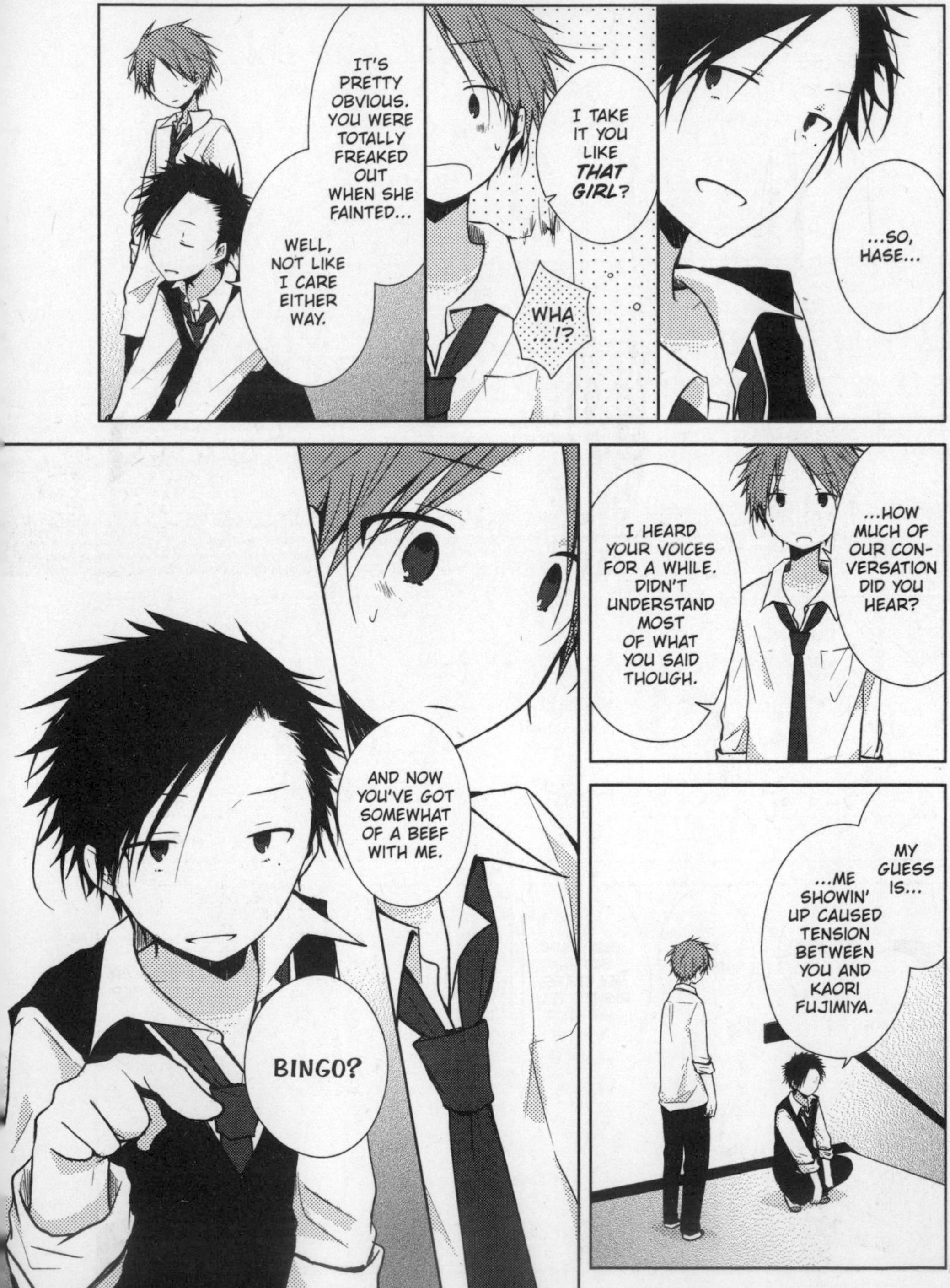
...SO, HASE...
I TAKE IT YOU LIKE *THAT GIRL*?
WHA ...!?
IT'S PRETTY OBVIOUS. YOU WERE TOTALLY FREAKED OUT WHEN SHE FAINTED...
WELL, NOT LIKE I CARE EITHER WAY.
...HOW MUCH OF OUR CON-VERSATION DID YOU HEAR?
I HEARD YOUR VOICES FOR A WHILE. DIDN'T UNDERSTAND MOST OF WHAT YOU SAID THOUGH.
MY GUESS IS...
...ME SHOWIN' UP CAUSED TENSION BETWEEN YOU AND KAORI FUJIMIYA.
AND NOW YOU'VE GOT SOMEWHAT OF A BEEF WITH ME.
BINGO?

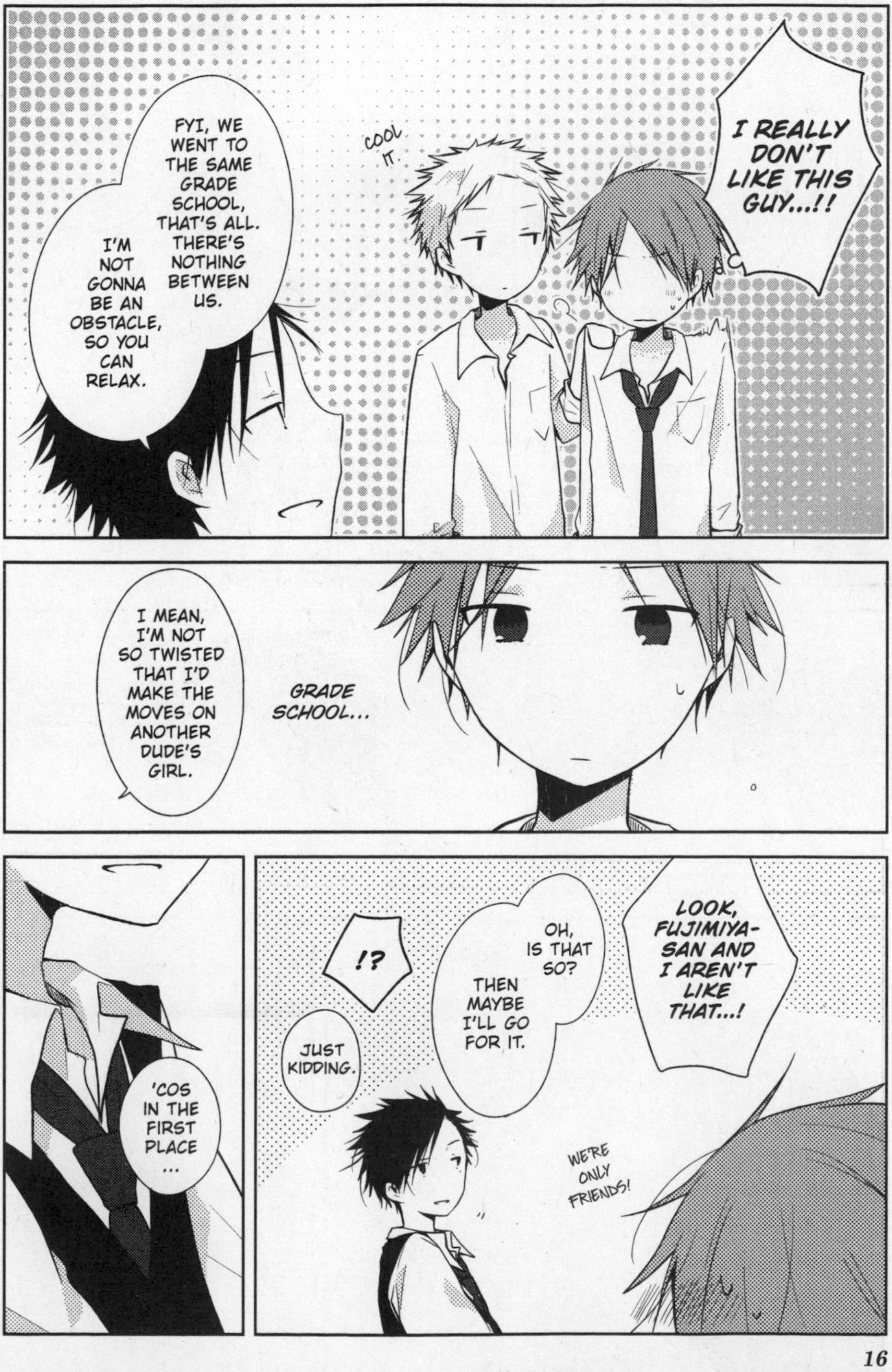
I REALLY DON'T LIKE THIS GUY...!!
COOL IT.
FYI, WE WENT TO THE SAME GRADE SCHOOL, THAT'S ALL. THERE'S NOTHING BETWEEN US.
I'M NOT GONNA BE AN OBSTACLE, SO YOU CAN RELAX.
GRADE SCHOOL...
I MEAN, I'M NOT SO TWISTED THAT I'D MAKE THE MOVES ON ANOTHER DUDE'S GIRL.
LOOK, FUJIMIYA-SAN AND I AREN'T LIKE THAT...!
WE'RE ONLY FRIENDS!
OH, IS THAT SO?
THEN MAYBE I'LL GO FOR IT.
!?
JUST KIDDING.
'COS IN THE FIRST PLACE ...

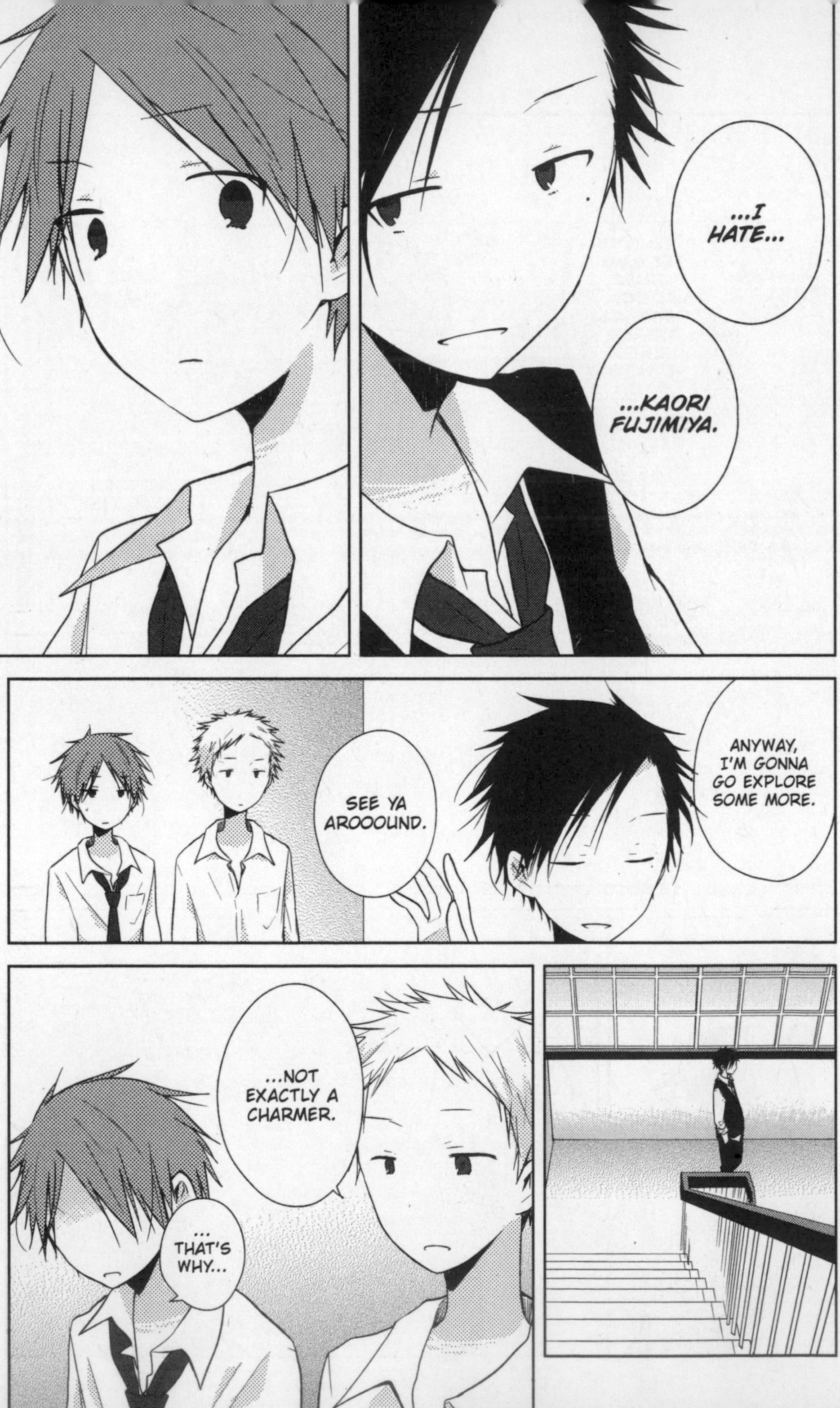
...I HATE...
...KAORI FUJIMIYA.
ANYWAY, I'M GONNA GO EXPLORE SOME MORE.
SEE YA AROOOUND.
...NOT EXACTLY A CHARMER.
...THAT'S WHY...

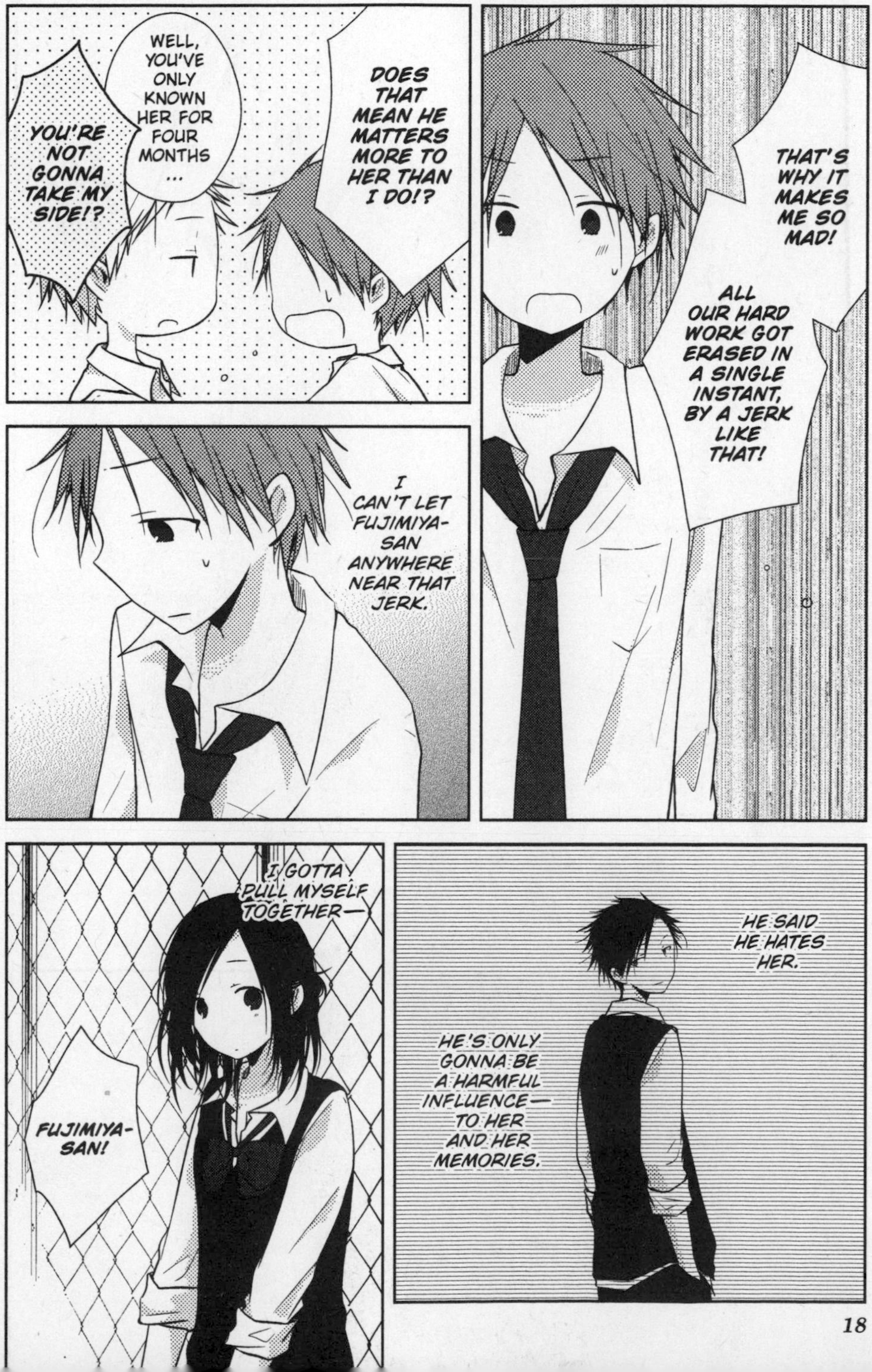
THAT'S WHY IT MAKES ME SO MAD!
ALL OUR HARD WORK GOT ERASED IN A SINGLE INSTANT, BY A JERK LIKE THAT!
DOES THAT MEAN HE MATTERS MORE TO HER THAN I DO!?
WELL, YOU'VE ONLY KNOWN HER FOR FOUR MONTHS ...
YOU'RE NOT GONNA TAKE MY SIDE!?
I CAN'T LET FUJIMIYA-SAN ANYWHERE NEAR THAT JERK.
HE SAID HE HATES HER.
HE'S ONLY GONNA BE A HARMFUL INFLUENCE— TO HER AND HER MEMORIES.
I GOTTA PULL MYSELF TOGETHER—
FUJIMIYA-SAN!

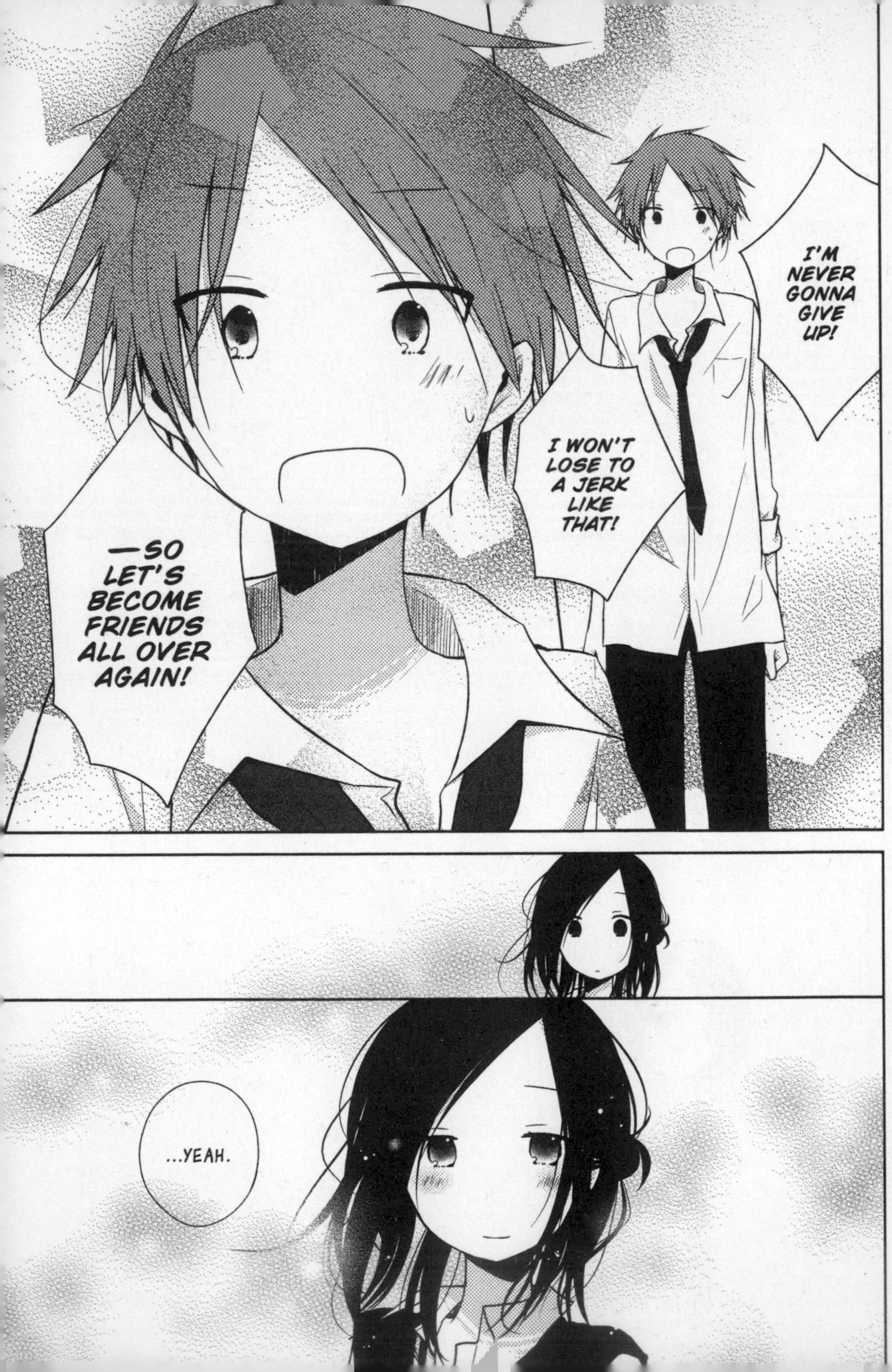
I'M NEVER GONNA GIVE UP!
I WON'T LOSE TO A JERK LIKE THAT!
—SO LET'S BECOME FRIENDS ALL OVER AGAIN!
...YEAH.

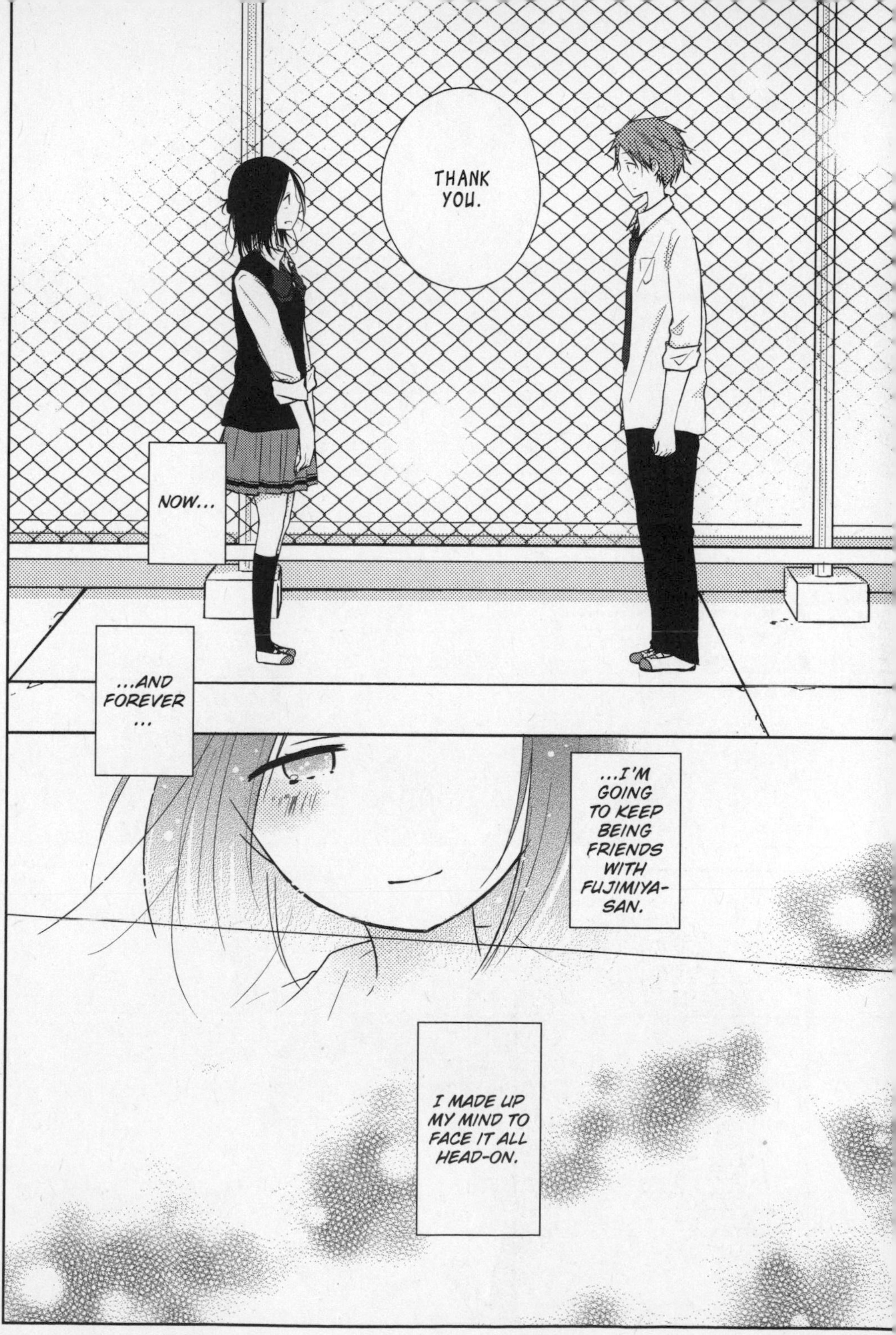
THANK YOU.
NOW...
...AND FOREVER...
...I'M GOING TO KEEP BEING FRIENDS WITH FUJIMIYA-SAN.
I MADE UP MY MIND TO FACE IT ALL HEAD-ON.

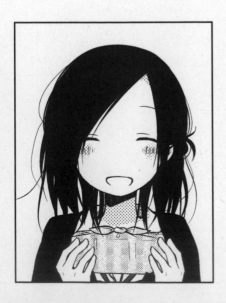

FOR AVOIDANCE PURPOSES

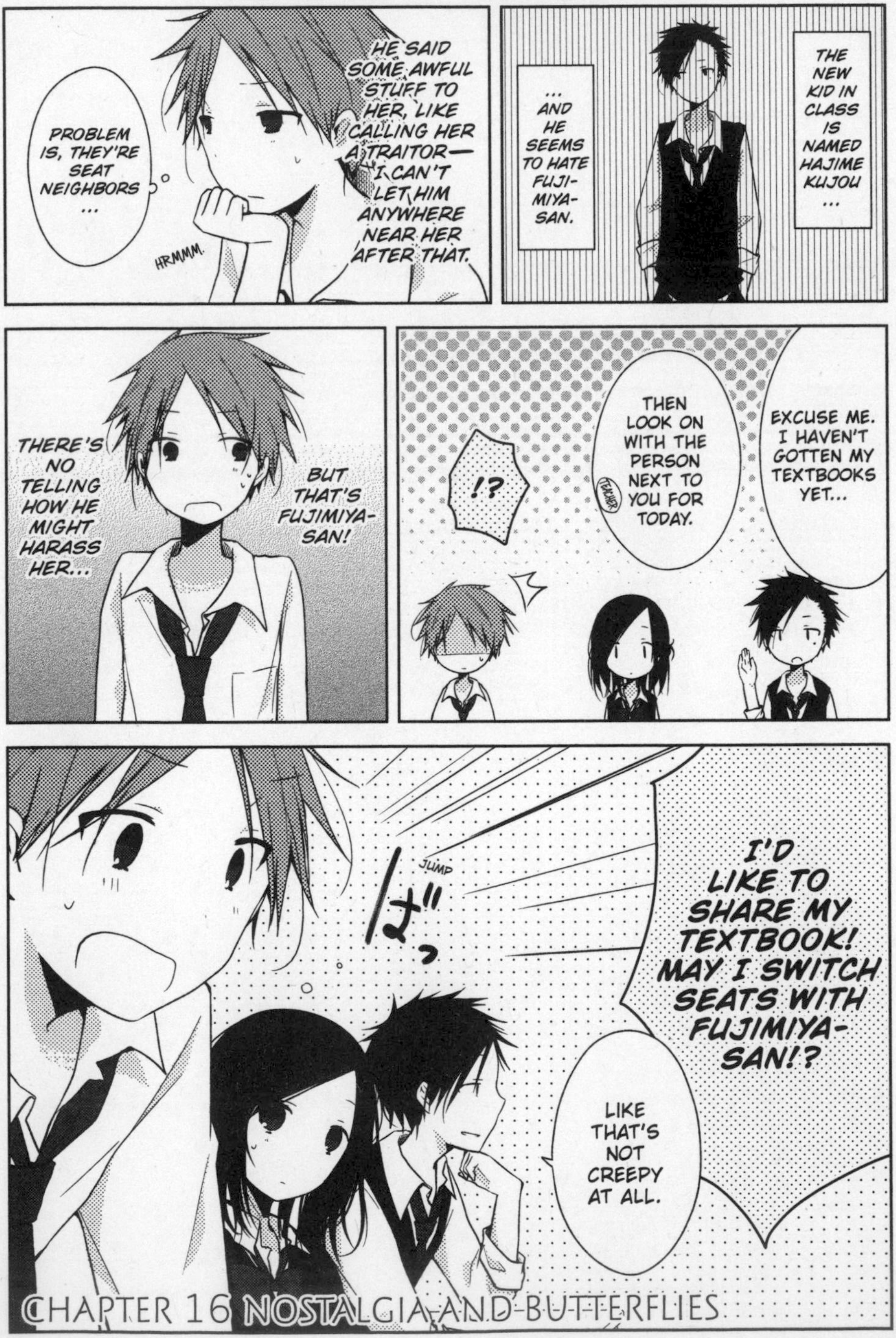
THE NEW KID IN CLASS IS NAMED HAJIME KUJOU...
...AND HE SEEMS TO HATE FUJIMIYA-SAN.
HE SAID SOME AWFUL STUFF TO HER, LIKE CALLING HER A TRAITOR—I CAN'T LET HIM ANYWHERE NEAR HER AFTER THAT.
PROBLEM IS, THEY'RE SEAT NEIGHBORS...
HRMMM.
EXCUSE ME. I HAVEN'T GOTTEN MY TEXTBOOKS YET...
TEACHER
THEN LOOK ON WITH THE PERSON NEXT TO YOU FOR TODAY.
!?
BUT THAT'S FUJIMIYA-SAN!
THERE'S NO TELLING HOW HE MIGHT HARASS HER...
I'D LIKE TO SHARE MY TEXTBOOK! MAY I SWITCH SEATS WITH FUJIMIYA-SAN!?
JUMP
ば
LIKE THAT'S NOT CREEPY AT ALL.
CHAPTER 16 NOSTALGIA AND BUTTERFLIES

HOSTILE ATMOSPHERE

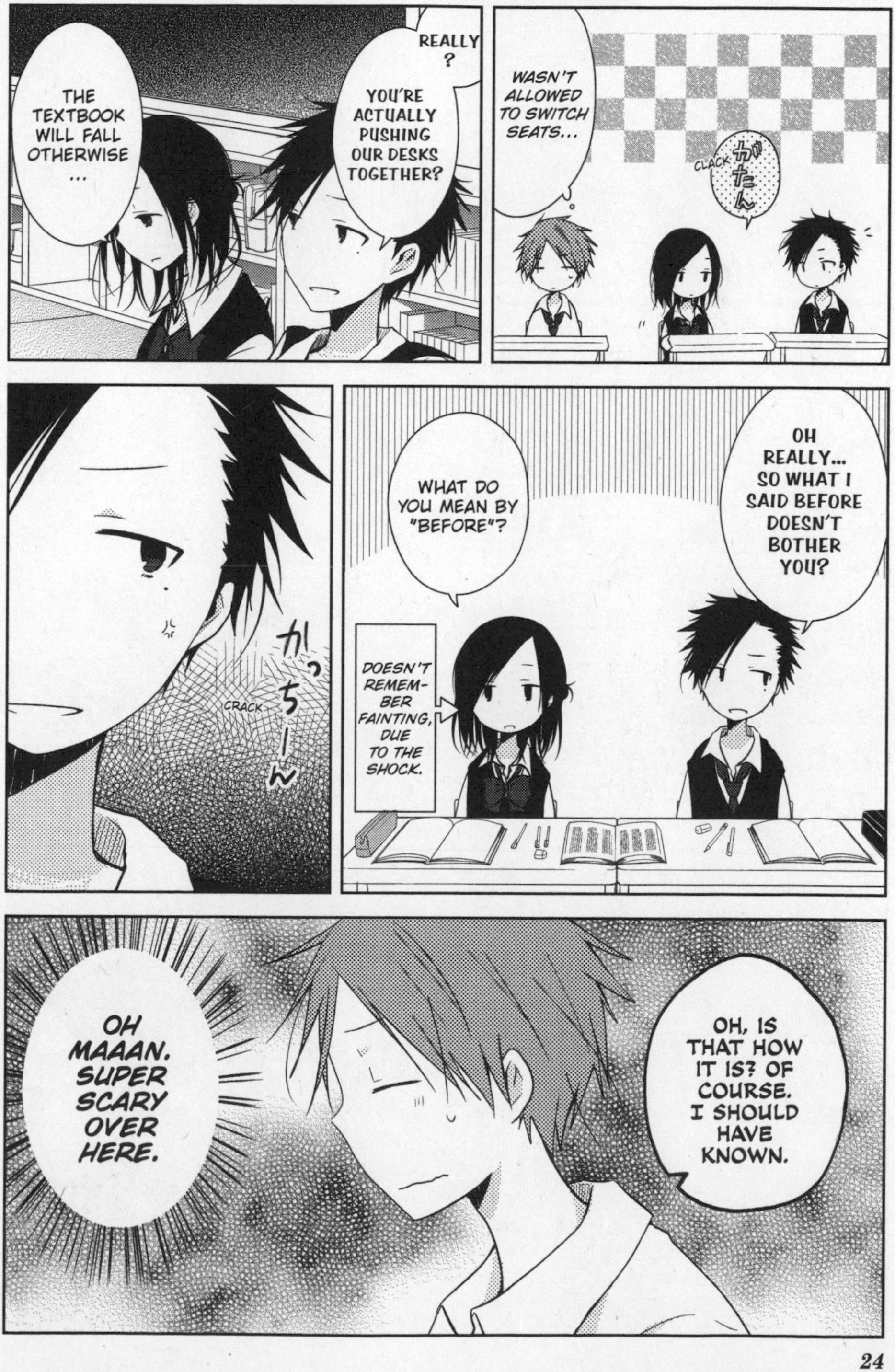
WASN'T ALLOWED TO SWITCH SEATS...
かたん
CLACK
REALLY?
YOU'RE ACTUALLY PUSHING OUR DESKS TOGETHER?
THE TEXTBOOK WILL FALL OTHERWISE...
OH REALLY... SO WHAT I SAID BEFORE DOESN'T BOTHER YOU?
WHAT DO YOU MEAN BY "BEFORE"?
DOESN'T REMEMBER FAINTING, DUE TO THE SHOCK.
かっちーん
CRACK
OH, IS THAT HOW IT IS? OF COURSE. I SHOULD HAVE KNOWN.
OH MAAAN. SUPER SCARY OVER HERE.

!? !? !?

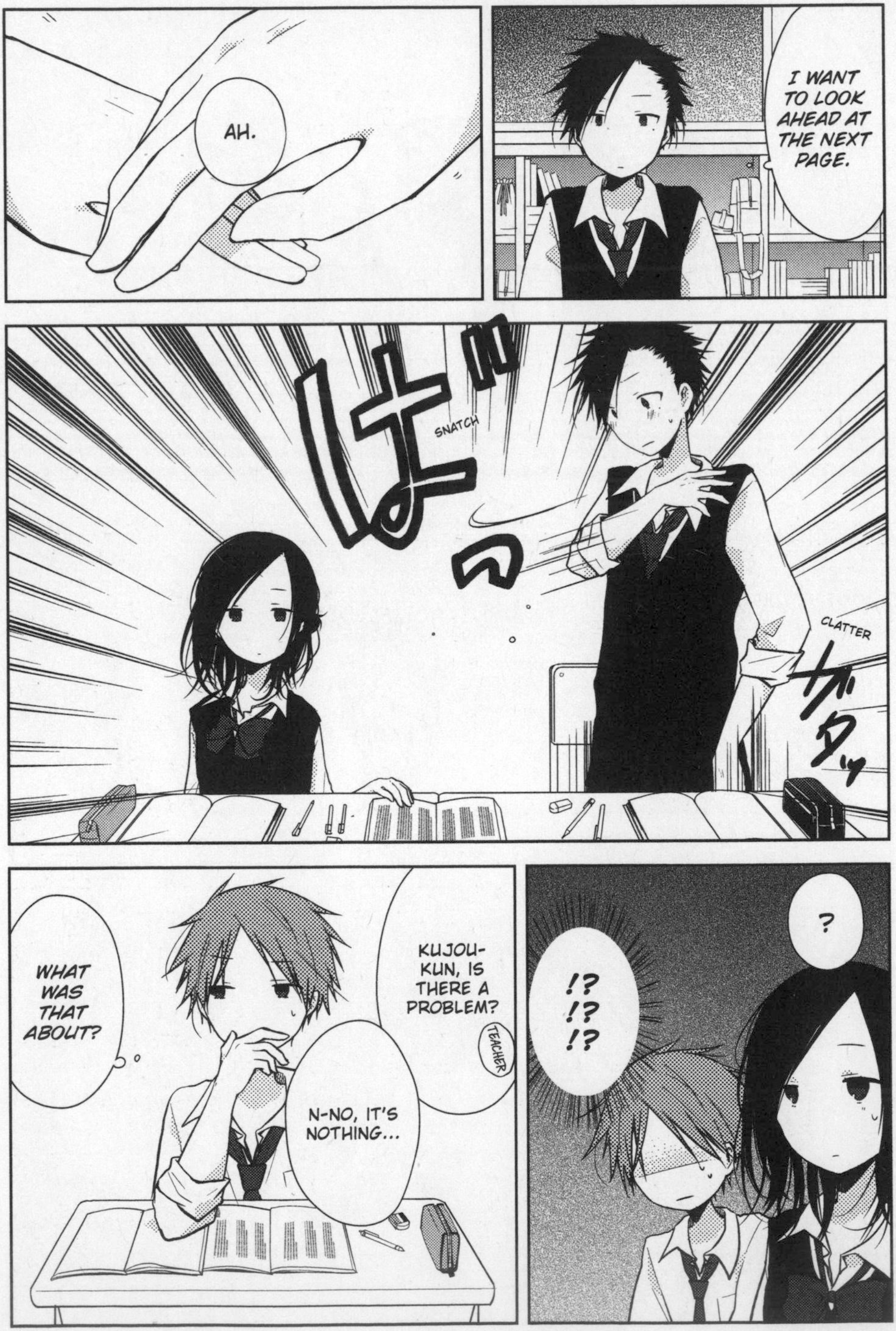
I WANT TO LOOK AHEAD AT THE NEXT PAGE.
AH.
ばっ
SNATCH
ガタッ
CLATTER
?
!? !? !?
KUJOU-KUN, IS THERE A PROBLEM?
TEACHER
N-NO, IT'S NOTHING...
WHAT WAS THAT ABOUT?

COULD IT BE...

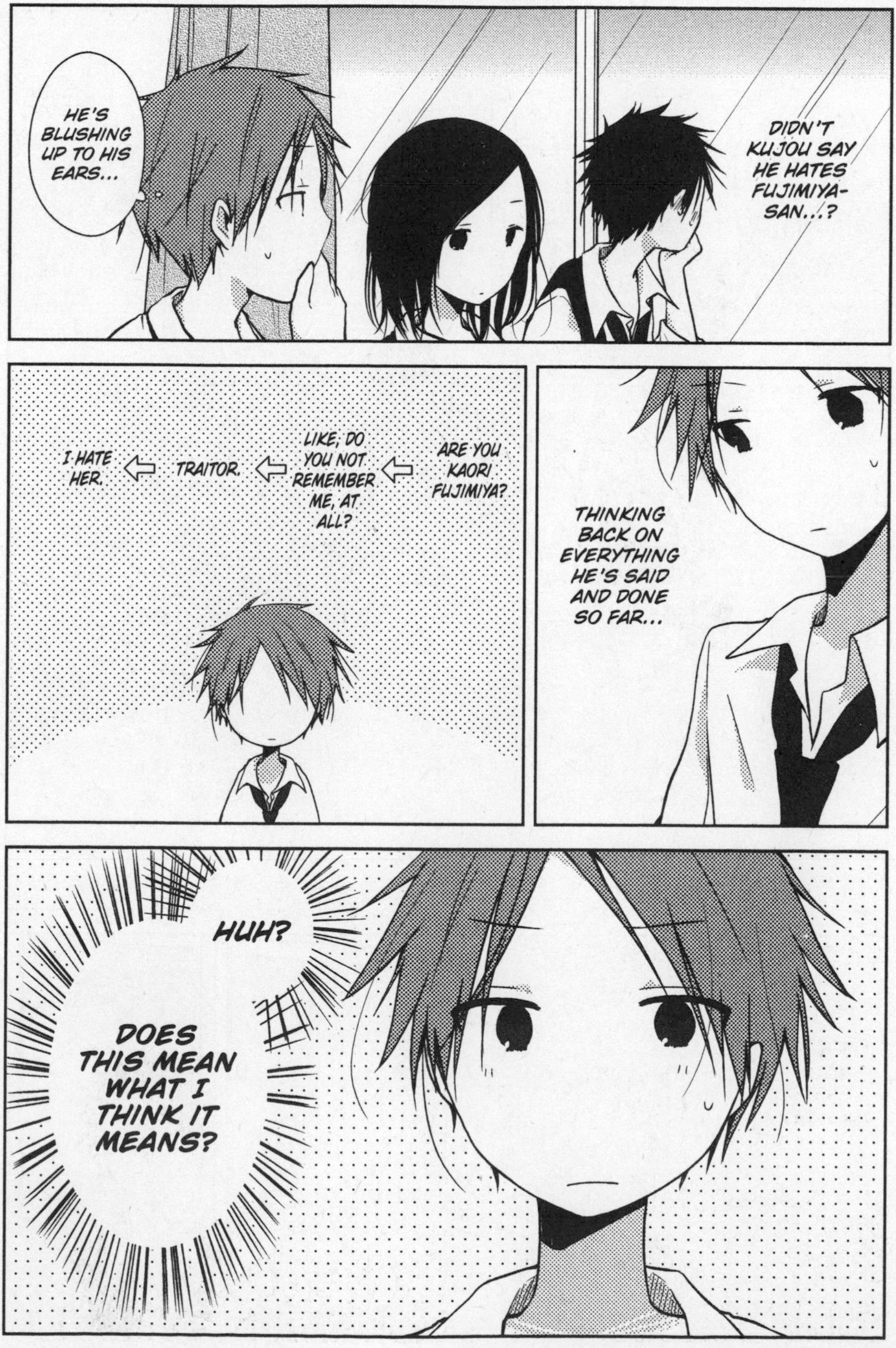
DIDN'T KUJOU SAY HE HATES FUJIMIYA-SAN...?
HE'S BLUSHING UP TO HIS EARS...
THINKING BACK ON EVERYTHING HE'S SAID AND DONE SO FAR...
ARE YOU KAORI FUJIMIYA?
LIKE, DO YOU NOT REMEMBER ME, AT ALL?
TRAITOR.
I HATE HER.
HUH?
DOES THIS MEAN WHAT I THINK IT MEANS?

PAUSE

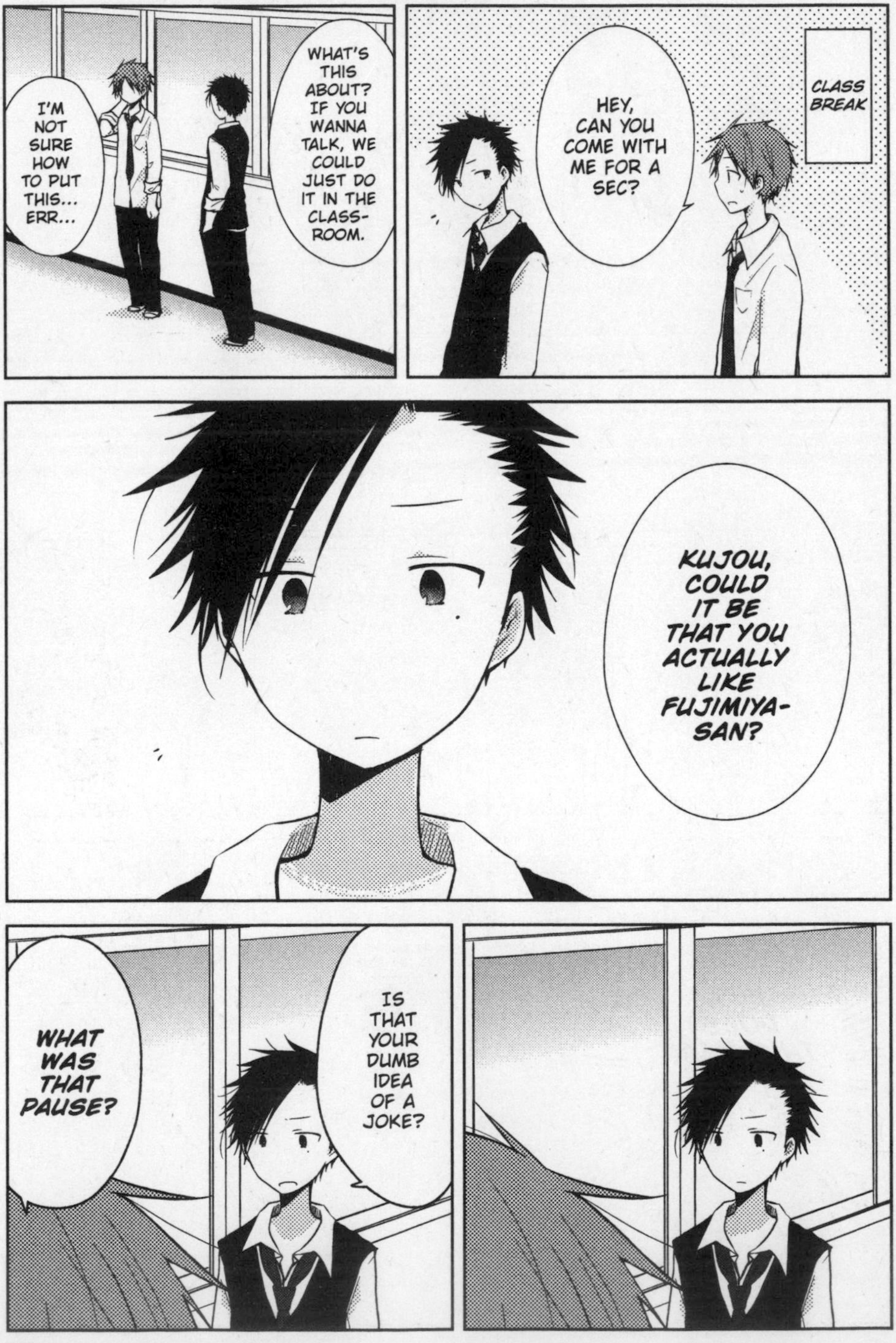

CLASS BREAK
HEY, CAN YOU COME WITH ME FOR A SEC?
WHAT'S THIS ABOUT? IF YOU WANNA TALK, WE COULD JUST DO IT IN THE CLASS-ROOM.
I'M NOT SURE HOW TO PUT THIS... ERR...
KUJOU, COULD IT BE THAT YOU ACTUALLY LIKE FUJIMIYA-SAN?
IS THAT YOUR DUMB IDEA OF A JOKE?
WHAT WAS THAT PAUSE?

ABOUT TO BLOW

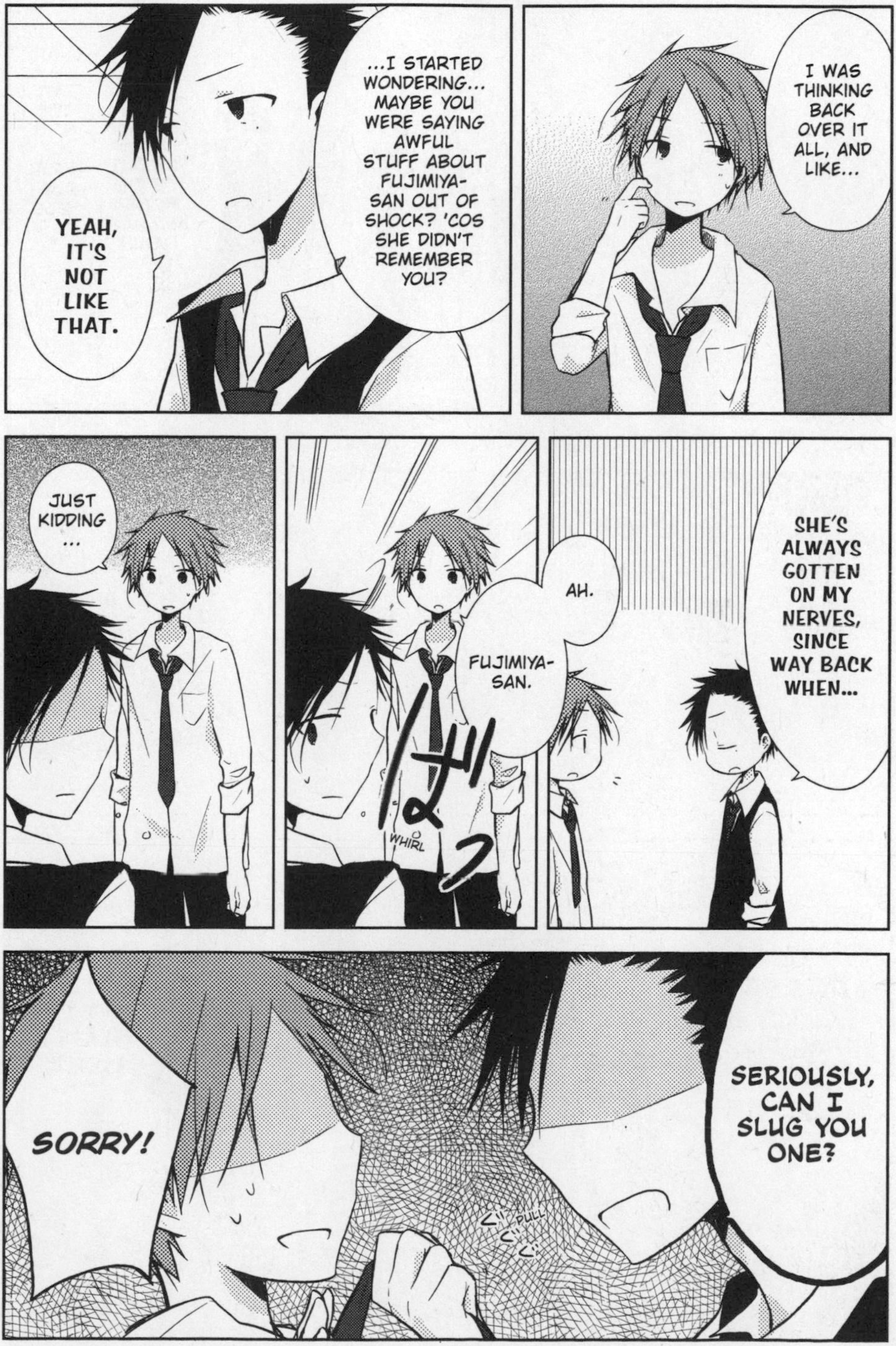
I WAS THINKING BACK OVER IT ALL, AND LIKE...
...I STARTED WONDERING... MAYBE YOU WERE SAYING AWFUL STUFF ABOUT FUJIMIYA-SAN OUT OF SHOCK? 'COS SHE DIDN'T REMEMBER YOU?
YEAH, IT'S NOT LIKE THAT.
SHE'S ALWAYS GOTTEN ON MY NERVES, SINCE WAY BACK WHEN...
AH.
FUJIMIYA-SAN.
WHIRL
JUST KIDDING...
SERIOUSLY, CAN I SLUG YOU ONE?
PULL
SORRY!

IF IT WAS REALLY LIKE THAT

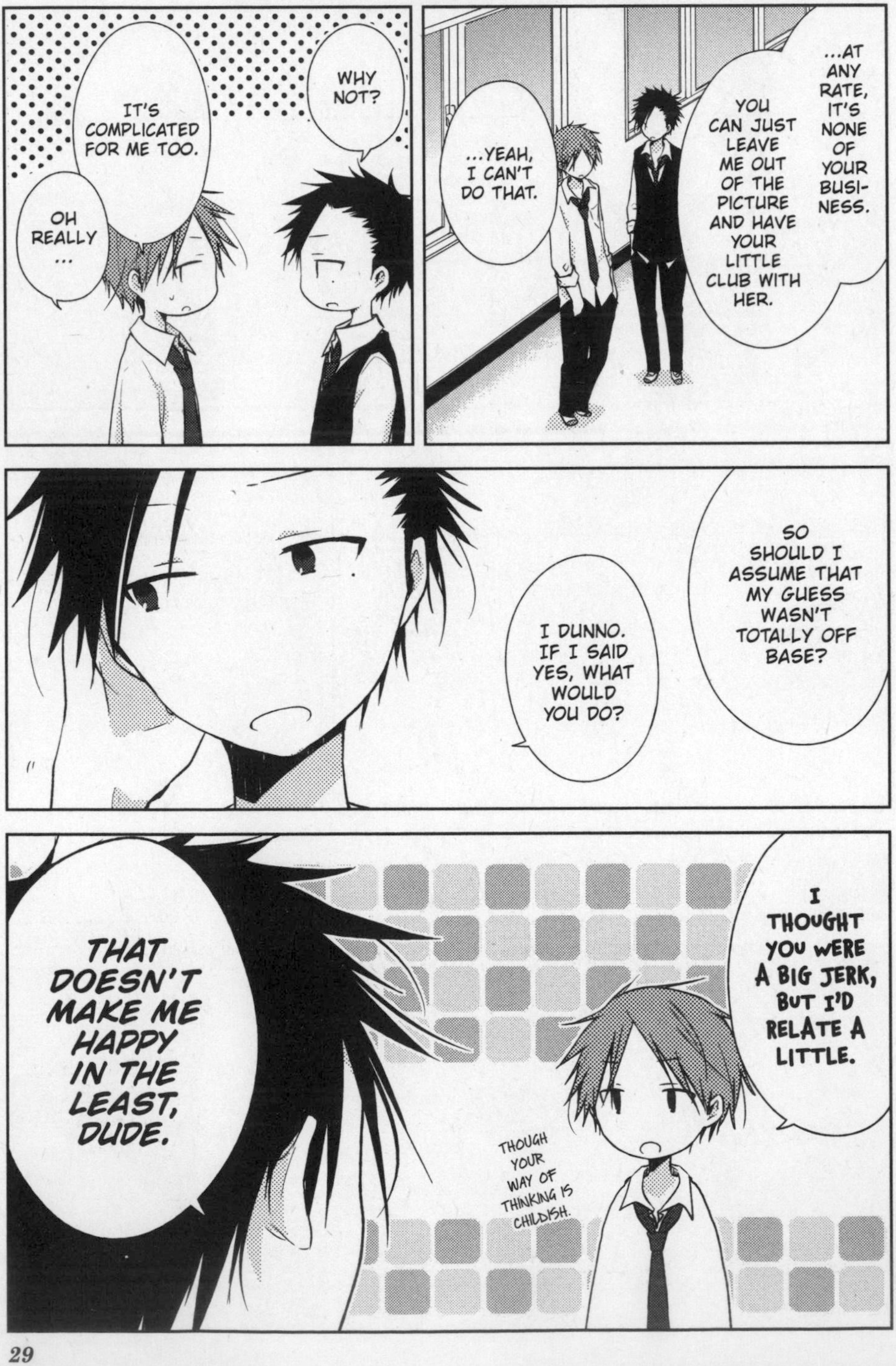
...AT ANY RATE, IT'S NONE OF YOUR BUSI-NESS.
YOU CAN JUST LEAVE ME OUT OF THE PICTURE AND HAVE YOUR LITTLE CLUB WITH HER.
...YEAH, I CAN'T DO THAT.
WHY NOT?
IT'S COMPLICATED FOR ME TOO.
OH REALLY ...
SO SHOULD I ASSUME THAT MY GUESS WASN'T TOTALLY OFF BASE?
I DUNNO. IF I SAID YES, WHAT WOULD YOU DO?
I THOUGHT YOU WERE A BIG JERK, BUT I'D RELATE A LITTLE.
THOUGH YOUR WAY OF THINKING IS CHILDISH.
THAT DOESN'T MAKE ME HAPPY IN THE LEAST, DUDE.

CAUGHT

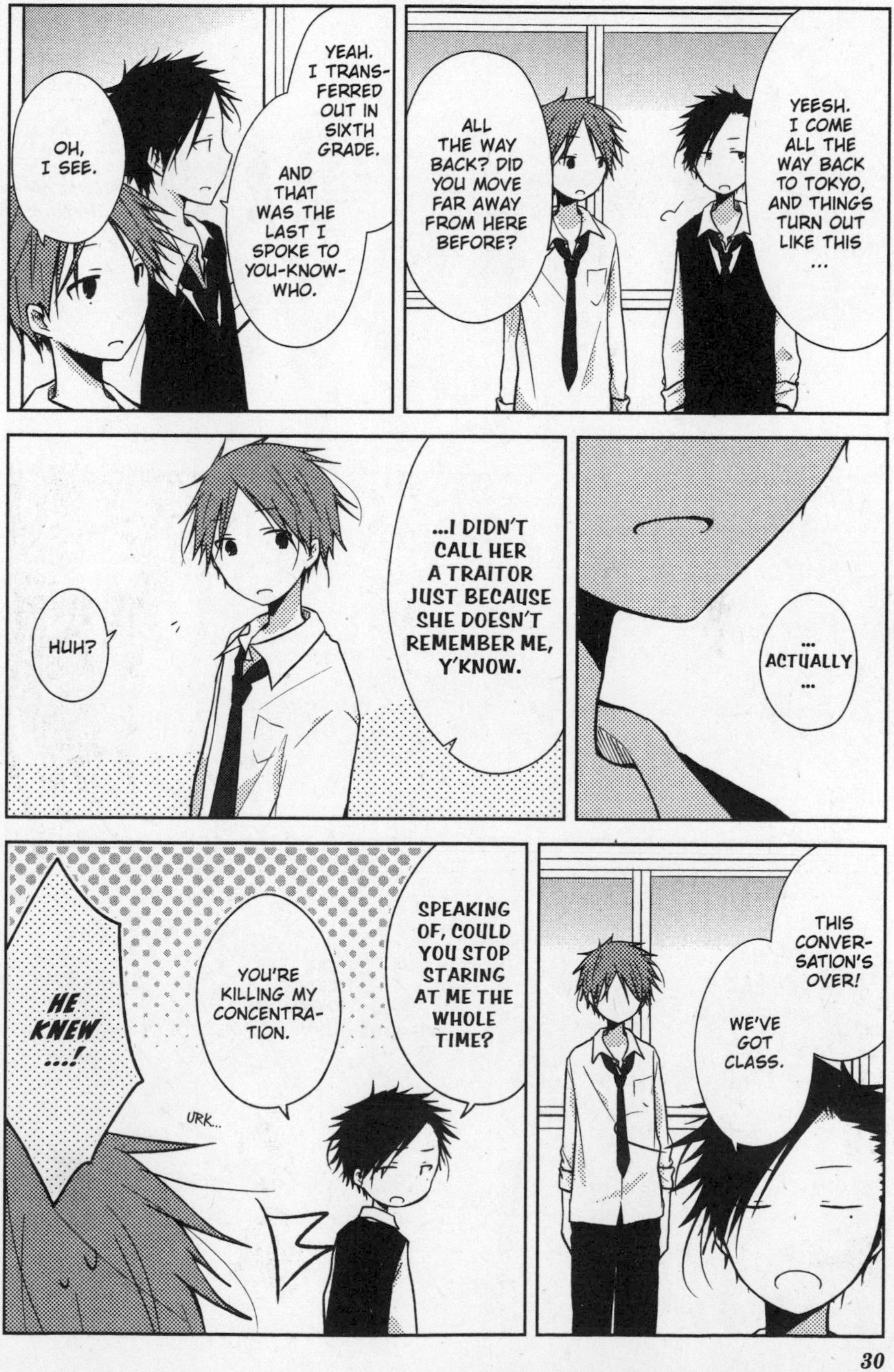
YEESH. I COME ALL THE WAY BACK TO TOKYO, AND THINGS TURN OUT LIKE THIS ...
ALL THE WAY BACK? DID YOU MOVE FAR AWAY FROM HERE BEFORE?
YEAH. I TRANSFERRED OUT IN SIXTH GRADE.
AND THAT WAS THE LAST I SPOKE TO YOU-KNOW-WHO.
OH, I SEE.
... ACTUALLY ...
...I DIDN'T CALL HER A TRAITOR JUST BECAUSE SHE DOESN'T REMEMBER ME, Y'KNOW.
HUH?
THIS CONVERSATION'S OVER!
WE'VE GOT CLASS.
SPEAKING OF, COULD YOU STOP STARING AT ME THE WHOLE TIME?
YOU'RE KILLING MY CONCENTRATION.
HE KNEW ...!
URK...

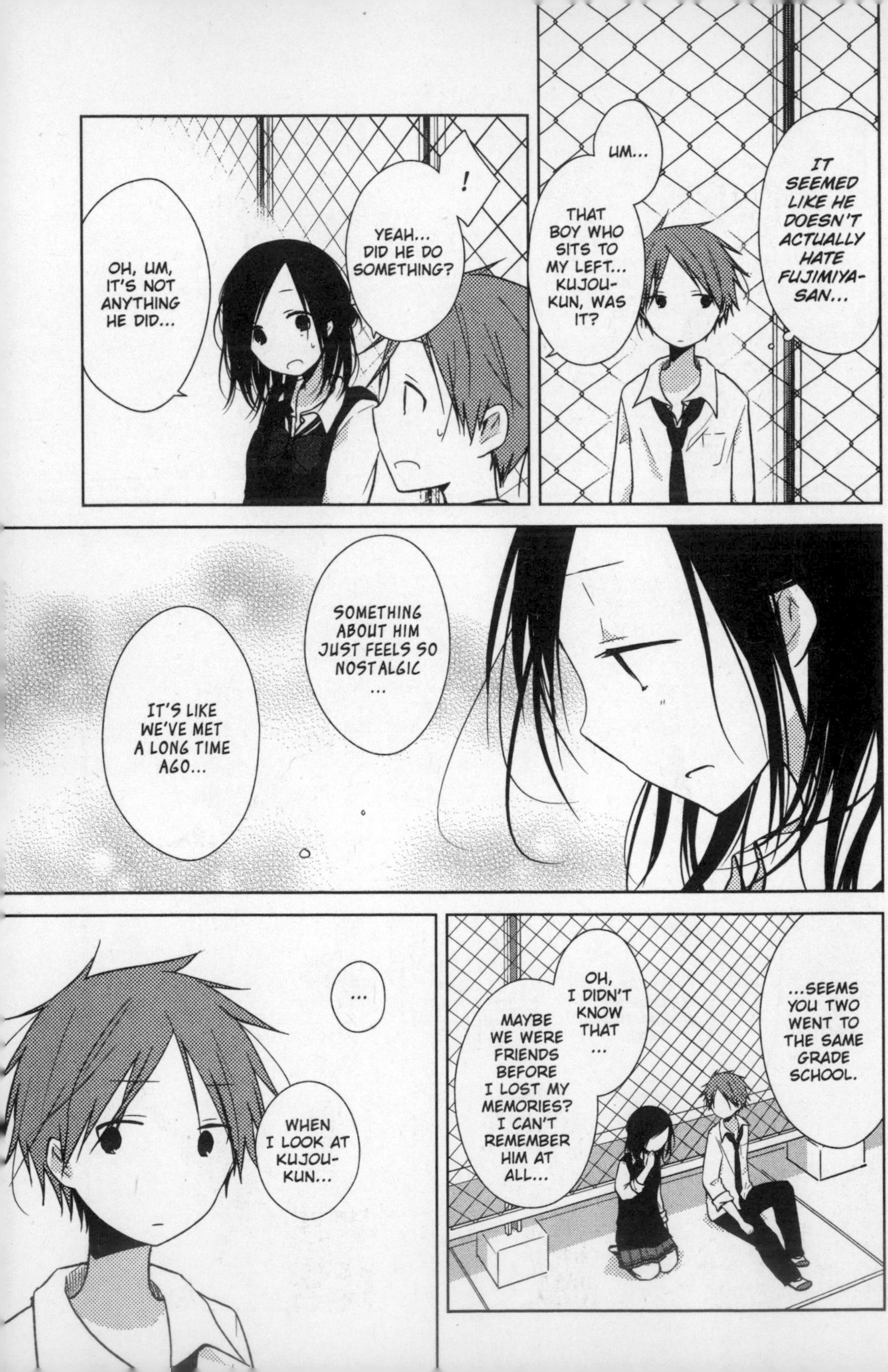
IT SEEMED LIKE HE DOESN'T ACTUALLY HATE FUJIMIYA-SAN...
UM...
THAT BOY WHO SITS TO MY LEFT... KUJOU-KUN, WAS IT?
!
YEAH... DID HE DO SOMETHING?
OH, UM, IT'S NOT ANYTHING HE DID...
SOMETHING ABOUT HIM JUST FEELS SO NOSTALGIC ...
IT'S LIKE WE'VE MET A LONG TIME AGO...
...SEEMS YOU TWO WENT TO THE SAME GRADE SCHOOL.
OH, I DIDN'T KNOW THAT ...
MAYBE WE WERE FRIENDS BEFORE I LOST MY MEMORIES? I CAN'T REMEMBER HIM AT ALL...
...
WHEN I LOOK AT KUJOU-KUN...

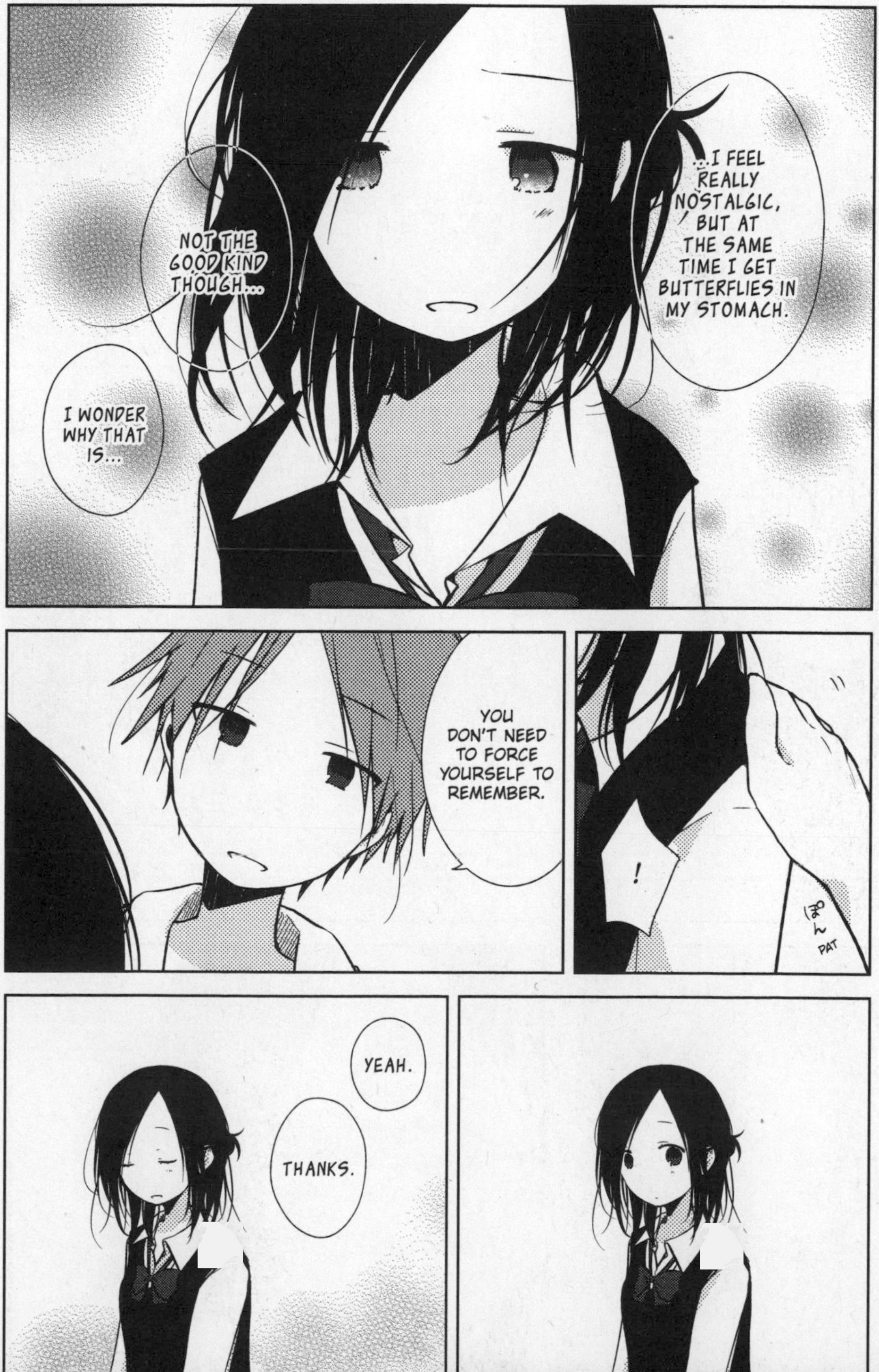
...I FEEL REALLY NOSTALGIC, BUT AT THE SAME TIME I GET BUTTERFLIES IN MY STOMACH.
NOT THE GOOD KIND THOUGH...
I WONDER WHY THAT IS...
!
ぽん
PAT
YOU DON'T NEED TO FORCE YOURSELF TO REMEMBER.
YEAH.
THANKS.

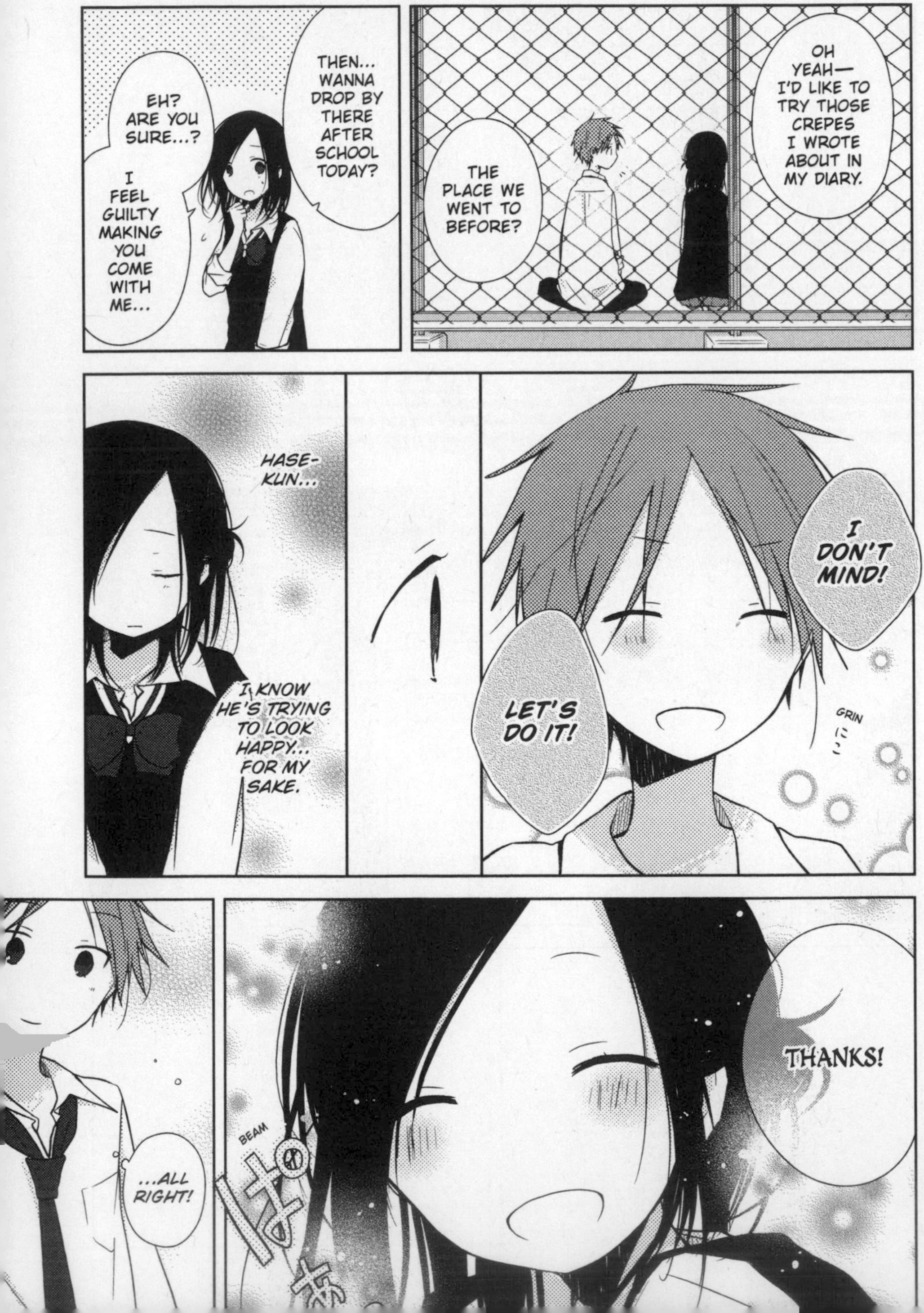
OH YEAH— I'D LIKE TO TRY THOSE CREPES I WROTE ABOUT IN MY DIARY.
THE PLACE WE WENT TO BEFORE?
THEN... WANNA DROP BY THERE AFTER SCHOOL TODAY?
EH? ARE YOU SURE...?
I FEEL GUILTY MAKING YOU COME WITH ME...
I DON'T MIND!
LET'S DO IT!
GRIN
にこ
HASE-KUN...
I KNOW HE'S TRYING TO LOOK HAPPY... FOR MY SAKE.
THANKS!
BEAM
...ALL RIGHT!

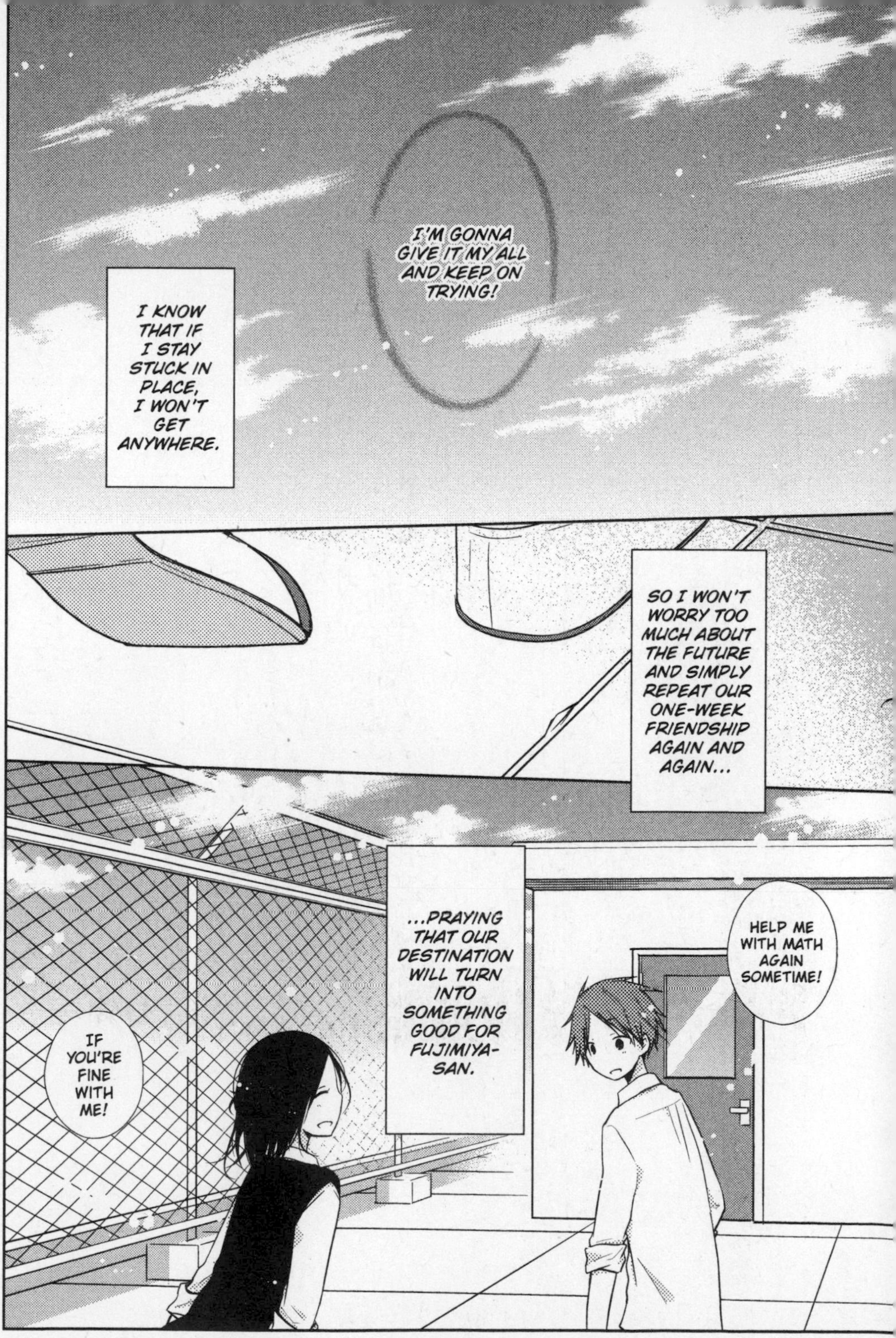
I'M GONNA GIVE IT MY ALL AND KEEP ON TRYING!
I KNOW THAT IF I STAY STUCK IN PLACE, I WON'T GET ANYWHERE.
SO I WON'T WORRY TOO MUCH ABOUT THE FUTURE AND SIMPLY REPEAT OUR ONE-WEEK FRIENDSHIP AGAIN AND AGAIN...
...PRAYING THAT OUR DESTINATION WILL TURN INTO SOMETHING GOOD FOR FUJIMIYA-SAN.
HELP ME WITH MATH AGAIN SOMETIME!
IF YOU'RE FINE WITH ME!

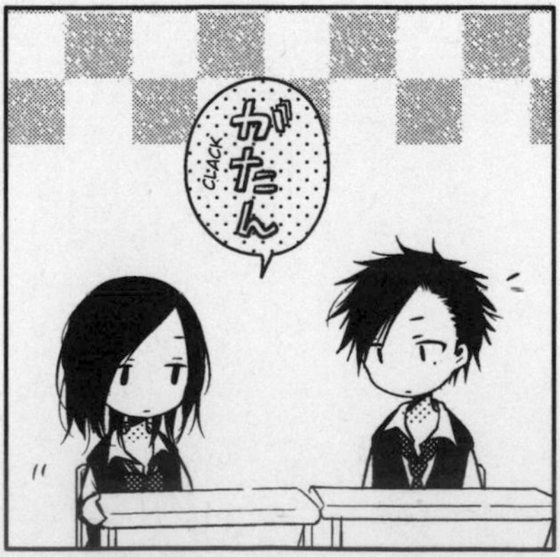
がたん
CLACK

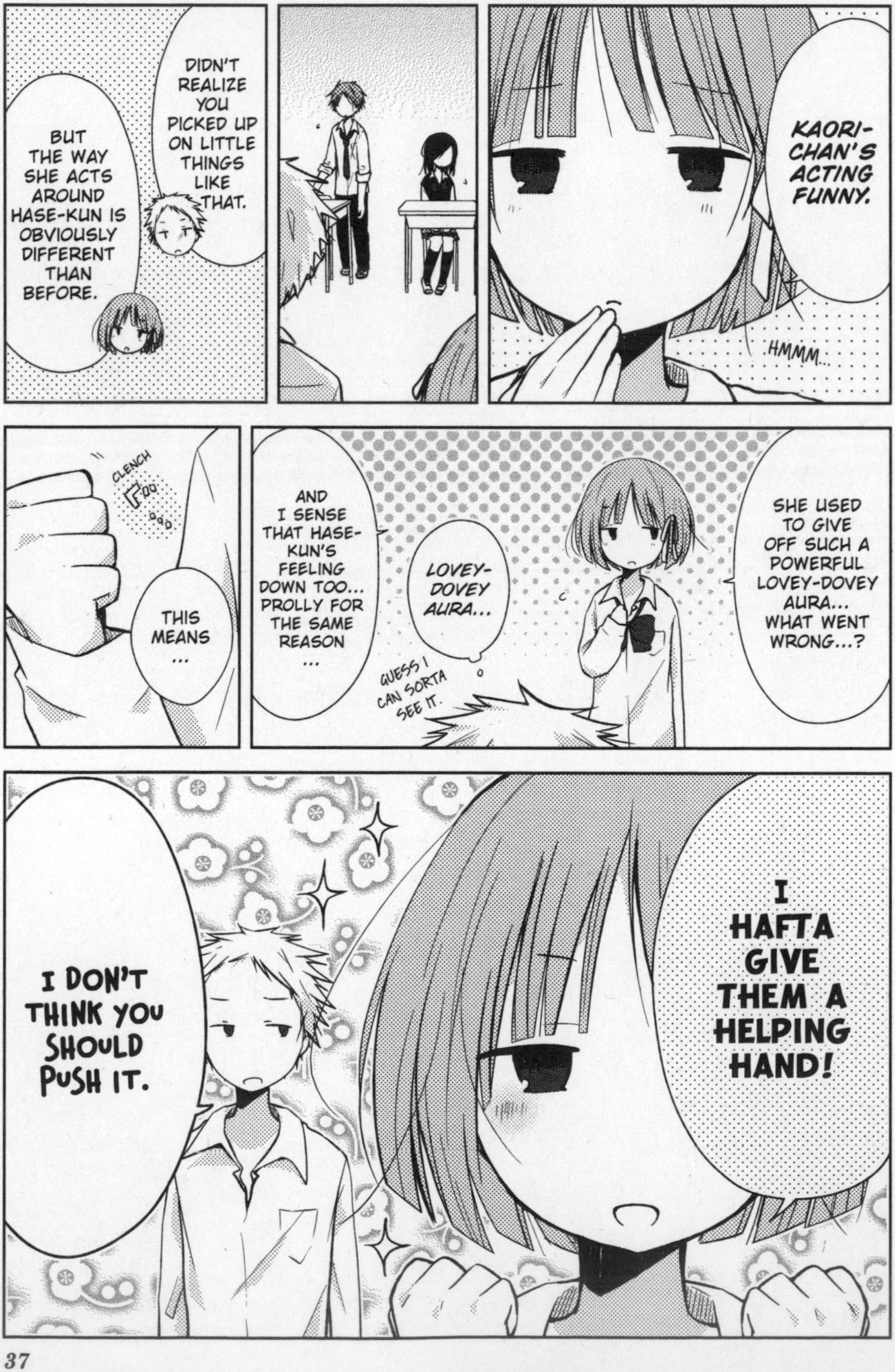
KAORI-CHAN'S ACTING FUNNY.
HMMM...
DIDN'T REALIZE YOU PICKED UP ON LITTLE THINGS LIKE THAT.
BUT THE WAY SHE ACTS AROUND HASE-KUN IS OBVIOUSLY DIFFERENT THAN BEFORE.
SHE USED TO GIVE OFF SUCH A POWERFUL LOVEY-DOVEY AURA... WHAT WENT WRONG...?
LOVEY-DOVEY AURA...
GUESS I CAN SORTA SEE IT.
AND I SENSE THAT HASE-KUN'S FEELING DOWN TOO... PROLLY FOR THE SAME REASON ...
CLENCH
THIS MEANS ...
I HAFTA GIVE THEM A HELPING HAND!
I DON'T THINK YOU SHOULD PUSH IT.

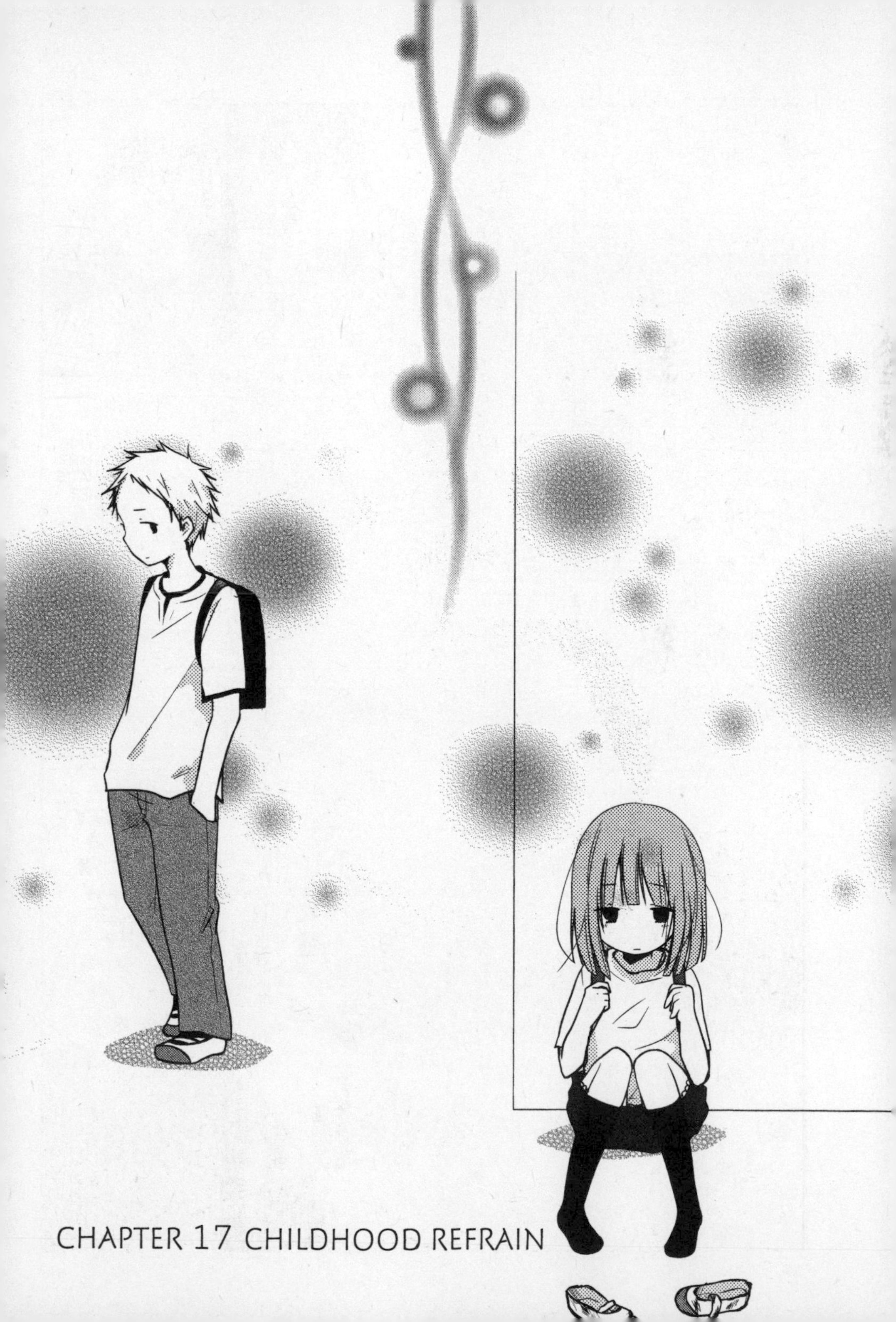

CHAPTER 17 CHILDHOOD REFRAIN

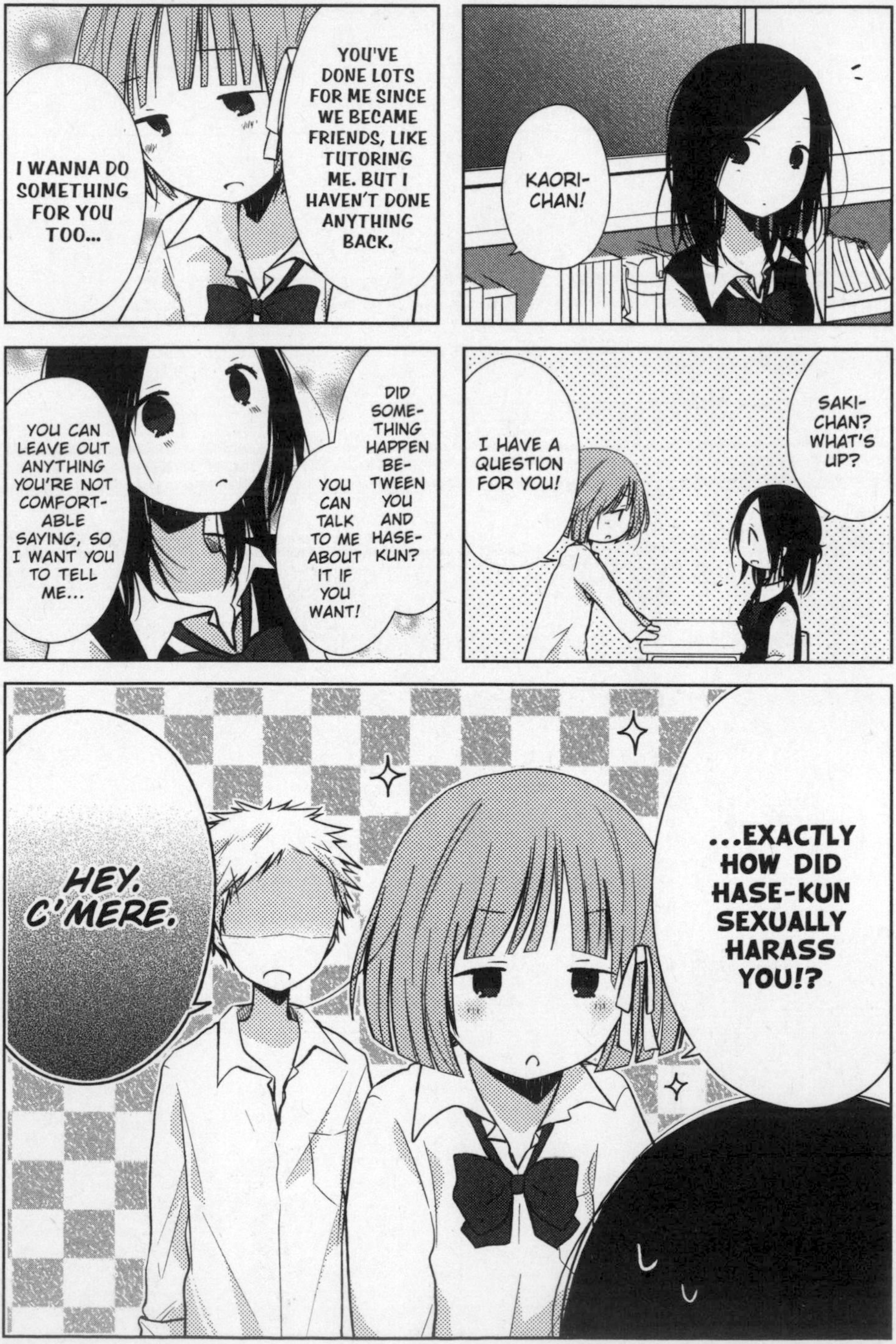
KAORI-CHAN!
YOU'VE DONE LOTS FOR ME SINCE WE BECAME FRIENDS, LIKE TUTORING ME. BUT I HAVEN'T DONE ANYTHING BACK.
I WANNA DO SOMETHING FOR YOU TOO...
SAKI-CHAN? WHAT'S UP?
I HAVE A QUESTION FOR YOU!
DID SOME-THING HAPPEN BE-TWEEN YOU AND HASE-KUN?
YOU CAN TALK TO ME ABOUT IT IF YOU WANT!
YOU CAN LEAVE OUT ANYTHING YOU'RE NOT COMFORT-ABLE SAYING, SO I WANT YOU TO TELL ME...
...EXACTLY HOW DID HASE-KUN SEXUALLY HARASS YOU!?
HEY. C'MERE.

ACCORDING TO HER IMAGINATION

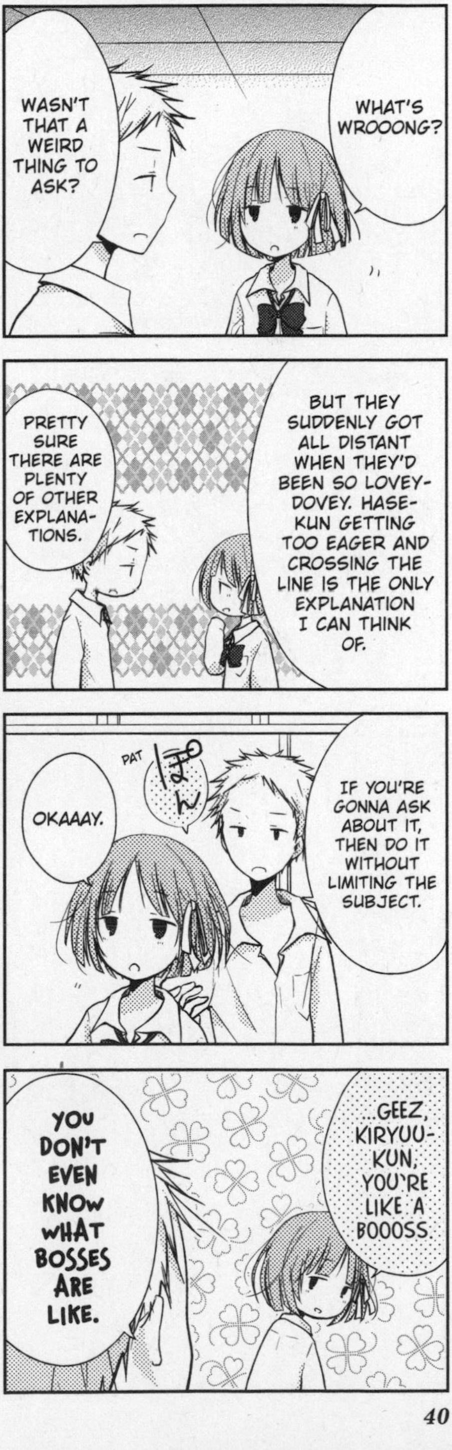
WHAT'S WROOONG?
WASN'T THAT A WEIRD THING TO ASK?
BUT THEY SUDDENLY GOT ALL DISTANT WHEN THEY'D BEEN SO LOVEY-DOVEY. HASE-KUN GETTING TOO EAGER AND CROSSING THE LINE IS THE ONLY EXPLANATION I CAN THINK OF.
PRETTY SURE THERE ARE PLENTY OF OTHER EXPLANATIONS.
IF YOU'RE GONNA ASK ABOUT IT, THEN DO IT WITHOUT LIMITING THE SUBJECT.
PAT
ぽん
OKAAAY.
...GEEZ, KIRYUU-KUN, YOU'RE LIKE A BOOOSS.
YOU DON'T EVEN KNOW WHAT BOSSES ARE LIKE.

NOTHING FOR IT

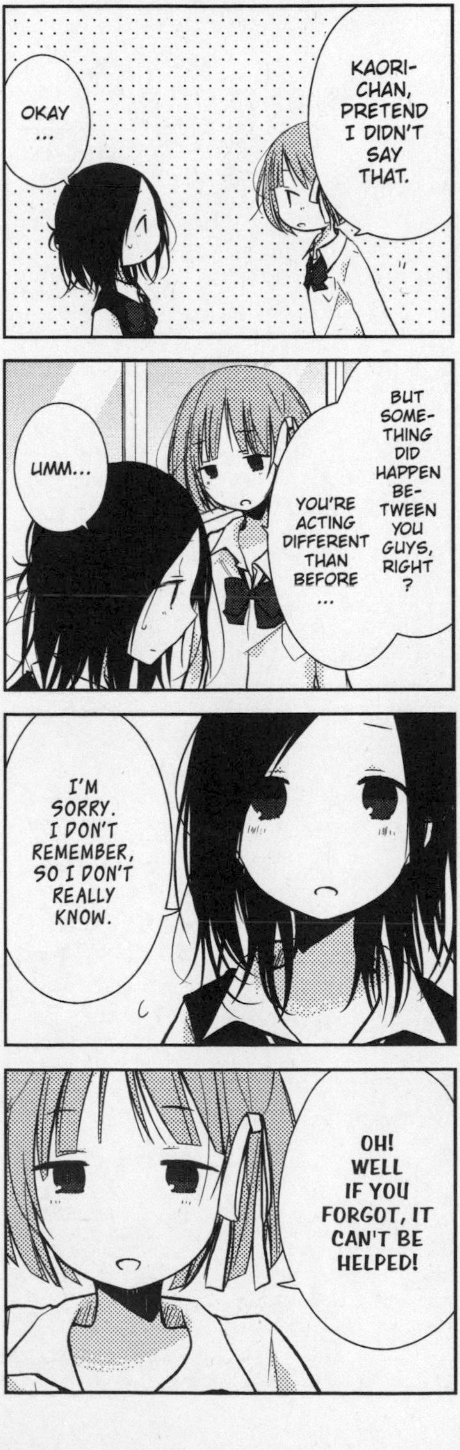
KAORI-CHAN, PRETEND I DIDN'T SAY THAT.
OKAY ...
BUT SOMETHING DID HAPPEN BETWEEN YOU GUYS, RIGHT?
YOU'RE ACTING DIFFERENT THAN BEFORE ...
UMM...
I'M SORRY. I DON'T REMEMBER, SO I DON'T REALLY KNOW.
OH! WELL IF YOU FORGOT, IT CAN'T BE HELPED!

AFTER ALL

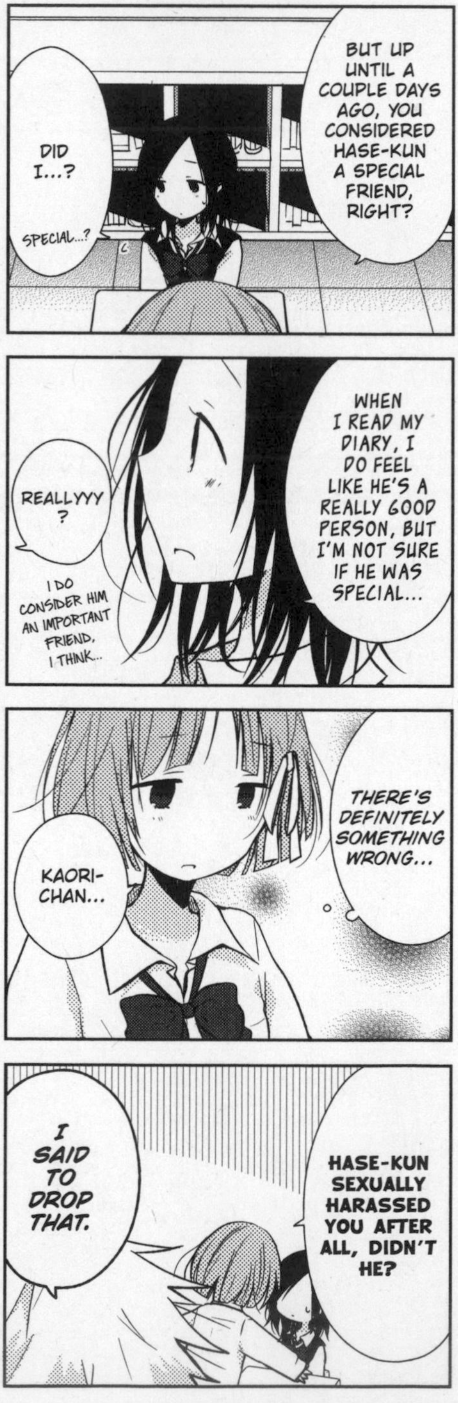
BUT UP UNTIL A COUPLE DAYS AGO, YOU CONSIDERED HASE-KUN A SPECIAL FRIEND, RIGHT?
DID I...?
SPECIAL...?
WHEN I READ MY DIARY, I DO FEEL LIKE HE'S A REALLY GOOD PERSON, BUT I'M NOT SURE IF HE WAS SPECIAL...
REALLYYY ?
I DO CONSIDER HIM AN IMPORTANT FRIEND, I THINK...
THERE'S DEFINITELY SOMETHING WRONG...
KAORI-CHAN...
HASE-KUN SEXUALLY HARASSED YOU AFTER ALL, DIDN'T HE?
I SAID TO DROP THAT.

STAB

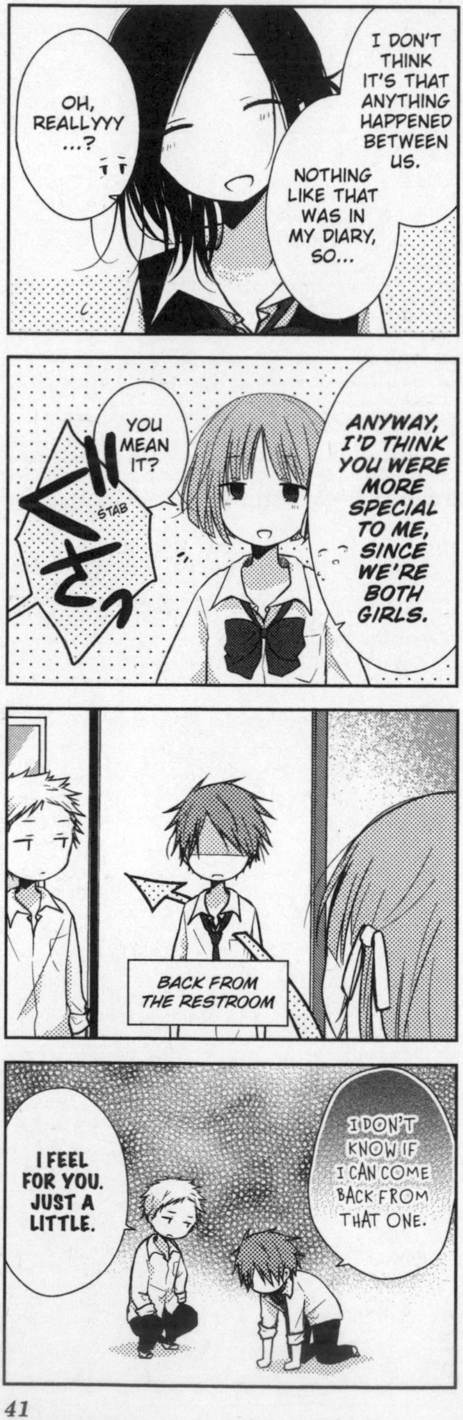
I DON'T THINK IT'S THAT ANYTHING HAPPENED BETWEEN US.
NOTHING LIKE THAT WAS IN MY DIARY, SO...
OH, REALLYYY ...?
ANYWAY, I'D THINK YOU WERE MORE SPECIAL TO ME, SINCE WE'RE BOTH GIRLS.
YOU MEAN IT?
STAB
BACK FROM THE RESTROOM
I DON'T KNOW IF I CAN COME BACK FROM THAT ONE.
I FEEL FOR YOU. JUST A LITTLE.

A FIXED THING

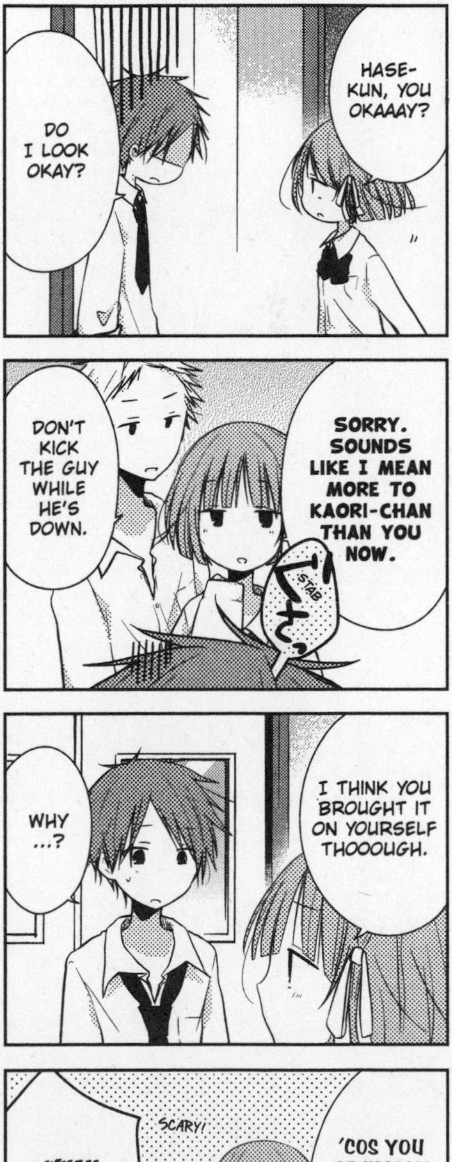
HASE-KUN, YOU OKAAAY?
DO I LOOK OKAY?
SORRY. SOUNDS LIKE I MEAN MORE TO KAORI-CHAN THAN YOU NOW.
STAB
DON'T KICK THE GUY WHILE HE'S DOWN.
I THINK YOU BROUGHT IT ON YOURSELF THOOOUGH.
WHY ...?
'COS YOU SEXUALLY HARASSED HER, DIDN'T YOU?
SCARY!
WHEN DID IT TURN INTO THAT!?

HAPPENS ALL THE TIME

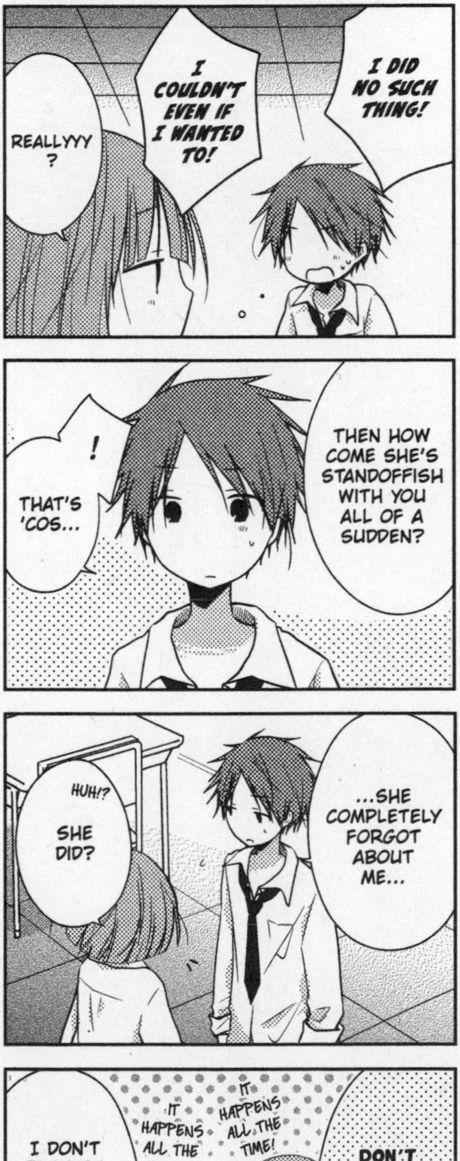
I DID NO SUCH THING!
I COULDN'T EVEN IF I WANTED TO!
REALLYYY?
THEN HOW COME SHE'S STANDOFFISH WITH YOU ALL OF A SUDDEN?
!
THAT'S 'COS...
...SHE COMPLETELY FORGOT ABOUT ME...
HUH!?
SHE DID?
DON'T BLAME HER TOO MUCH FOR FORGETTING, OKAY?
IT HAPPENS ALL THE TIME!
IT HAPPENS ALL THE TIME...?
I DON'T PLAN ON IT, BUT HEARING THAT COMING FROM YOU IS KINDA...

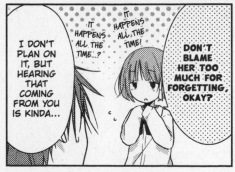

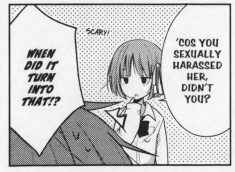

ALL THAT

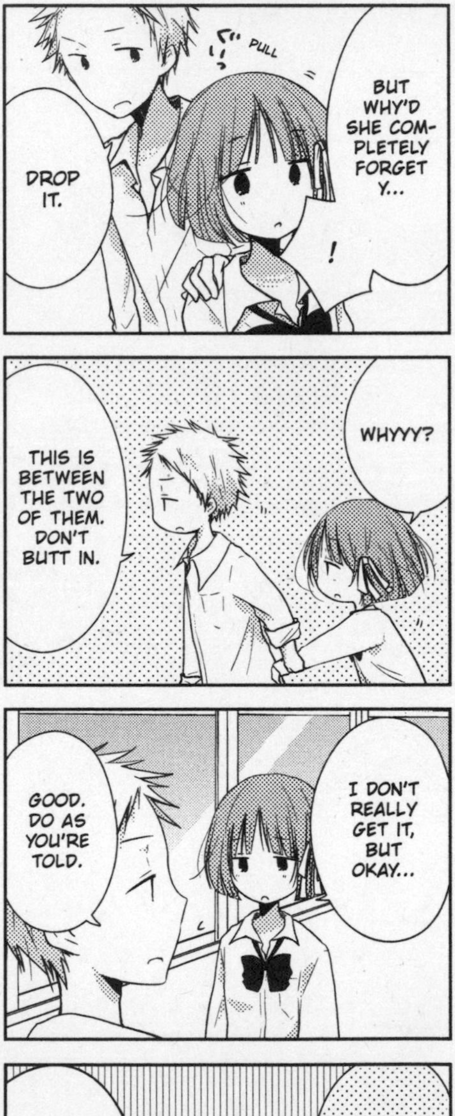
BUT WHY'D SHE COMPLETELY FORGET Y...
PULL
DROP IT.
WHYYY?
THIS IS BETWEEN THE TWO OF THEM. DON'T BUTT IN.
I DON'T REALLY GET IT, BUT OKAY...
GOOD. DO AS YOU'RE TOLD.
THEN IN EXCHANGE, FEED ME A FUN TOPIC.
WAS ALL THAT JUST YOU KILLING TIME?

HIDDEN AGENDA

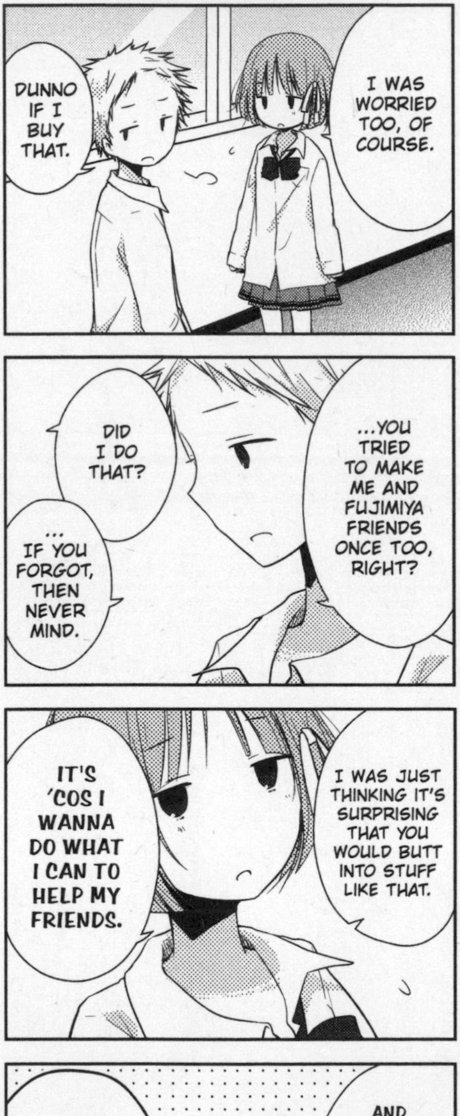
I WAS WORRIED TOO, OF COURSE.
DUNNO IF I BUY THAT.
...YOU TRIED TO MAKE ME AND FUJIMIYA FRIENDS ONCE TOO, RIGHT?
DID I DO THAT?
... IF YOU FORGOT, THEN NEVER MIND.
I WAS JUST THINKING IT'S SURPRISING THAT YOU WOULD BUTT INTO STUFF LIKE THAT.
IT'S 'COS I WANNA DO WHAT I CAN TO HELP MY FRIENDS.
AND THEN, IT'D BE GREAT IF WE BECAME EVEN CLOSER, AND I COULD GET FAWNED ON EVEN MORE.
SO IN THE END IT'S ALL TO HELP YOURSELF?

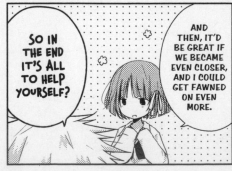

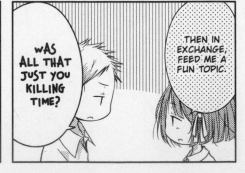

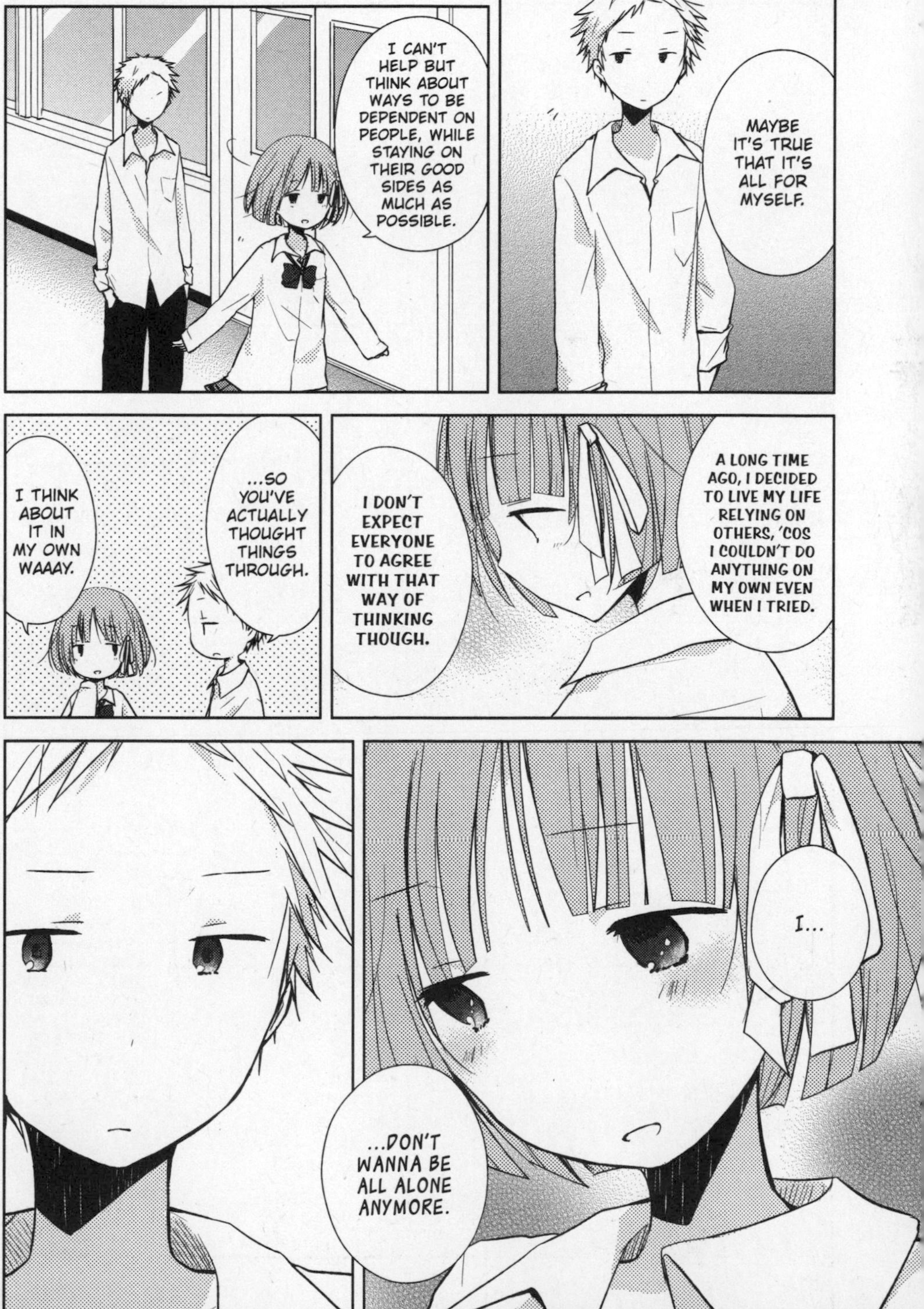
MAYBE IT'S TRUE THAT IT'S ALL FOR MYSELF.
I CAN'T HELP BUT THINK ABOUT WAYS TO BE DEPENDENT ON PEOPLE, WHILE STAYING ON THEIR GOOD SIDES AS MUCH AS POSSIBLE.
A LONG TIME AGO, I DECIDED TO LIVE MY LIFE RELYING ON OTHERS, 'COS I COULDN'T DO ANYTHING ON MY OWN EVEN WHEN I TRIED.
I DON'T EXPECT EVERYONE TO AGREE WITH THAT WAY OF THINKING THOUGH.
...SO YOU'VE ACTUALLY THOUGHT THINGS THROUGH.
I THINK ABOUT IT IN MY OWN WAAAY.
I...
...DON'T WANNA BE ALL ALONE ANYMORE.

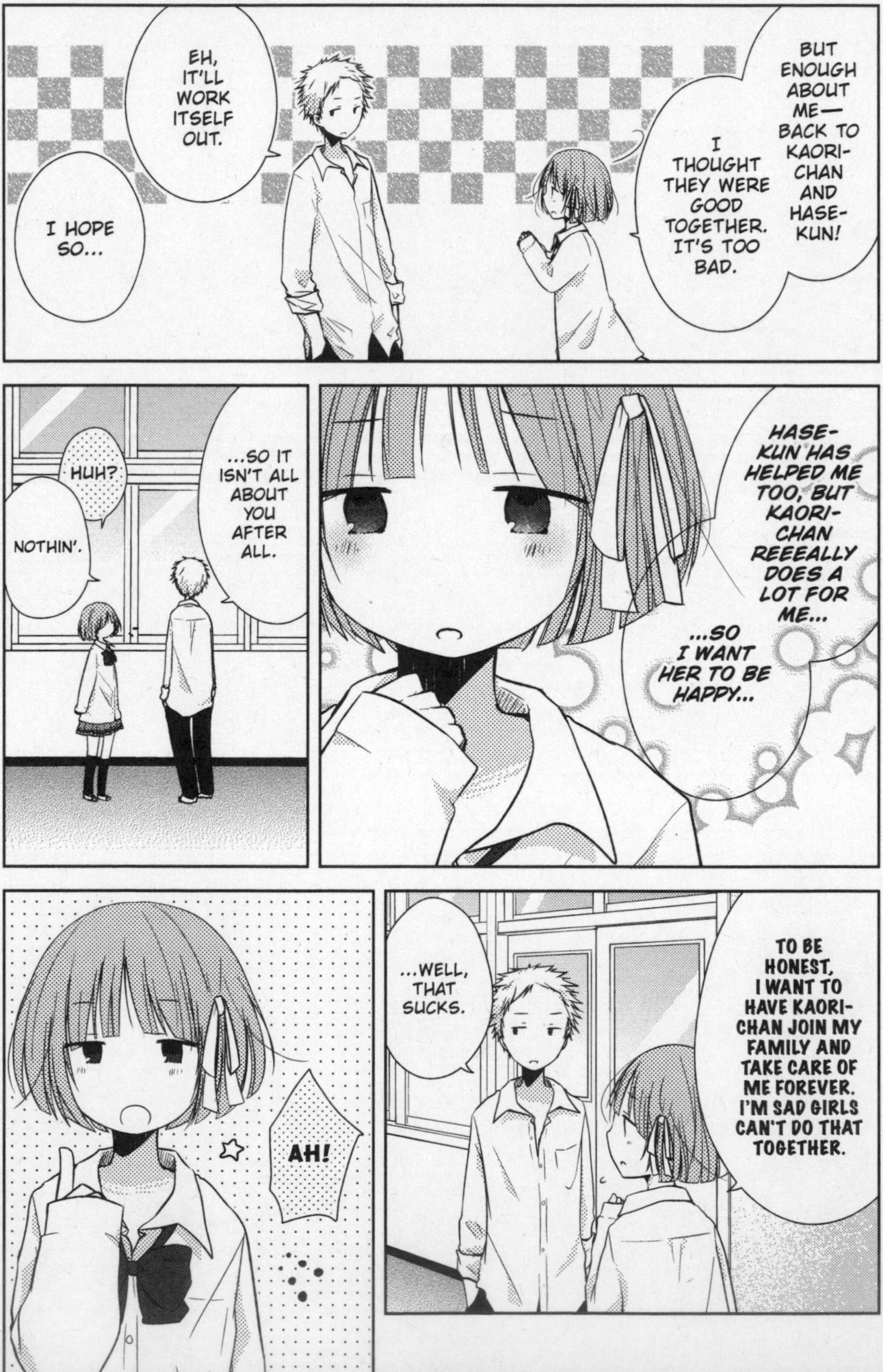
BUT ENOUGH ABOUT ME— BACK TO KAORI-CHAN AND HASE-KUN!
I THOUGHT THEY WERE GOOD TOGETHER. IT'S TOO BAD.
EH, IT'LL WORK ITSELF OUT.
I HOPE SO...
HASE-KUN HAS HELPED ME TOO, BUT KAORI-CHAN REEEALLY DOES A LOT FOR ME...
...SO I WANT HER TO BE HAPPY...
...SO IT ISN'T ALL ABOUT YOU AFTER ALL.
HUH?
NOTHIN'.
TO BE HONEST, I WANT TO HAVE KAORI-CHAN JOIN MY FAMILY AND TAKE CARE OF ME FOREVER. I'M SAD GIRLS CAN'T DO THAT TOGETHER.
...WELL, THAT SUCKS.
AH!

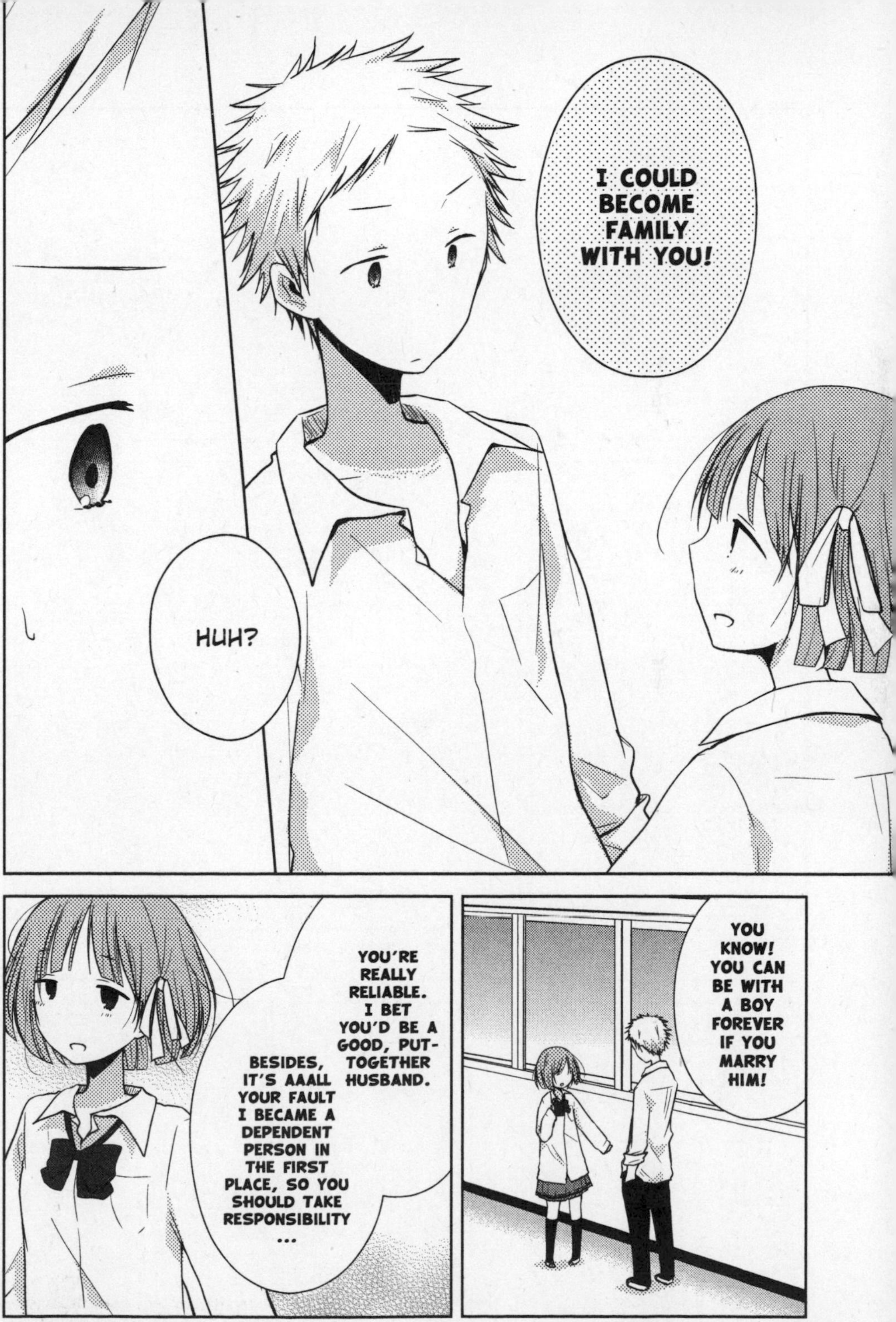
I COULD BECOME FAMILY WITH YOU!
HUH?
YOU KNOW! YOU CAN BE WITH A BOY FOREVER IF YOU MARRY HIM!
YOU'RE REALLY RELIABLE. I BET YOU'D BE A GOOD, PUT-TOGETHER HUSBAND.
BESIDES, IT'S AAALL YOUR FAULT I BECAME A DEPENDENT PERSON IN THE FIRST PLACE, SO YOU SHOULD TAKE RESPONSIBILITY ...

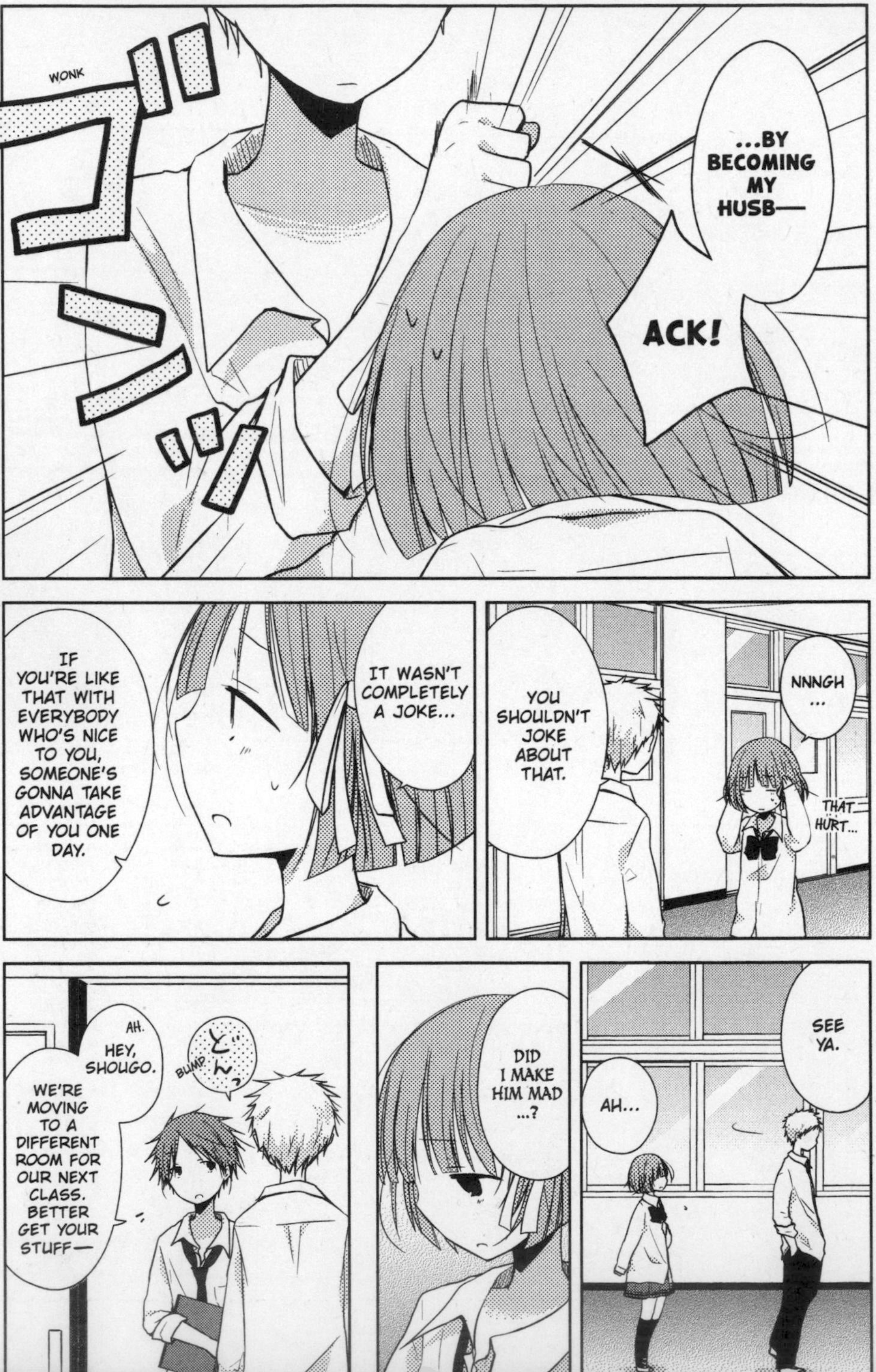
...BY BECOMING MY HUSB—
WONK
ゴンッ
ACK!
NNNGH...
THAT HURT...
YOU SHOULDN'T JOKE ABOUT THAT.
IT WASN'T COMPLETELY A JOKE...
IF YOU'RE LIKE THAT WITH EVERYBODY WHO'S NICE TO YOU, SOMEONE'S GONNA TAKE ADVANTAGE OF YOU ONE DAY.
SEE YA.
AH...
DID I MAKE HIM MAD ...?
どん
BUMP
AH.
HEY, SHOUGO.
WE'RE MOVING TO A DIFFERENT ROOM FOR OUR NEXT CLASS. BETTER GET YOUR STUFF—

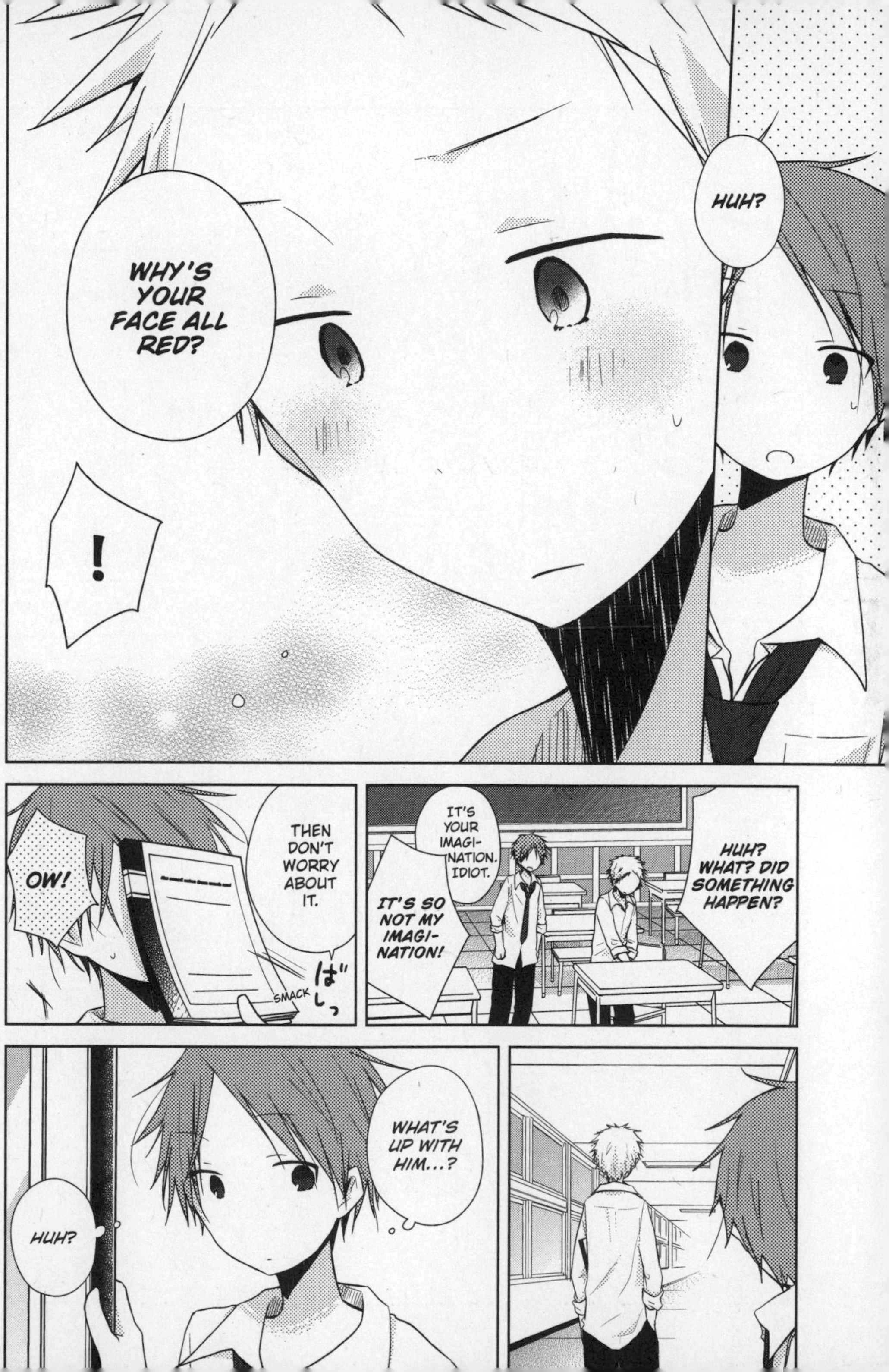
HUH?
WHY'S YOUR FACE ALL RED?
!
HUH? WHAT? DID SOMETHING HAPPEN?
IT'S YOUR IMAGINATION. IDIOT.
IT'S SO NOT MY IMAGINATION!
THEN DON'T WORRY ABOUT IT.
ばしっ
SMACK
OW!
WHAT'S UP WITH HIM...?
HUH?

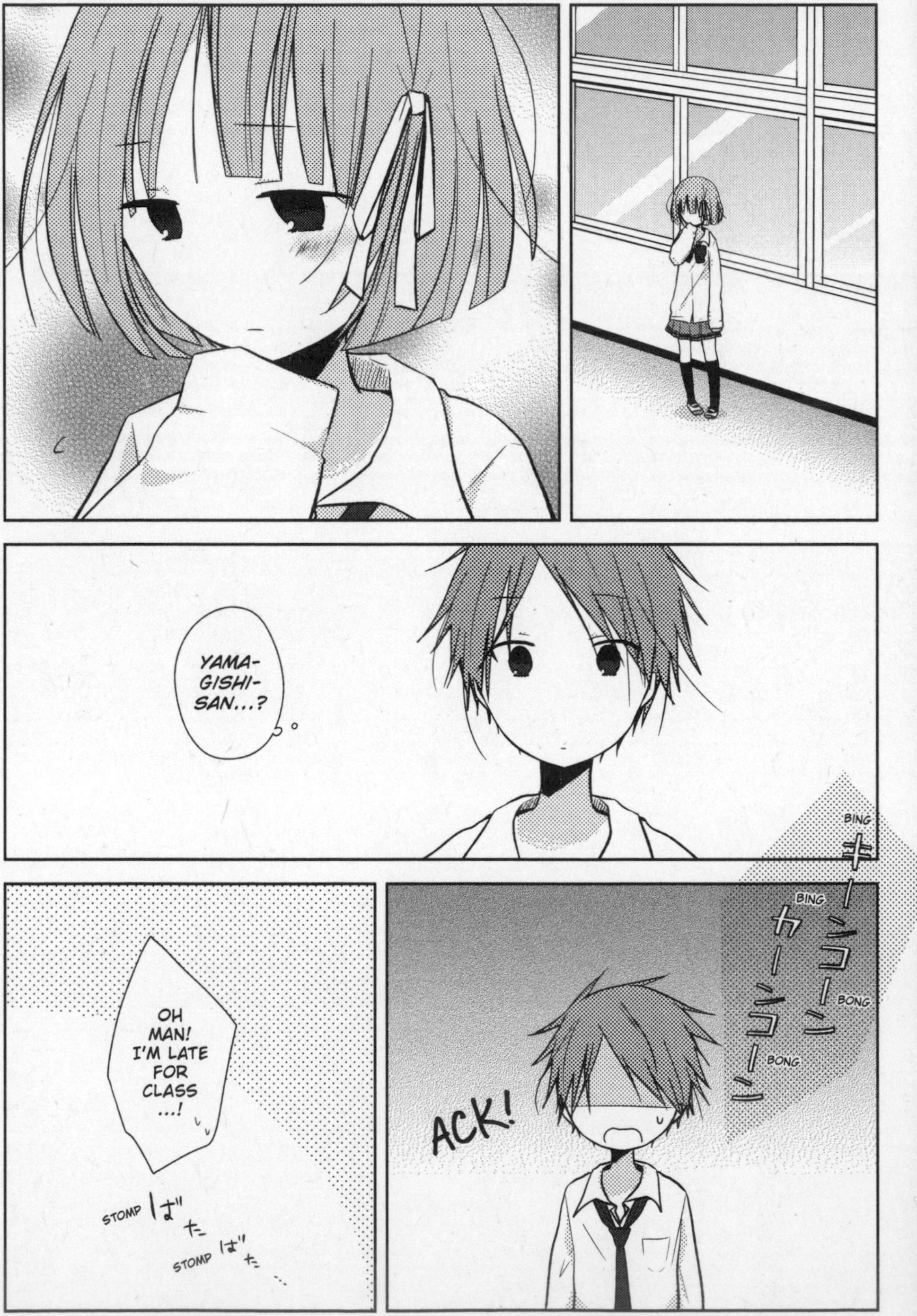
YAMA-GISHI-SAN...?
BING
キーンコーン
BING
カーンコーン
BONG
BONG
ACK!
OH MAN! I'M LATE FOR CLASS ...!
STOMP ばた
STOMP ばた

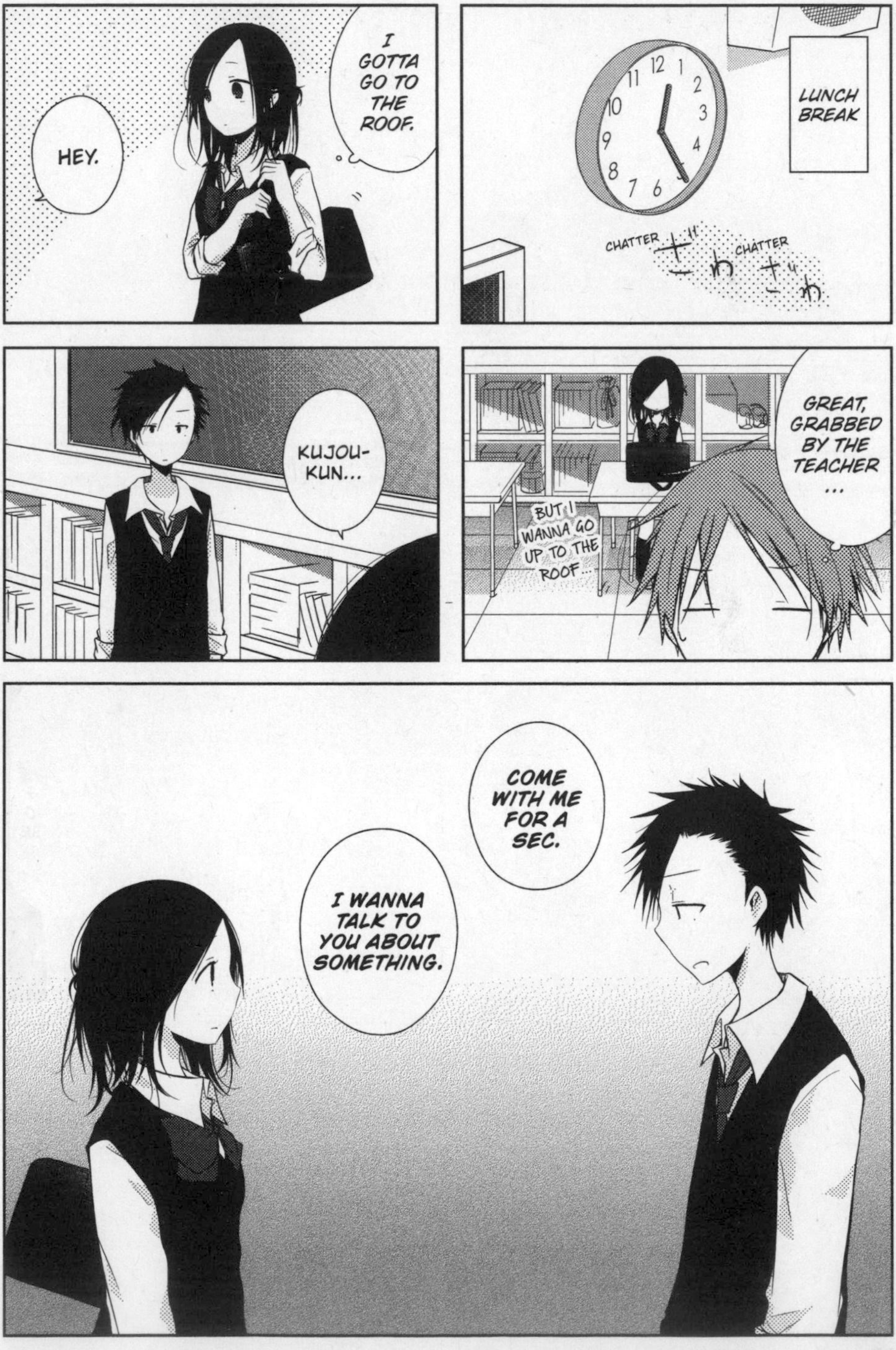
LUNCH BREAK
CHATTER
CHATTER
I GOTTA GO TO THE ROOF.
HEY.
GREAT, GRABBED BY THE TEACHER...
BUT I WANNA GO UP TO THE ROOF...
KUJOU-KUN...
COME WITH ME FOR A SEC.
I WANNA TALK TO YOU ABOUT SOMETHING.

CHAPTER 18 THIRD-WHEEL RHAPSODY

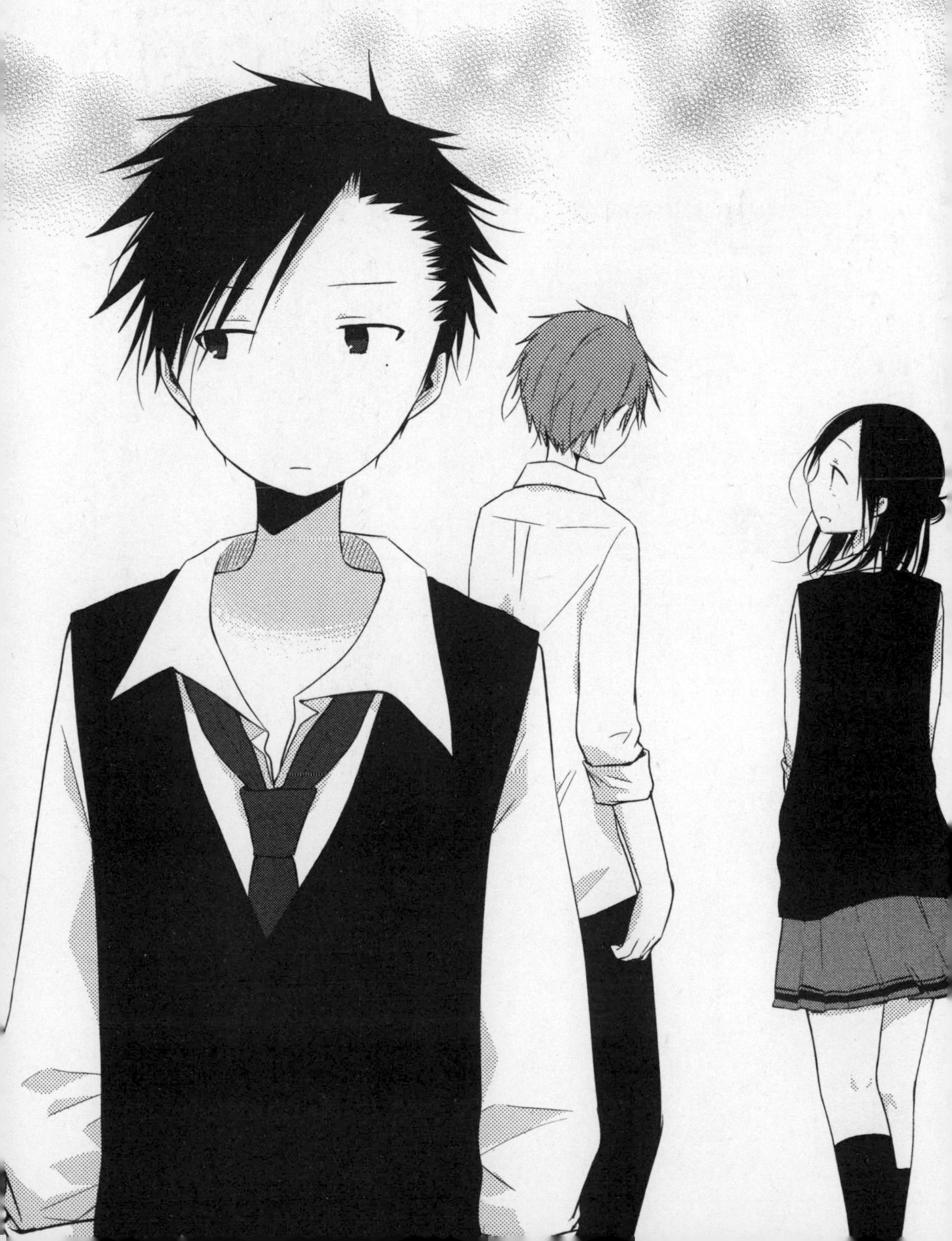

CALLED OUT

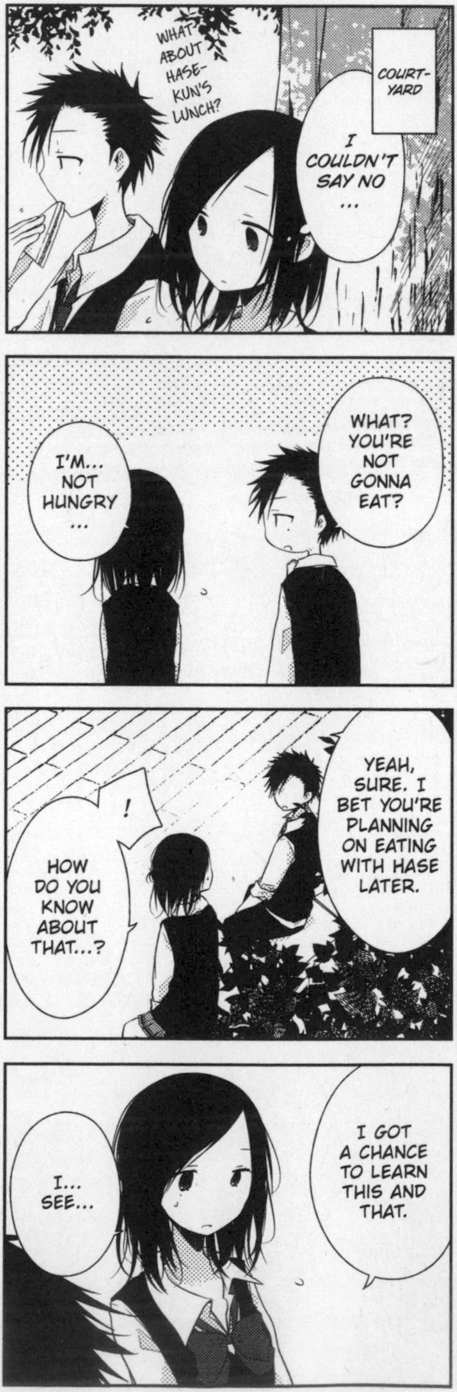
COURT-YARD
I COULDN'T SAY NO ...
WHAT ABOUT HASE-KUN'S LUNCH?
WHAT? YOU'RE NOT GONNA EAT?
I'M... NOT HUNGRY ...
YEAH, SURE. I BET YOU'RE PLANNING ON EATING WITH HASE LATER.
!
HOW DO YOU KNOW ABOUT THAT...?
I GOT A CHANCE TO LEARN THIS AND THAT.
I... SEE...

BECAUSE WE'RE FRIENDS

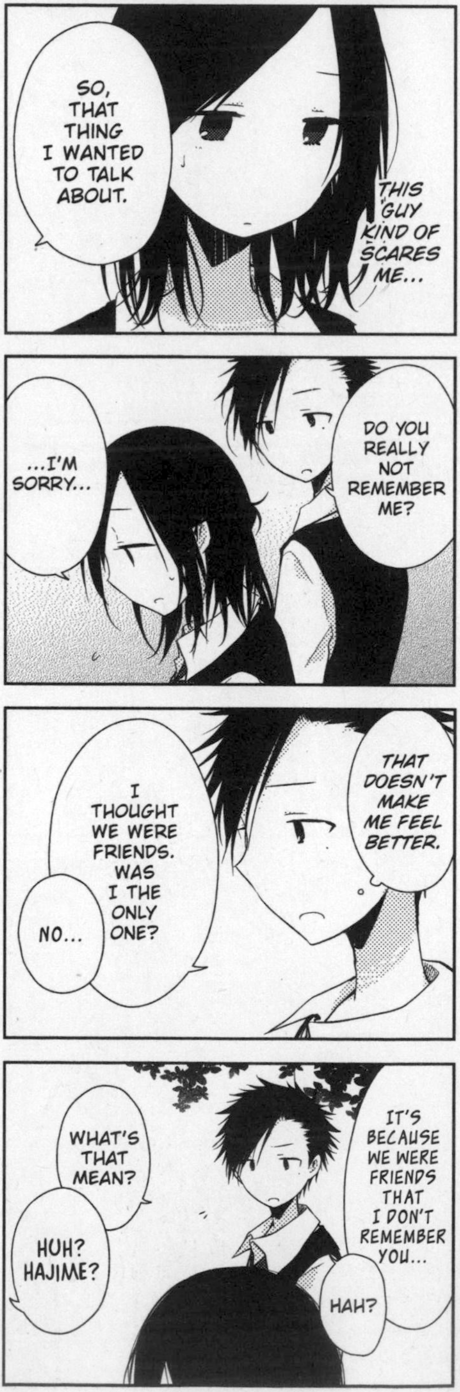
THIS GUY KIND OF SCARES ME...
SO, THAT THING I WANTED TO TALK ABOUT.
DO YOU REALLY NOT REMEMBER ME?
...I'M SORRY...
THAT DOESN'T MAKE ME FEEL BETTER.
I THOUGHT WE WERE FRIENDS. WAS I THE ONLY ONE?
NO...
IT'S BECAUSE WE WERE FRIENDS THAT I DON'T REMEMBER YOU...
HAH?
WHAT'S THAT MEAN?
HUH? HAJIME?

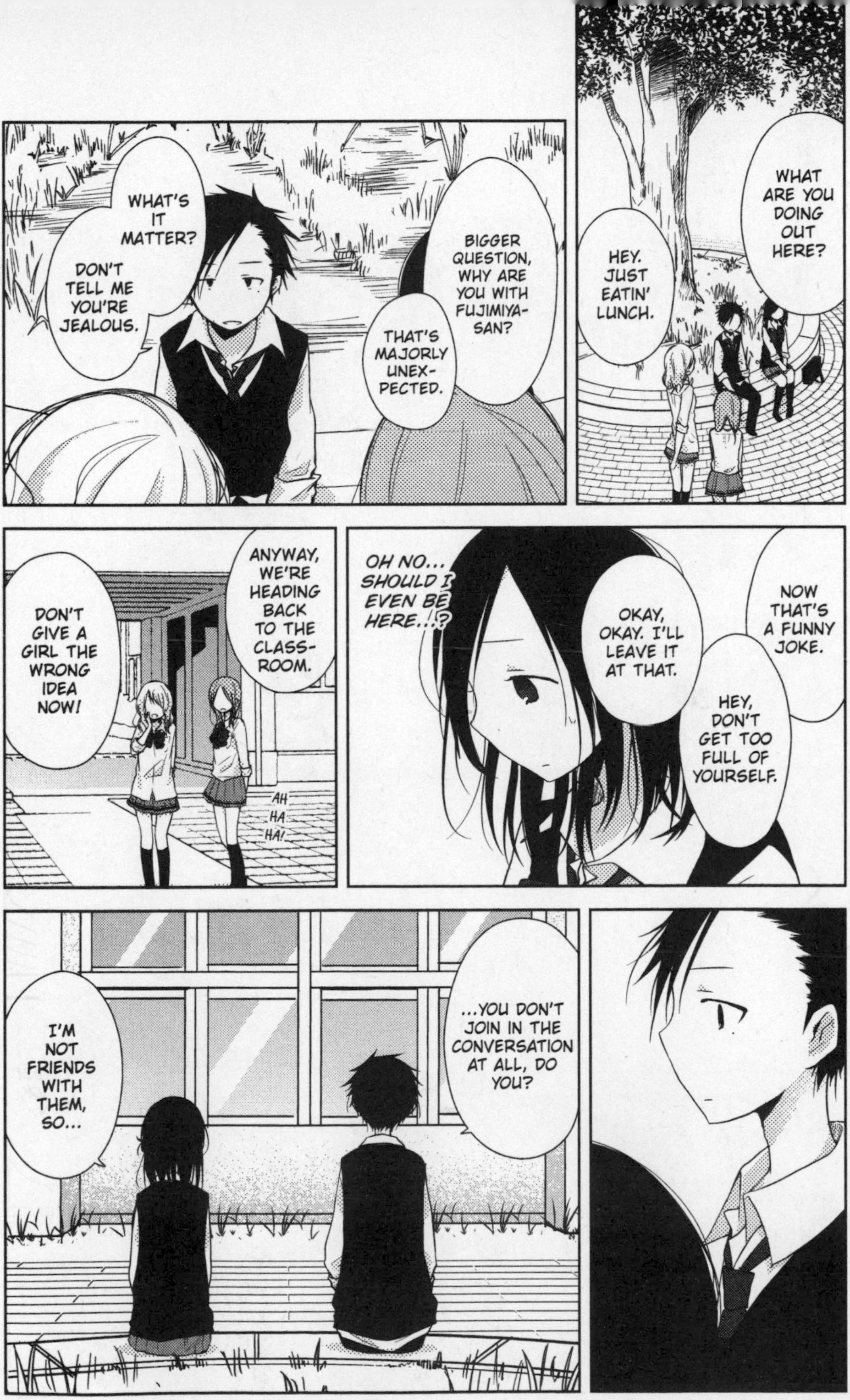
WHAT ARE YOU DOING OUT HERE?
HEY. JUST EATIN' LUNCH.
BIGGER QUESTION, WHY ARE YOU WITH FUJIMIYA-SAN?
THAT'S MAJORLY UNEXPECTED.
WHAT'S IT MATTER?
DON'T TELL ME YOU'RE JEALOUS.
NOW THAT'S A FUNNY JOKE.
HEY, DON'T GET TOO FULL OF YOURSELF.
OKAY, OKAY. I'LL LEAVE IT AT THAT.
OH NO... SHOULD I EVEN BE HERE...!?
ANYWAY, WE'RE HEADING BACK TO THE CLASS-ROOM.
DON'T GIVE A GIRL THE WRONG IDEA NOW!
AH HA HA!
...YOU DON'T JOIN IN THE CONVERSATION AT ALL, DO YOU?
I'M NOT FRIENDS WITH THEM, SO...

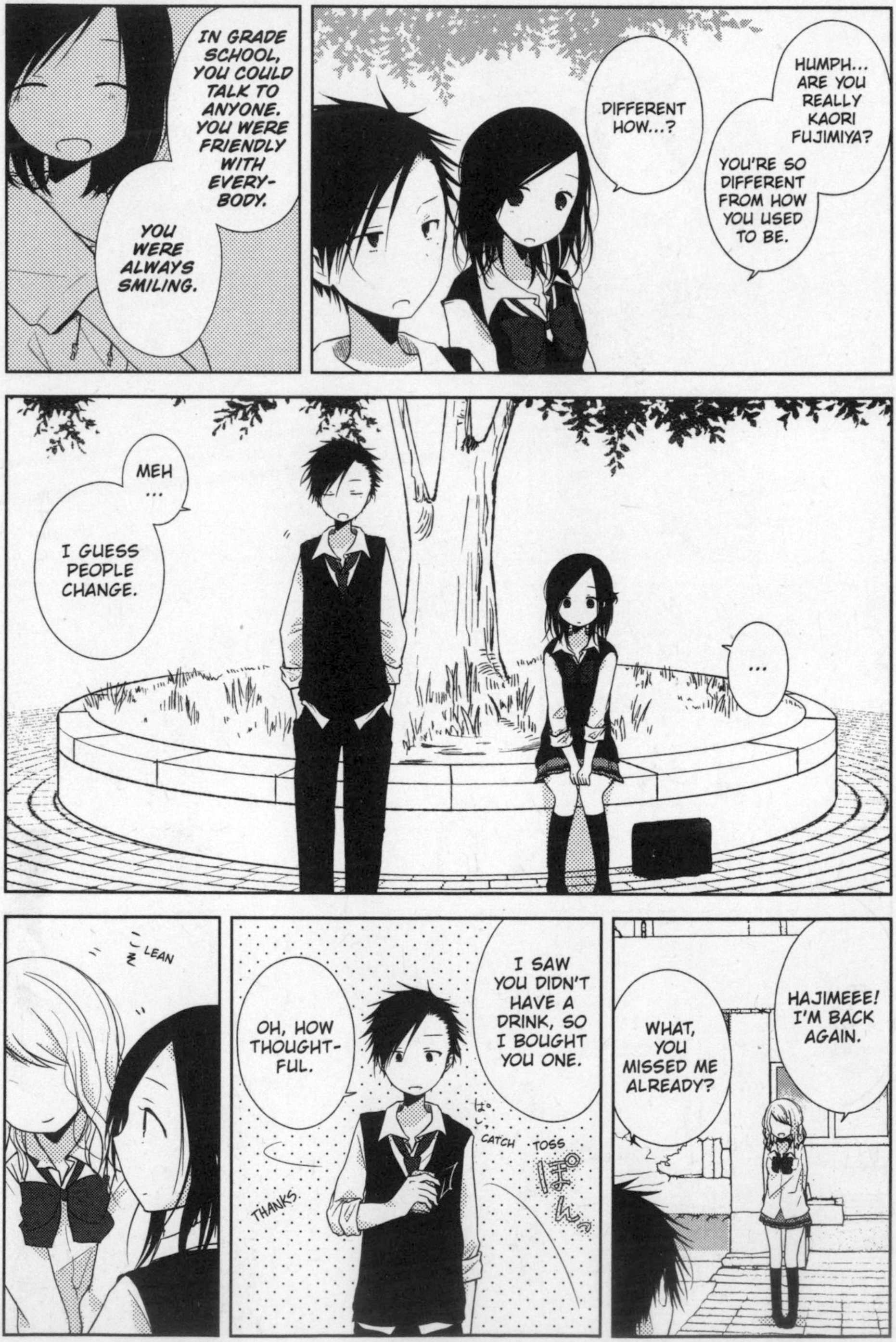
HUMPH... ARE YOU REALLY KAORI FUJIMIYA?
YOU'RE SO DIFFERENT FROM HOW YOU USED TO BE.
DIFFERENT HOW...?
IN GRADE SCHOOL, YOU COULD TALK TO ANYONE. YOU WERE FRIENDLY WITH EVERY-BODY.
YOU WERE ALWAYS SMILING.
MEH ...
I GUESS PEOPLE CHANGE.
...
HAJIMEEE! I'M BACK AGAIN.
WHAT, YOU MISSED ME ALREADY?
I SAW YOU DIDN'T HAVE A DRINK, SO I BOUGHT YOU ONE.
TOSS
CATCH
OH, HOW THOUGHTFUL.
THANKS.
LEAN

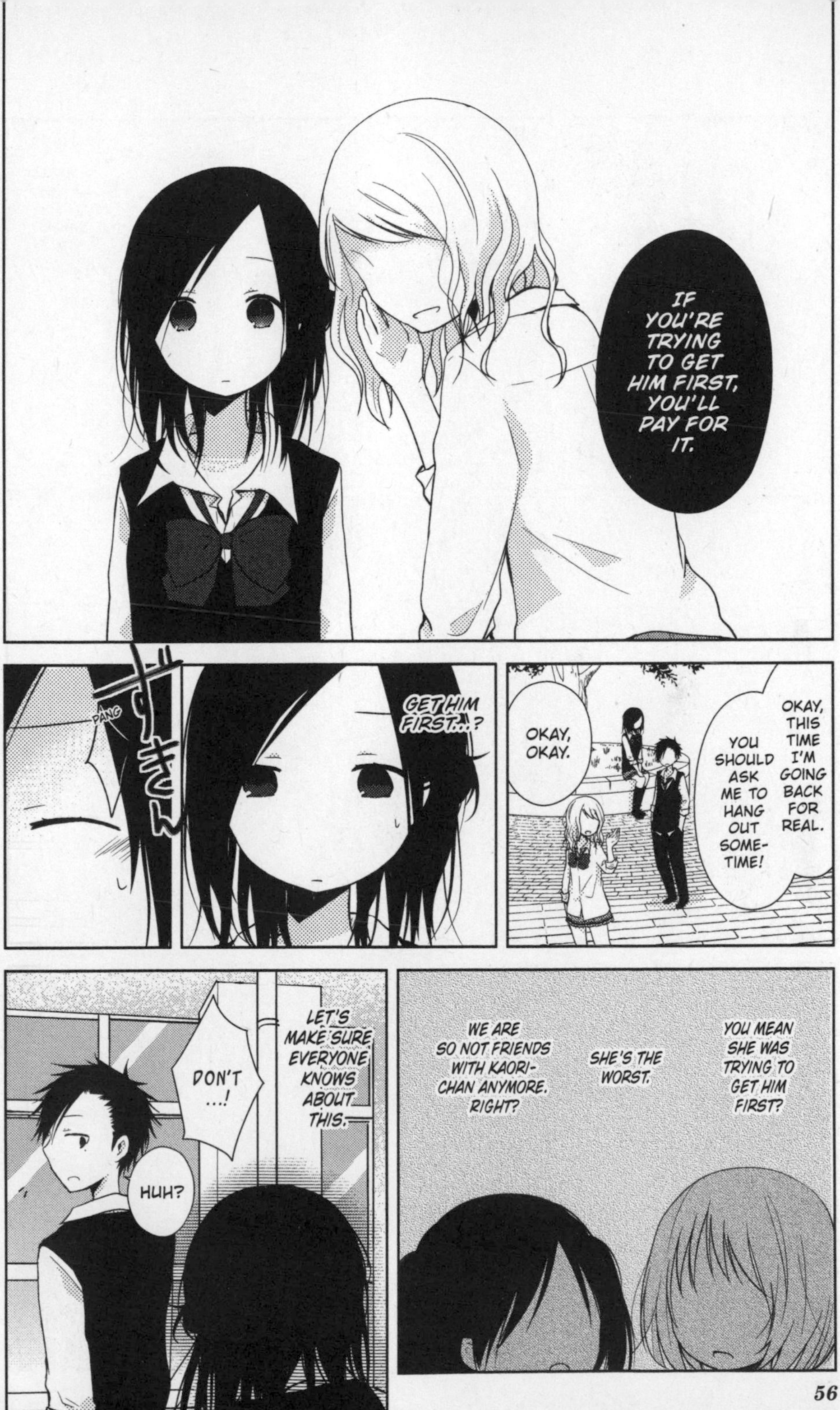
IF YOU'RE TRYING TO GET HIM FIRST, YOU'LL PAY FOR IT.
OKAY, THIS TIME I'M GOING BACK FOR REAL.
YOU SHOULD ASK ME TO HANG OUT SOMETIME!
OKAY, OKAY.
GET HIM FIRST...?
PANG
ずきん
YOU MEAN SHE WAS TRYING TO GET HIM FIRST?
SHE'S THE WORST.
WE ARE SO NOT FRIENDS WITH KAORI-CHAN ANYMORE. RIGHT?
LET'S MAKE SURE EVERYONE KNOWS ABOUT THIS.
DON'T ...!
HUH?

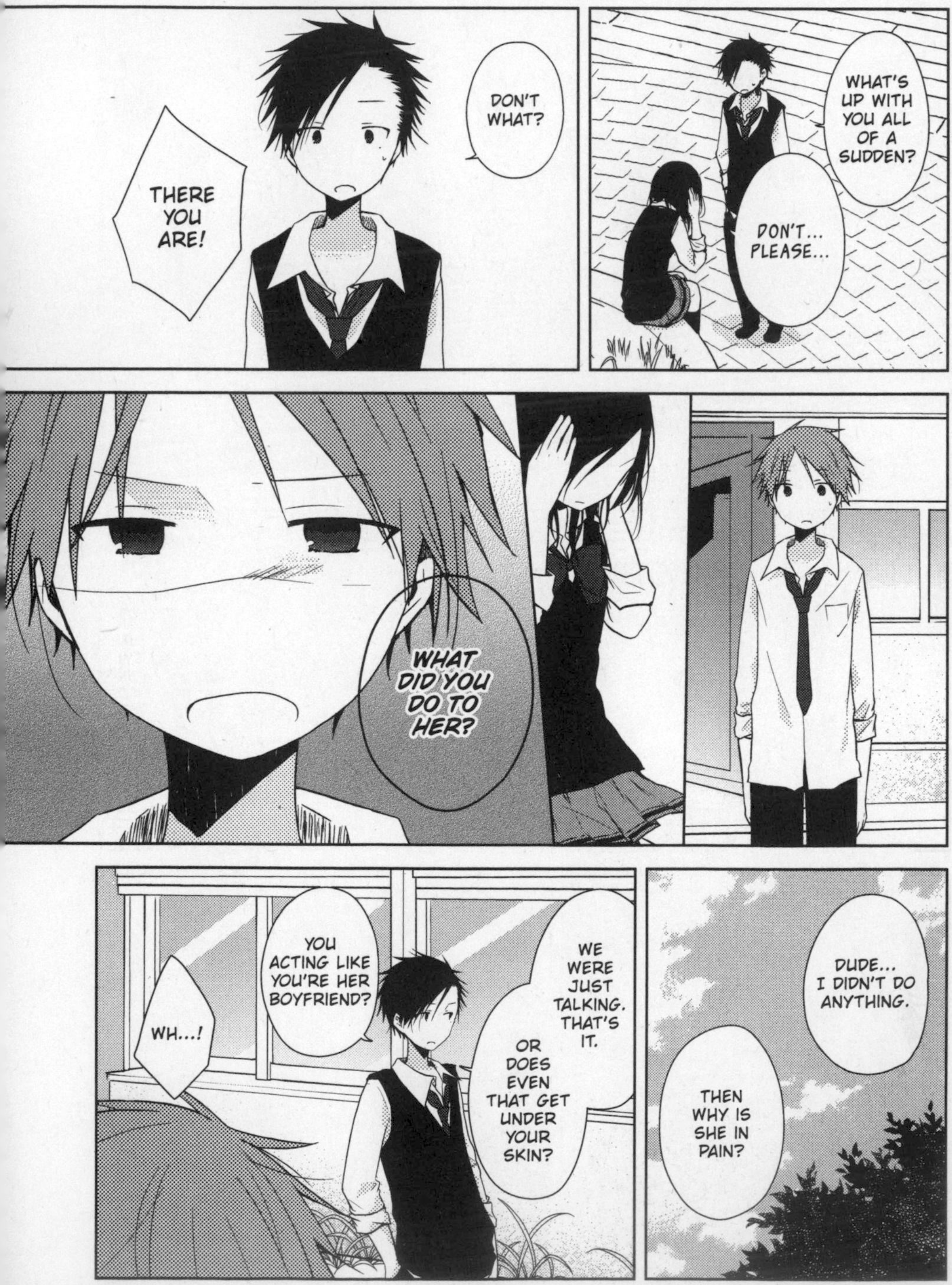

WHAT'S UP WITH YOU ALL OF A SUDDEN?
DON'T... PLEASE...
DON'T WHAT?
THERE YOU ARE!
WHAT DID YOU DO TO HER?
DUDE... I DIDN'T DO ANYTHING.
THEN WHY IS SHE IN PAIN?
WE WERE JUST TALKING. THAT'S IT.
OR DOES EVEN THAT GET UNDER YOUR SKIN?
YOU ACTING LIKE YOU'RE HER BOYFRIEND?
WH...!

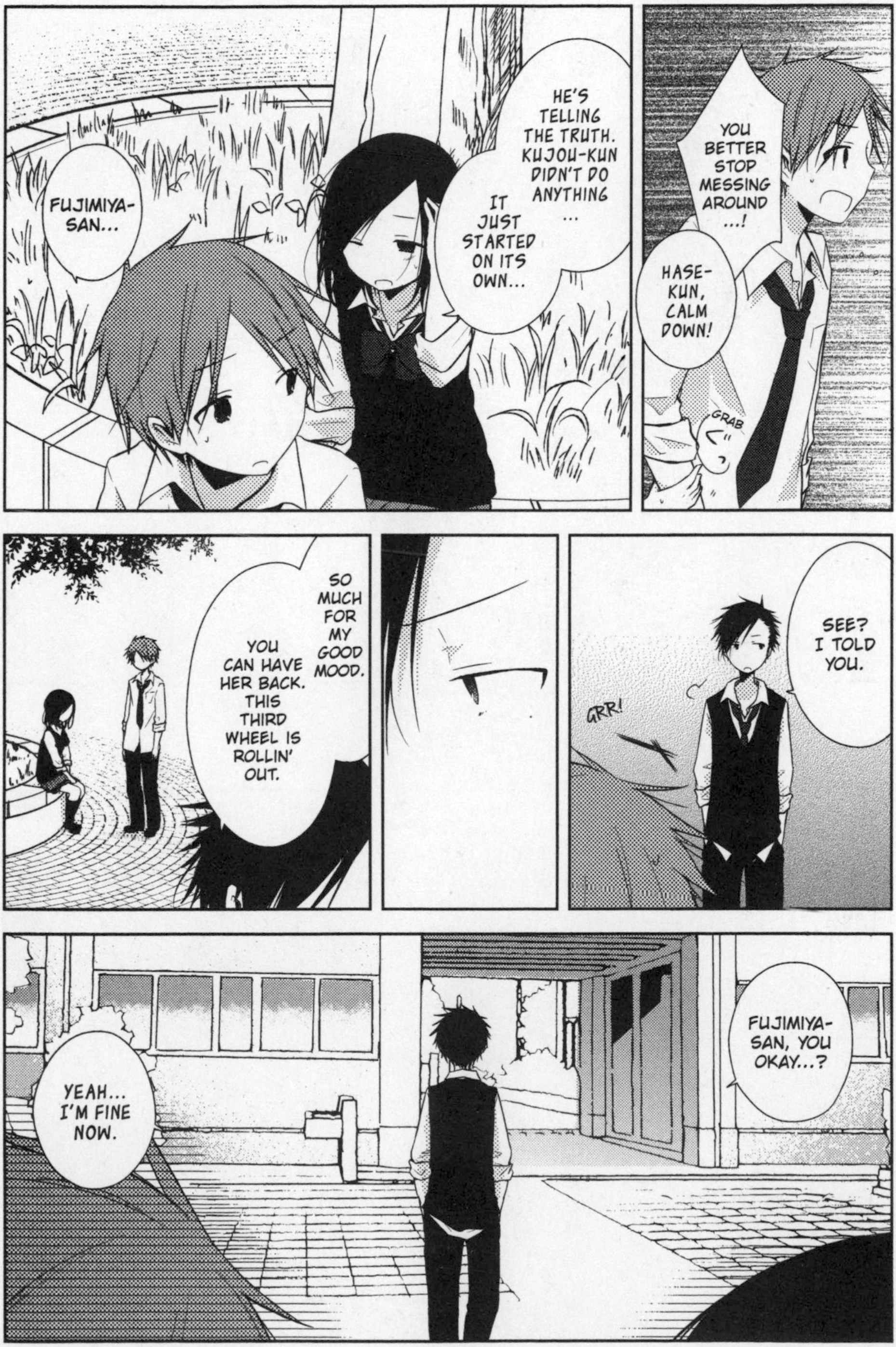
YOU BETTER STOP MESSING AROUND ...!
HASE-KUN, CALM DOWN!
GRAB
HE'S TELLING THE TRUTH. KUJOU-KUN DIDN'T DO ANYTHING ...
IT JUST STARTED ON ITS OWN...
FUJIMIYA-SAN...
SEE? I TOLD YOU.
GRR!
SO MUCH FOR MY GOOD MOOD.
YOU CAN HAVE HER BACK. THIS THIRD WHEEL IS ROLLIN' OUT.
FUJIMIYA-SAN, YOU OKAY...?
YEAH... I'M FINE NOW.

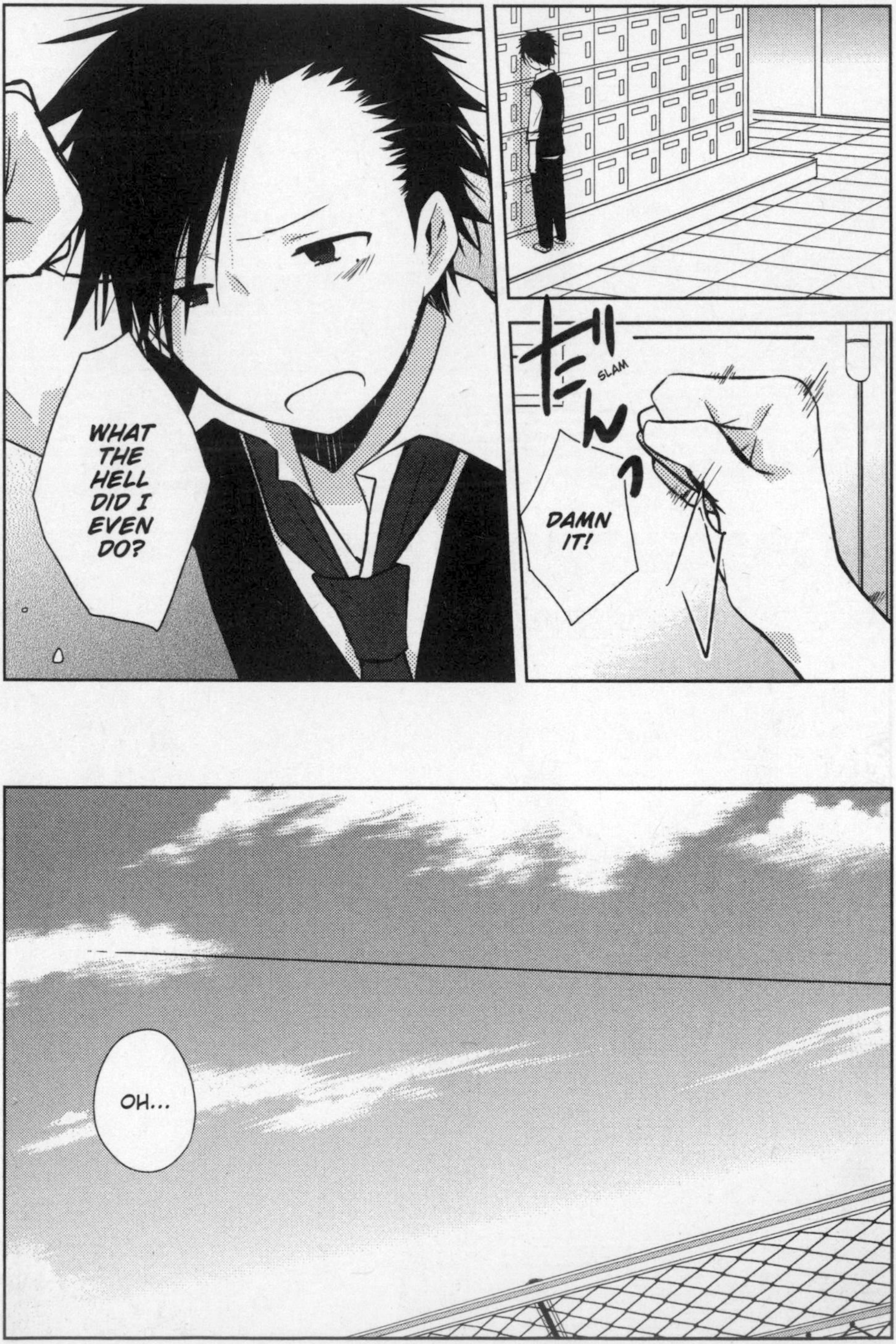
だんっ
SLAM
DAMN IT!
WHAT THE HELL DID I EVEN DO?
OH...

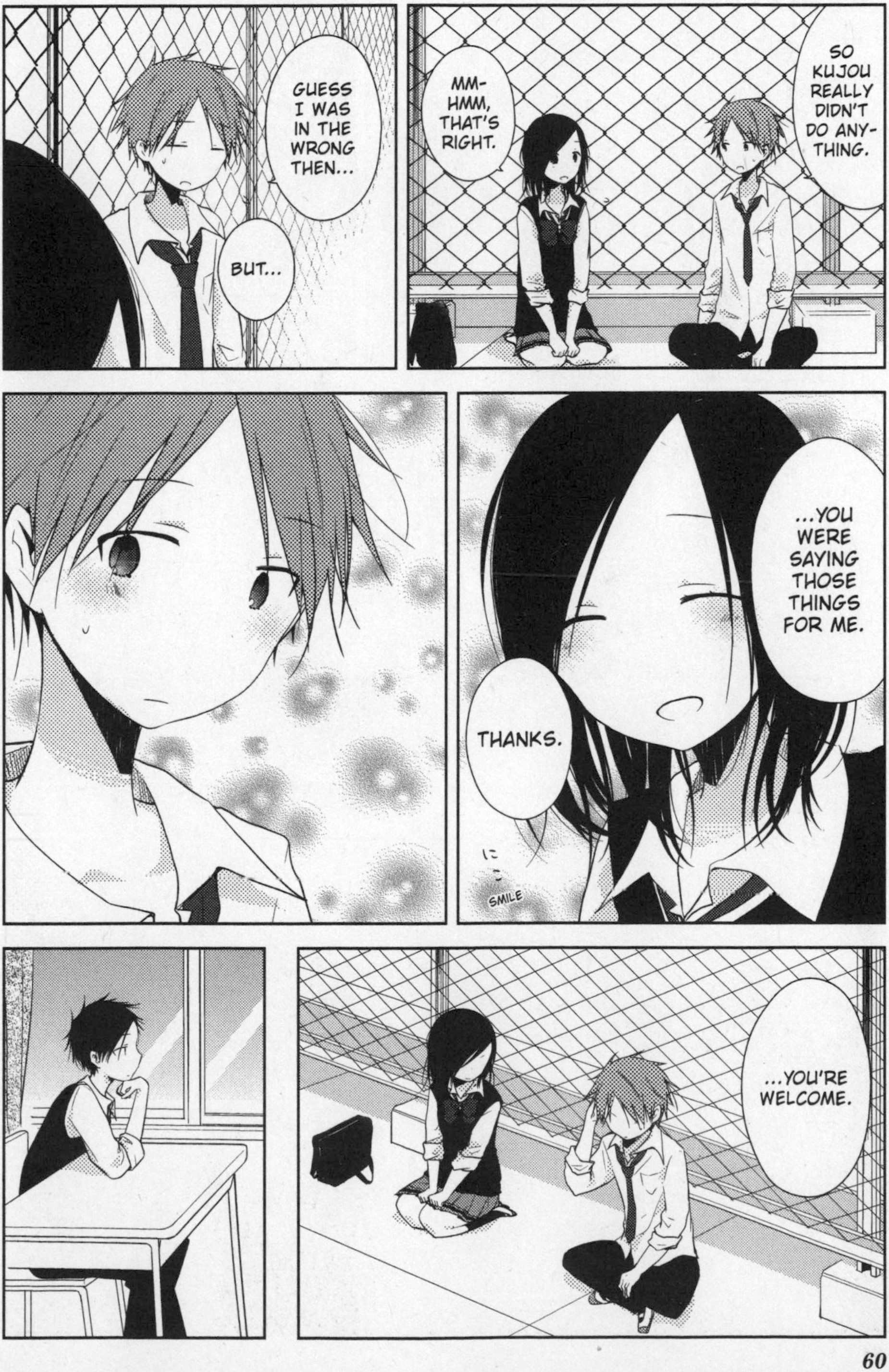
SO KUJOU REALLY DIDN'T DO ANY-THING.
MM-HMM, THAT'S RIGHT.
GUESS I WAS IN THE WRONG THEN...
BUT...
...YOU WERE SAYING THOSE THINGS FOR ME.
THANKS.
にこ
SMILE
...YOU'RE WELCOME.

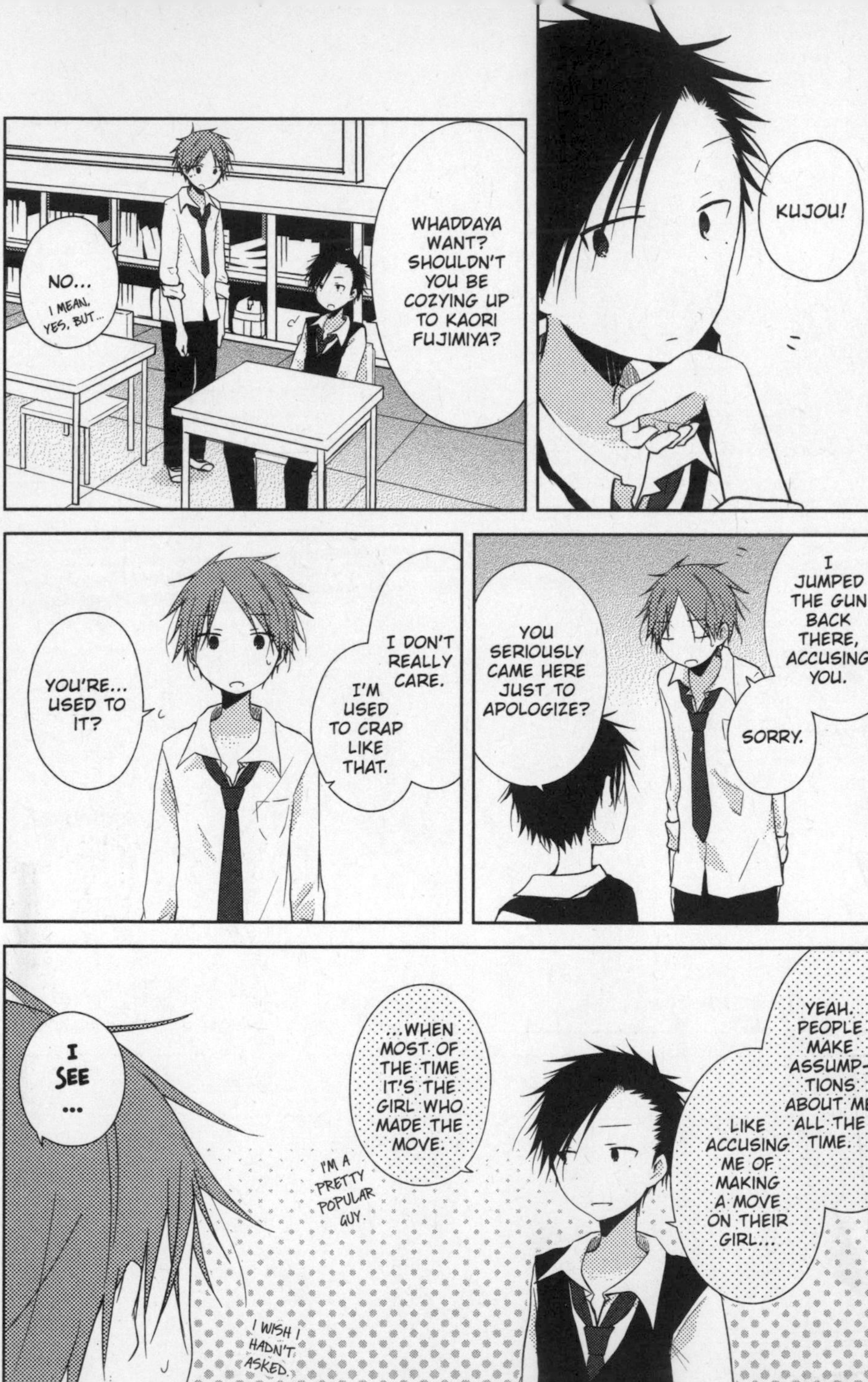
KUJOU!
WHADDAYA WANT? SHOULDN'T YOU BE COZYING UP TO KAORI FUJIMIYA?
NO... I MEAN, YES, BUT...
I JUMPED THE GUN BACK THERE, ACCUSING YOU.
SORRY.
YOU SERIOUSLY CAME HERE JUST TO APOLOGIZE?
I DON'T REALLY CARE.
I'M USED TO CRAP LIKE THAT.
YOU'RE... USED TO IT?
YEAH. PEOPLE MAKE ASSUMP-TIONS ABOUT ME ALL THE TIME.
LIKE ACCUSING ME OF MAKING A MOVE ON THEIR GIRL...
...WHEN MOST OF THE TIME IT'S THE GIRL WHO MADE THE MOVE.
I'M A PRETTY POPULAR GUY.
I SEE...
I WISH I HADN'T ASKED.

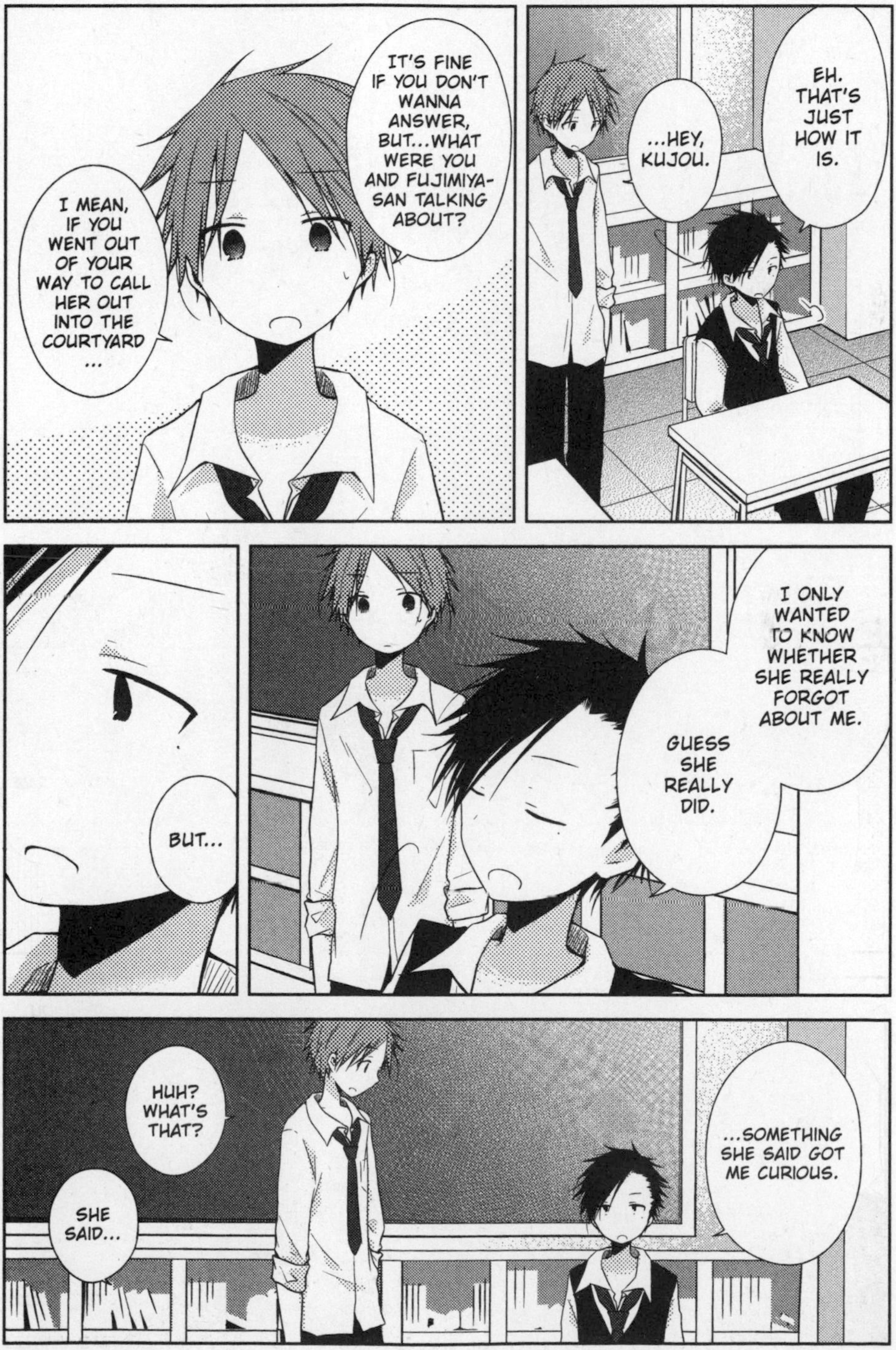
EH. THAT'S JUST HOW IT IS.
...HEY, KUJOU.
IT'S FINE IF YOU DON'T WANNA ANSWER, BUT...WHAT WERE YOU AND FUJIMIYA-SAN TALKING ABOUT?
I MEAN, IF YOU WENT OUT OF YOUR WAY TO CALL HER OUT INTO THE COURTYARD...
I ONLY WANTED TO KNOW WHETHER SHE REALLY FORGOT ABOUT ME.
GUESS SHE REALLY DID.
BUT...
...SOMETHING SHE SAID GOT ME CURIOUS.
HUH? WHAT'S THAT?
SHE SAID...

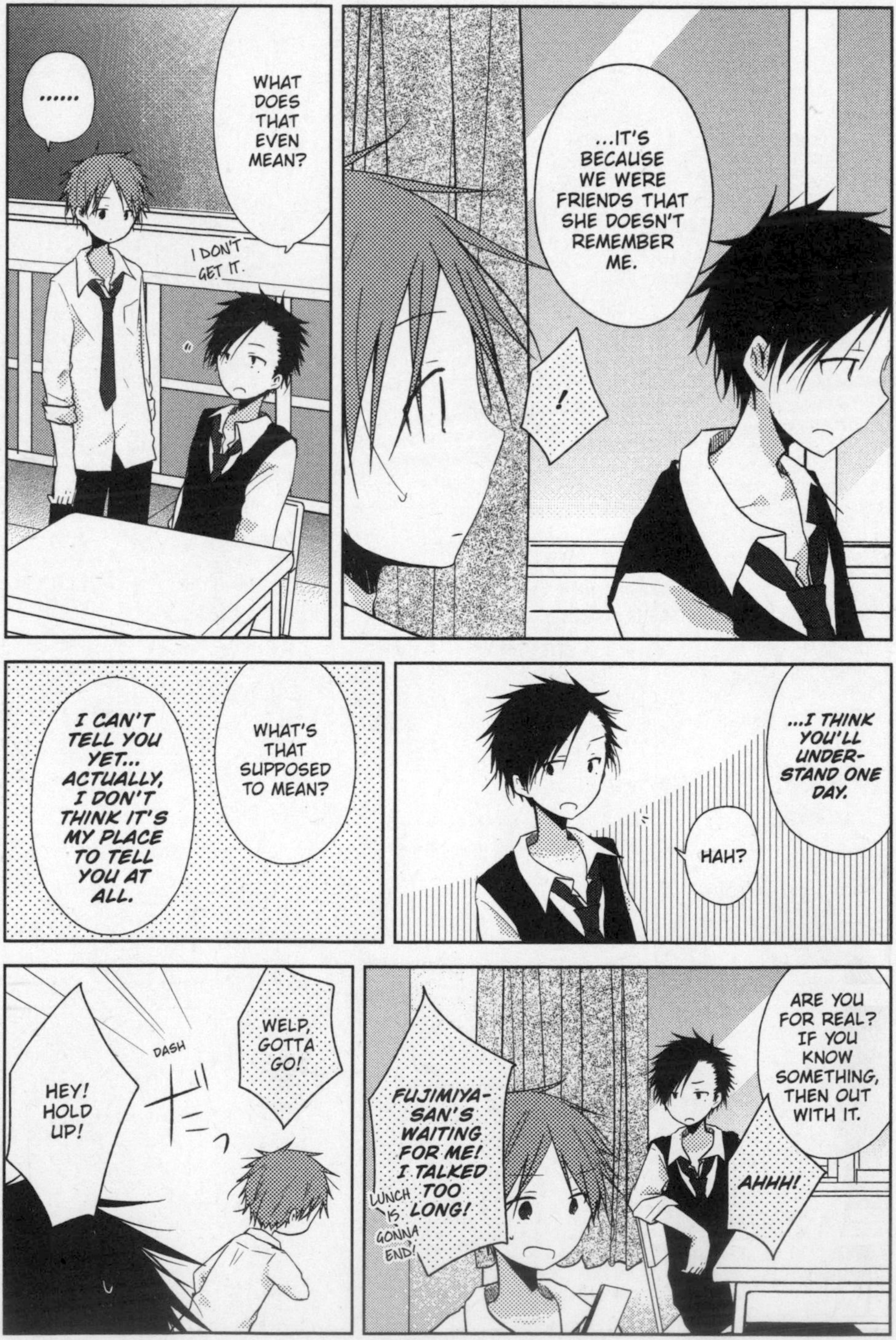
...IT'S BECAUSE WE WERE FRIENDS THAT SHE DOESN'T REMEMBER ME.
!
WHAT DOES THAT EVEN MEAN?
......
I DON'T GET IT.
...I THINK YOU'LL UNDER-STAND ONE DAY.
HAH?
WHAT'S THAT SUPPOSED TO MEAN?
I CAN'T TELL YOU YET... ACTUALLY, I DON'T THINK IT'S MY PLACE TO TELL YOU AT ALL.
ARE YOU FOR REAL? IF YOU KNOW SOMETHING, THEN OUT WITH IT.
AHHH!
FUJIMIYA-SAN'S WAITING FOR ME! I TALKED TOO LONG!
LUNCH IS GONNA END!
WELP, GOTTA GO!
DASH
HEY! HOLD UP!

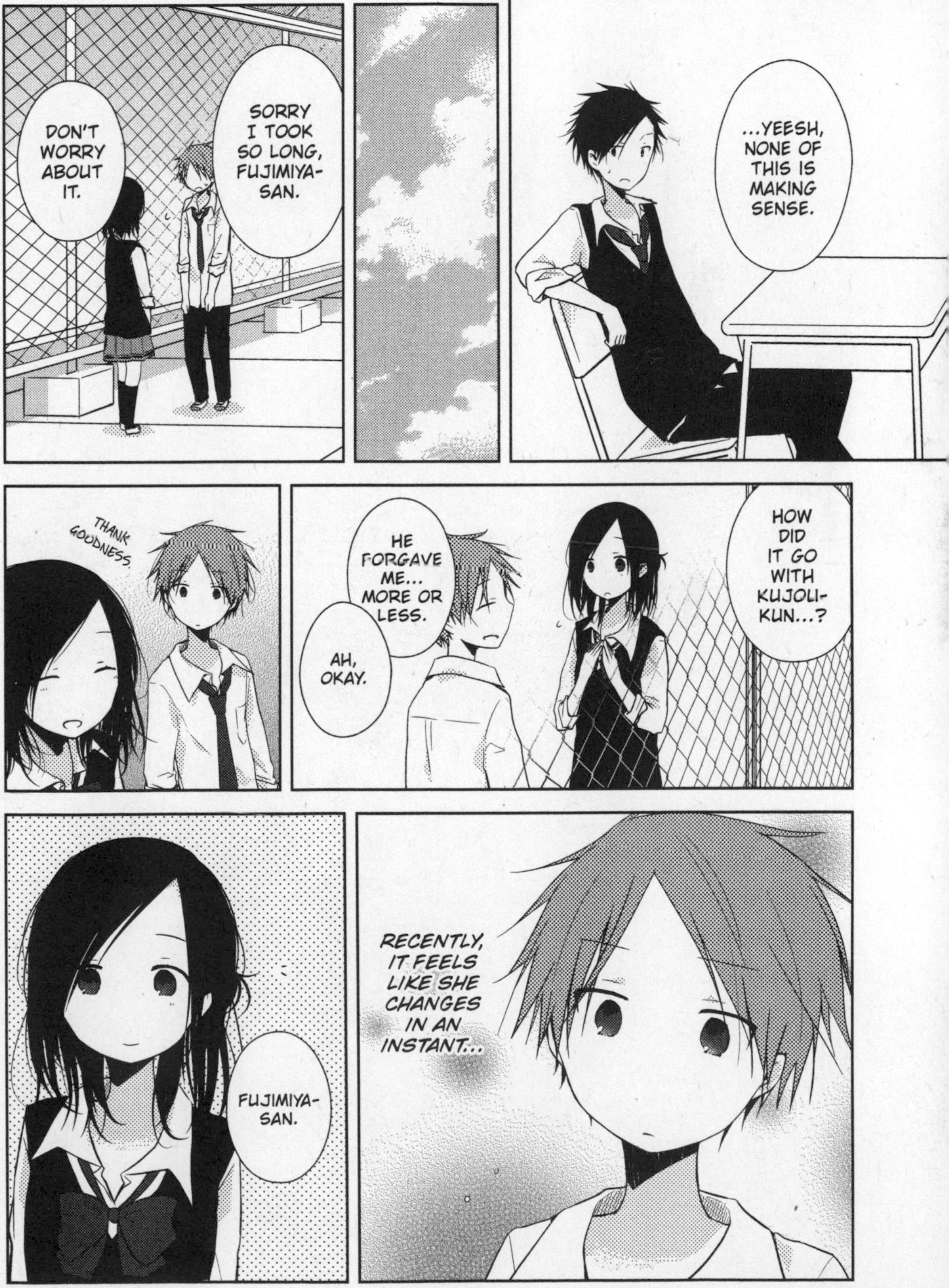
...YEESH, NONE OF THIS IS MAKING SENSE.
SORRY I TOOK SO LONG, FUJIMIYA-SAN.
DON'T WORRY ABOUT IT.
HOW DID IT GO WITH KUJOU-KUN...?
HE FORGAVE ME... MORE OR LESS.
AH, OKAY.
THANK GOODNESS.
RECENTLY, IT FEELS LIKE SHE CHANGES IN AN INSTANT...
FUJIMIYA-SAN.

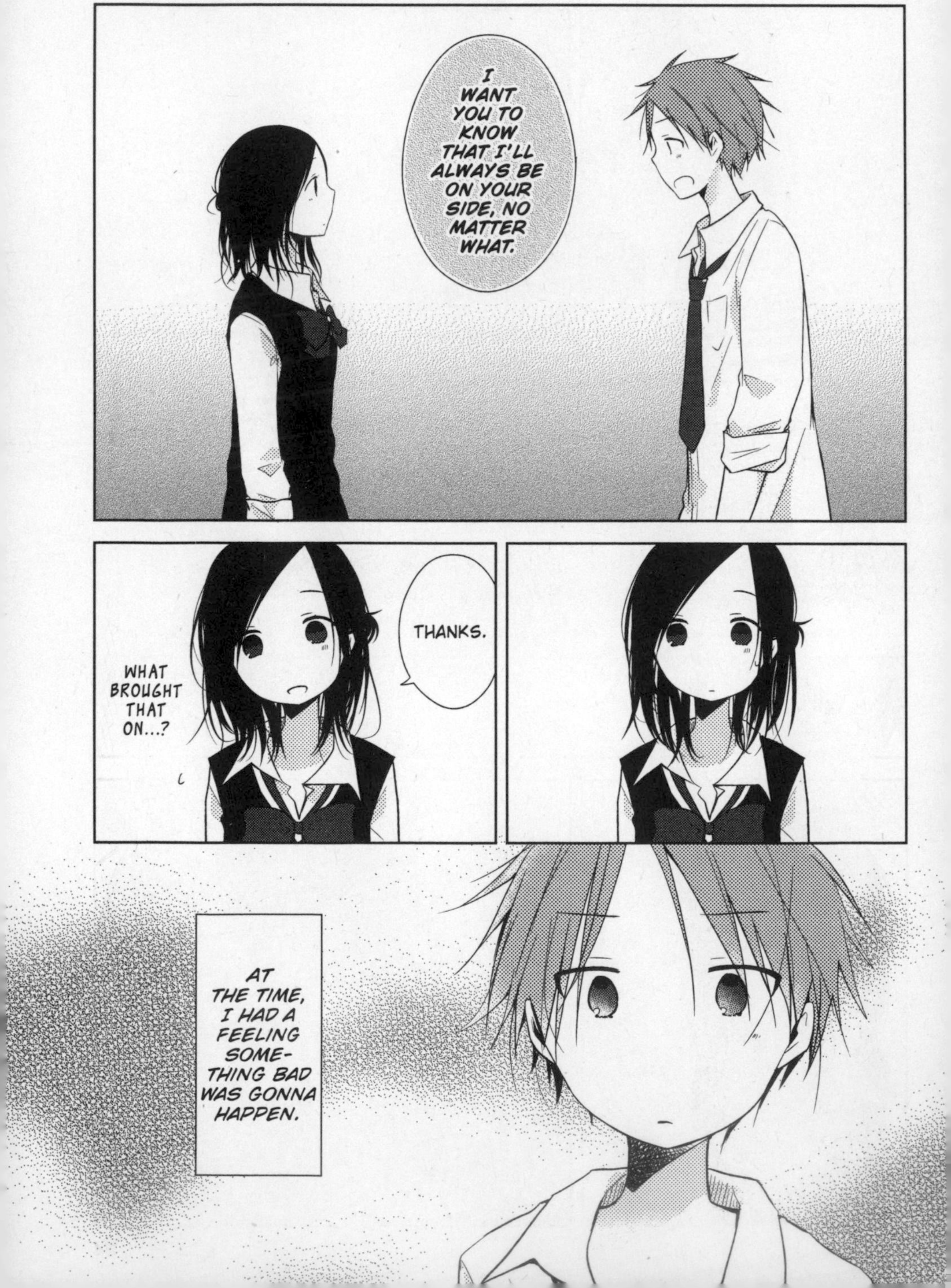
I WANT YOU TO KNOW THAT I'LL ALWAYS BE ON YOUR SIDE, NO MATTER WHAT.
THANKS.
WHAT BROUGHT THAT ON...?
AT THE TIME, I HAD A FEELING SOME-THING BAD WAS GONNA HAPPEN.

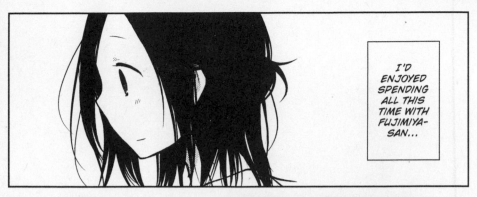

I'D ENJOYED SPENDING ALL THIS TIME WITH FUJIMIYA-SAN...

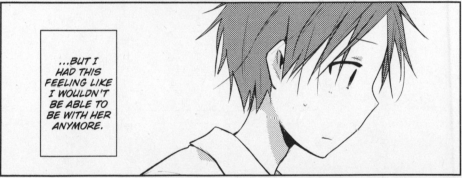

...BUT I HAD THIS FEELING LIKE I WOULDN'T BE ABLE TO BE WITH HER ANYMORE.

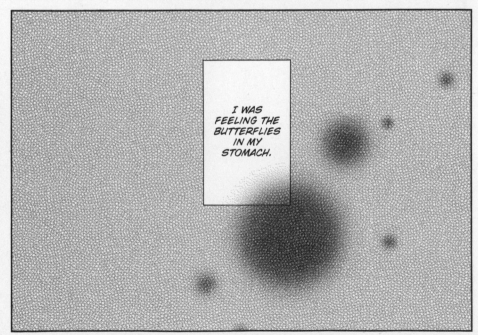

I WAS FEELING THE BUTTERFLIES IN MY STOMACH.

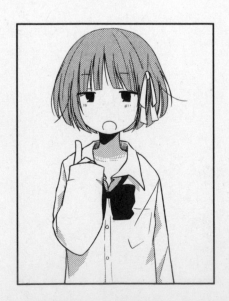

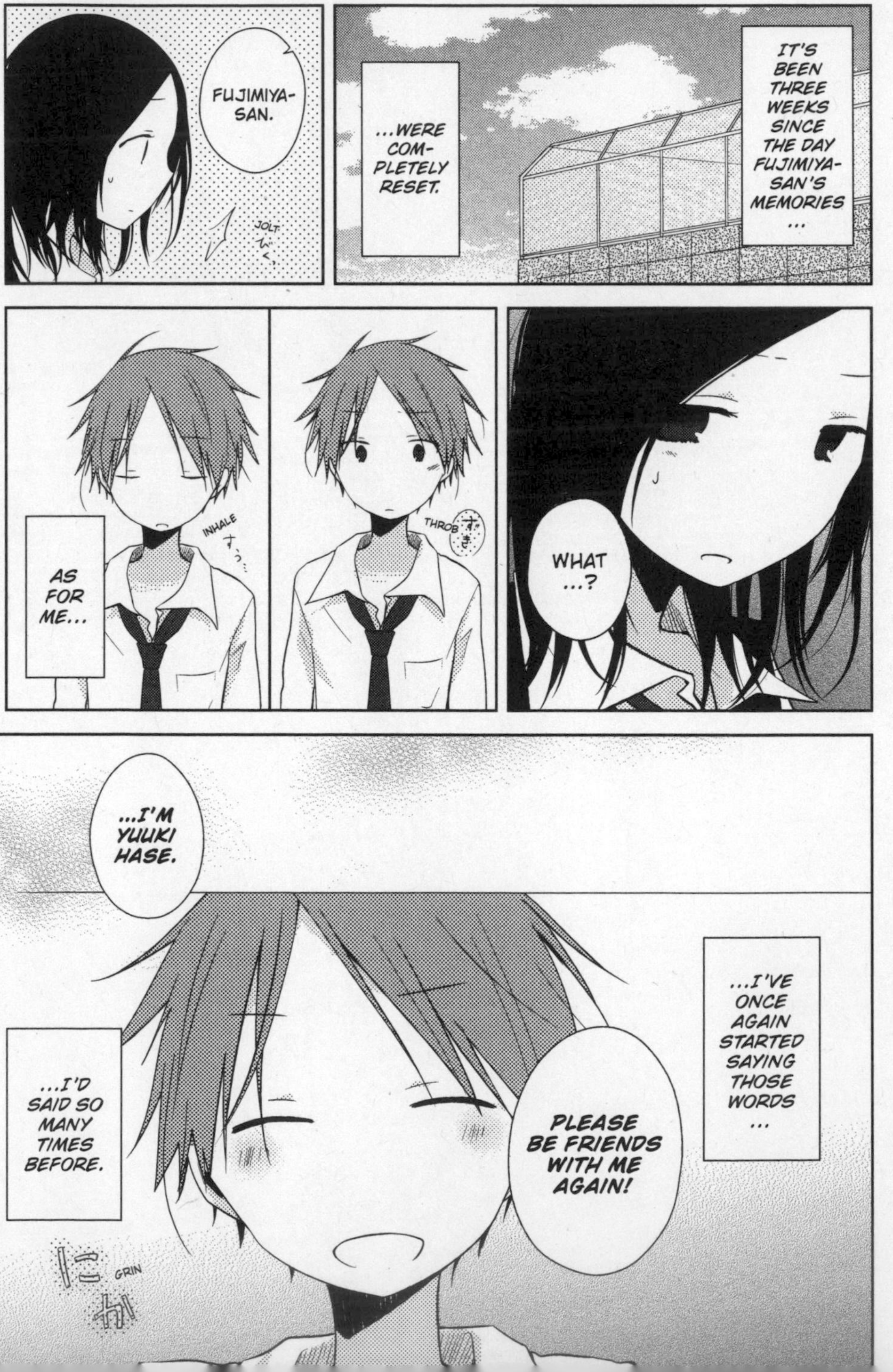
IT'S BEEN THREE WEEKS SINCE THE DAY FUJIMIYA-SAN'S MEMORIES ...
...WERE COMPLETELY RESET.
FUJIMIYA-SAN.
JOLT
WHAT ...?
THROB
INHALE
AS FOR ME...
...I'M YUUKI HASE.
...I'VE ONCE AGAIN STARTED SAYING THOSE WORDS ...
PLEASE BE FRIENDS WITH ME AGAIN!
...I'D SAID SO MANY TIMES BEFORE.
GRIN

CHAPTER 19 FORMULA FOR ENJOYMENT

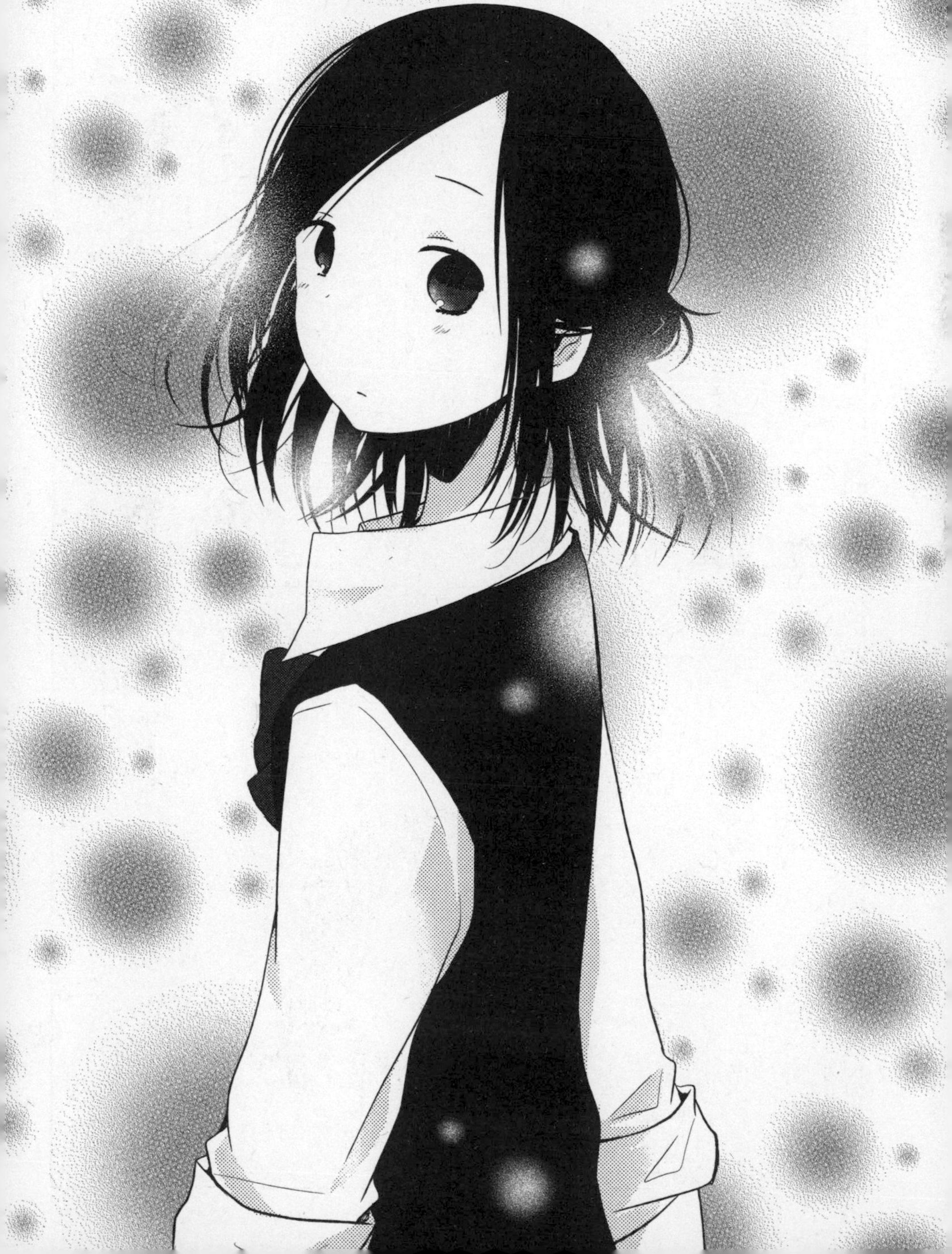

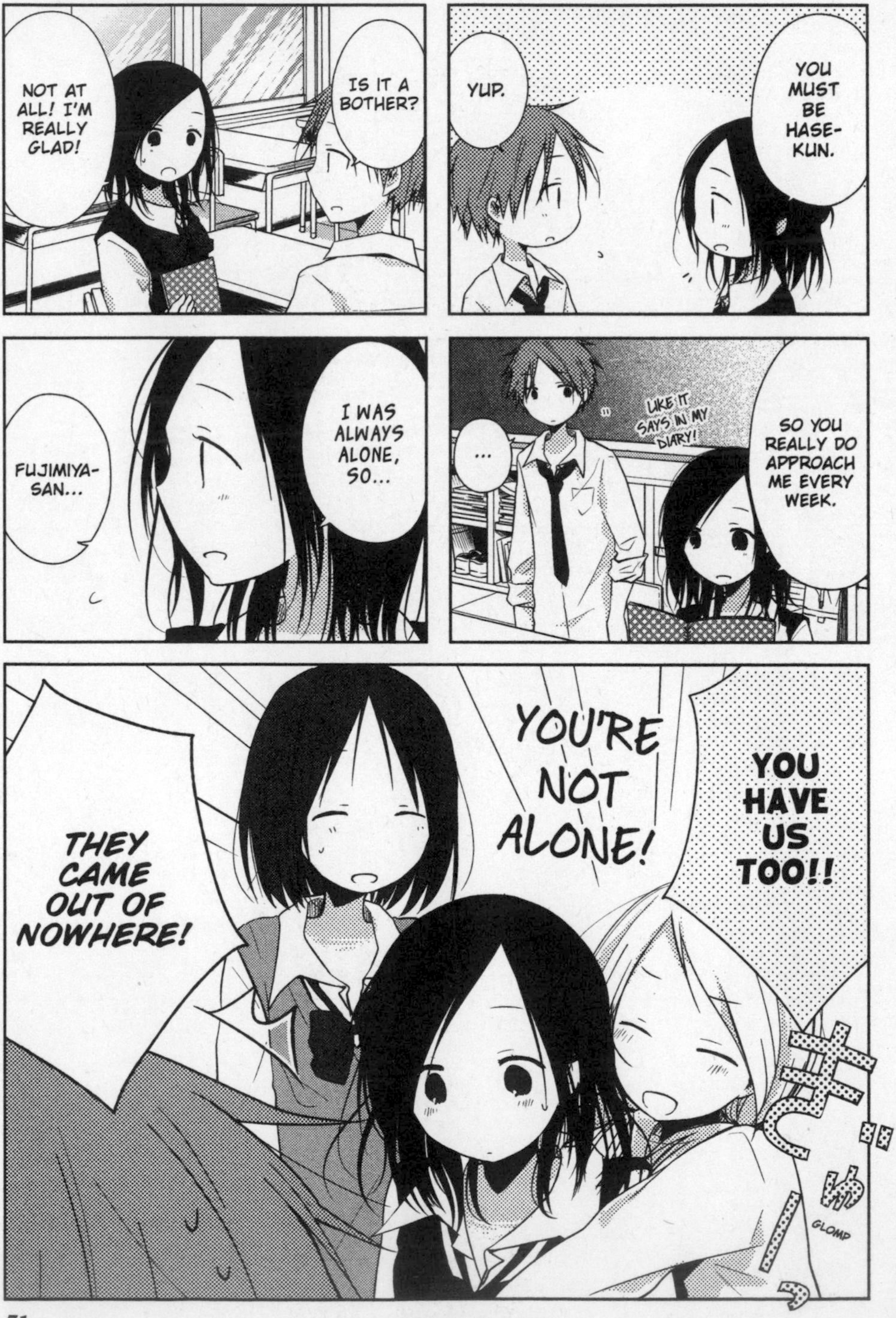
YOU MUST BE HASE-KUN.
YUP.
IS IT A BOTHER?
NOT AT ALL! I'M REALLY GLAD!
SO YOU REALLY DO APPROACH ME EVERY WEEK.
LIKE IT SAYS IN MY DIARY!
...
I WAS ALWAYS ALONE, SO...
FUJIMIYA-SAN...
YOU HAVE US TOO!!
YOU'RE NOT ALONE!
THEY CAME OUT OF NOWHERE!
GLOMP

CULTURE FESTIVAL

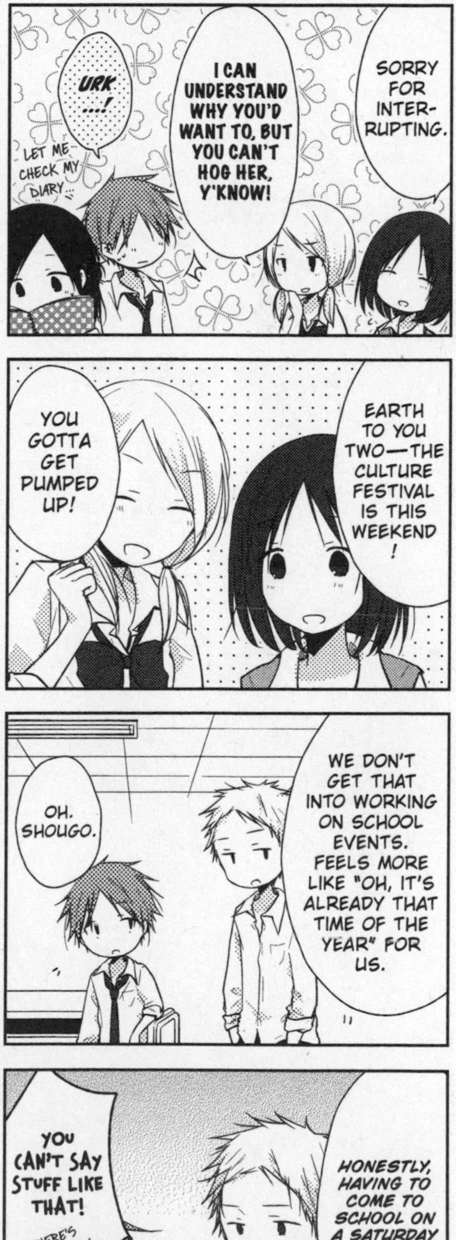
SORRY FOR INTER-RUPTING.
I CAN UNDERSTAND WHY YOU'D WANT TO, BUT YOU CAN'T HOG HER, Y'KNOW!
URK ...!
LET ME CHECK MY DIARY...
EARTH TO YOU TWO—THE CULTURE FESTIVAL IS THIS WEEKEND!
YOU GOTTA GET PUMPED UP!
WE DON'T GET THAT INTO WORKING ON SCHOOL EVENTS. FEELS MORE LIKE "OH, IT'S ALREADY THAT TIME OF THE YEAR" FOR US.
OH. SHOUGO.
HONESTLY, HAVING TO COME TO SCHOOL ON A SATURDAY MAKES THE WHOLE THING A HASSLE.
YOU CAN'T SAY STUFF LIKE THAT!
WHERE'S YOUR SCHOOL SPIRIT!?

FAVOR

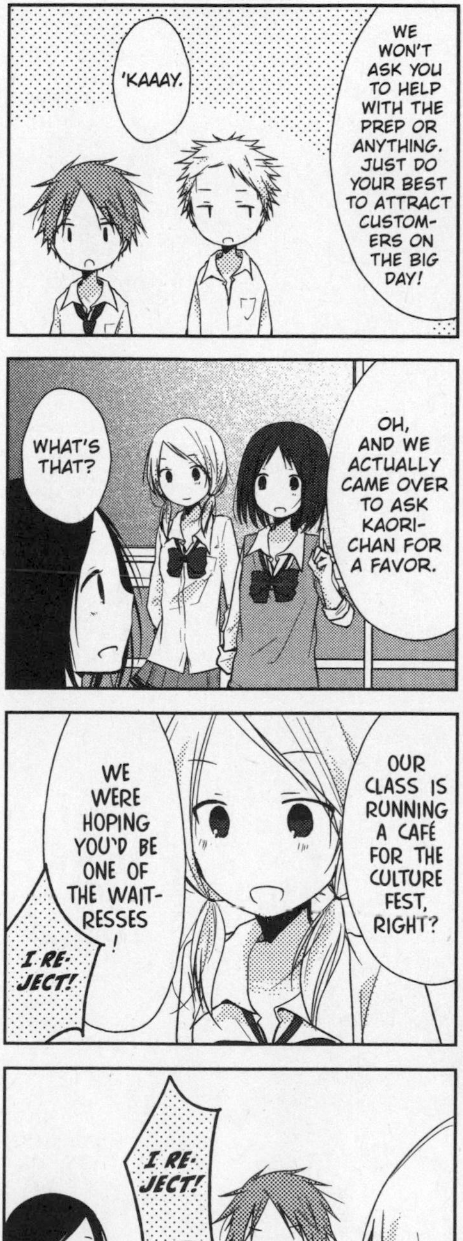
WE WON'T ASK YOU TO HELP WITH THE PREP OR ANYTHING. JUST DO YOUR BEST TO ATTRACT CUSTOMERS ON THE BIG DAY!
'KAAAY.
OH, AND WE ACTUALLY CAME OVER TO ASK KAORI-CHAN FOR A FAVOR.
WHAT'S THAT?
OUR CLASS IS RUNNING A CAFÉ FOR THE CULTURE FEST, RIGHT?
WE WERE HOPING YOU'D BE ONE OF THE WAIT-RESSES!
I RE-JECT!
I RE-JECT!

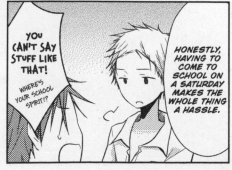

WAITRESS

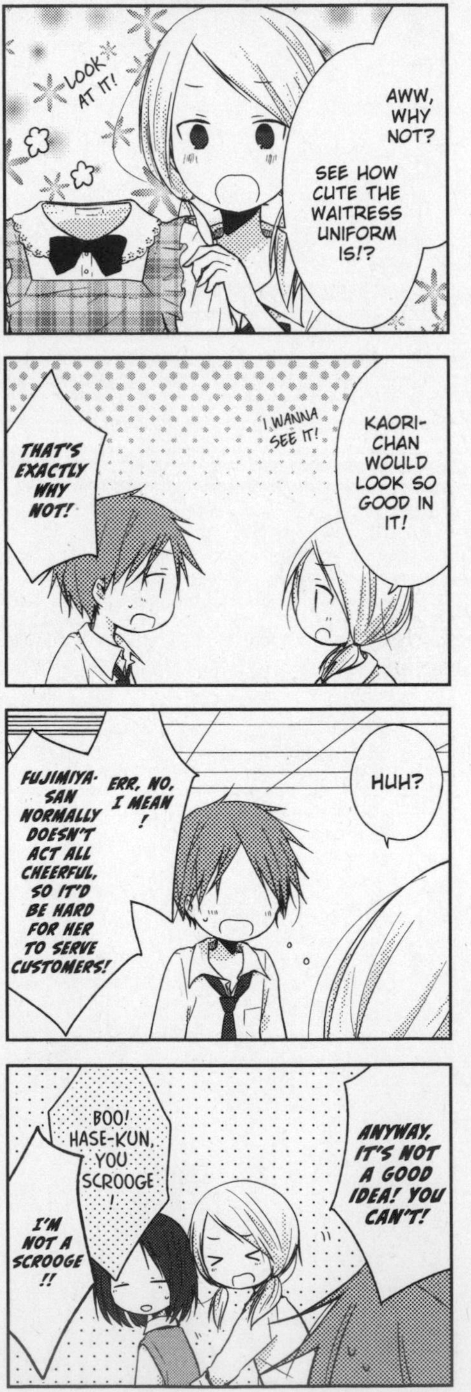
AWW, WHY NOT?
SEE HOW CUTE THE WAITRESS UNIFORM IS!?
LOOK AT IT!
KAORI-CHAN WOULD LOOK SO GOOD IN IT!
I WANNA SEE IT!
THAT'S EXACTLY WHY NOT!
HUH?
ERR, NO, I MEAN!
FUJIMIYA-SAN NORMALLY DOESN'T ACT ALL CHEERFUL, SO IT'D BE HARD FOR HER TO SERVE CUSTOMERS!
ANYWAY, IT'S NOT A GOOD IDEA! YOU CAN'T!
BOO! HASE-KUN, YOU SCROOGE!
I'M NOT A SCROOGE!!

SOMEHOW

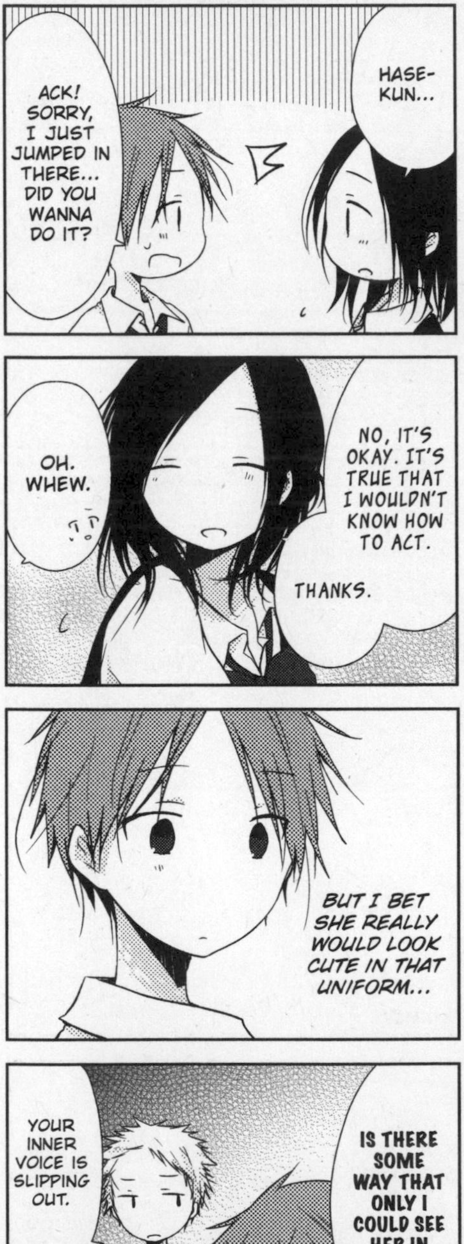
HASE-KUN...
ACK! SORRY, I JUST JUMPED IN THERE... DID YOU WANNA DO IT?
NO, IT'S OKAY. IT'S TRUE THAT I WOULDN'T KNOW HOW TO ACT.
THANKS.
OH. WHEW.
BUT I BET SHE REALLY WOULD LOOK CUTE IN THAT UNIFORM...
IS THERE SOME WAY THAT ONLY I COULD SEE HER IN IT...?
YOUR INNER VOICE IS SLIPPING OUT.
CREEP

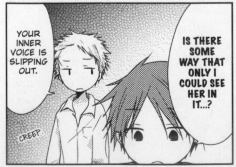

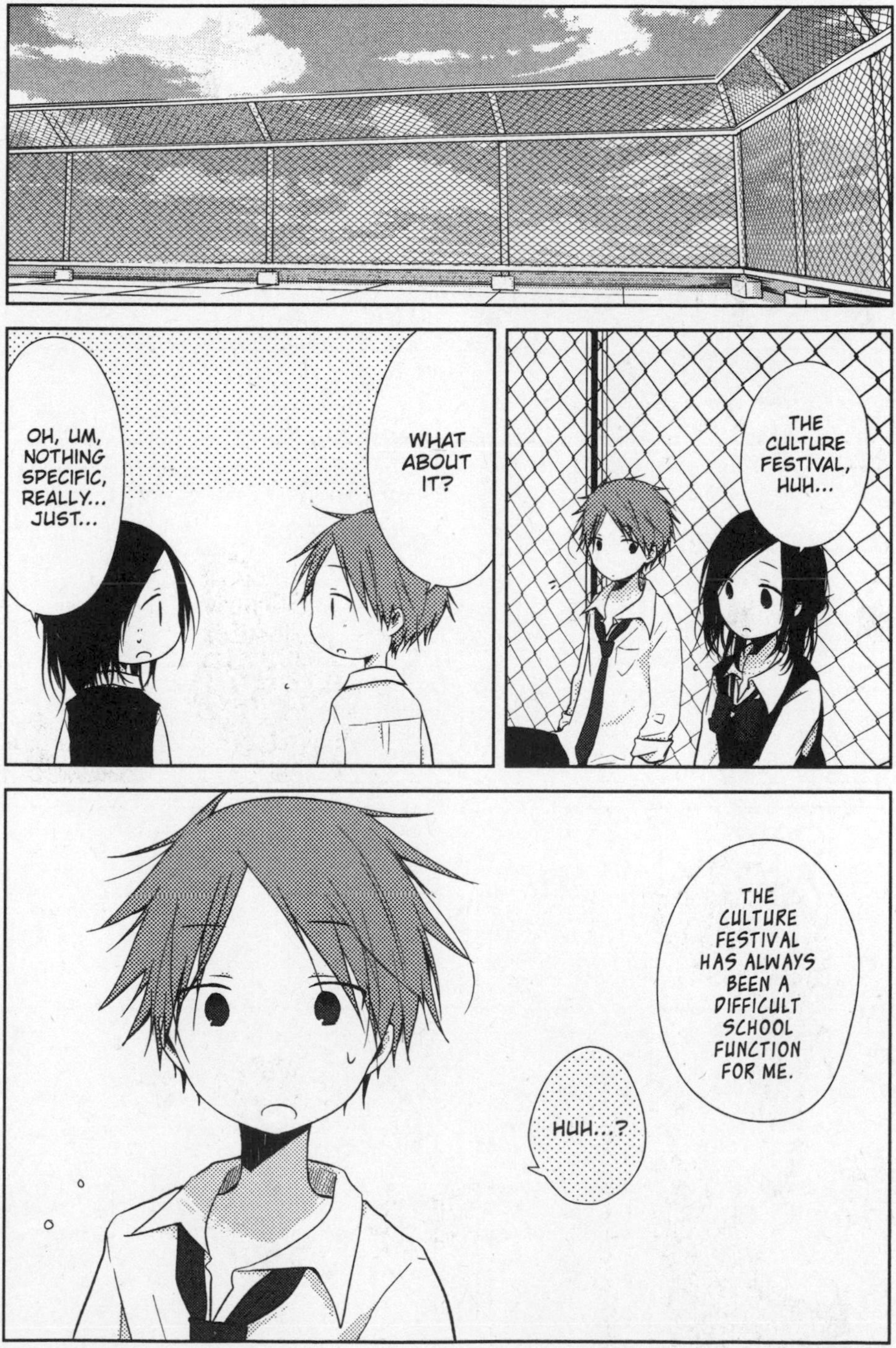
THE CULTURE FESTIVAL, HUH...
WHAT ABOUT IT?
OH, UM, NOTHING SPECIFIC, REALLY... JUST...
THE CULTURE FESTIVAL HAS ALWAYS BEEN A DIFFICULT SCHOOL FUNCTION FOR ME.
HUH...?

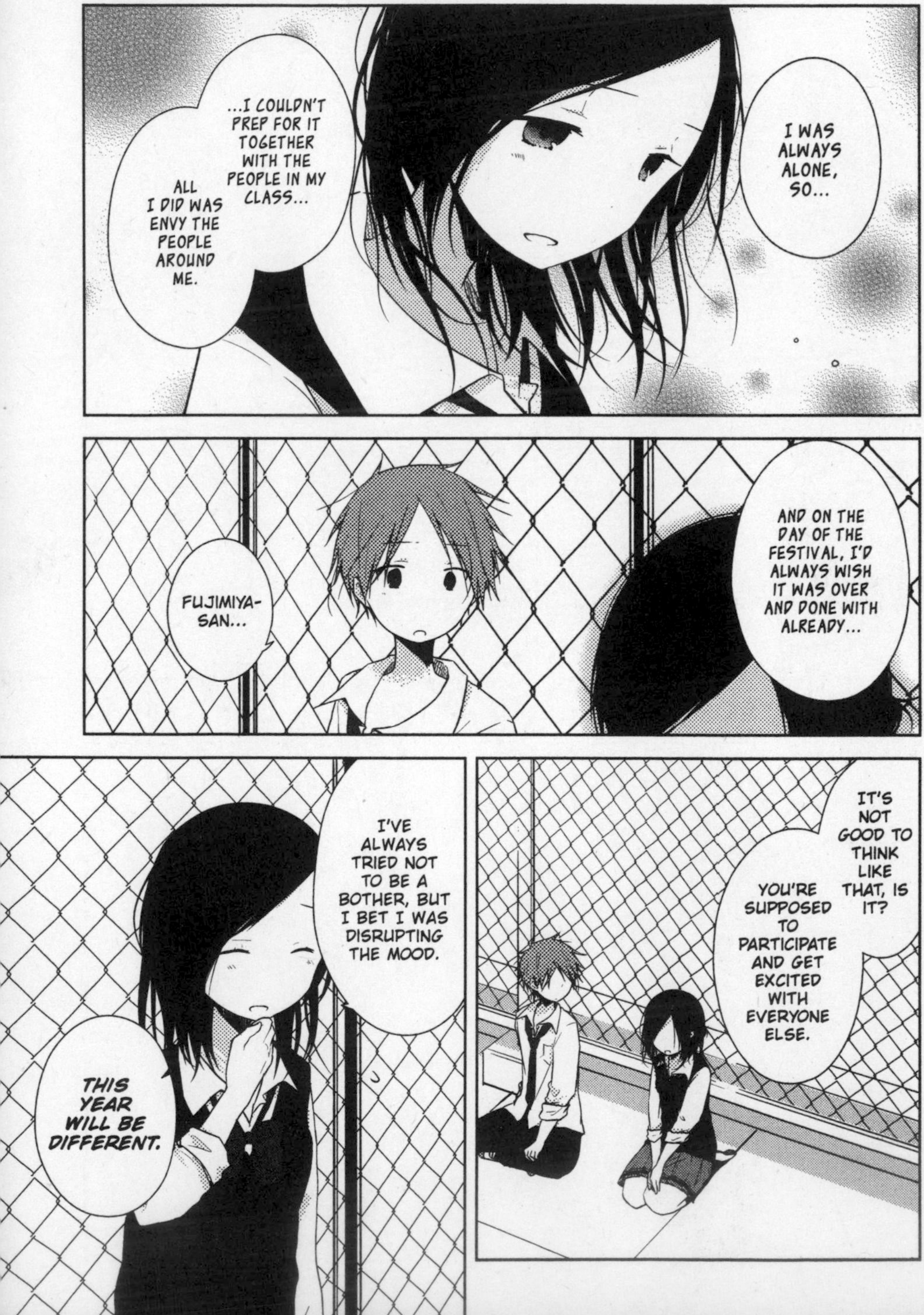
I WAS ALWAYS ALONE, SO...
...I COULDN'T PREP FOR IT TOGETHER WITH THE PEOPLE IN MY CLASS...
ALL I DID WAS ENVY THE PEOPLE AROUND ME.
AND ON THE DAY OF THE FESTIVAL, I'D ALWAYS WISH IT WAS OVER AND DONE WITH ALREADY...
FUJIMIYA-SAN...
IT'S NOT GOOD TO THINK LIKE THAT, IS IT?
YOU'RE SUPPOSED TO PARTICIPATE AND GET EXCITED WITH EVERYONE ELSE.
I'VE ALWAYS TRIED NOT TO BE A BOTHER, BUT I BET I WAS DISRUPTING THE MOOD.
THIS YEAR WILL BE DIFFERENT.

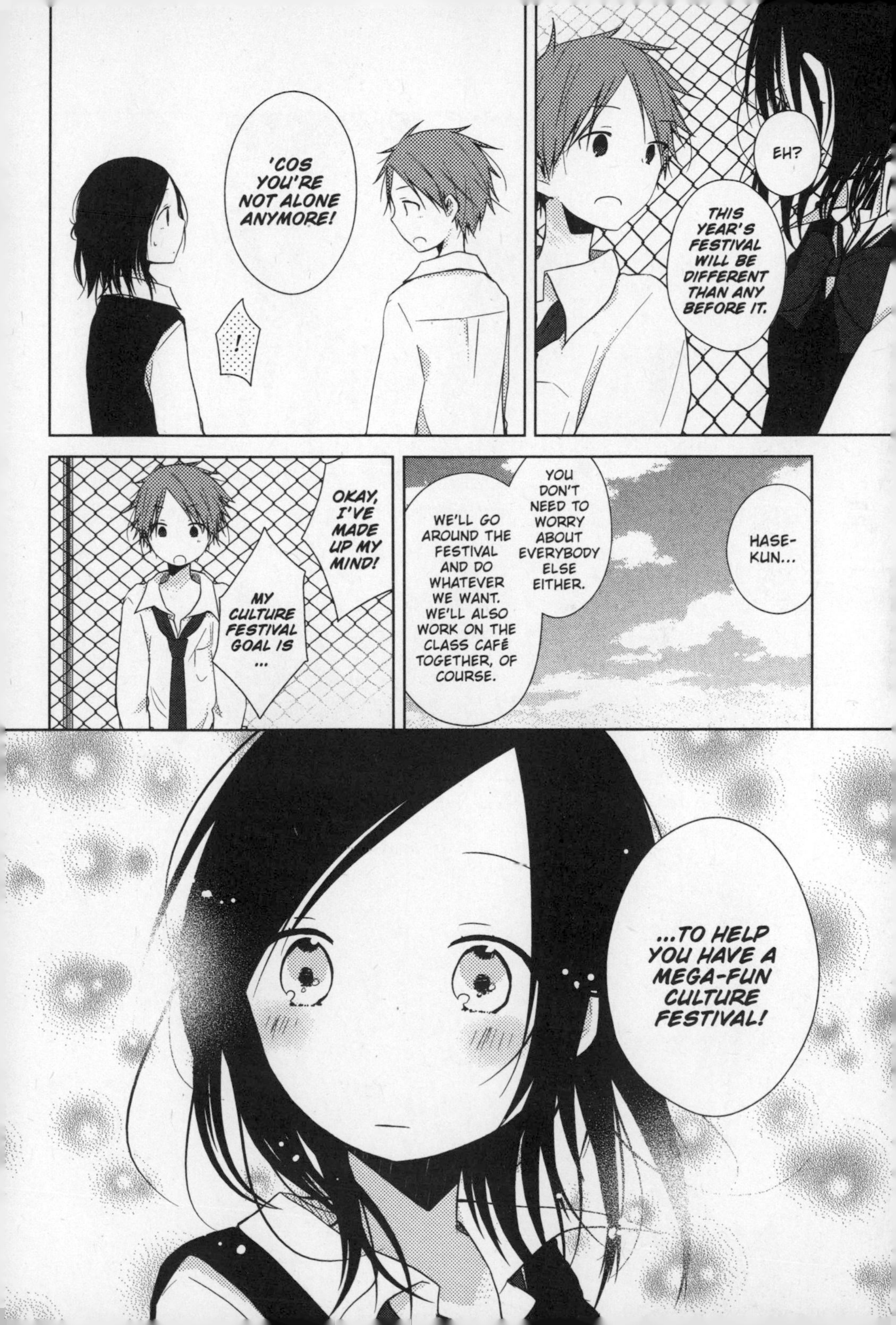
EH?
THIS YEAR'S FESTIVAL WILL BE DIFFERENT THAN ANY BEFORE IT.
'COS YOU'RE NOT ALONE ANYMORE!
!
HASE-KUN...
YOU DON'T NEED TO WORRY ABOUT EVERYBODY ELSE EITHER.
WE'LL GO AROUND THE FESTIVAL AND DO WHATEVER WE WANT. WE'LL ALSO WORK ON THE CLASS CAFÉ TOGETHER, OF COURSE.
OKAY, I'VE MADE UP MY MIND!
MY CULTURE FESTIVAL GOAL IS ...
...TO HELP YOU HAVE A MEGA-FUN CULTURE FESTIVAL!

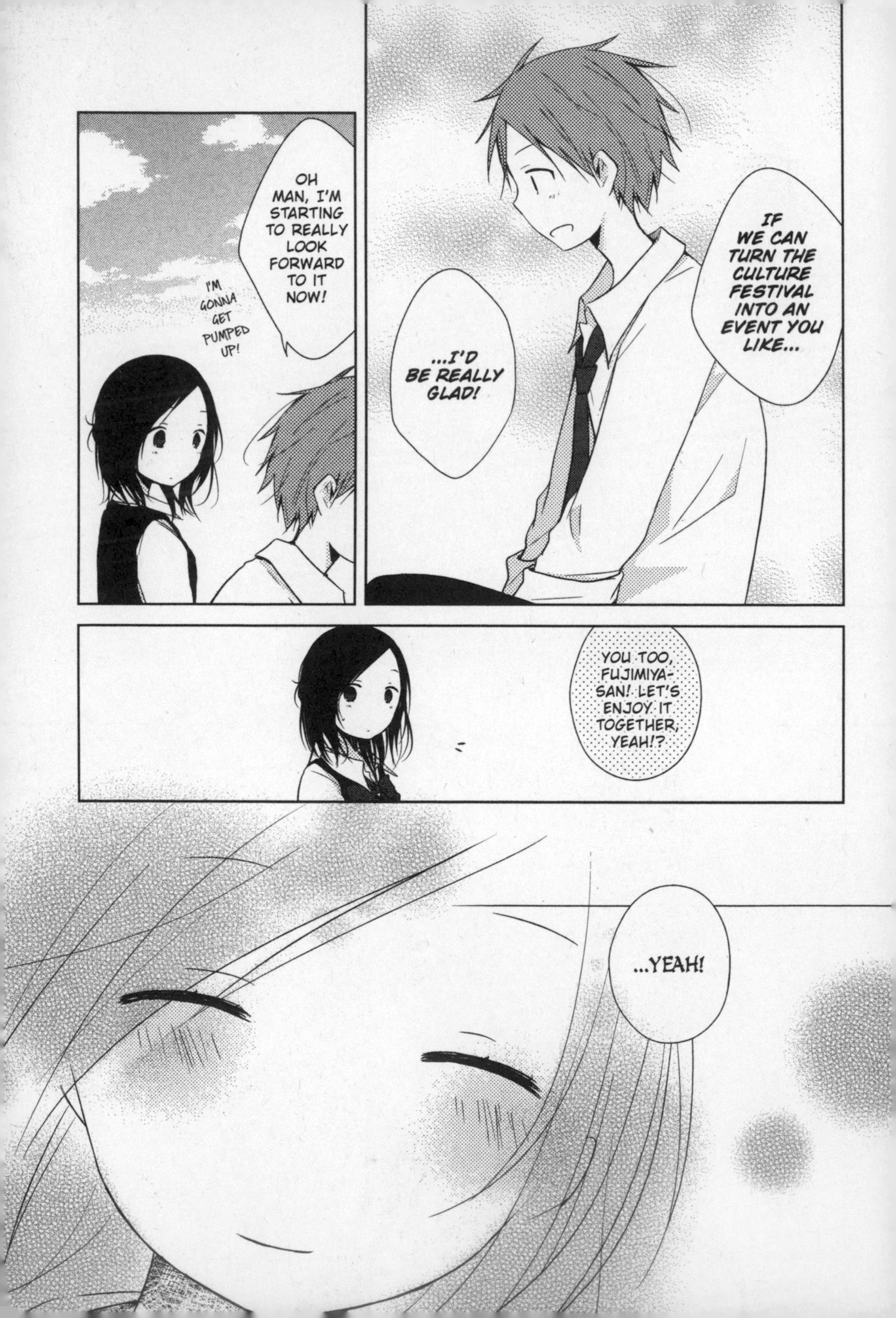
IF WE CAN TURN THE CULTURE FESTIVAL INTO AN EVENT YOU LIKE...
...I'D BE REALLY GLAD!
OH MAN, I'M STARTING TO REALLY LOOK FORWARD TO IT NOW!
I'M GONNA GET PUMPED UP!
YOU TOO, FUJIMIYA-SAN! LET'S ENJOY IT TOGETHER, YEAH!?
...YEAH!

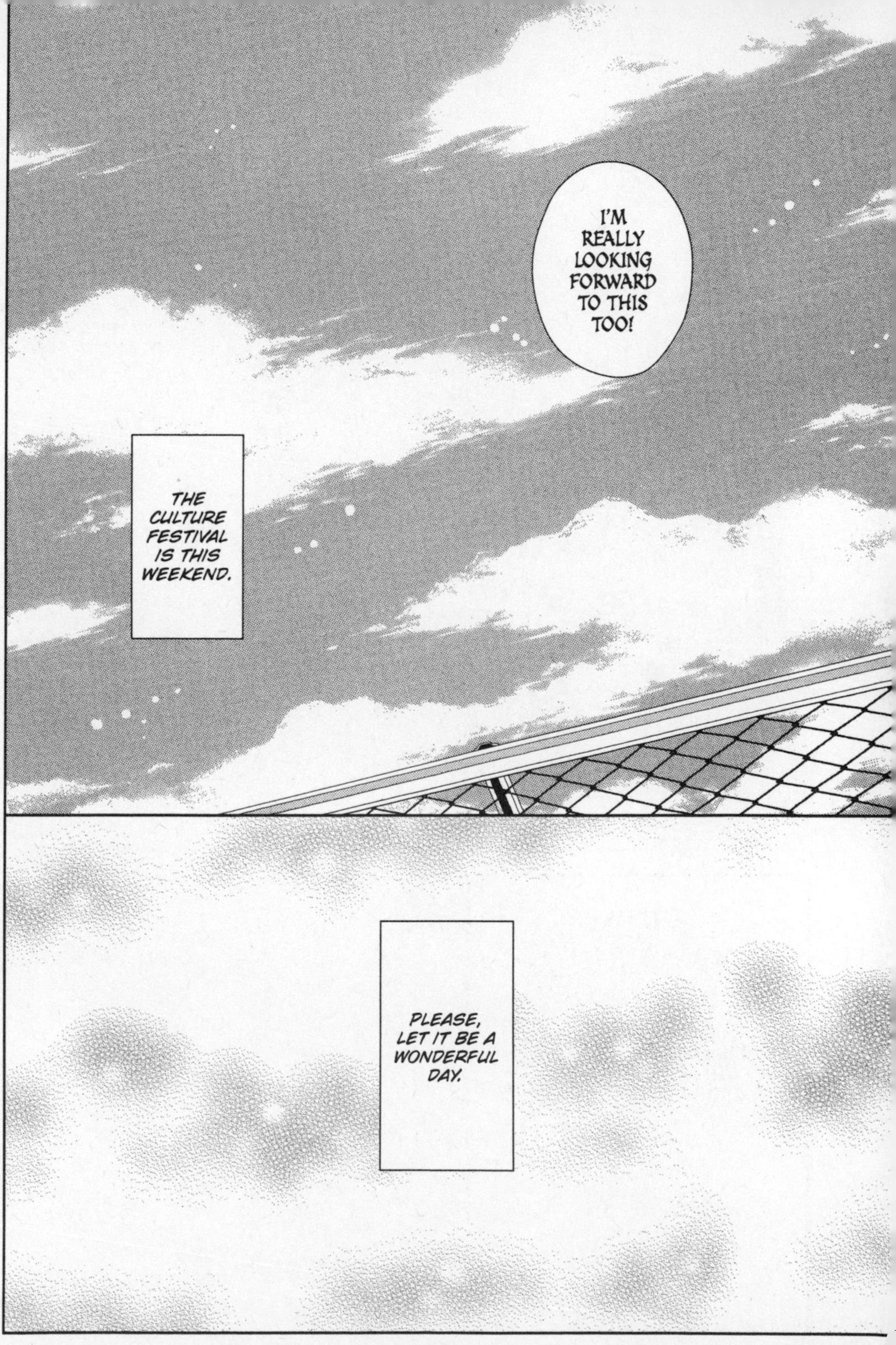
I'M REALLY LOOKING FORWARD TO THIS TOO!
THE CULTURE FESTIVAL IS THIS WEEKEND.
PLEASE, LET IT BE A WONDERFUL DAY.

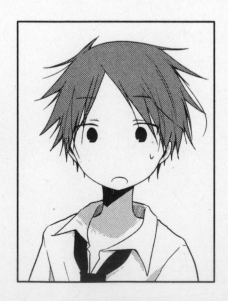

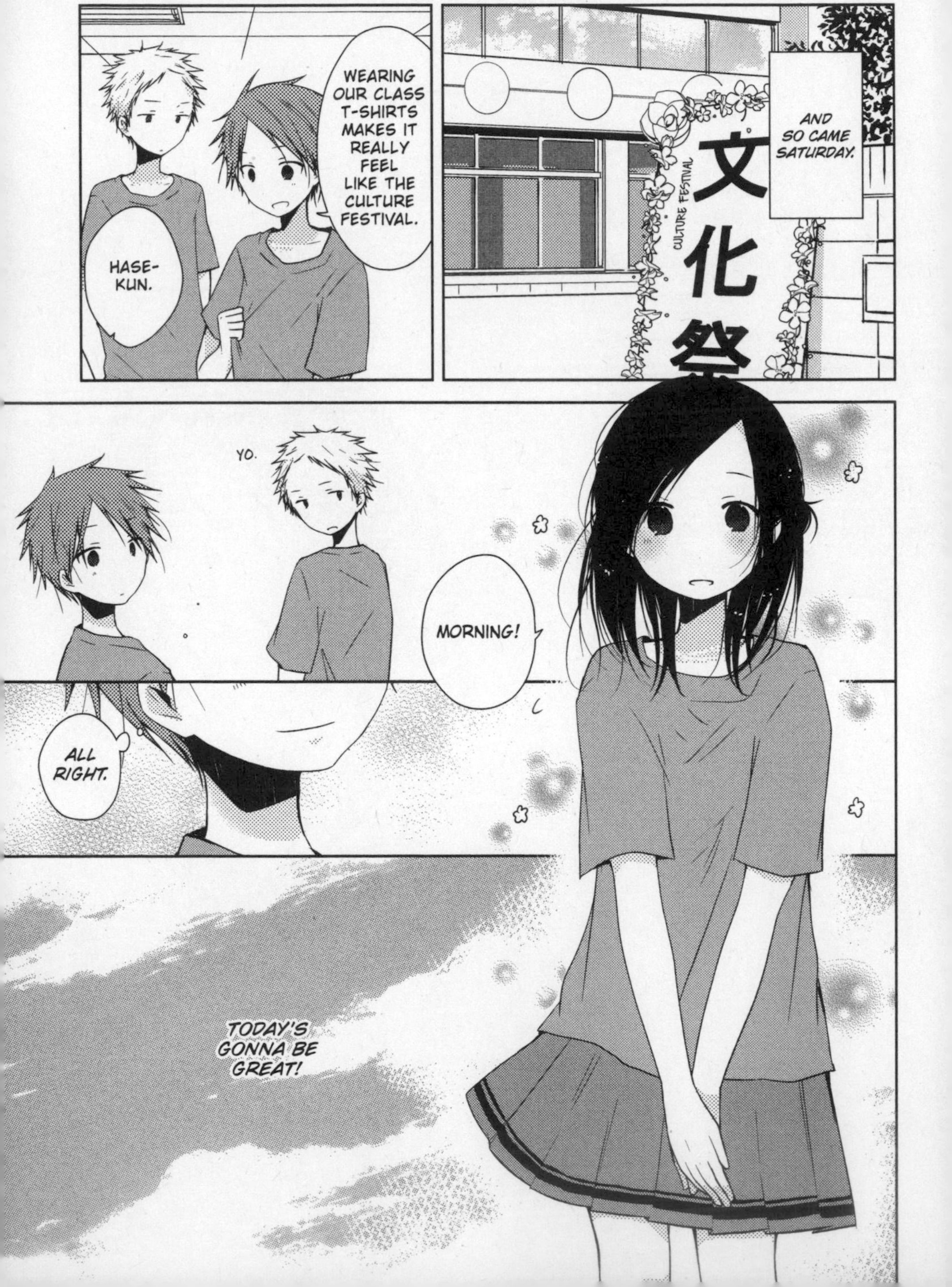
AND SO CAME SATURDAY.
文化祭
CULTURE FESTIVAL
WEARING OUR CLASS T-SHIRTS MAKES IT REALLY FEEL LIKE THE CULTURE FESTIVAL.
HASE-KUN.
MORNING!
YO.
ALL RIGHT.
TODAY'S GONNA BE GREAT!

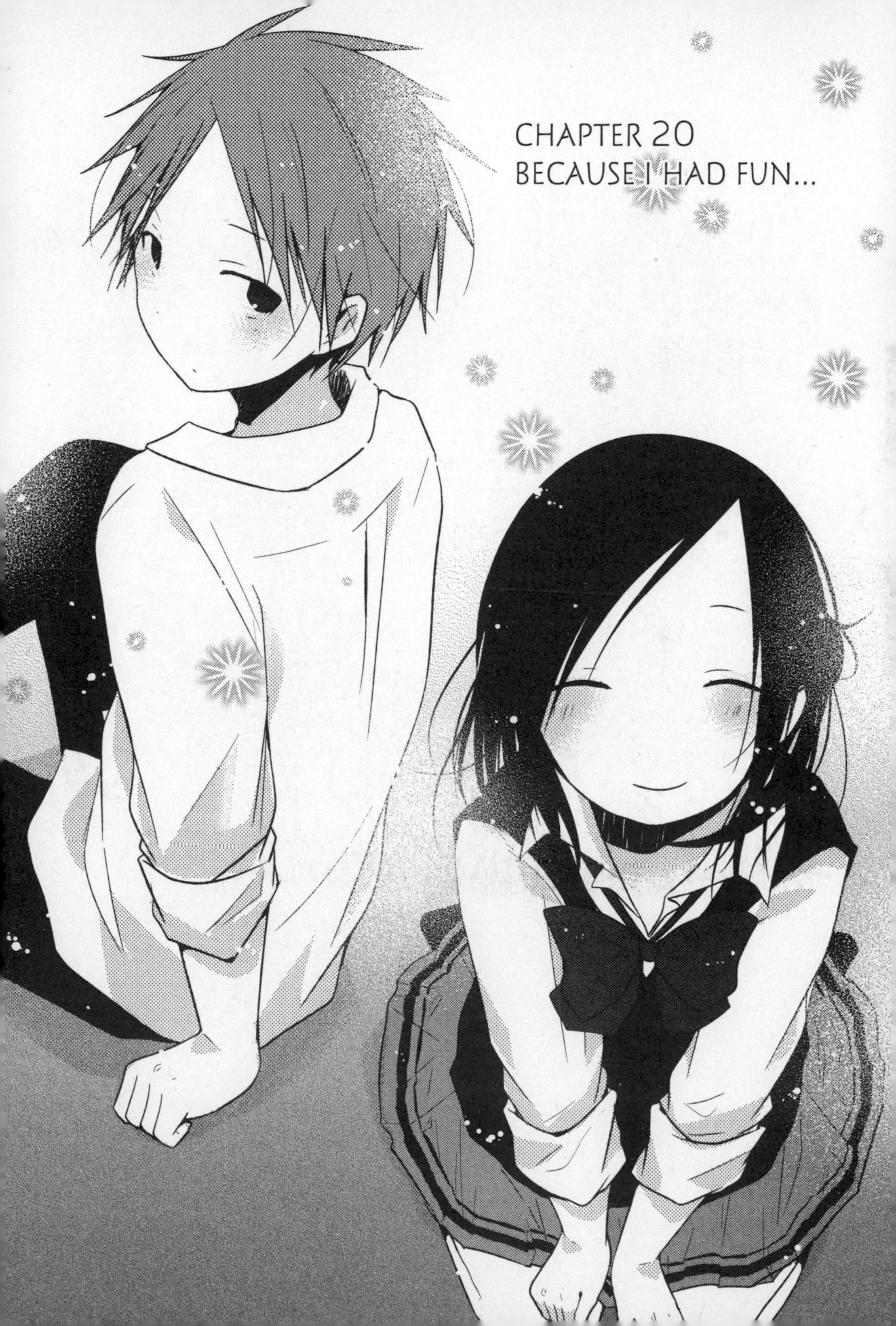
CHAPTER 20
BECAUSE I HAD FUN...

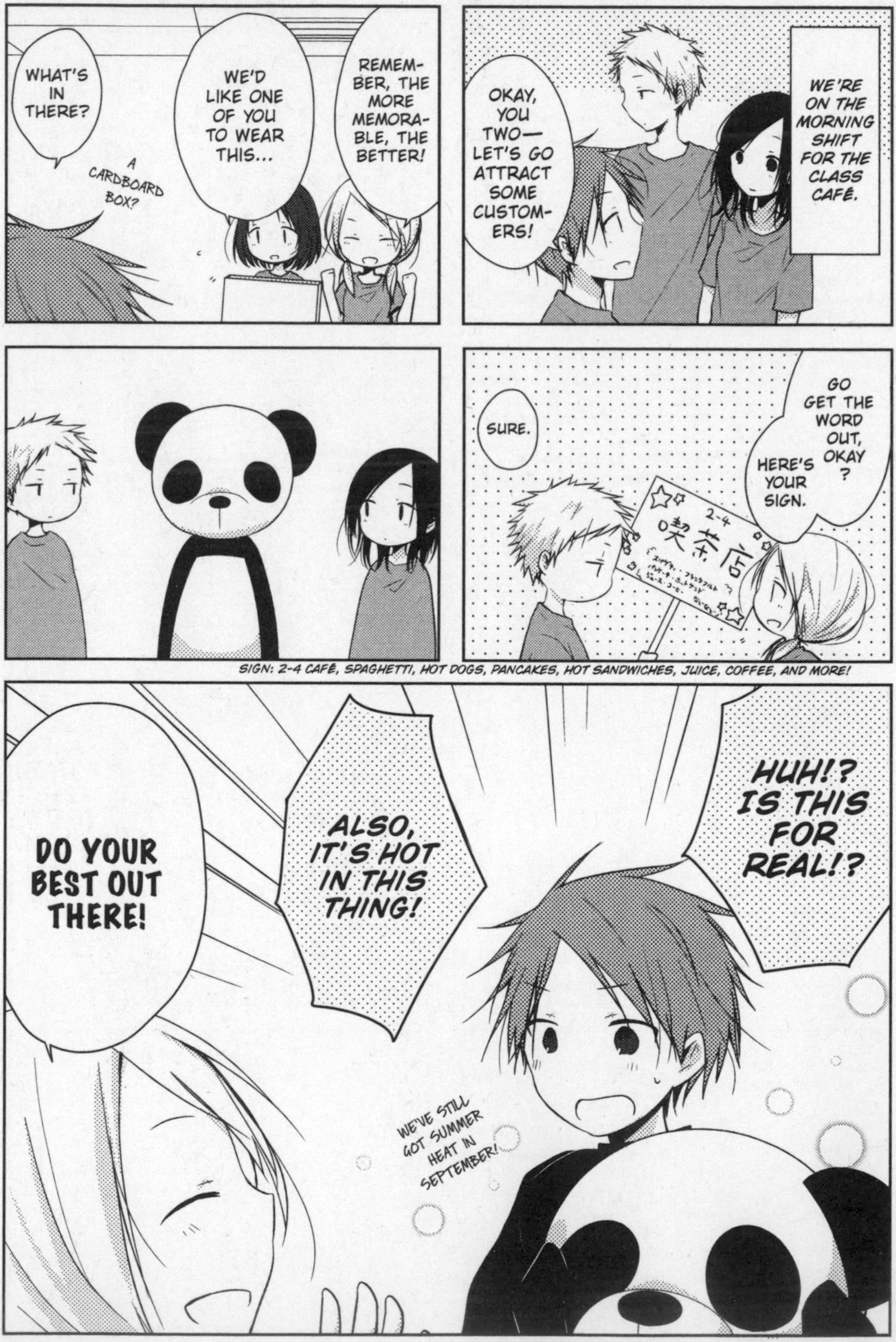
WE'RE ON THE MORNING SHIFT FOR THE CLASS CAFÉ.
OKAY, YOU TWO— LET'S GO ATTRACT SOME CUSTOMERS!
REMEMBER, THE MORE MEMORABLE, THE BETTER!
WE'D LIKE ONE OF YOU TO WEAR THIS...
WHAT'S IN THERE?
A CARDBOARD BOX?
GO GET THE WORD OUT, OKAY?
HERE'S YOUR SIGN.
SURE.
2-4
喫茶店
SIGN: 2-4 CAFÉ, SPAGHETTI, HOT DOGS, PANCAKES, HOT SANDWICHES, JUICE, COFFEE, AND MORE!
HUH!? IS THIS FOR REAL!?
ALSO, IT'S HOT IN THIS THING!
WE'VE STILL GOT SUMMER HEAT IN SEPTEMBER!
DO YOUR BEST OUT THERE!

GAP

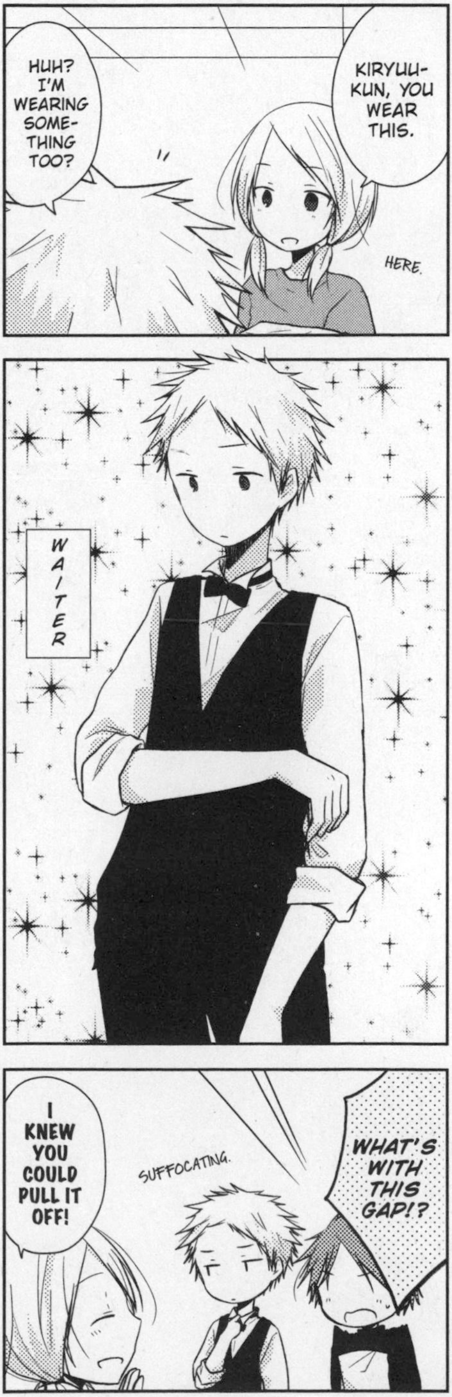
KIRYUU-KUN, YOU WEAR THIS.
HUH? I'M WEARING SOMETHING TOO?
HERE.
WAITER
WHAT'S WITH THIS GAP!?
SUFFOCATING.
I KNEW YOU COULD PULL IT OFF!

AS ALWAYS

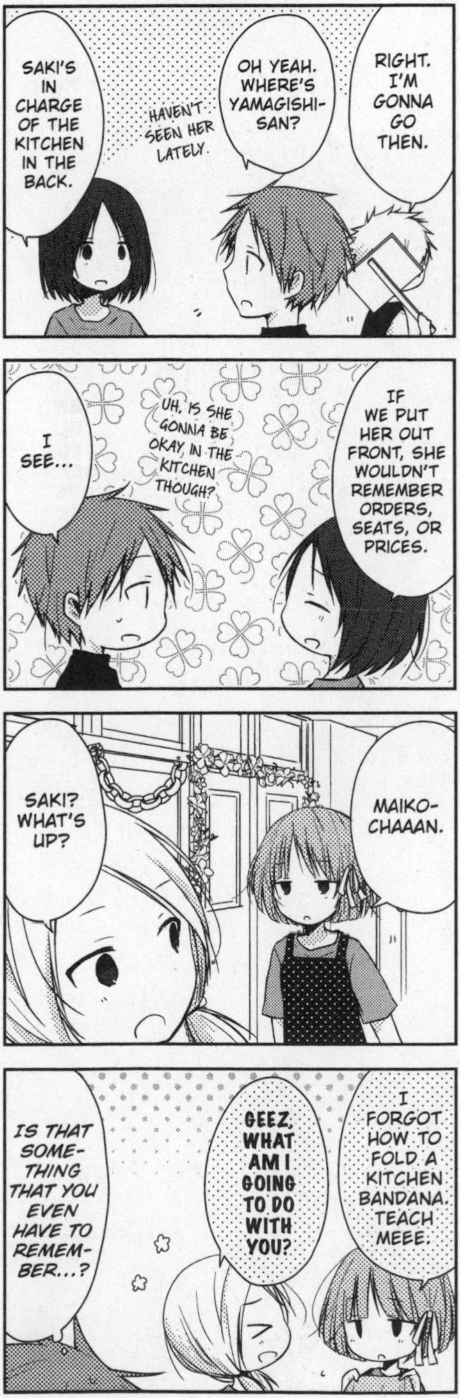
RIGHT. I'M GONNA GO THEN.
OH YEAH. WHERE'S YAMAGISHI-SAN?
HAVEN'T SEEN HER LATELY.
SAKI'S IN CHARGE OF THE KITCHEN IN THE BACK.
IF WE PUT HER OUT FRONT, SHE WOULDN'T REMEMBER ORDERS, SEATS, OR PRICES.
UH, IS SHE GONNA BE OKAY, IN THE KITCHEN THOUGH?
I SEE...
MAIKO-CHAAAN.
SAKI? WHAT'S UP?
I FORGOT HOW TO FOLD A KITCHEN BANDANA. TEACH MEEE.
GEEZ, WHAT AM I GOING TO DO WITH YOU?
IS THAT SOMETHING THAT YOU EVEN HAVE TO REMEMBER...?

EASY TO IMAGINE

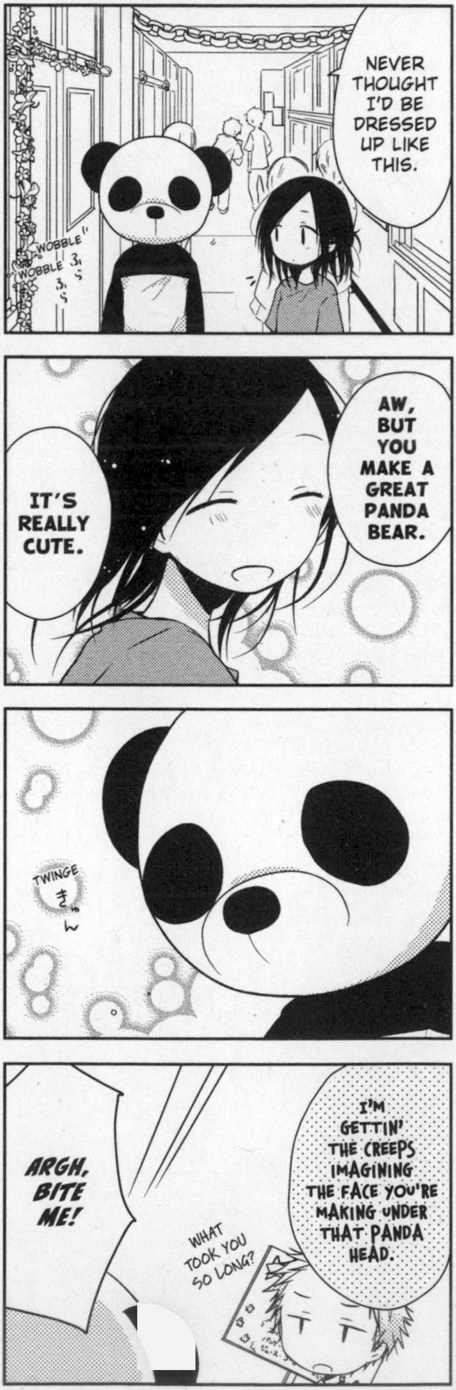

NEVER THOUGHT I'D BE DRESSED UP LIKE THIS.
WOBBLE WOBBLE
AW, BUT YOU MAKE A GREAT PANDA BEAR.
IT'S REALLY CUTE.
TWINGE
I'M GETTIN' THE CREEPS IMAGINING THE FACE YOU'RE MAKING UNDER THAT PANDA HEAD.
WHAT TOOK YOU SO LONG?
ARGH, BITE ME!

ATTRACTING CUSTOMERS

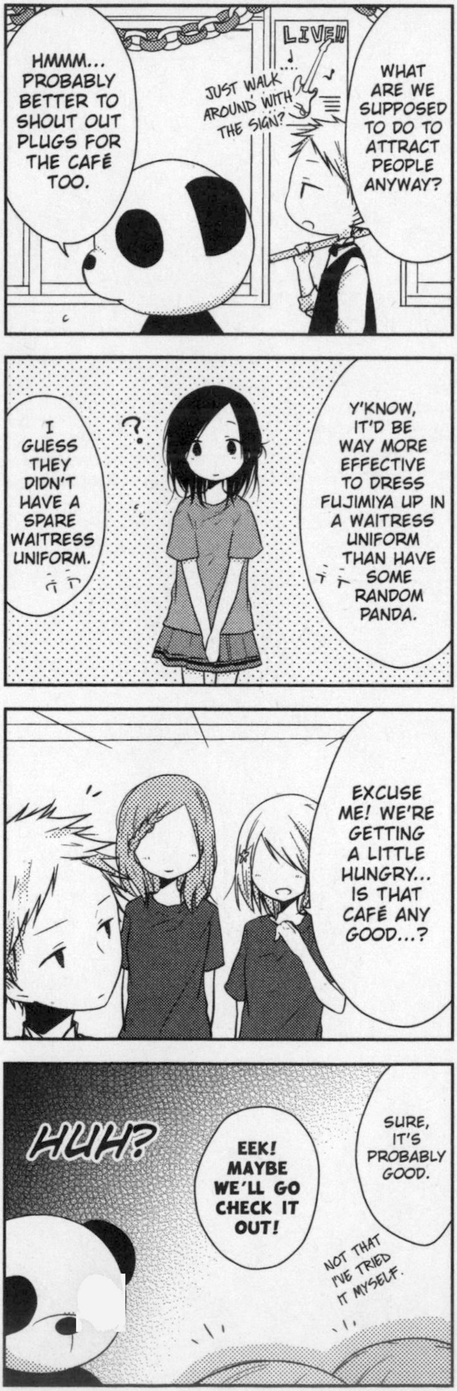

WHAT ARE WE SUPPOSED TO DO TO ATTRACT PEOPLE ANYWAY?
LIVE!!
JUST WALK AROUND WITH THE SIGN?
HMMM... PROBABLY BETTER TO SHOUT OUT PLUGS FOR THE CAFÉ TOO.
Y'KNOW, IT'D BE WAY MORE EFFECTIVE TO DRESS FUJIMIYA UP IN A WAITRESS UNIFORM THAN HAVE SOME RANDOM PANDA.
I GUESS THEY DIDN'T HAVE A SPARE WAITRESS UNIFORM.
EXCUSE ME! WE'RE GETTING A LITTLE HUNGRY... IS THAT CAFÉ ANY GOOD...?
SURE, IT'S PROBABLY GOOD.
NOT THAT I'VE TRIED IT MYSELF.
EEK! MAYBE WE'LL GO CHECK IT OUT!
HUH?

CHERRY-PICKING

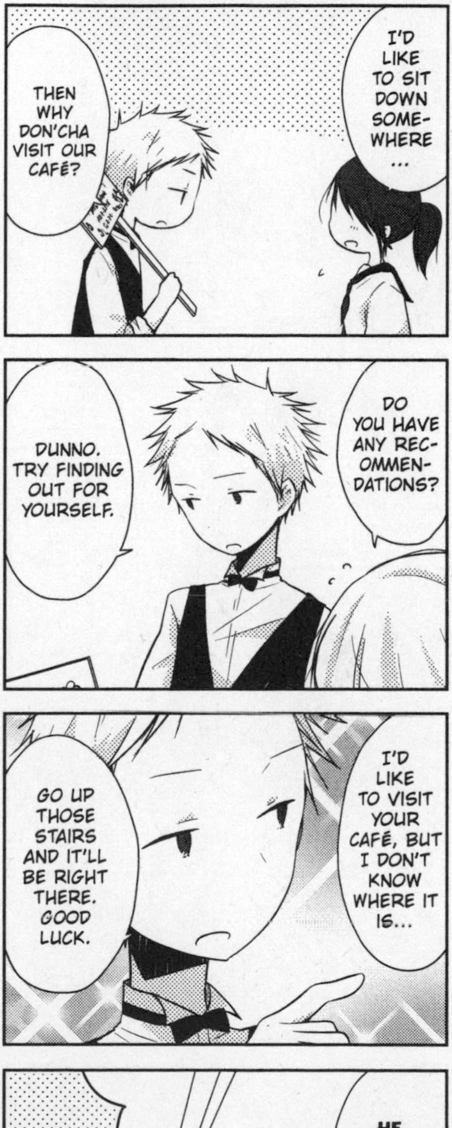
I'D LIKE TO SIT DOWN SOME-WHERE ...
THEN WHY DON'CHA VISIT OUR CAFÉ?
DO YOU HAVE ANY REC-OMMEN-DATIONS?
DUNNO. TRY FINDING OUT FOR YOURSELF.
I'D LIKE TO VISIT YOUR CAFÉ, BUT I DON'T KNOW WHERE IT IS...
GO UP THOSE STAIRS AND IT'LL BE RIGHT THERE. GOOD LUCK.
HE TOLD ME "GOOD LUCK"!
EEK!
WHAT'S THE POINT OF ME BEING HERE!?
WHAT'S THE POINT OF THE PANDA!?

PANDA BEAR

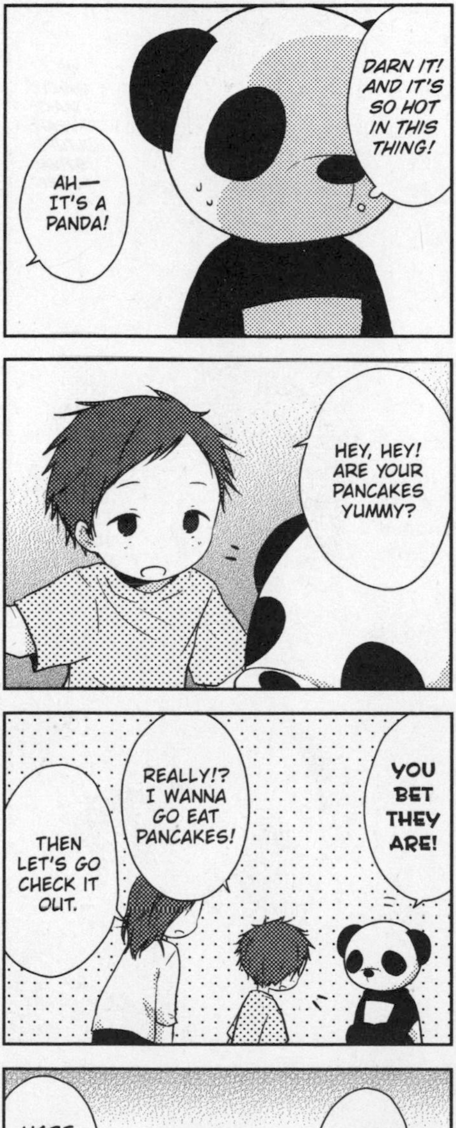
DARN IT! AND IT'S SO HOT IN THIS THING!
AH— IT'S A PANDA!
HEY, HEY! ARE YOUR PANCAKES YUMMY?
YOU BET THEY ARE!
REALLY!? I WANNA GO EAT PANCAKES!
THEN LET'S GO CHECK IT OUT.
YAAAY!
HASE-KUN'S TRYING HARD TOO...

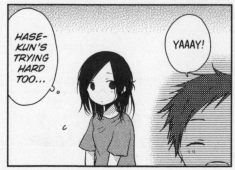

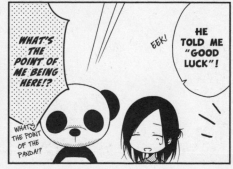

I'LL MAKE AN EFFORT

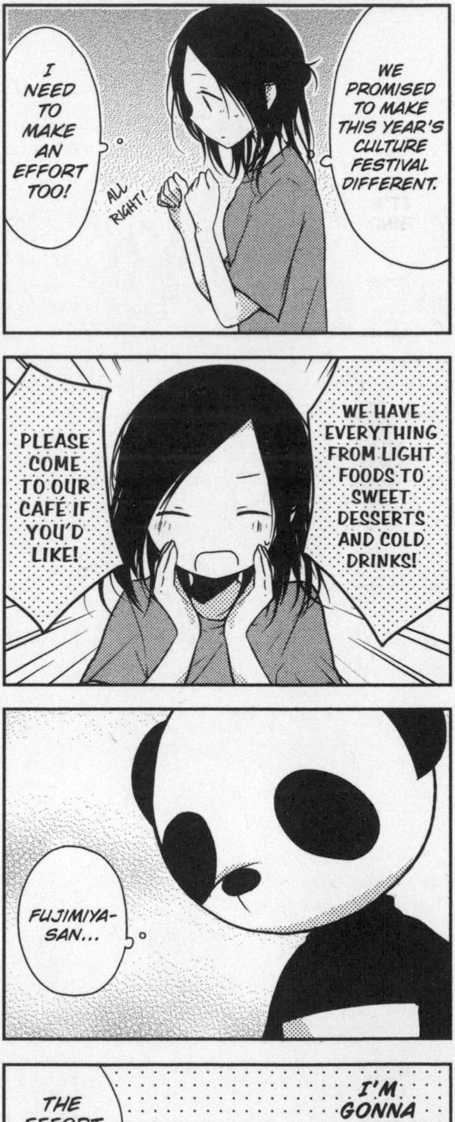
WE PROMISED TO MAKE THIS YEAR'S CULTURE FESTIVAL DIFFERENT.
ALL RIGHT!
I NEED TO MAKE AN EFFORT TOO!
WE HAVE EVERYTHING FROM LIGHT FOODS TO SWEET DESSERTS AND COLD DRINKS!
PLEASE COME TO OUR CAFÉ IF YOU'D LIKE!
FUJIMIYA-SAN...
I'M GONNA TRY HARDER TOO!
PLEASE AND THANK YOU!
PLEASE CHECK US OUT!
PROBABLY SHOULDN'T SAY SO MYSELF, BUT...
THE EFFORT GAP BETWEEN ME AND THEM IS HUGE.

THUMBS UP

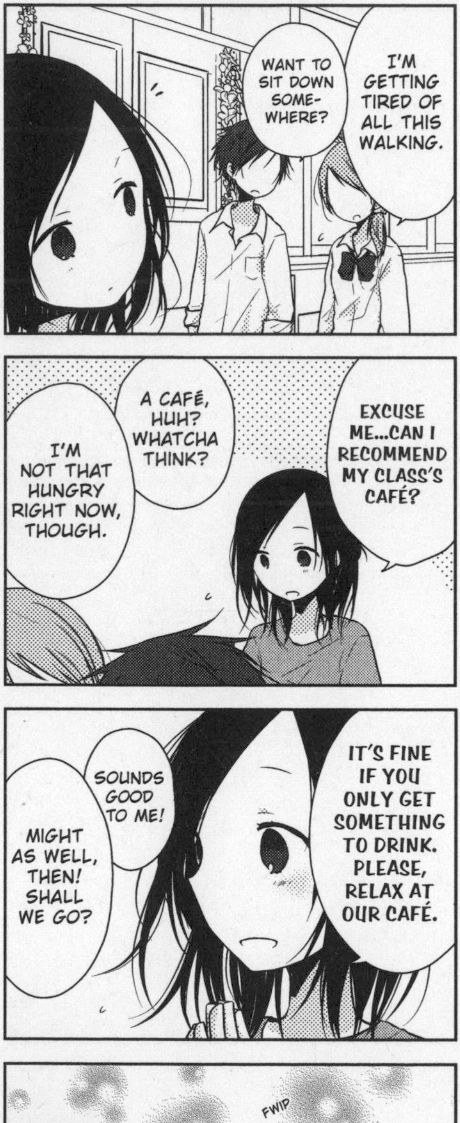
I'M GETTING TIRED OF ALL THIS WALKING.
WANT TO SIT DOWN SOME-WHERE?
EXCUSE ME...CAN I RECOMMEND MY CLASS'S CAFÉ?
A CAFÉ, HUH? WHATCHA THINK?
I'M NOT THAT HUNGRY RIGHT NOW, THOUGH.
IT'S FINE IF YOU ONLY GET SOMETHING TO DRINK. PLEASE, RELAX AT OUR CAFÉ.
SOUNDS GOOD TO ME!
MIGHT AS WELL, THEN! SHALL WE GO?
FWIP
EH HEH HEH!

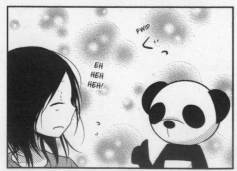

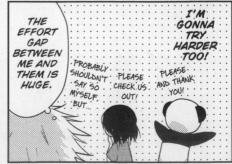

UNEXPECTED EMERGENCY

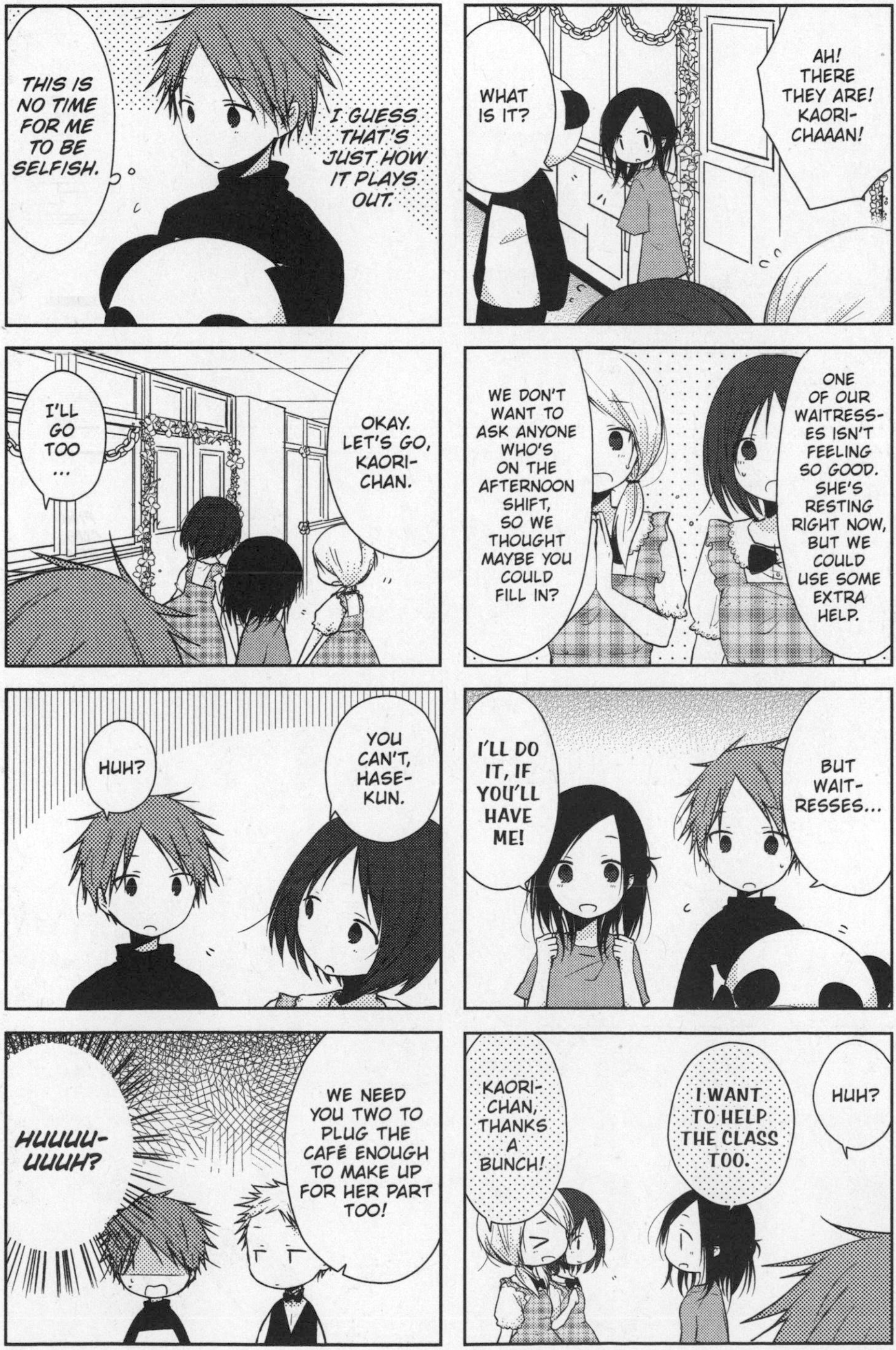
AH! THERE THEY ARE! KAORI-CHAAAN!
WHAT IS IT?
ONE OF OUR WAITRESSES ISN'T FEELING SO GOOD. SHE'S RESTING RIGHT NOW, BUT WE COULD USE SOME EXTRA HELP.
WE DON'T WANT TO ASK ANYONE WHO'S ON THE AFTERNOON SHIFT, SO WE THOUGHT MAYBE YOU COULD FILL IN?
BUT WAITRESSES...
I'LL DO IT, IF YOU'LL HAVE ME!
HUH?
I WANT TO HELP THE CLASS TOO.
KAORI-CHAN, THANKS A BUNCH!
I GUESS THAT'S JUST HOW IT PLAYS OUT.
THIS IS NO TIME FOR ME TO BE SELFISH.
OKAY. LET'S GO, KAORI-CHAN.
I'LL GO TOO...
YOU CAN'T, HASE-KUN.
HUH?
WE NEED YOU TWO TO PLUG THE CAFÉ ENOUGH TO MAKE UP FOR HER PART TOO!
HUUUU-UUUH?

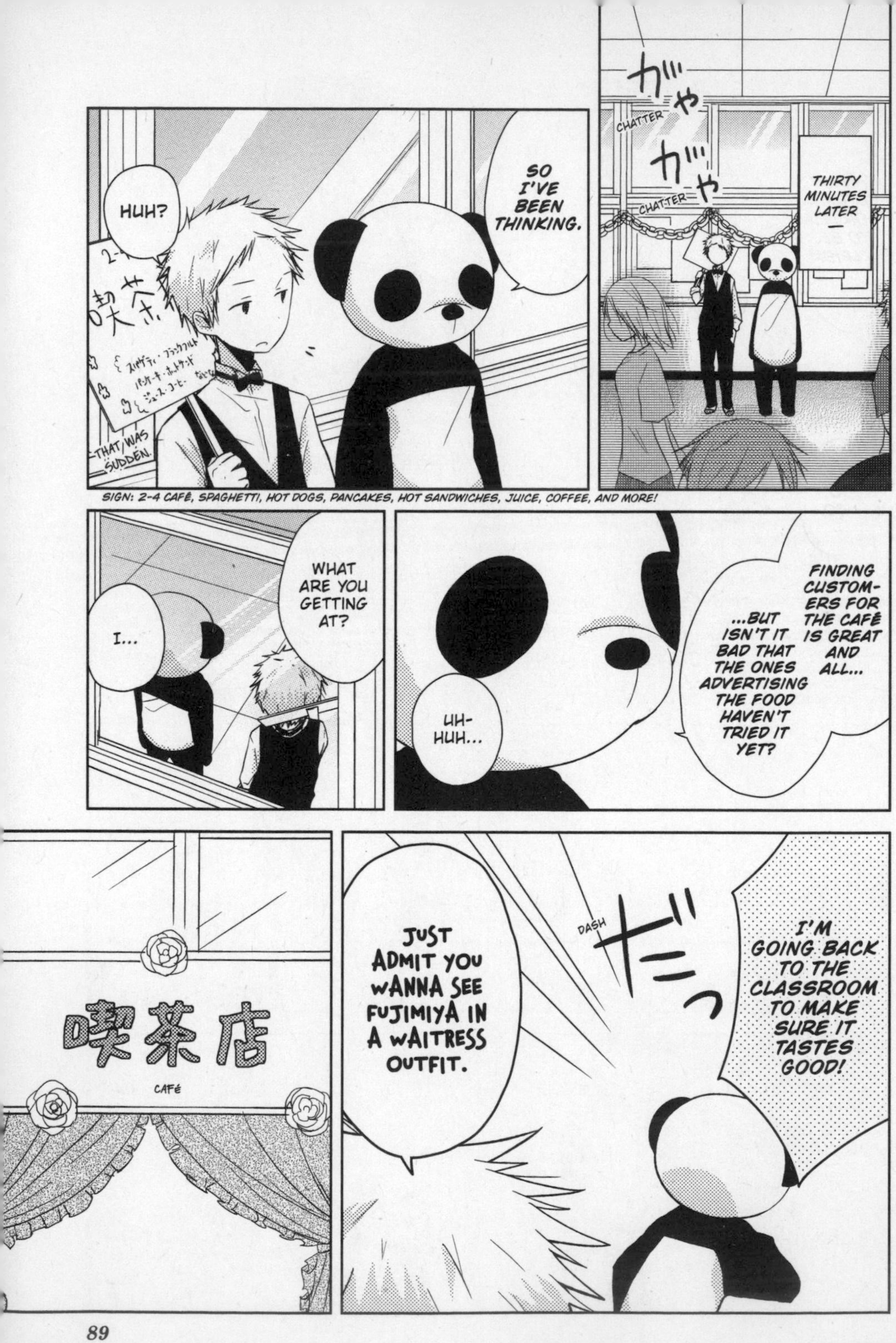
CHATTER
CHATTER
THIRTY MINUTES LATER—
SO I'VE BEEN THINKING.
HUH?
THAT WAS SUDDEN.
SIGN: 2-4 CAFÉ, SPAGHETTI, HOT DOGS, PANCAKES, HOT SANDWICHES, JUICE, COFFEE, AND MORE!
FINDING CUSTOMERS FOR THE CAFÉ IS GREAT AND ALL...
...BUT ISN'T IT BAD THAT THE ONES ADVERTISING THE FOOD HAVEN'T TRIED IT YET?
UH-HUH...
WHAT ARE YOU GETTING AT?
I...
I'M GOING BACK TO THE CLASSROOM TO MAKE SURE IT TASTES GOOD!
DASH
JUST ADMIT YOU WANNA SEE FUJIMIYA IN A WAITRESS OUTFIT.
喫茶店
CAFÉ

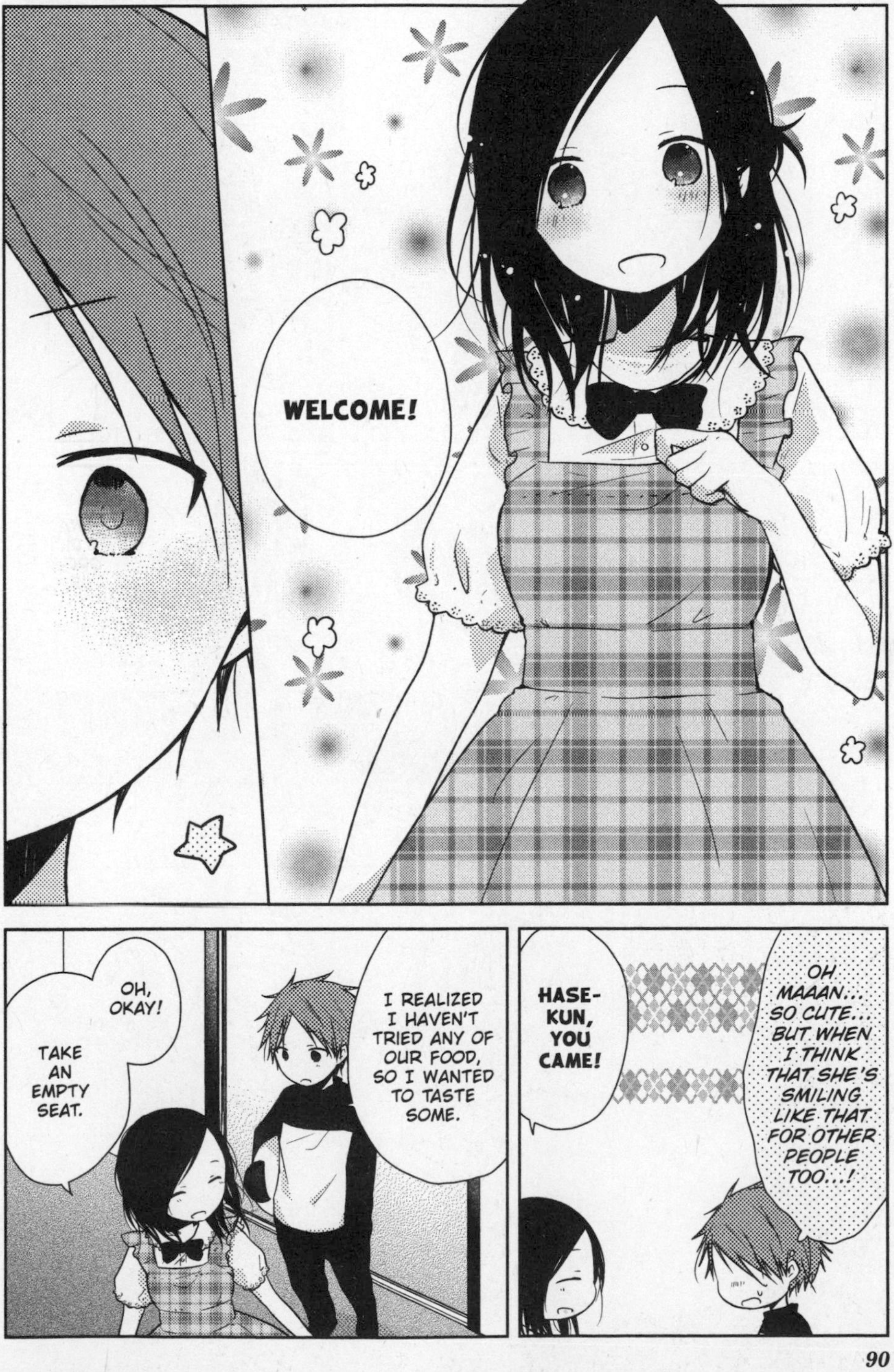
WELCOME!
OH MAAAN... SO CUTE... BUT WHEN I THINK THAT SHE'S SMILING LIKE THAT FOR OTHER PEOPLE TOO...!
HASE-KUN, YOU CAME!
I REALIZED I HAVEN'T TRIED ANY OF OUR FOOD, SO I WANTED TO TASTE SOME.
OH, OKAY!
TAKE AN EMPTY SEAT.

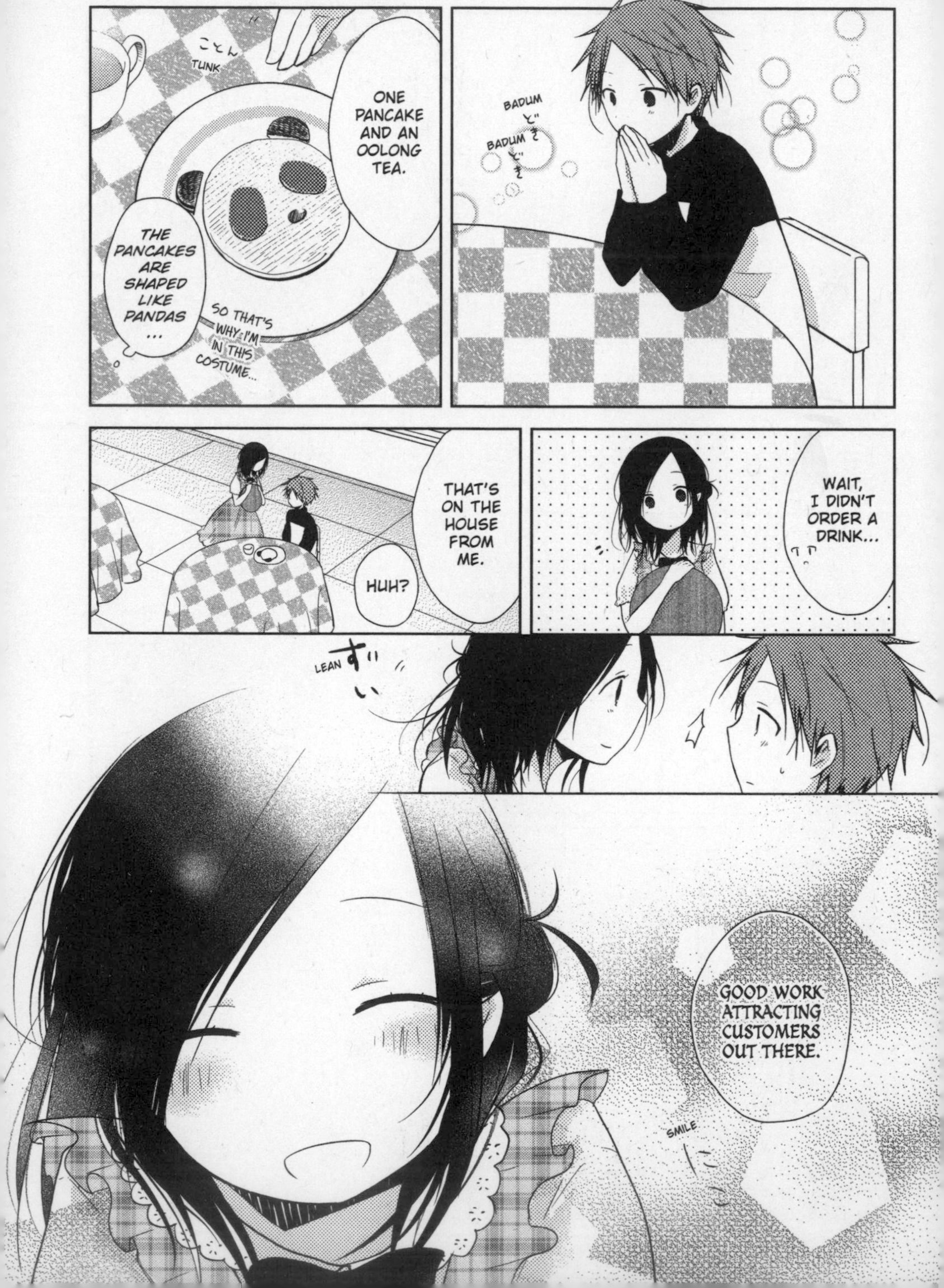

BADUM
BADUM
ことん
TUNK
ONE PANCAKE AND AN OOLONG TEA.
THE PANCAKES ARE SHAPED LIKE PANDAS...
SO THAT'S WHY I'M IN THIS COSTUME...
WAIT, I DIDN'T ORDER A DRINK...
THAT'S ON THE HOUSE FROM ME.
HUH?
LEAN
GOOD WORK ATTRACTING CUSTOMERS OUT THERE.
SMILE

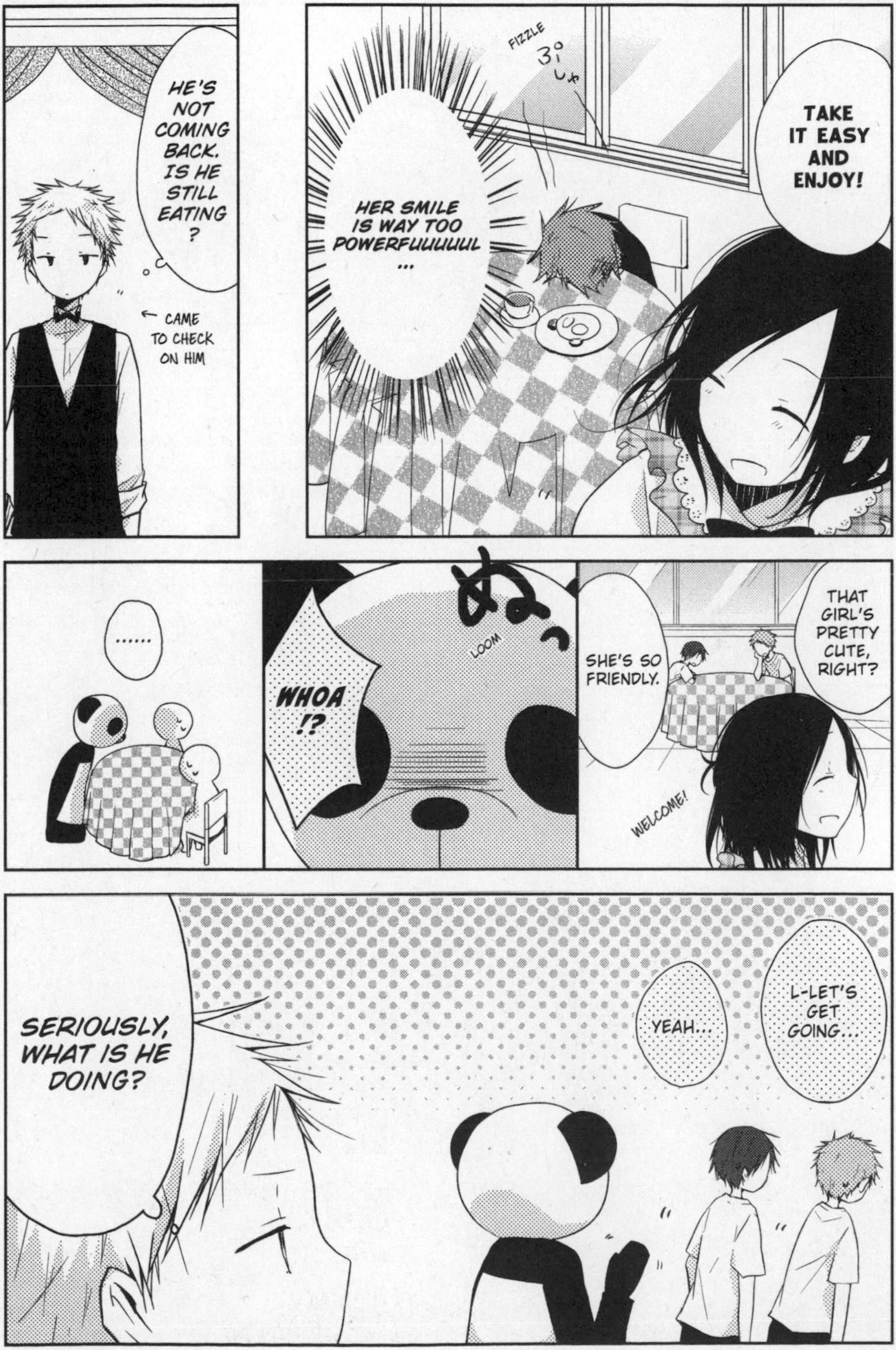
TAKE IT EASY AND ENJOY!
FIZZLE
HER SMILE IS WAY TOO POWERFUUUUUL ...
HE'S NOT COMING BACK. IS HE STILL EATING?
← CAME TO CHECK ON HIM
THAT GIRL'S PRETTY CUTE, RIGHT?
SHE'S SO FRIENDLY.
WELCOME!
ぬっ
LOOM
WHOA !?
......
L-LET'S GET GOING...
YEAH...
SERIOUSLY, WHAT IS HE DOING?

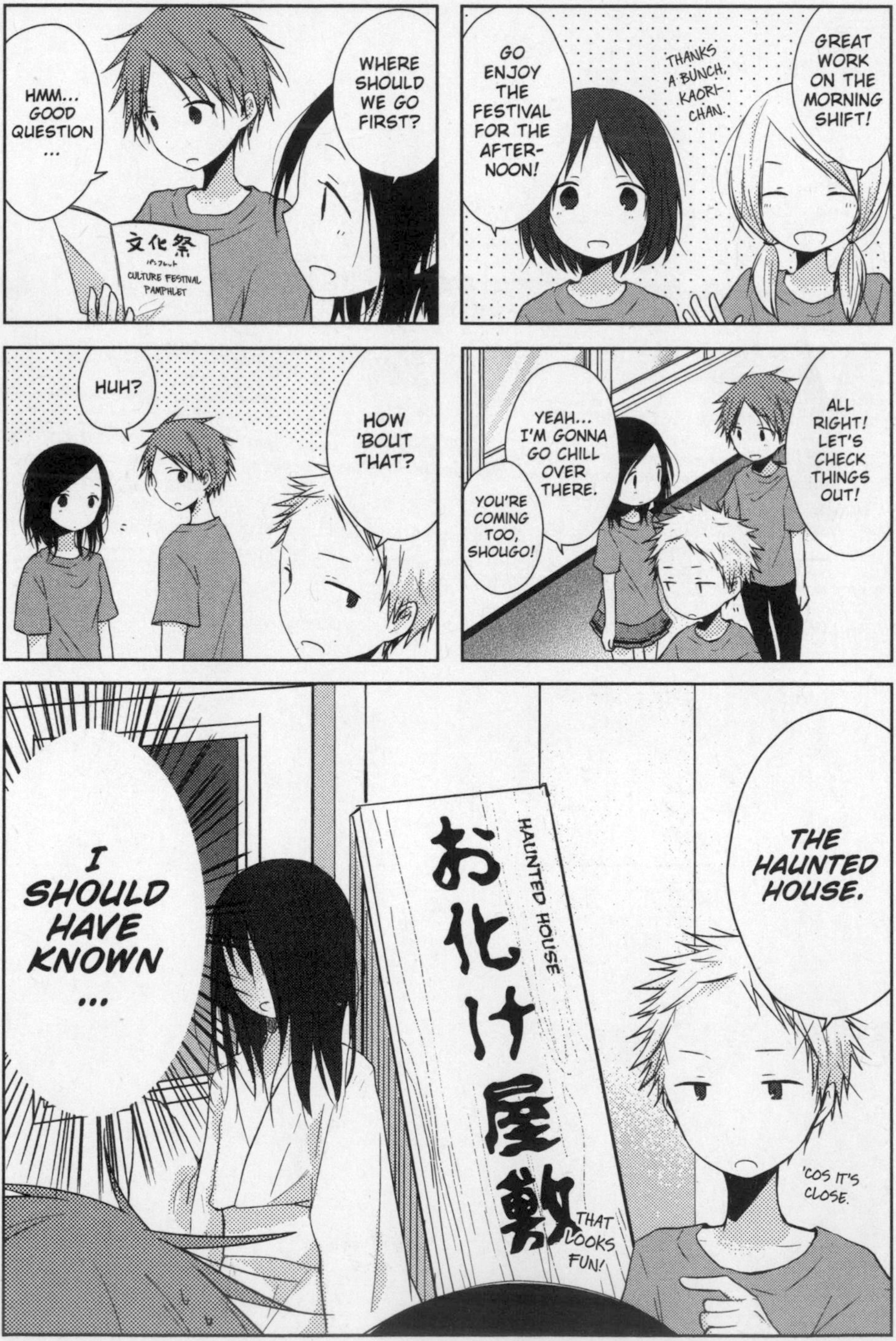
GREAT WORK ON THE MORNING SHIFT!
THANKS A BUNCH, KAORI-CHAN.
GO ENJOY THE FESTIVAL FOR THE AFTER-NOON!
WHERE SHOULD WE GO FIRST?
HMM... GOOD QUESTION ...
文化祭
パンフレット
CULTURE FESTIVAL PAMPHLET
ALL RIGHT! LET'S CHECK THINGS OUT!
YEAH... I'M GONNA GO CHILL OVER THERE.
YOU'RE COMING TOO, SHOUGO!
HOW 'BOUT THAT?
HUH?
THE HAUNTED HOUSE.
'COS IT'S CLOSE.
お化け屋敷
HAUNTED HOUSE
THAT LOOKS FUN!
I SHOULD HAVE KNOWN ...

HAUNTED HOUSE

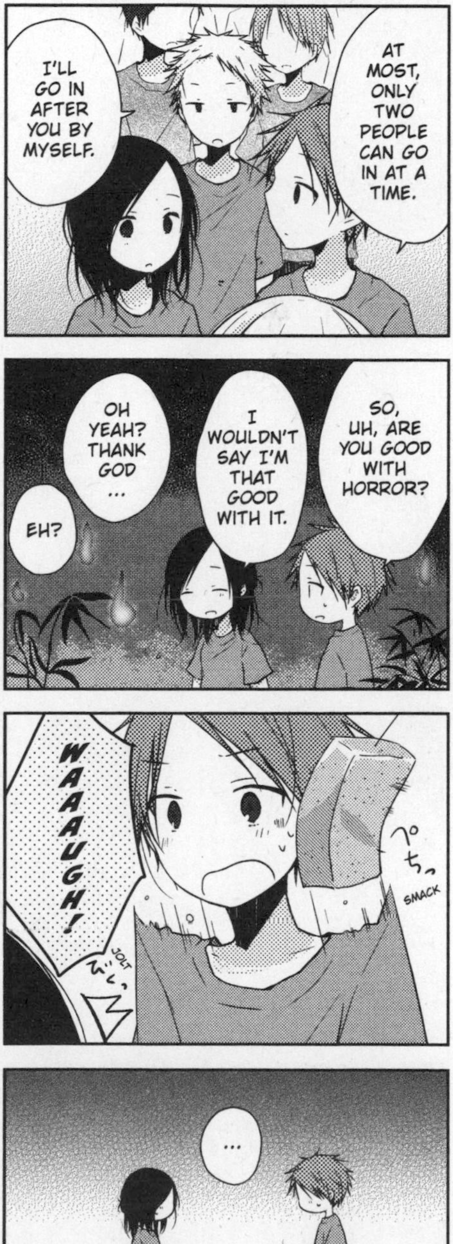
AT MOST, ONLY TWO PEOPLE CAN GO IN AT A TIME.
I'LL GO IN AFTER YOU BY MYSELF.
SO, UH, ARE YOU GOOD WITH HORROR?
I WOULDN'T SAY I'M THAT GOOD WITH IT.
OH YEAH? THANK GOD ...
EH?
SMACK
WAAAUGH!
JOLT
...

SCARED

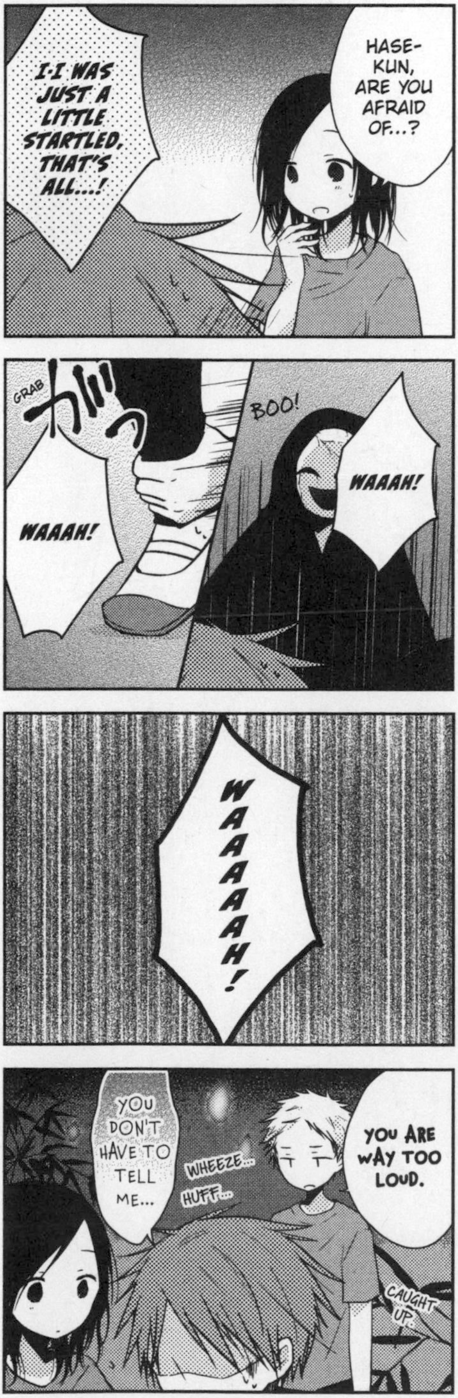
HASE-KUN, ARE YOU AFRAID OF...?
I-I WAS JUST A LITTLE STARTLED, THAT'S ALL...!
BOO!
WAAAH!
GRAB
WAAAH!
WAAAAAAH!
YOU ARE WAY TOO LOUD.
WHEEZE... HUFF...
YOU DON'T HAVE TO TELL ME...
CAUGHT UP.

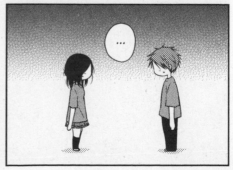

WHAT SHOULD I...

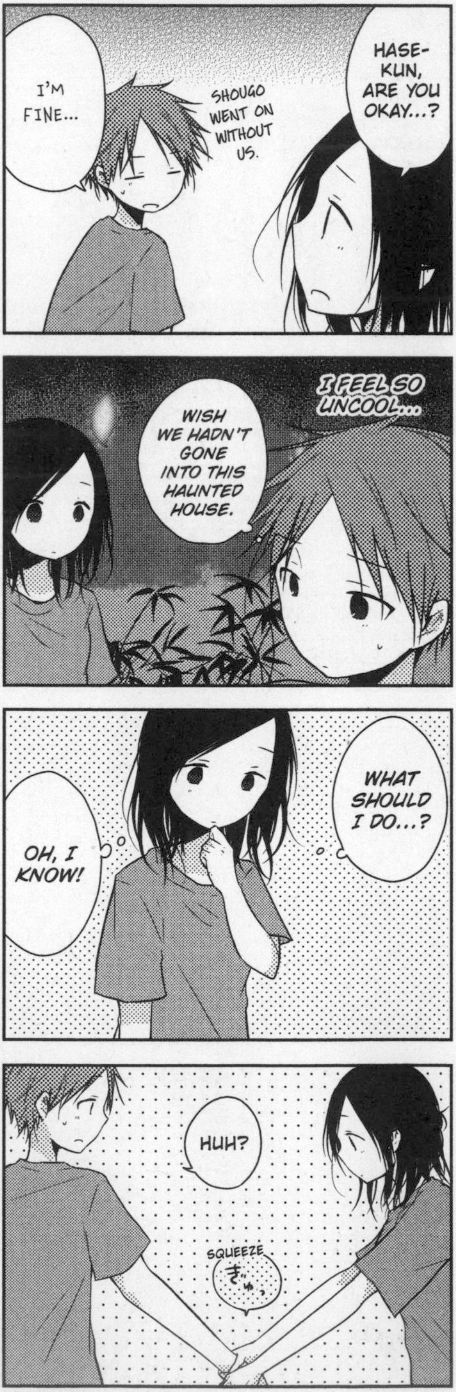
HASE-KUN, ARE YOU OKAY...?
SHOUGO WENT ON WITHOUT US.
I'M FINE...
I FEEL SO UNCOOL...
WISH WE HADN'T GONE INTO THIS HAUNTED HOUSE.
WHAT SHOULD I DO...?
OH, I KNOW!
HUH?
SQUEEZE
ぎゅっ

A WAY TO FORGET FEAR

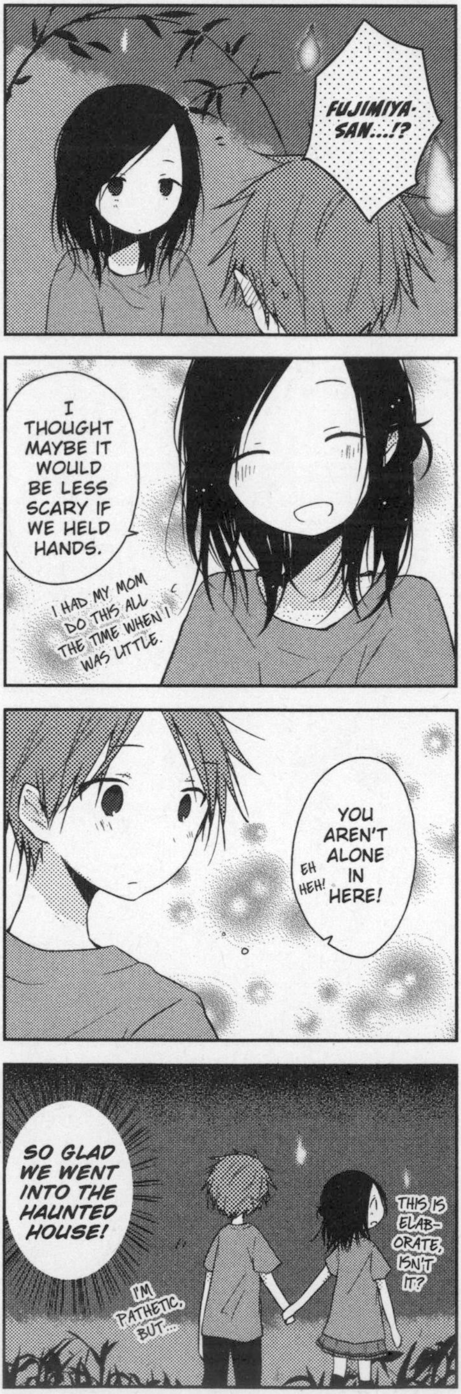
FUJIMIYA-SAN...!?
I THOUGHT MAYBE IT WOULD BE LESS SCARY IF WE HELD HANDS.
I HAD MY MOM DO THIS ALL THE TIME WHEN I WAS LITTLE.
YOU AREN'T ALONE IN HERE!
EH HEH!
THIS IS ELABORATE, ISN'T IT?
SO GLAD WE WENT INTO THE HAUNTED HOUSE!
I'M PATHETIC, BUT...

STRANGE

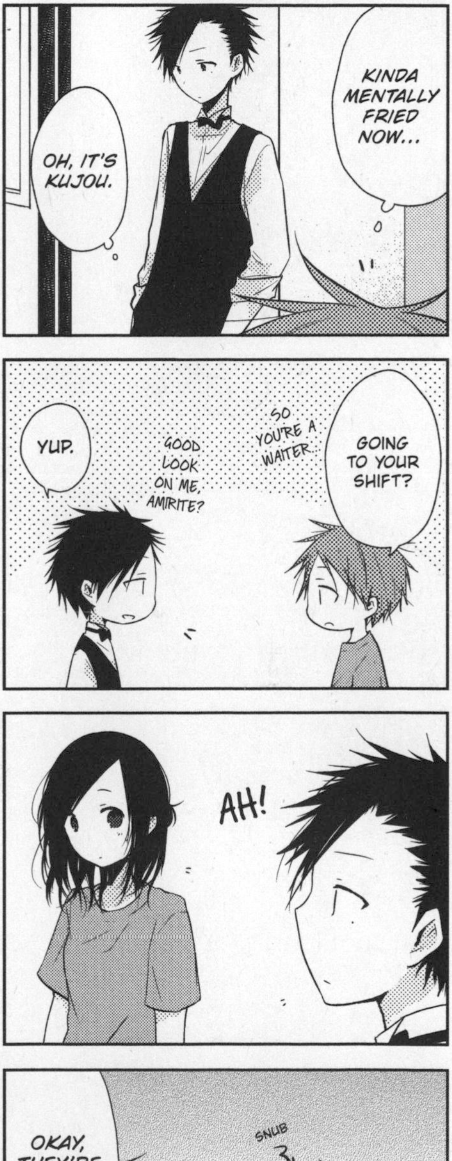
KINDA MENTALLY FRIED NOW...
OH, IT'S KUJOU.
GOING TO YOUR SHIFT?
SO YOU'RE A WAITER
GOOD LOOK ON ME, AMIRITE?
YUP.
AH!
SNUB
OKAY, THEY'RE ACTING KINDA STRANGE ...

CORNER BOOTH

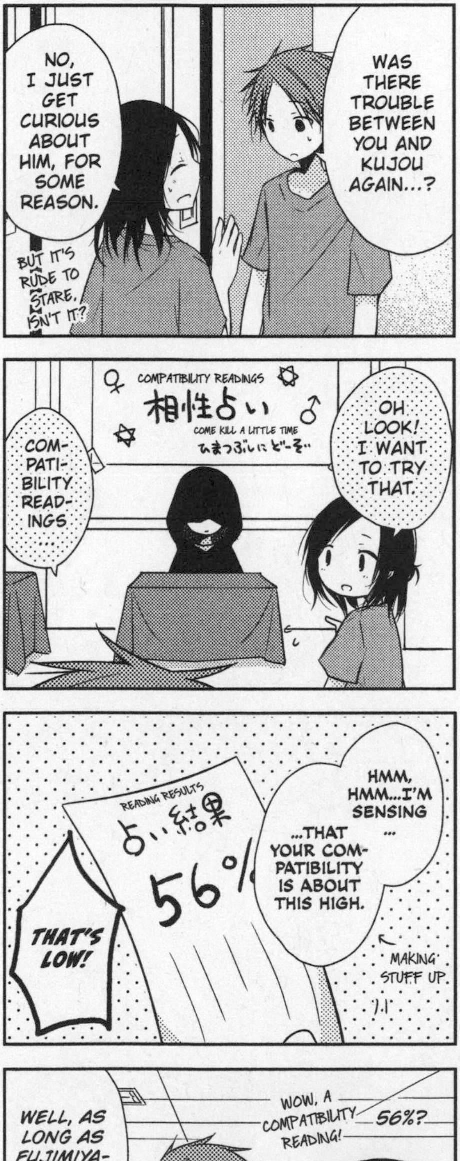
WAS THERE TROUBLE BETWEEN YOU AND KUJOU AGAIN...?
NO, I JUST GET CURIOUS ABOUT HIM, FOR SOME REASON.
BUT IT'S RUDE TO STARE, ISN'T IT?
OH LOOK! I WANT TO TRY THAT.
COMPATIBILITY READINGS
相性占い
COME KILL A LITTLE TIME
ひまつぶしにどーぞ
COM-PATI-BILITY READ-INGS...
HMM, HMM...I'M SENSING ...
...THAT YOUR COM-PATIBILITY IS ABOUT THIS HIGH.
MAKING STUFF UP
READING RESULTS
占い結果
56%
THAT'S LOW!
56%?
WOW, A COMPATIBILITY READING!
WELL, AS LONG AS FUJIMIYA-SAN IS HAPPY, THEN I AM TOO.
BUT 56%...?

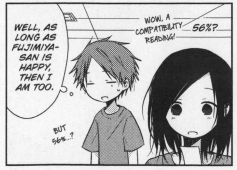

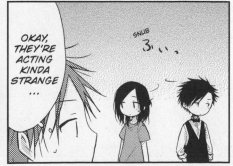

GIANT MAZE

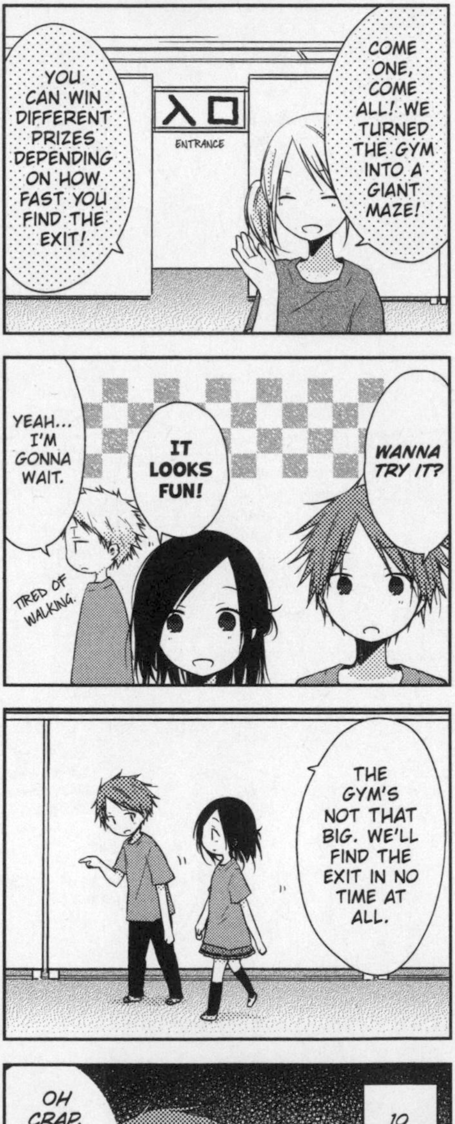
COME ONE, COME ALL! WE TURNED THE GYM INTO A GIANT MAZE!
入口
ENTRANCE
YOU CAN WIN DIFFERENT PRIZES DEPENDING ON HOW FAST YOU FIND THE EXIT!
WANNA TRY IT?
IT LOOKS FUN!
YEAH... I'M GONNA WAIT.
TIRED OF WALKING.
THE GYM'S NOT THAT BIG. WE'LL FIND THE EXIT IN NO TIME AT ALL.
10 MIN-UTES LATER
OH CRAP. WE'RE NOT FINDING THE EXIT.

DISAPPEARANCE

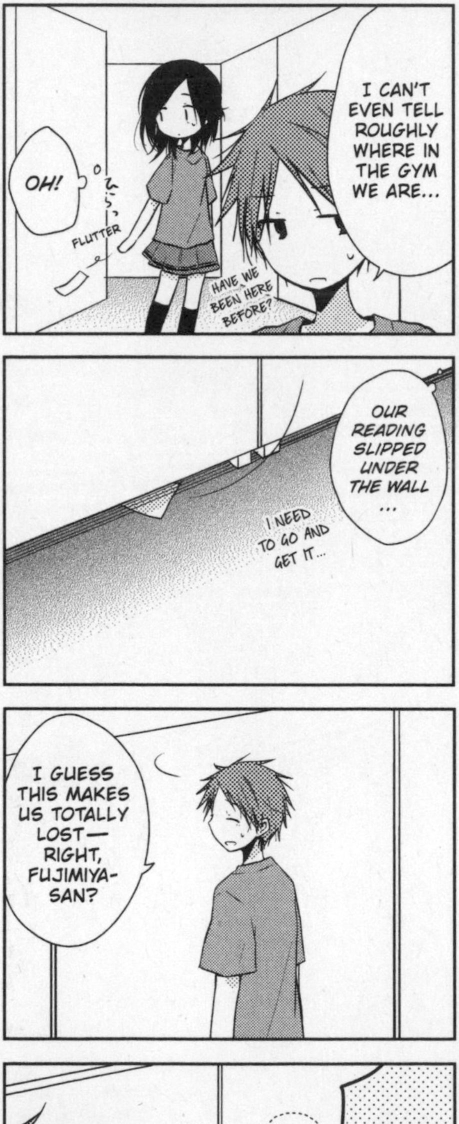
I CAN'T EVEN TELL ROUGHLY WHERE IN THE GYM WE ARE...
HAVE WE BEEN HERE BEFORE?
OH!
FLUTTER
OUR READING SLIPPED UNDER THE WALL ...
I NEED TO GO AND GET IT...
I GUESS THIS MAKES US TOTALLY LOST—RIGHT, FUJIMIYA-SAN?
WAIT, SHE'S GONE!?

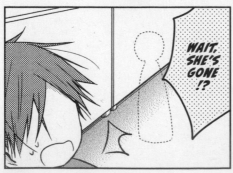

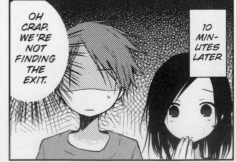

MARCO POLO

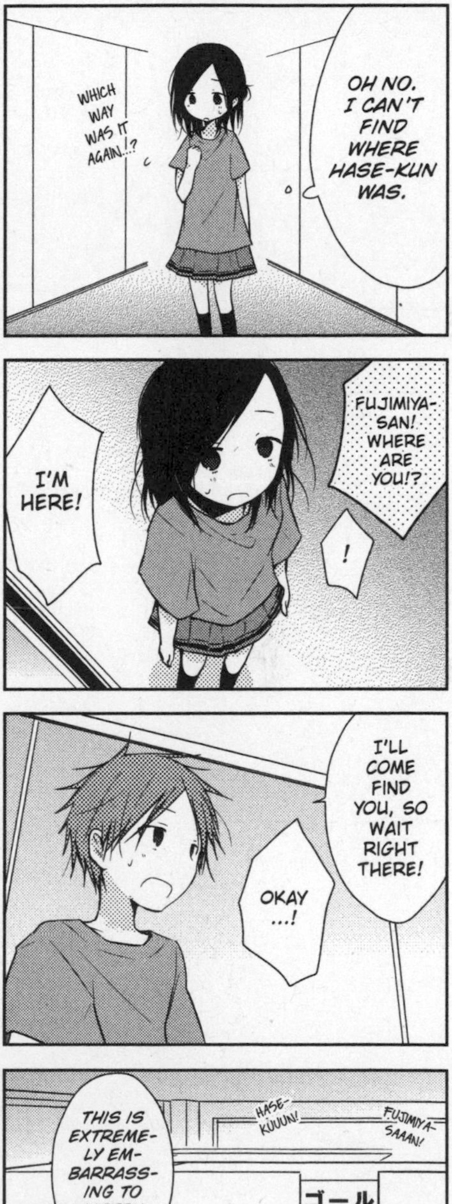
OH NO. I CAN'T FIND WHERE HASE-KUN WAS.
WHICH WAY WAS IT AGAIN...!?
FUJIMIYA-SAN! WHERE ARE YOU!?
I'M HERE!
!
I'LL COME FIND YOU, SO WAIT RIGHT THERE!
OKAY ...!
FUJIMIYA-SAAAN!
HASE-KUUUN!
THIS IS EXTREMELY EMBARRASSING TO LISTEN TO.
ゴール
EXIT
LOUD AND CLEAR

EXIT

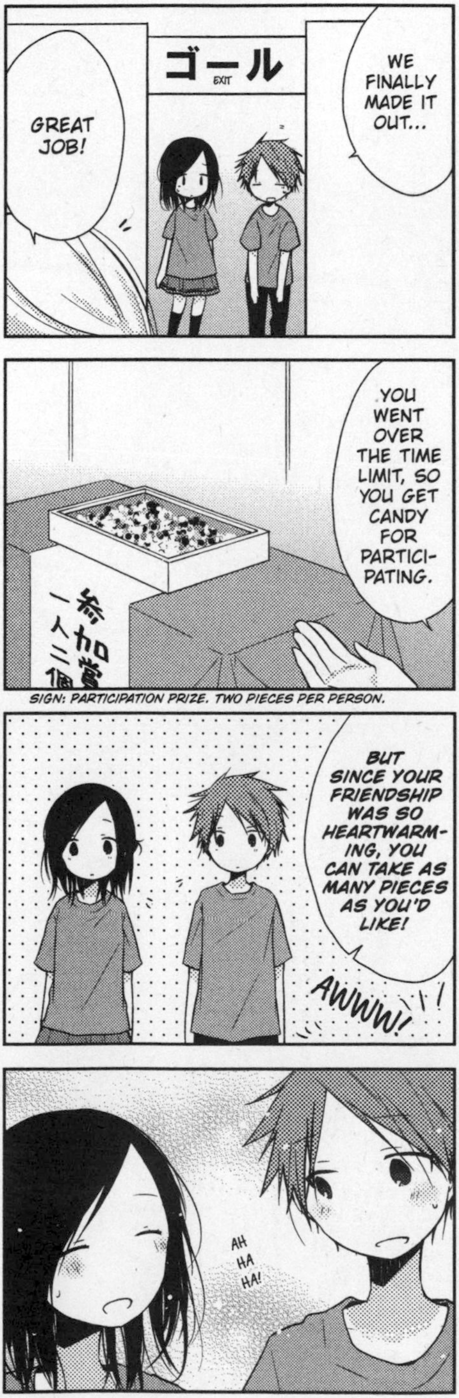
ゴール
EXIT
WE FINALLY MADE IT OUT...
GREAT JOB!
YOU WENT OVER THE TIME LIMIT, SO YOU GET CANDY FOR PARTICIPATING.
参加賞
一人二個
SIGN: PARTICIPATION PRIZE. TWO PIECES PER PERSON.
BUT SINCE YOUR FRIENDSHIP WAS SO HEARTWARMING, YOU CAN TAKE AS MANY PIECES AS YOU'D LIKE!
AWWW!
AH HA HA!

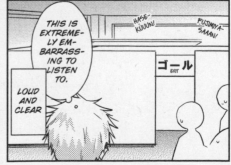

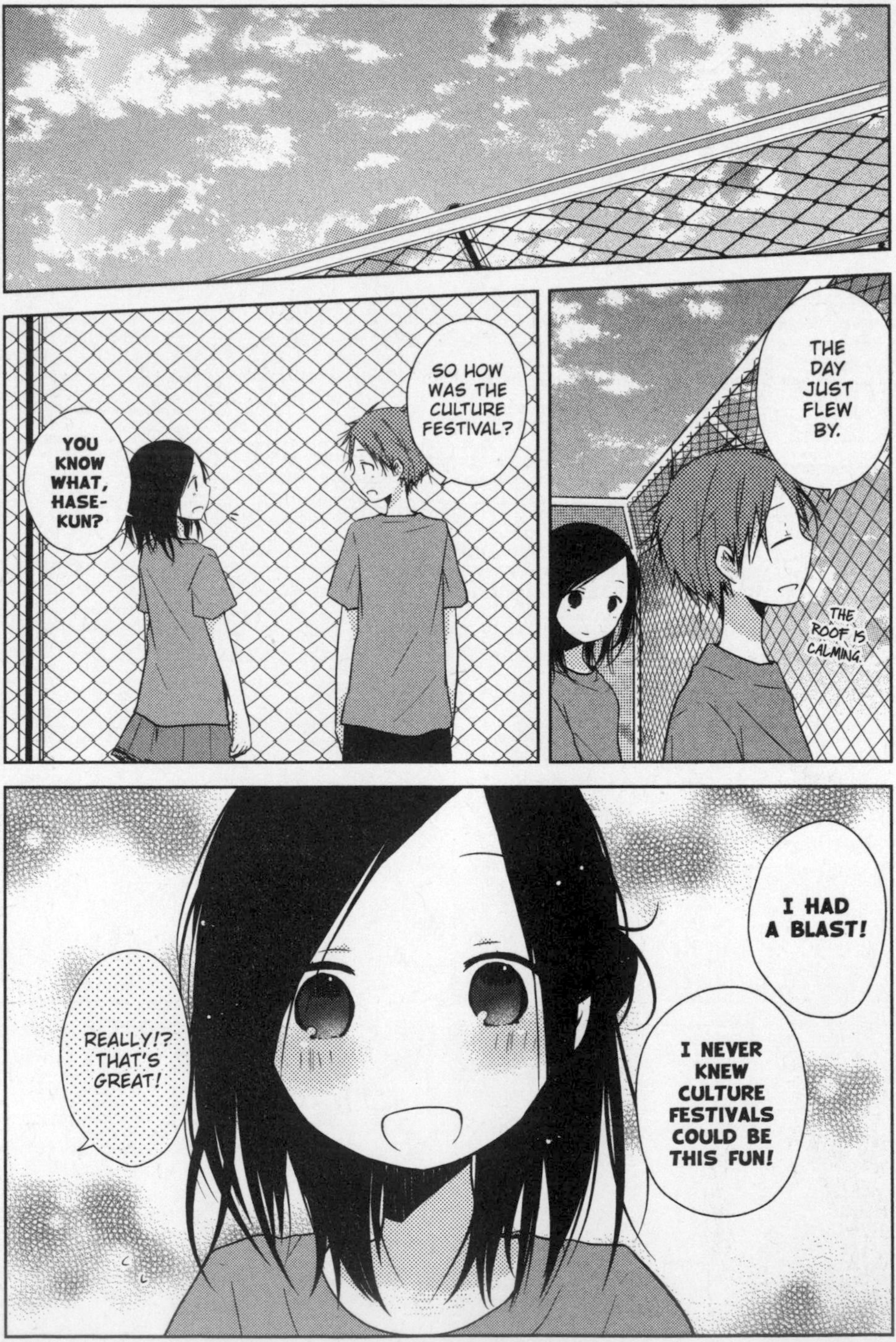
THE DAY JUST FLEW BY.
THE ROOF IS CALMING.
SO HOW WAS THE CULTURE FESTIVAL?
YOU KNOW WHAT, HASE-KUN?
I HAD A BLAST!
I NEVER KNEW CULTURE FESTIVALS COULD BE THIS FUN!
REALLY!? THAT'S GREAT!

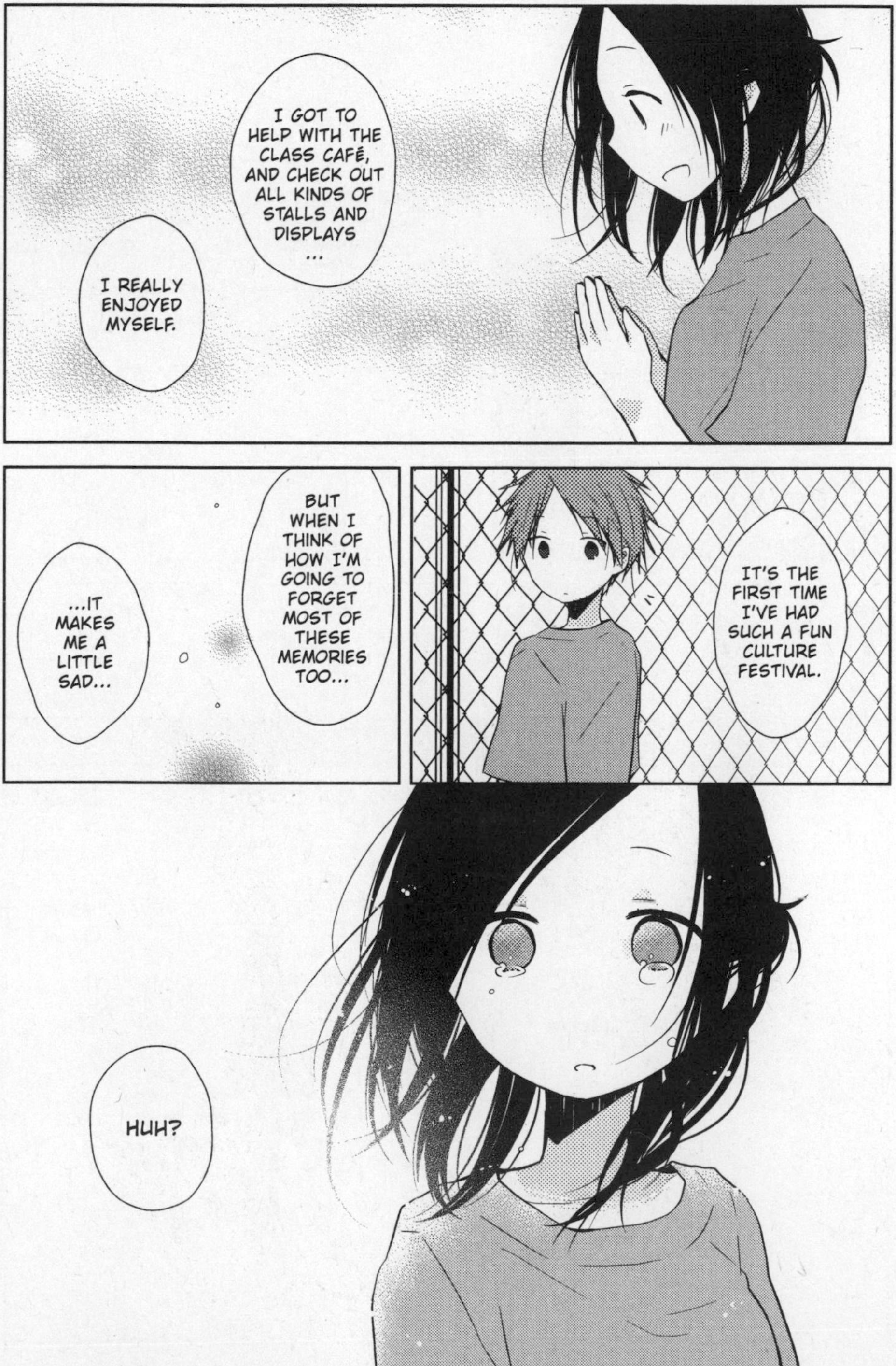
I GOT TO HELP WITH THE CLASS CAFÉ, AND CHECK OUT ALL KINDS OF STALLS AND DISPLAYS ...
I REALLY ENJOYED MYSELF.
IT'S THE FIRST TIME I'VE HAD SUCH A FUN CULTURE FESTIVAL.
BUT WHEN I THINK OF HOW I'M GOING TO FORGET MOST OF THESE MEMORIES TOO...
...IT MAKES ME A LITTLE SAD...
HUH?

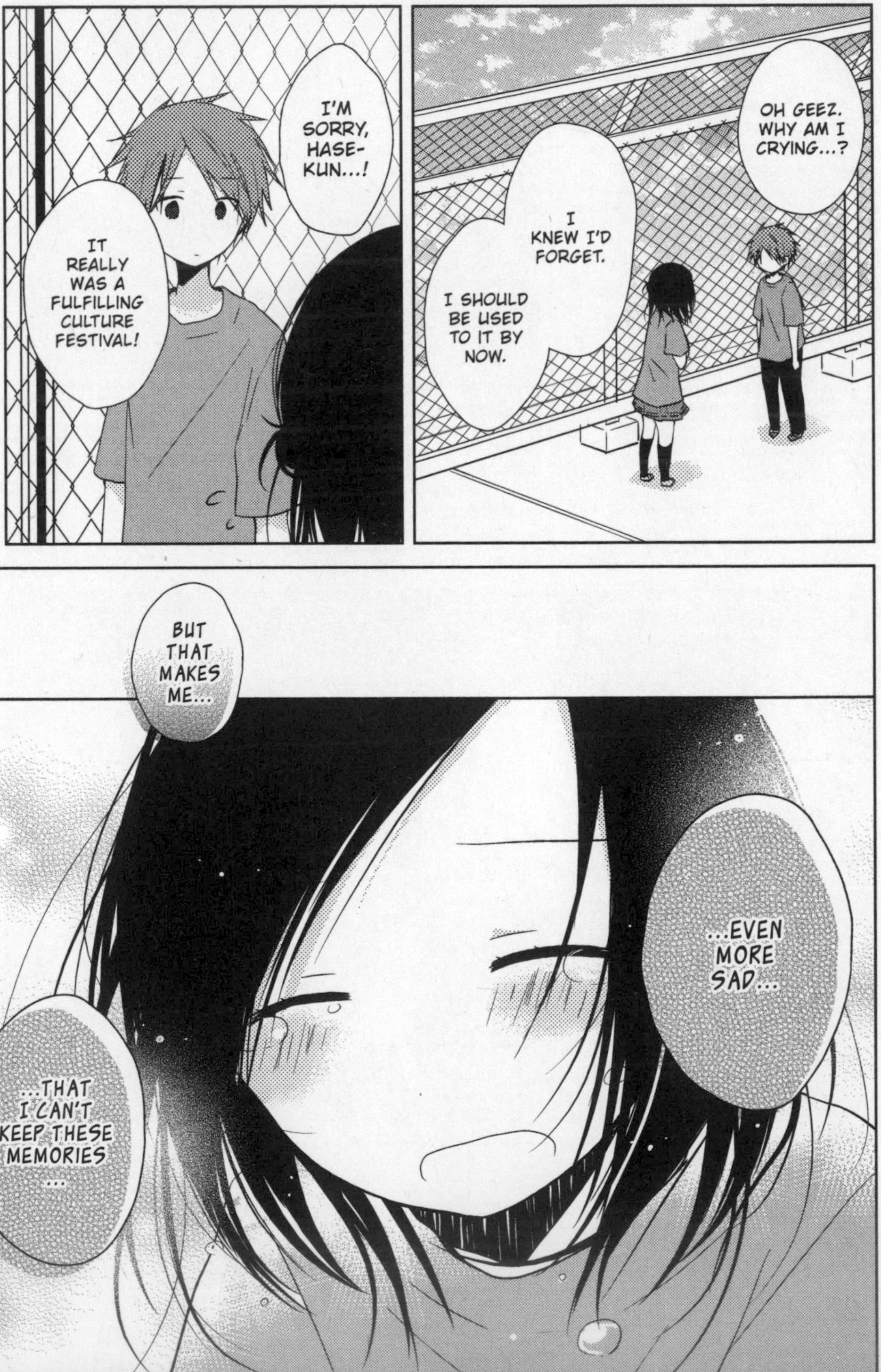
OH GEEZ. WHY AM I CRYING...?
I KNEW I'D FORGET.
I SHOULD BE USED TO IT BY NOW.
I'M SORRY, HASE-KUN...!
IT REALLY WAS A FULFILLING CULTURE FESTIVAL!
BUT THAT MAKES ME...
...EVEN MORE SAD...
...THAT I CAN'T KEEP THESE MEMORIES...

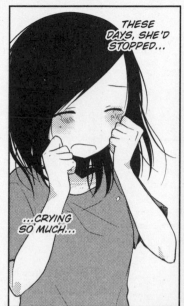

THESE DAYS, SHE'D STOPPED...

...CRYING SO MUCH...

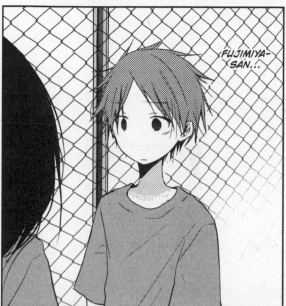

FUJIMIYA-SAN...

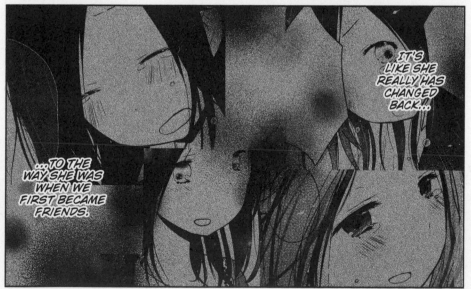

IT'S LIKE SHE REALLY HAS CHANGED BACK...

...TO THE WAY SHE WAS WHEN WE FIRST BECAME FRIENDS.

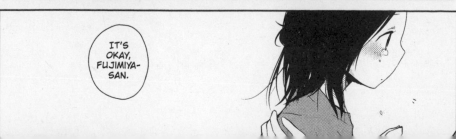

IT'S OKAY, FUJIMIYA-SAN.

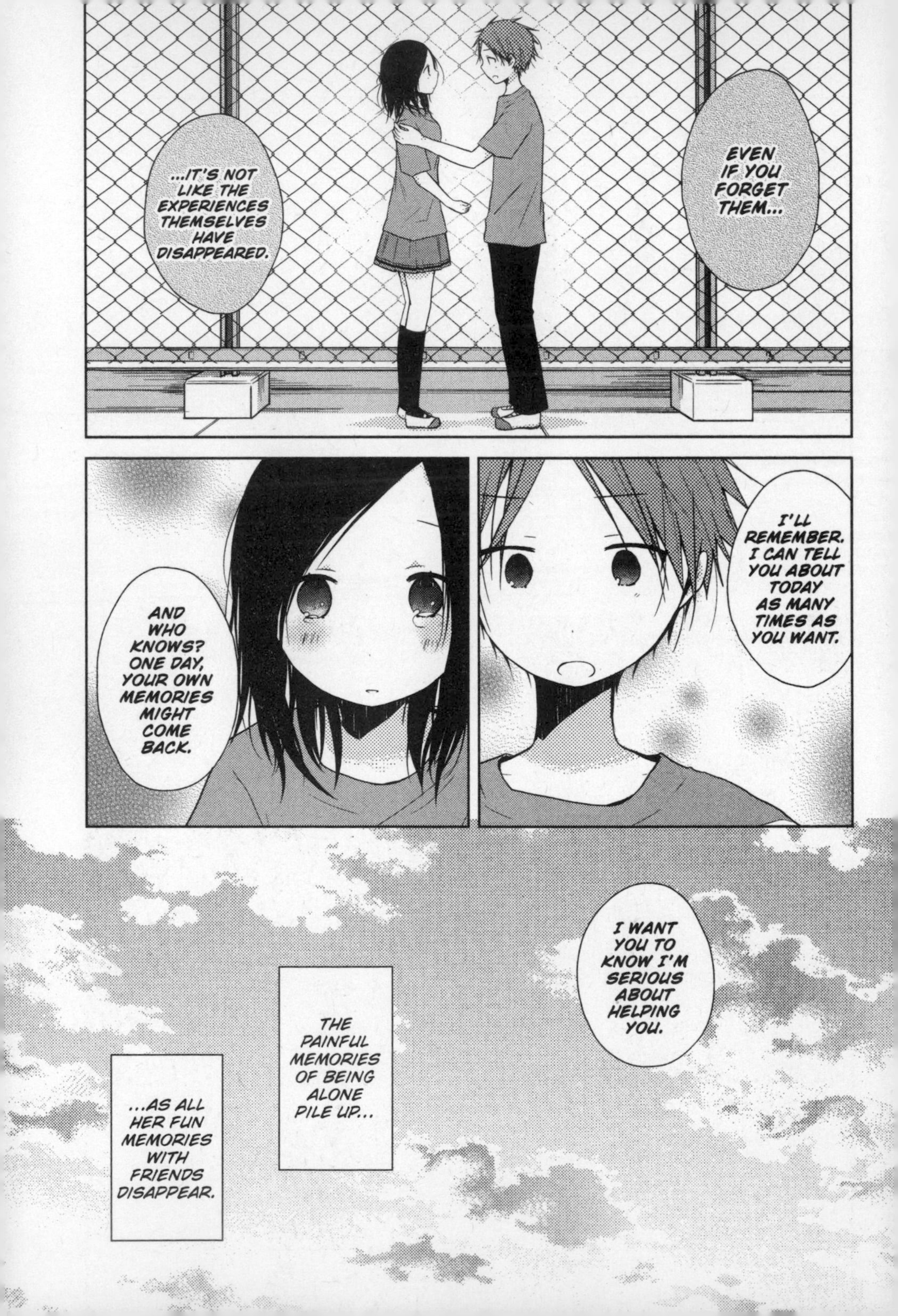
EVEN IF YOU FORGET THEM...
...IT'S NOT LIKE THE EXPERIENCES THEMSELVES HAVE DISAPPEARED.
I'LL REMEMBER. I CAN TELL YOU ABOUT TODAY AS MANY TIMES AS YOU WANT.
AND WHO KNOWS? ONE DAY, YOUR OWN MEMORIES MIGHT COME BACK.
I WANT YOU TO KNOW I'M SERIOUS ABOUT HELPING YOU.
THE PAINFUL MEMORIES OF BEING ALONE PILE UP...
...AS ALL HER FUN MEMORIES WITH FRIENDS DISAPPEAR.

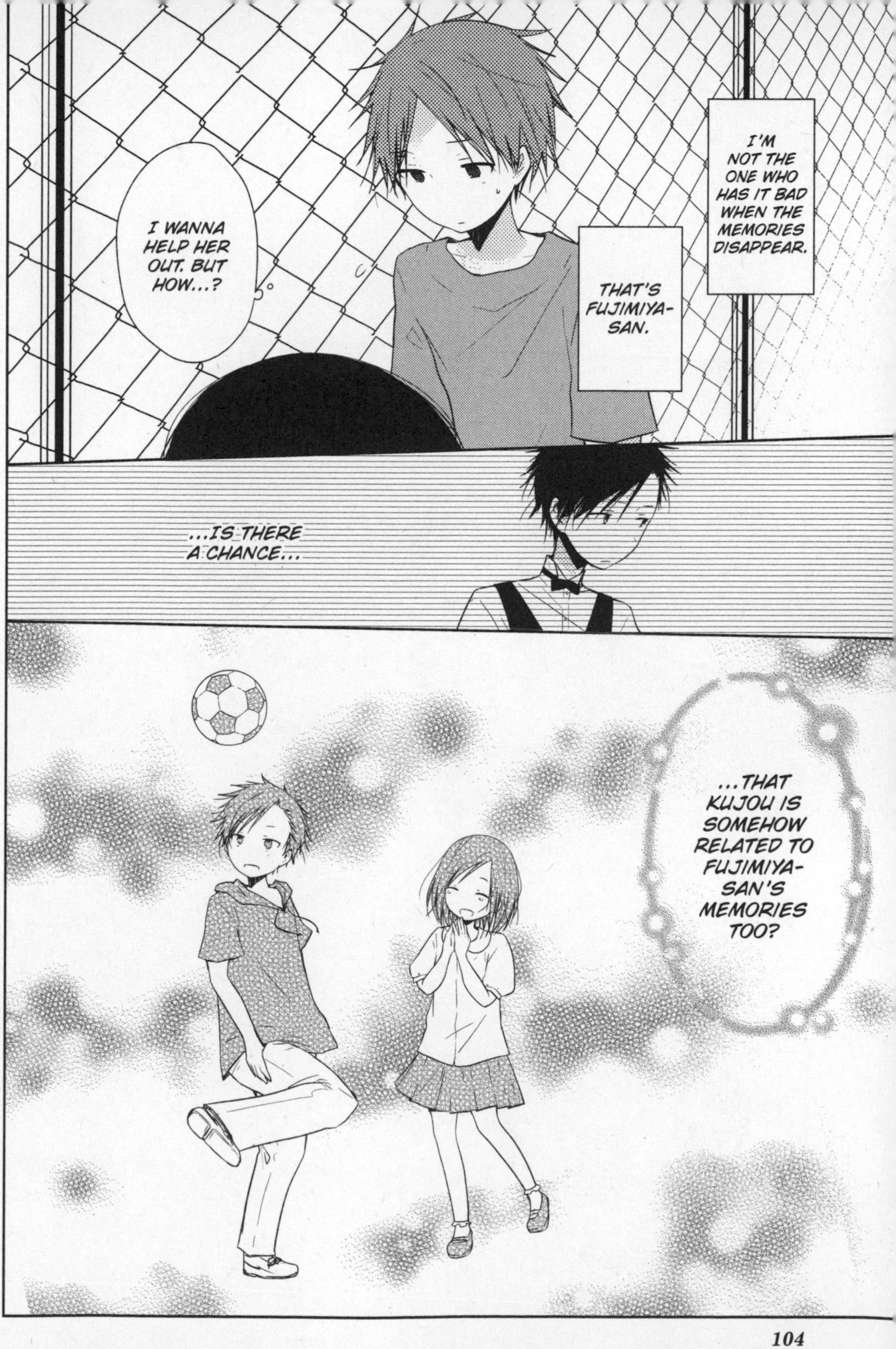
I'M NOT THE ONE WHO HAS IT BAD WHEN THE MEMORIES DISAPPEAR.
THAT'S FUJIMIYA-SAN.
I WANNA HELP HER OUT. BUT HOW...?
...IS THERE A CHANCE...
...THAT KUJOU IS SOMEHOW RELATED TO FUJIMIYA-SAN'S MEMORIES TOO?

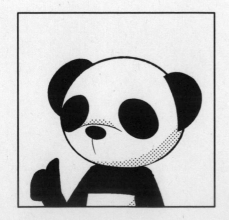

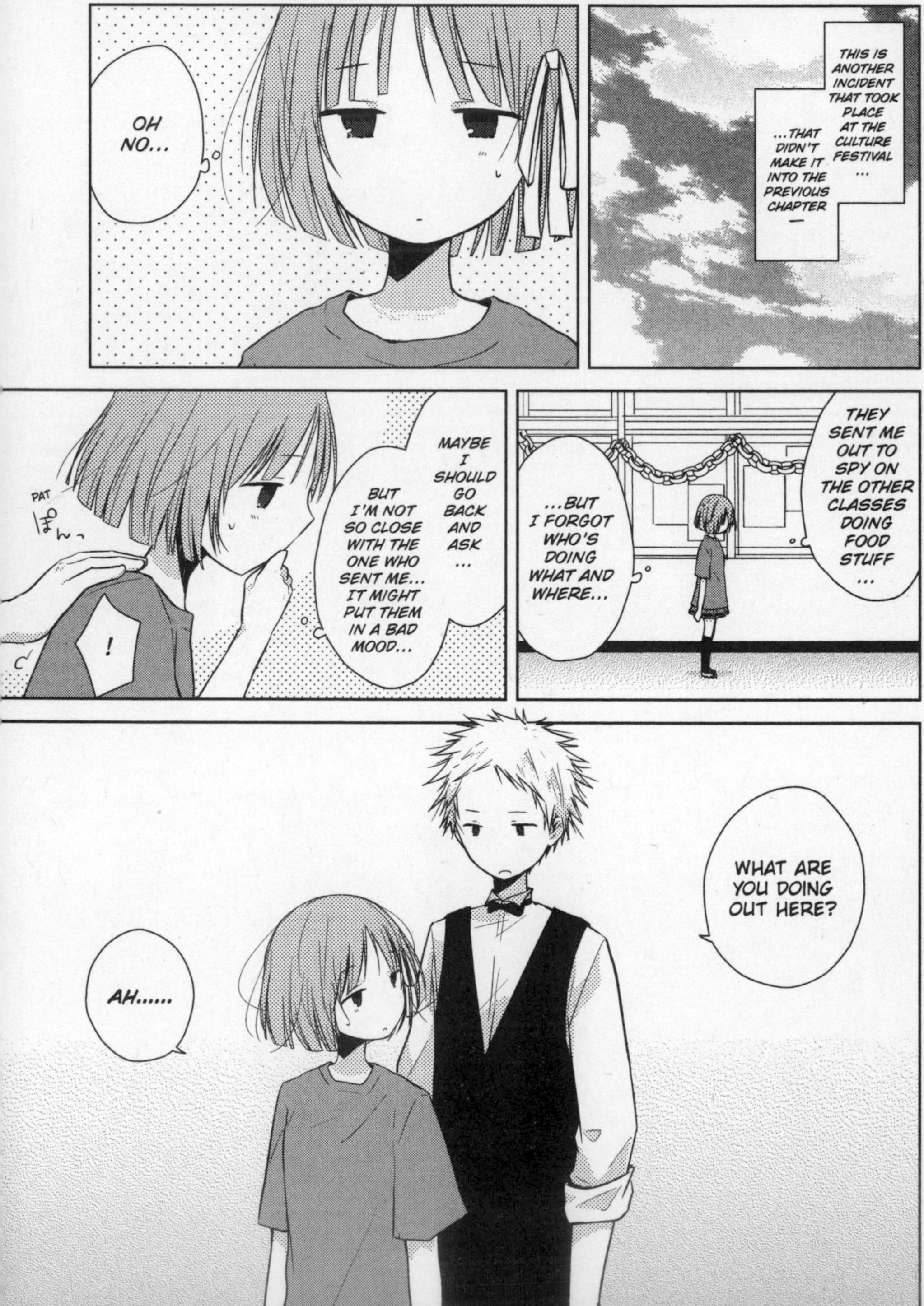
THIS IS ANOTHER INCIDENT THAT TOOK PLACE AT THE CULTURE FESTIVAL...
...THAT DIDN'T MAKE IT INTO THE PREVIOUS CHAPTER —
OH NO...
THEY SENT ME OUT TO SPY ON THE OTHER CLASSES DOING FOOD STUFF...
...BUT I FORGOT WHO'S DOING WHAT AND WHERE...
MAYBE I SHOULD GO BACK AND ASK...
BUT I'M NOT SO CLOSE WITH THE ONE WHO SENT ME... IT MIGHT PUT THEM IN A BAD MOOD...
PAT
ぽん
!
WHAT ARE YOU DOING OUT HERE?
AH......

CHAPTER 21 RING ROLLING STONES

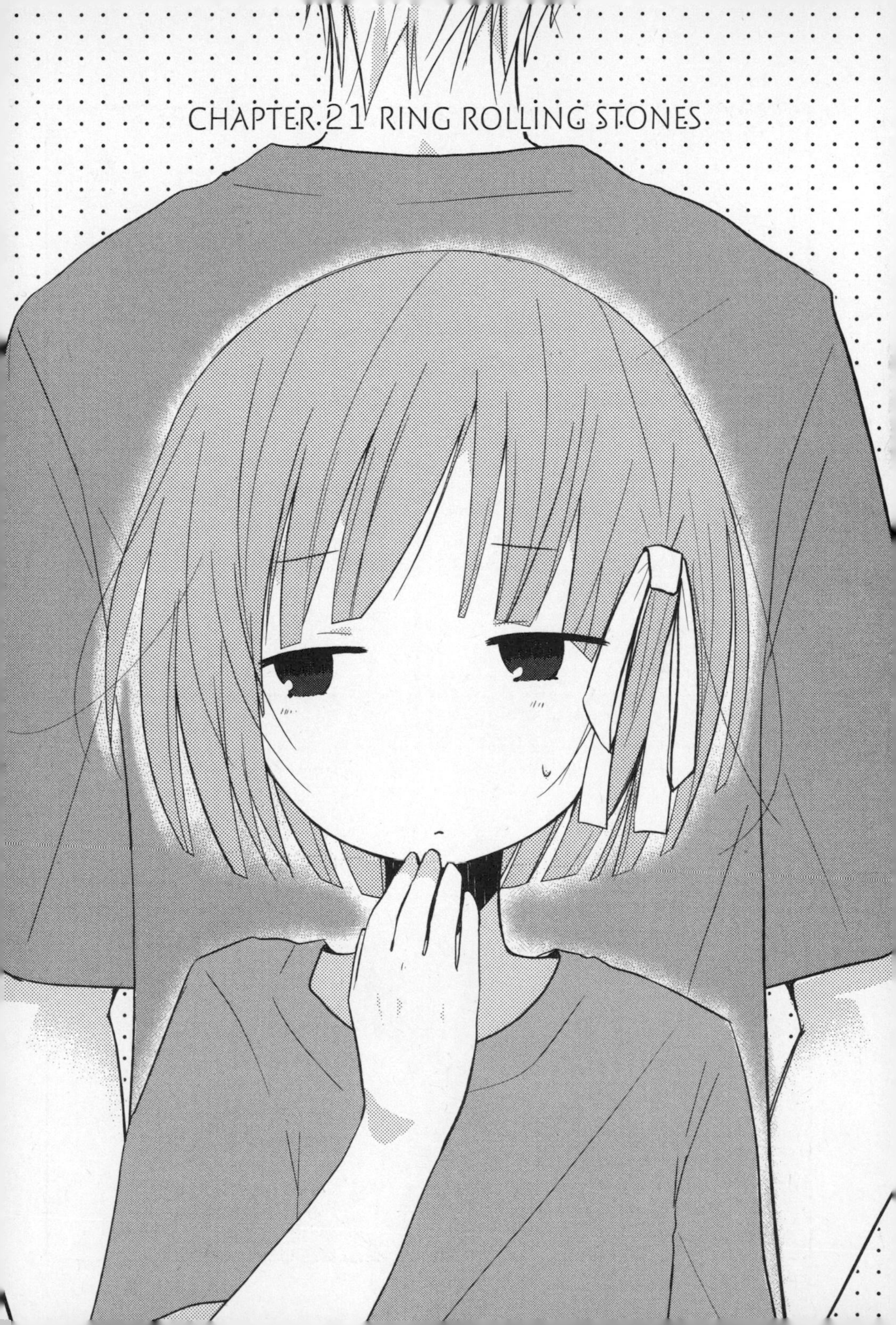

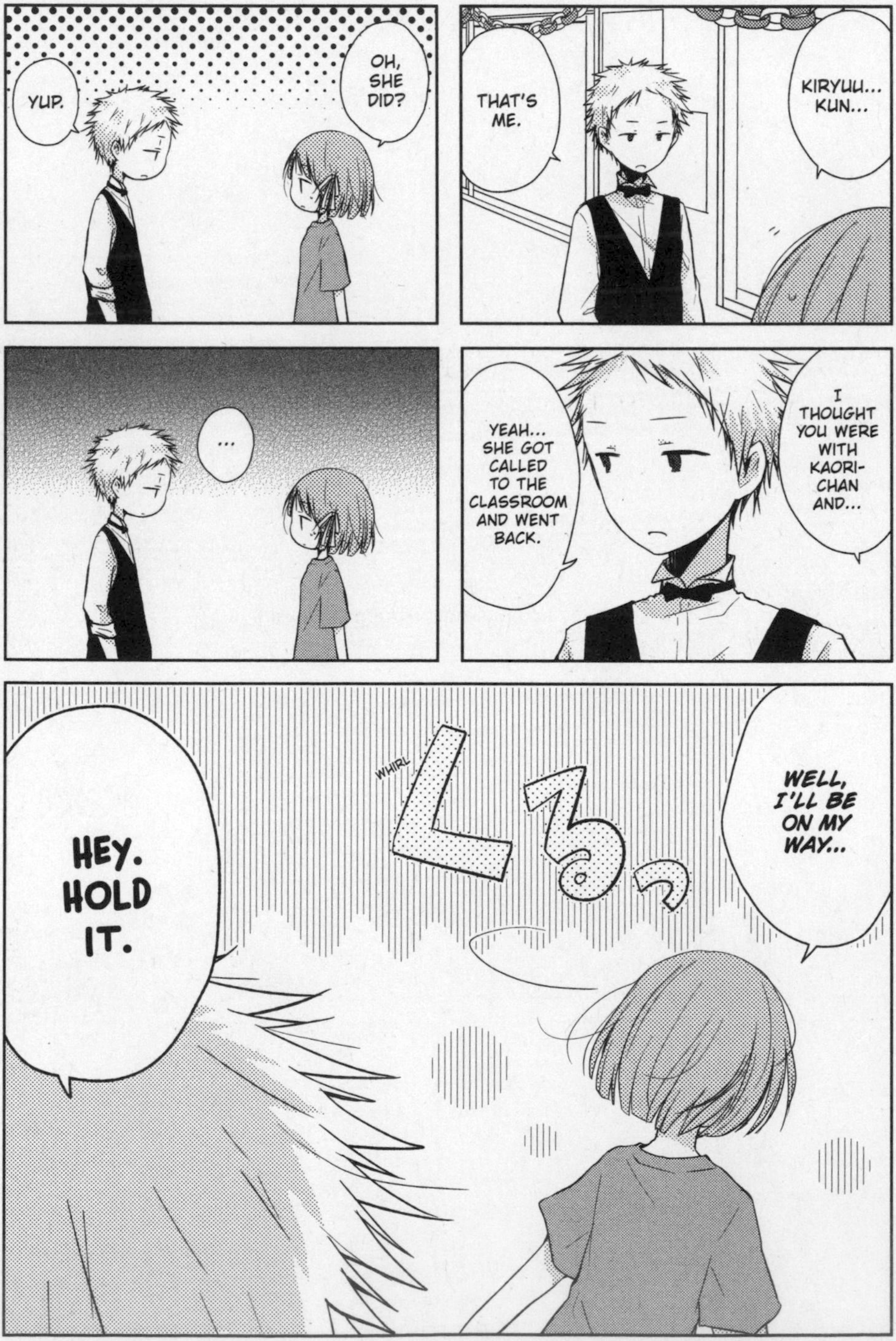
KIRYUU... KUN...
THAT'S ME.
OH, SHE DID?
YUP.
I THOUGHT YOU WERE WITH KAORI-CHAN AND...
YEAH... SHE GOT CALLED TO THE CLASSROOM AND WENT BACK.
...
WELL, I'LL BE ON MY WAY...
WHIRL
くるっ
HEY. HOLD IT.

GOT THAT IMPRESSION

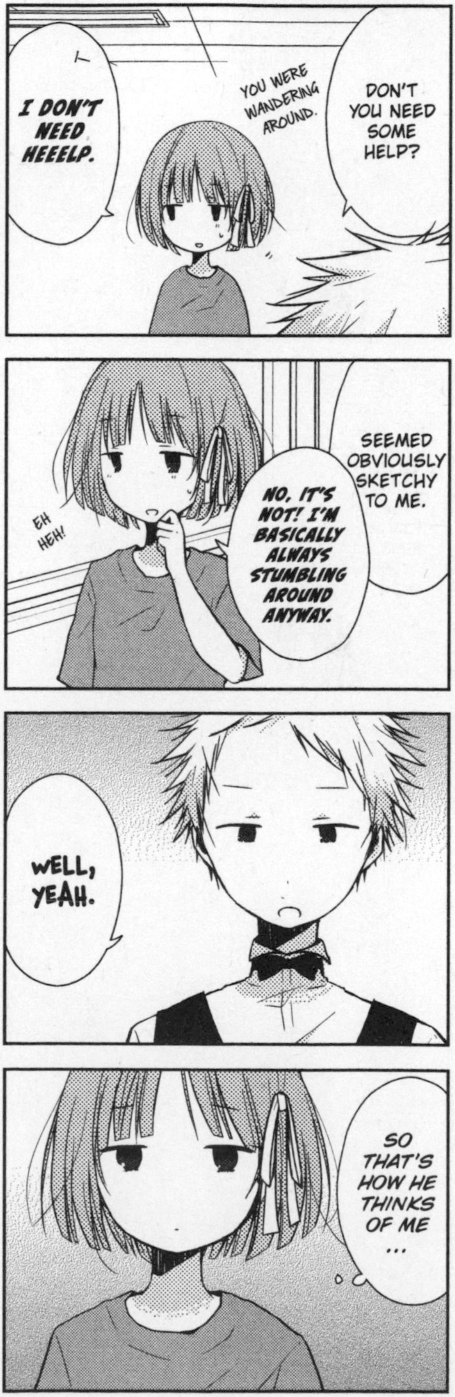
DON'T YOU NEED SOME HELP?
YOU WERE WANDERING AROUND.
I DON'T NEED HEEELP.
SEEMED OBVIOUSLY SKETCHY TO ME.
NO, IT'S NOT! I'M BASICALLY ALWAYS STUMBLING AROUND ANYWAY.
EH HEH!
WELL, YEAH.
SO THAT'S HOW HE THINKS OF ME ...

ABNORMAL

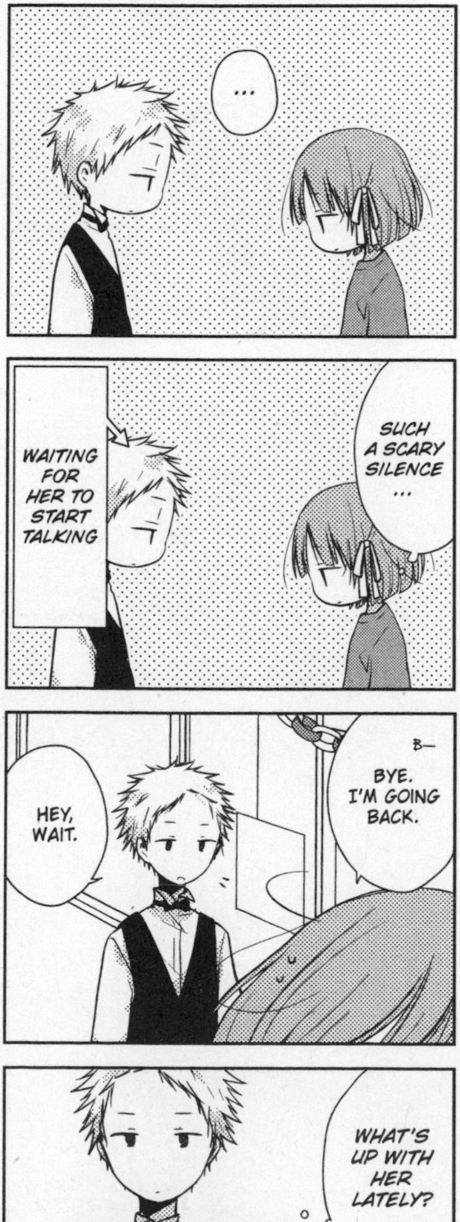
...
SUCH A SCARY SILENCE ...
WAITING FOR HER TO START TALKING
B—
BYE. I'M GOING BACK.
HEY, WAIT.
WHAT'S UP WITH HER LATELY?

THAT'S THE PROBLEM

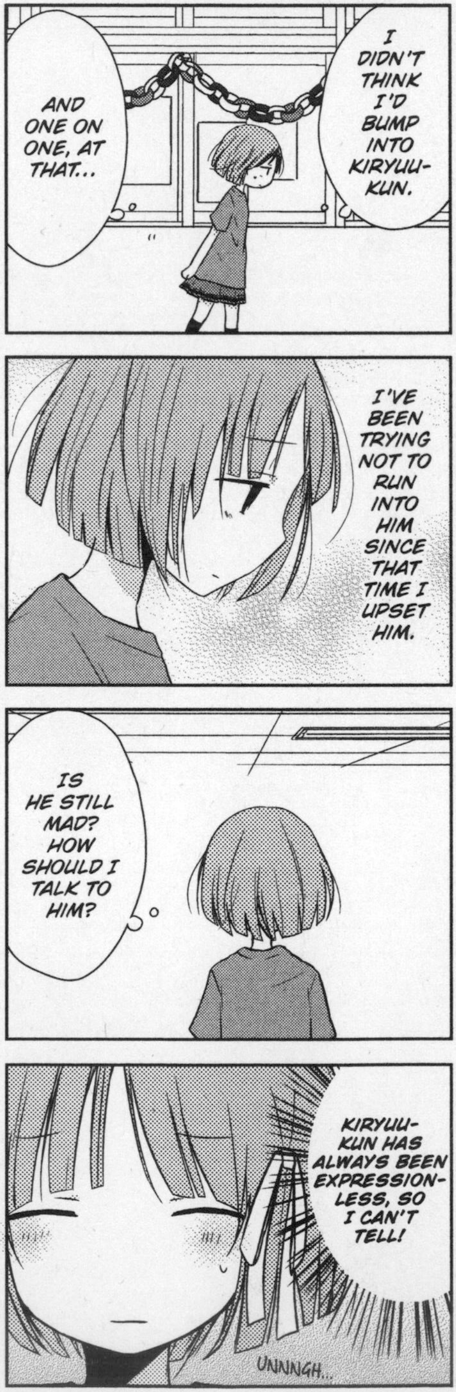
I DIDN'T THINK I'D BUMP INTO KIRYUU-KUN.
AND ONE ON ONE, AT THAT...
I'VE BEEN TRYING NOT TO RUN INTO HIM SINCE THAT TIME I UPSET HIM.
IS HE STILL MAD? HOW SHOULD I TALK TO HIM?
KIRYUU-KUN HAS ALWAYS BEEN EXPRESSION-LESS, SO I CAN'T TELL!
UNNNGH...

NOTICES

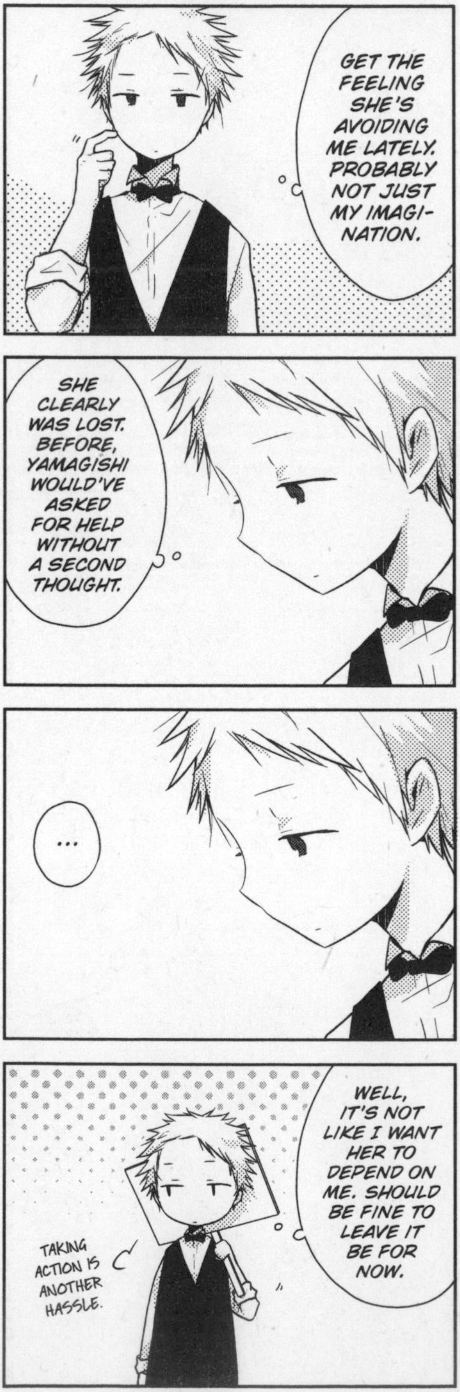
GET THE FEELING SHE'S AVOIDING ME LATELY. PROBABLY NOT JUST MY IMAGI-NATION.
SHE CLEARLY WAS LOST. BEFORE, YAMAGISHI WOULD'VE ASKED FOR HELP WITHOUT A SECOND THOUGHT.
...
WELL, IT'S NOT LIKE I WANT HER TO DEPEND ON ME. SHOULD BE FINE TO LEAVE IT BE FOR NOW.
TAKING ACTION IS ANOTHER HASSLE.

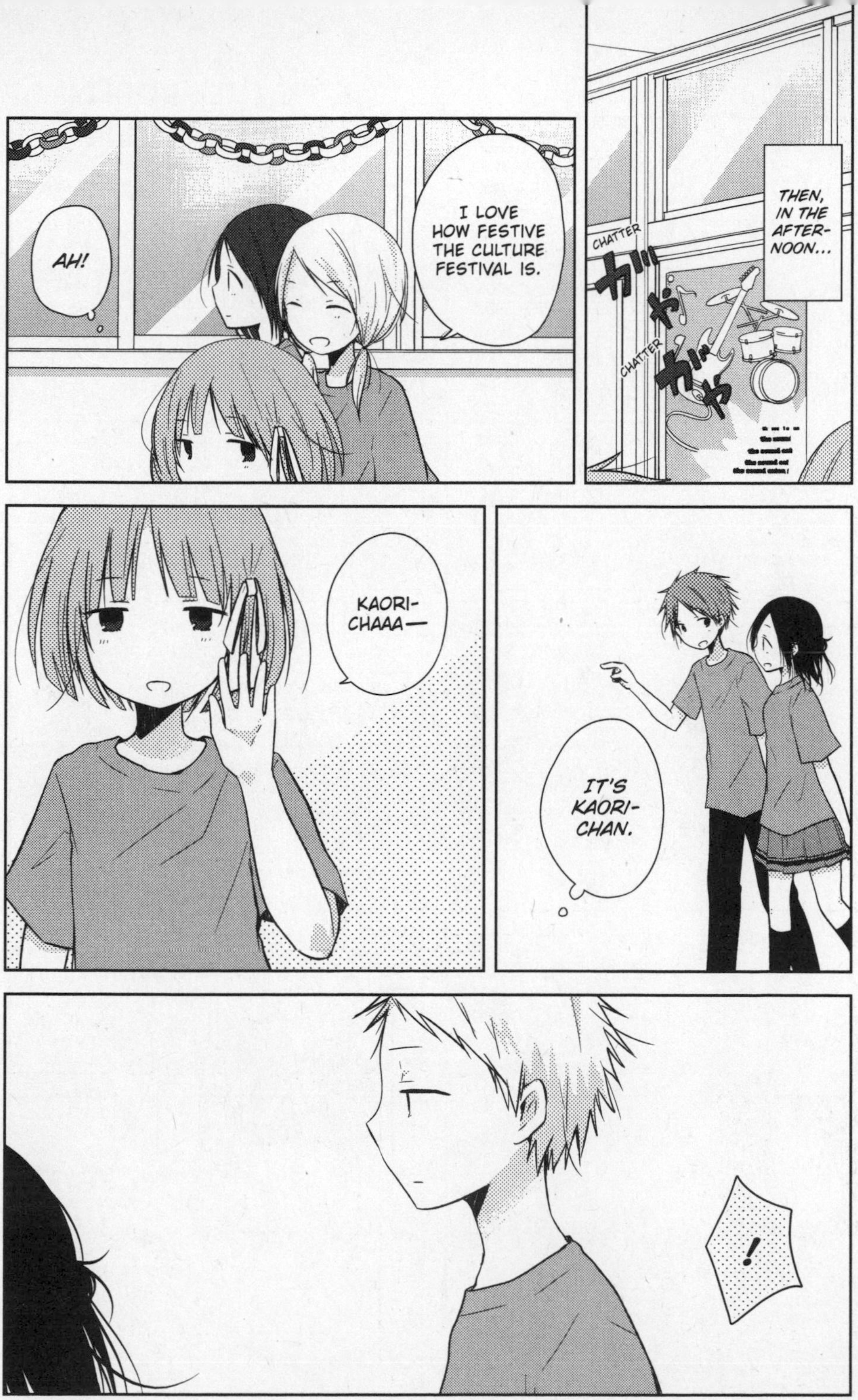
THEN, IN THE AFTERNOON...
CHATTER
CHATTER
I LOVE HOW FESTIVE THE CULTURE FESTIVAL IS.
AH!
IT'S KAORI-CHAN.
KAORI-CHAAA—
!

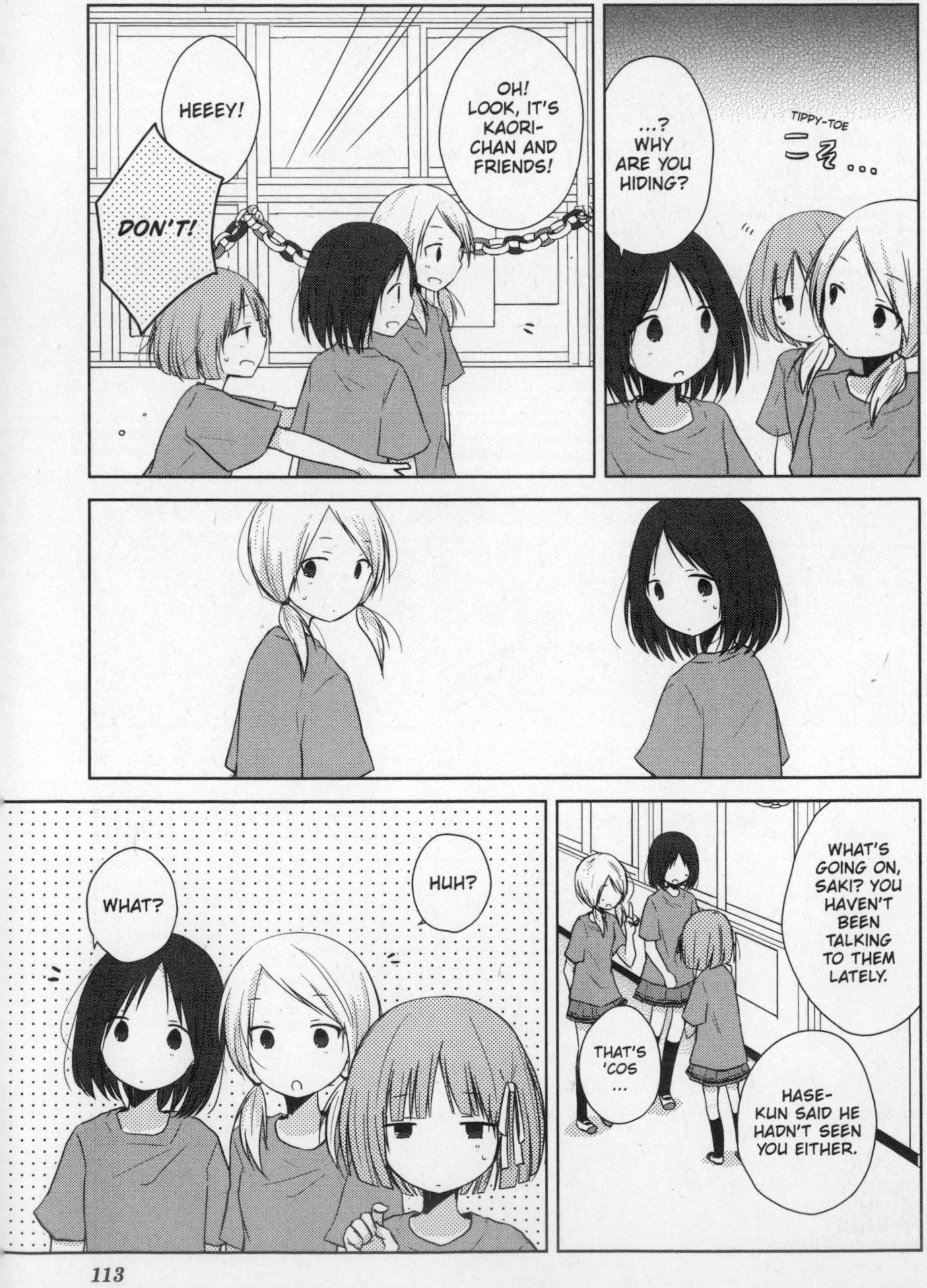
...? WHY ARE YOU HIDING?
TIPPY-TOE
OH! LOOK, IT'S KAORI-CHAN AND FRIENDS!
HEEEY!
DON'T!
WHAT'S GOING ON, SAKI? YOU HAVEN'T BEEN TALKING TO THEM LATELY.
HASE-KUN SAID HE HADN'T SEEN YOU EITHER.
THAT'S 'COS ...
HUH?
WHAT?

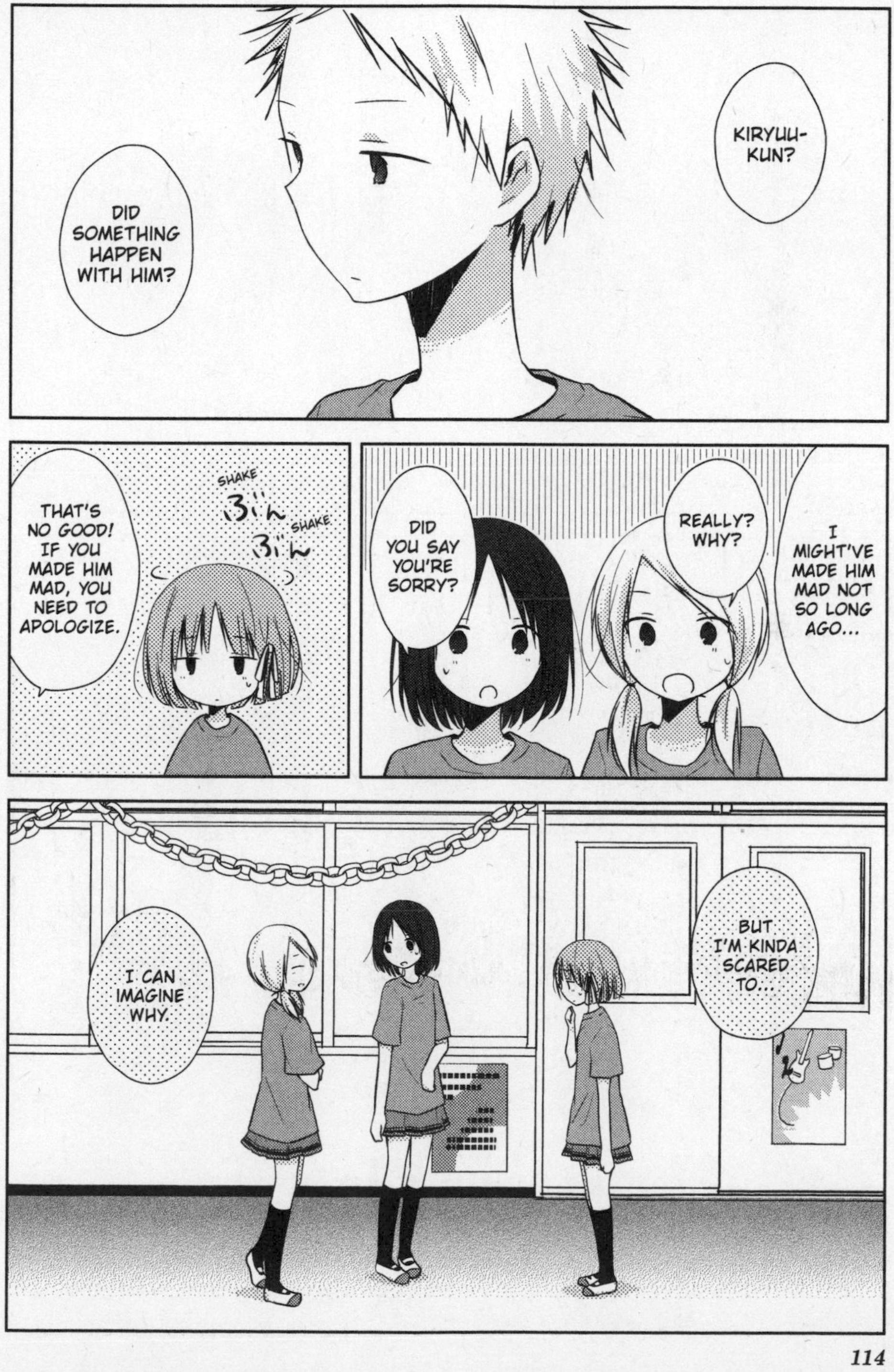
KIRYUU-KUN?
DID SOMETHING HAPPEN WITH HIM?
I MIGHT'VE MADE HIM MAD NOT SO LONG AGO...
REALLY? WHY?
DID YOU SAY YOU'RE SORRY?
SHAKE ぶん
SHAKE ぶん
THAT'S NO GOOD! IF YOU MADE HIM MAD, YOU NEED TO APOLOGIZE.
BUT I'M KINDA SCARED TO...
I CAN IMAGINE WHY.

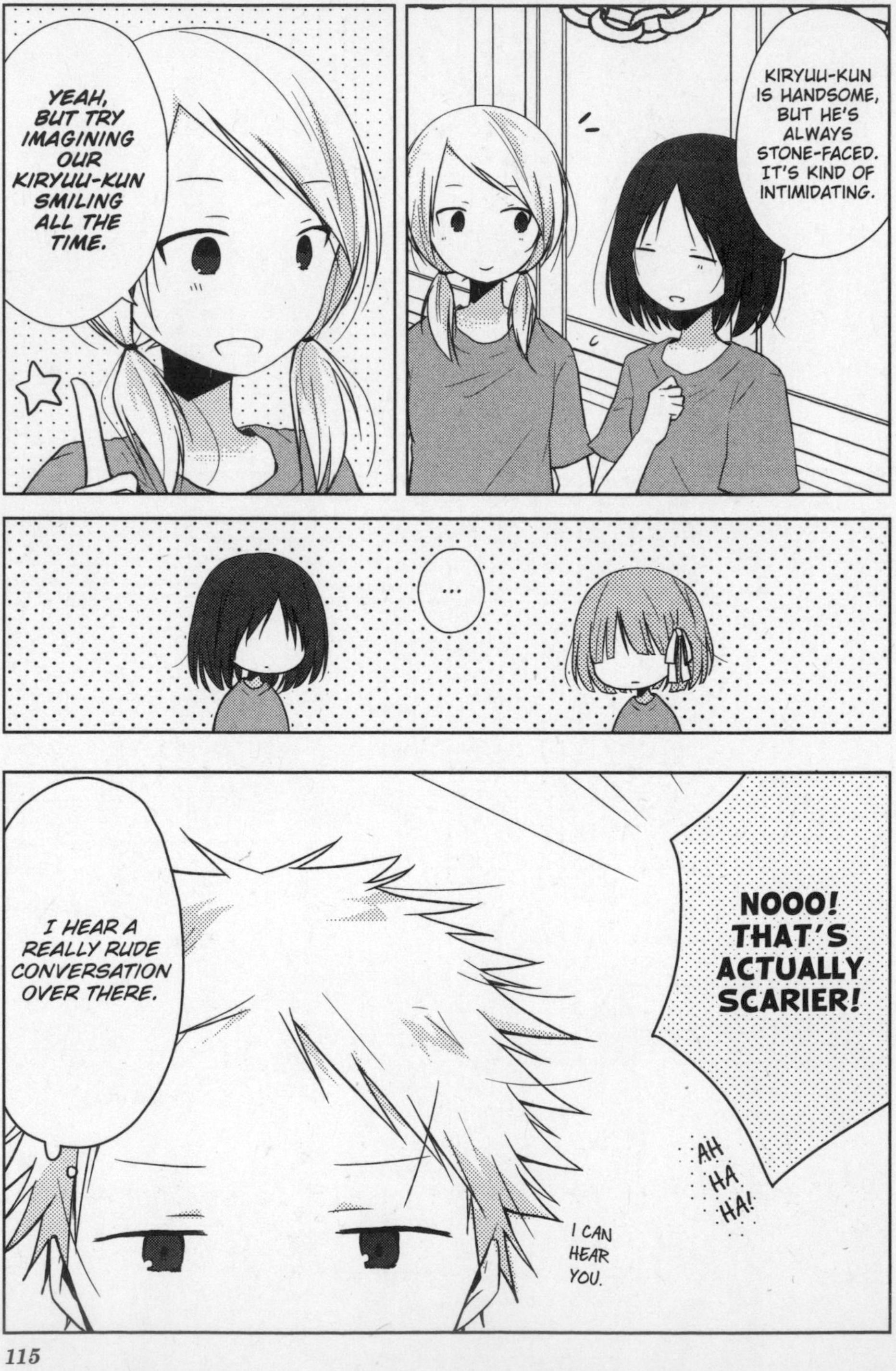
KIRYUU-KUN IS HANDSOME, BUT HE'S ALWAYS STONE-FACED. IT'S KIND OF INTIMIDATING.
YEAH, BUT TRY IMAGINING OUR KIRYUU-KUN SMILING ALL THE TIME.
...
NOOO! THAT'S ACTUALLY SCARIER!
AH HA HA!
I CAN HEAR YOU.
I HEAR A REALLY RUDE CONVERSATION OVER THERE.

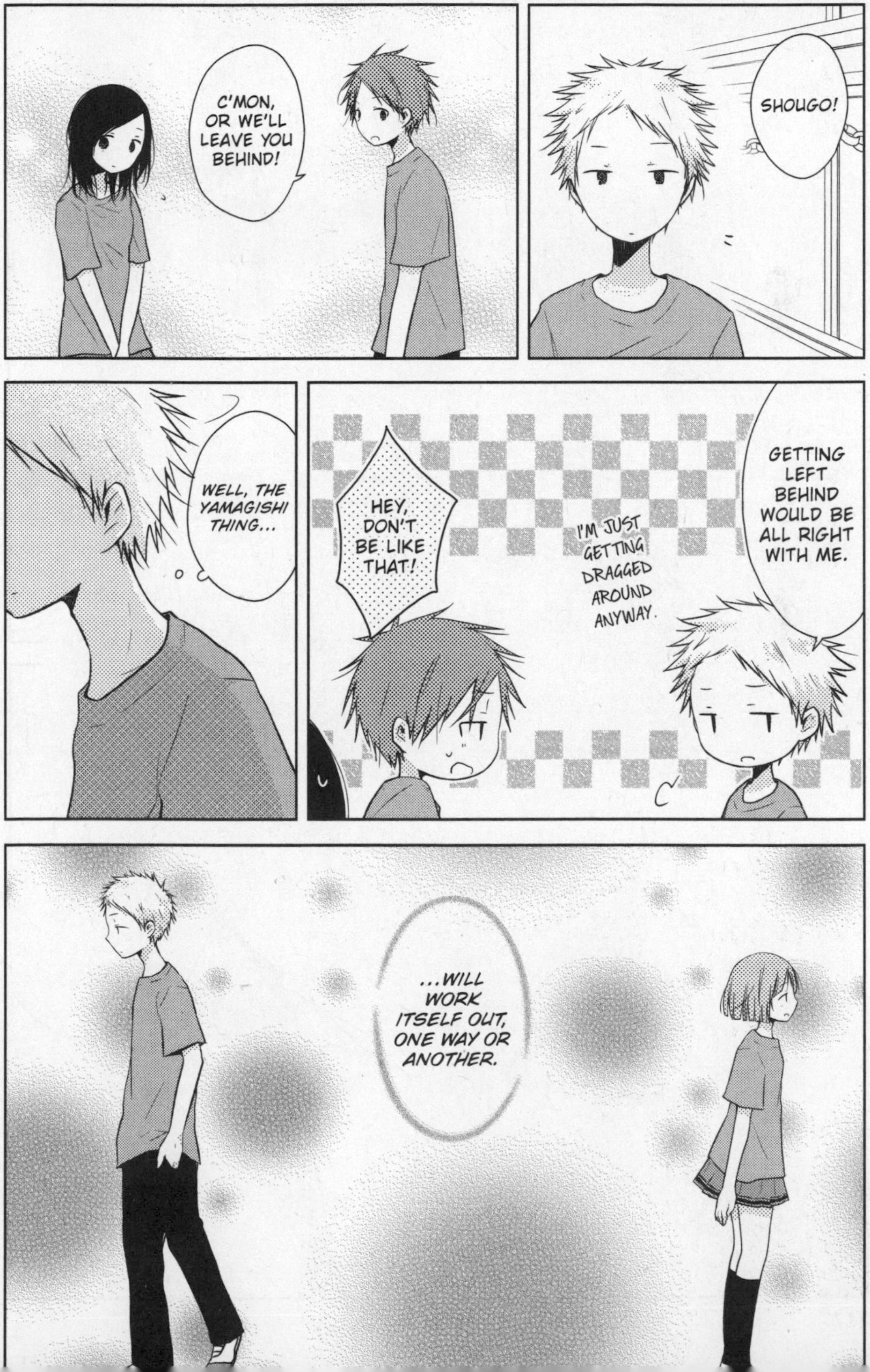
SHOUGO!
C'MON, OR WE'LL LEAVE YOU BEHIND!
GETTING LEFT BEHIND WOULD BE ALL RIGHT WITH ME.
I'M JUST GETTING DRAGGED AROUND ANYWAY.
HEY, DON'T BE LIKE THAT!
WELL, THE YAMAGISHI THING...
...WILL WORK ITSELF OUT, ONE WAY OR ANOTHER.

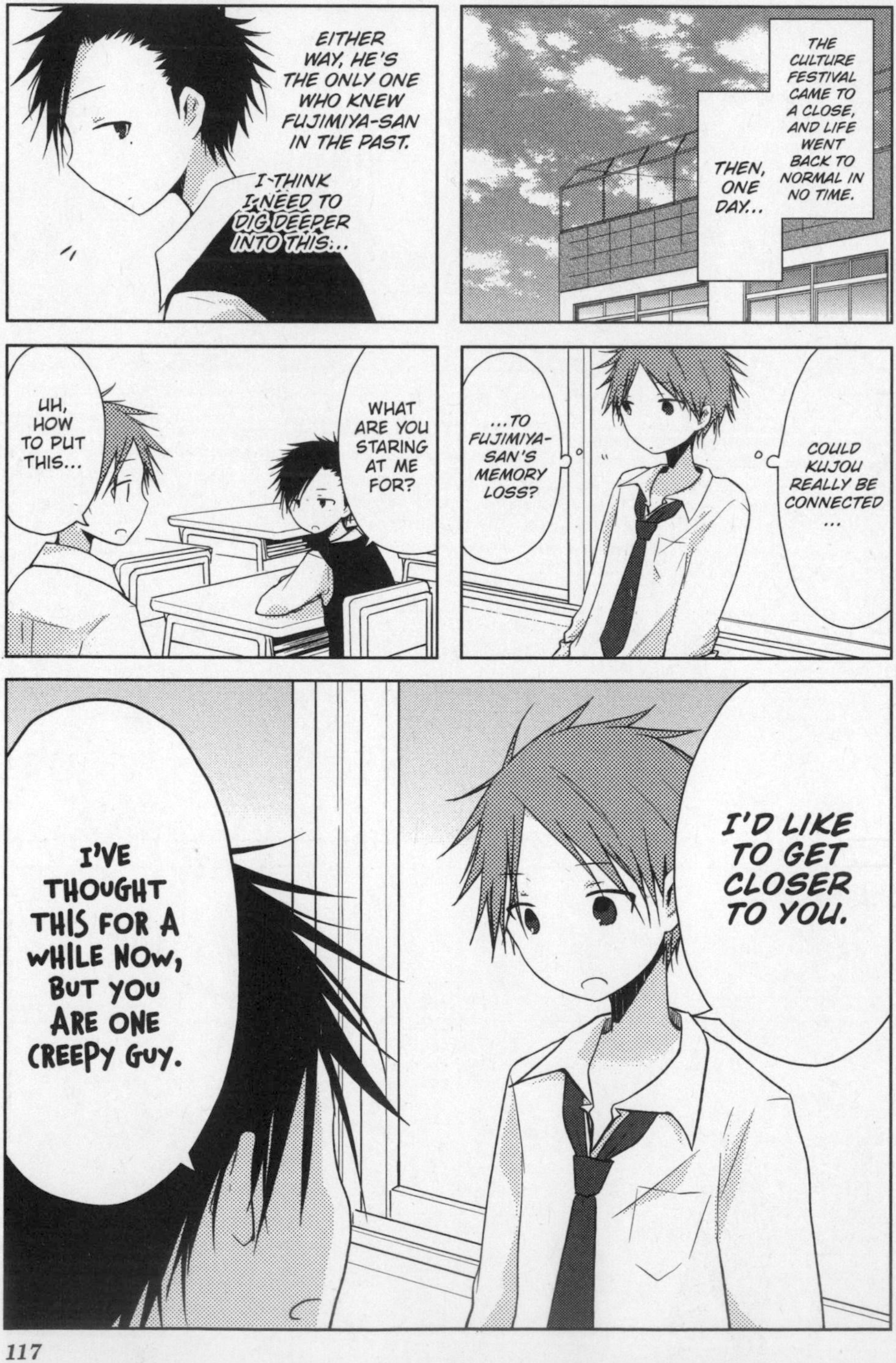
THE CULTURE FESTIVAL CAME TO A CLOSE, AND LIFE WENT BACK TO NORMAL IN NO TIME.
THEN, ONE DAY...
EITHER WAY, HE'S THE ONLY ONE WHO KNEW FUJIMIYA-SAN IN THE PAST.
I THINK I NEED TO DIG DEEPER INTO THIS...
COULD KUJOU REALLY BE CONNECTED...
...TO FUJIMIYA-SAN'S MEMORY LOSS?
WHAT ARE YOU STARING AT ME FOR?
UH, HOW TO PUT THIS...
I'D LIKE TO GET CLOSER TO YOU.
I'VE THOUGHT THIS FOR A WHILE NOW, BUT YOU ARE ONE CREEPY GUY.

FUN 1

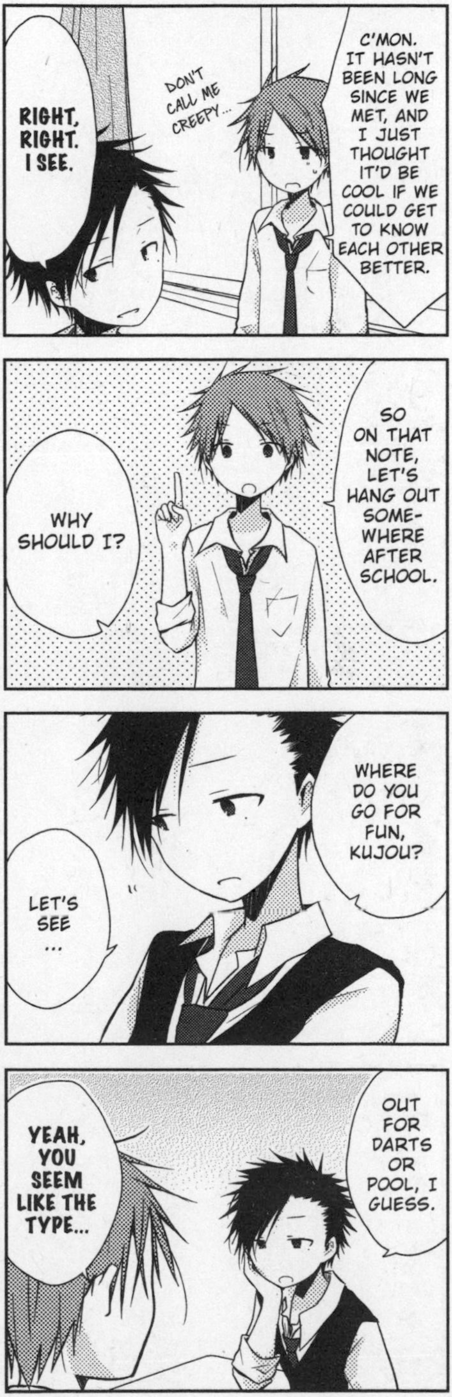
C'MON. IT HASN'T BEEN LONG SINCE WE MET, AND I JUST THOUGHT IT'D BE COOL IF WE COULD GET TO KNOW EACH OTHER BETTER.
DON'T CALL ME CREEPY...
RIGHT, RIGHT. I SEE.
SO ON THAT NOTE, LET'S HANG OUT SOME-WHERE AFTER SCHOOL.
WHY SHOULD I?
WHERE DO YOU GO FOR FUN, KUJOU?
LET'S SEE ...
OUT FOR DARTS OR POOL, I GUESS.
YEAH, YOU SEEM LIKE THE TYPE...

FUN 2

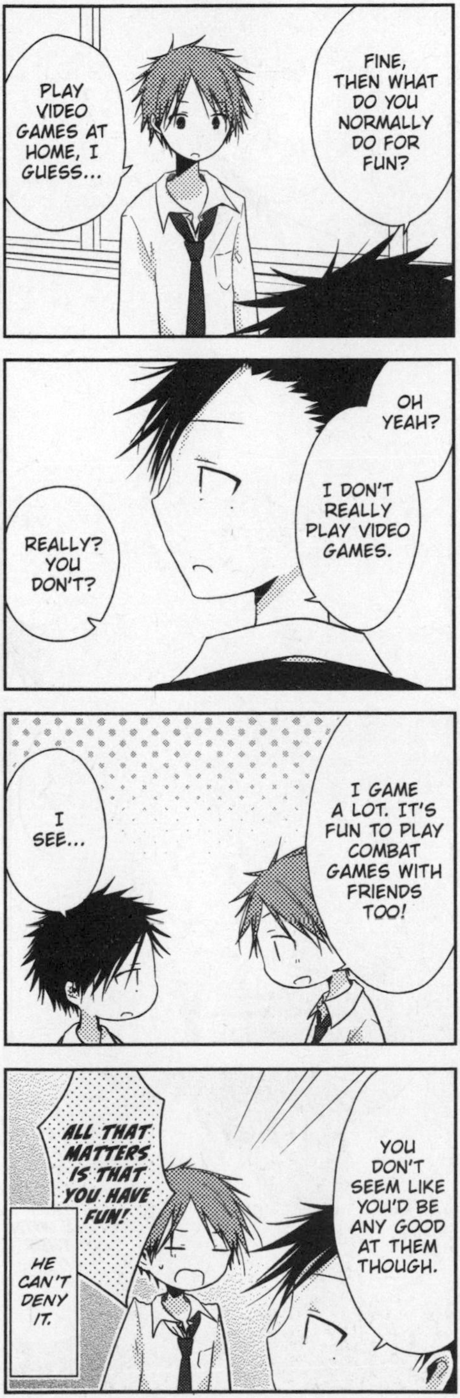
FINE, THEN WHAT DO YOU NORMALLY DO FOR FUN?
PLAY VIDEO GAMES AT HOME, I GUESS...
OH YEAH?
I DON'T REALLY PLAY VIDEO GAMES.
REALLY? YOU DON'T?
I GAME A LOT. IT'S FUN TO PLAY COMBAT GAMES WITH FRIENDS TOO!
I SEE...
YOU DON'T SEEM LIKE YOU'D BE ANY GOOD AT THEM THOUGH.
ALL THAT MATTERS IS THAT YOU HAVE FUN!
HE CAN'T DENY IT.

A REASON NOT TO GO

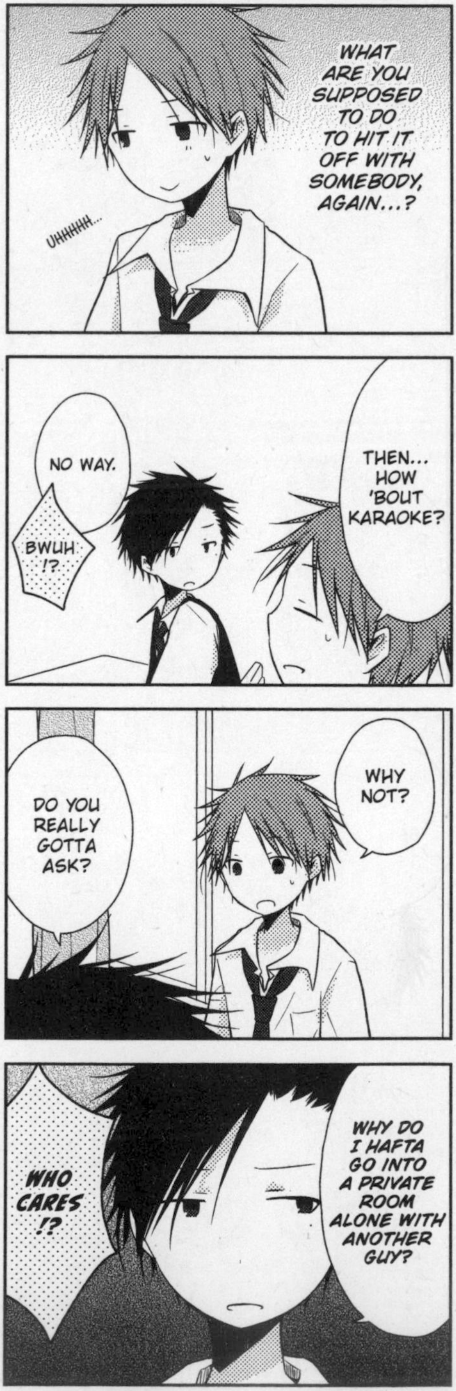
WHAT ARE YOU SUPPOSED TO DO TO HIT IT OFF WITH SOMEBODY, AGAIN...?
UHHHHH...
THEN... HOW 'BOUT KARAOKE?
NO WAY.
BWUH !?
WHY NOT?
DO YOU REALLY GOTTA ASK?
WHY DO I HAFTA GO INTO A PRIVATE ROOM ALONE WITH ANOTHER GUY?
WHO CARES !?

THE REAL REASON

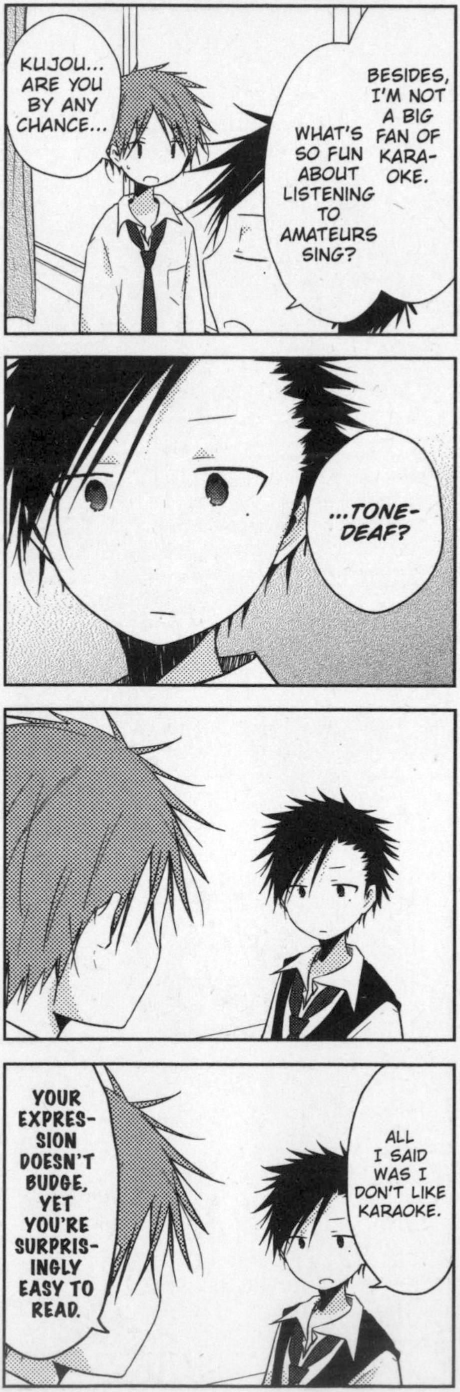
BESIDES, I'M NOT A BIG FAN OF KARAOKE.
WHAT'S SO FUN ABOUT LISTENING TO AMATEURS SING?
KUJOU... ARE YOU BY ANY CHANCE...
...TONE-DEAF?
ALL I SAID WAS I DON'T LIKE KARAOKE.
YOUR EXPRESSION DOESN'T BUDGE, YET YOU'RE SURPRISINGLY EASY TO READ.

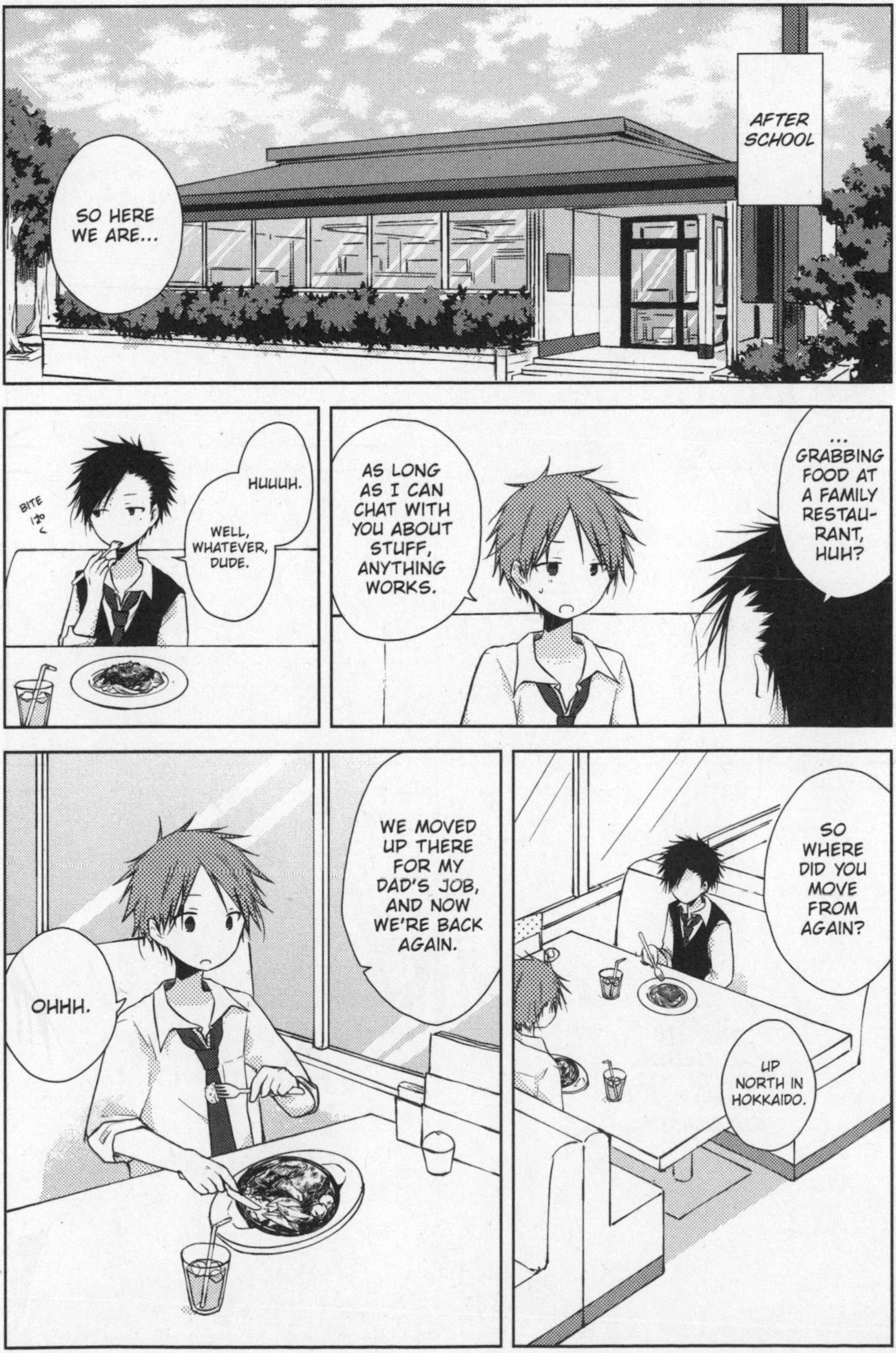
AFTER SCHOOL
SO HERE WE ARE...
...GRABBING FOOD AT A FAMILY RESTAURANT, HUH?
AS LONG AS I CAN CHAT WITH YOU ABOUT STUFF, ANYTHING WORKS.
HUUUH.
WELL, WHATEVER, DUDE.
BITE
SO WHERE DID YOU MOVE FROM AGAIN?
UP NORTH IN HOKKAIDO.
WE MOVED UP THERE FOR MY DAD'S JOB, AND NOW WE'RE BACK AGAIN.
OHHH.

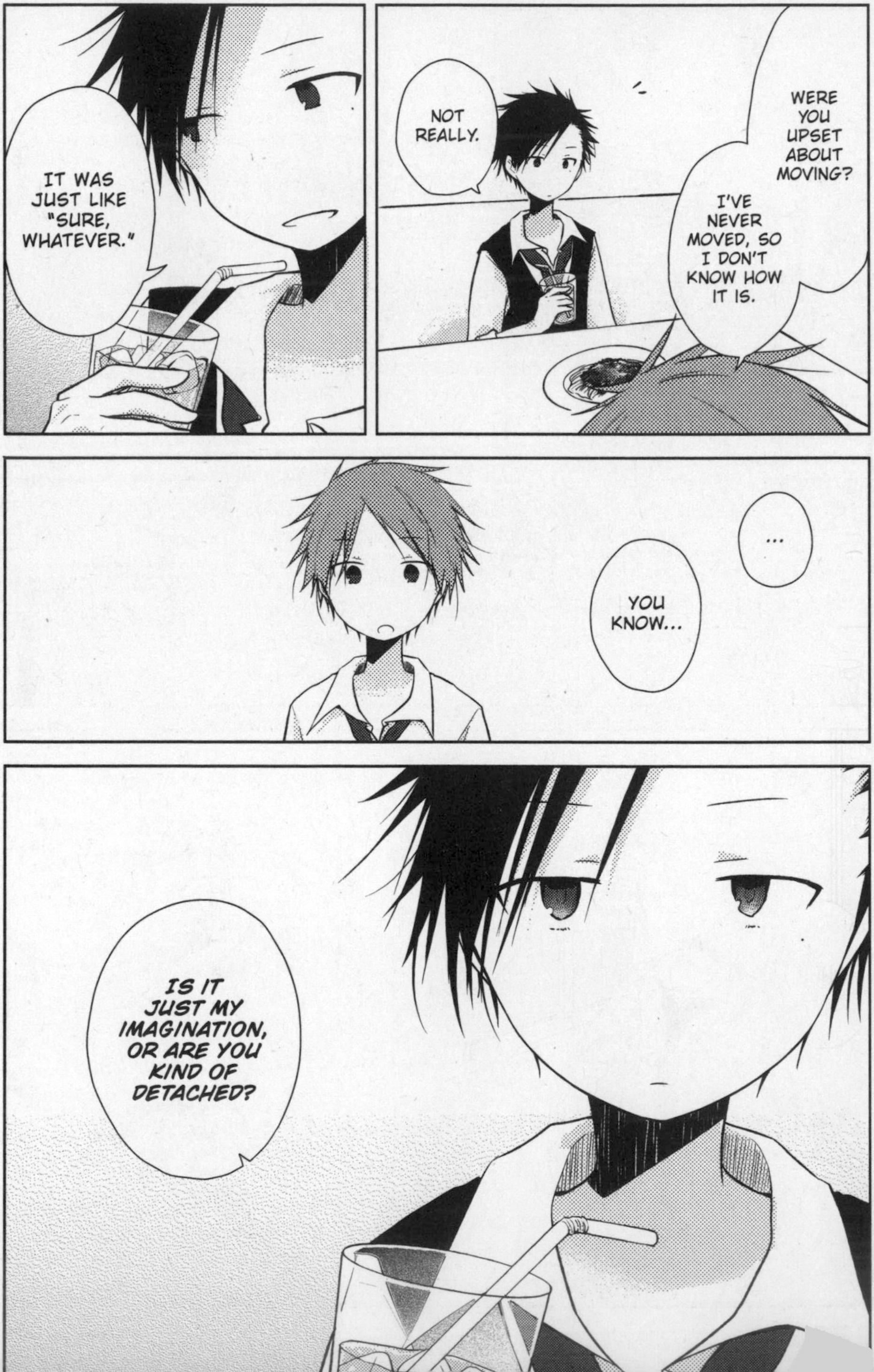
WERE YOU UPSET ABOUT MOVING?
I'VE NEVER MOVED, SO I DON'T KNOW HOW IT IS.
NOT REALLY.
IT WAS JUST LIKE "SURE, WHATEVER."
...
YOU KNOW...
IS IT JUST MY IMAGINATION, OR ARE YOU KIND OF DETACHED?

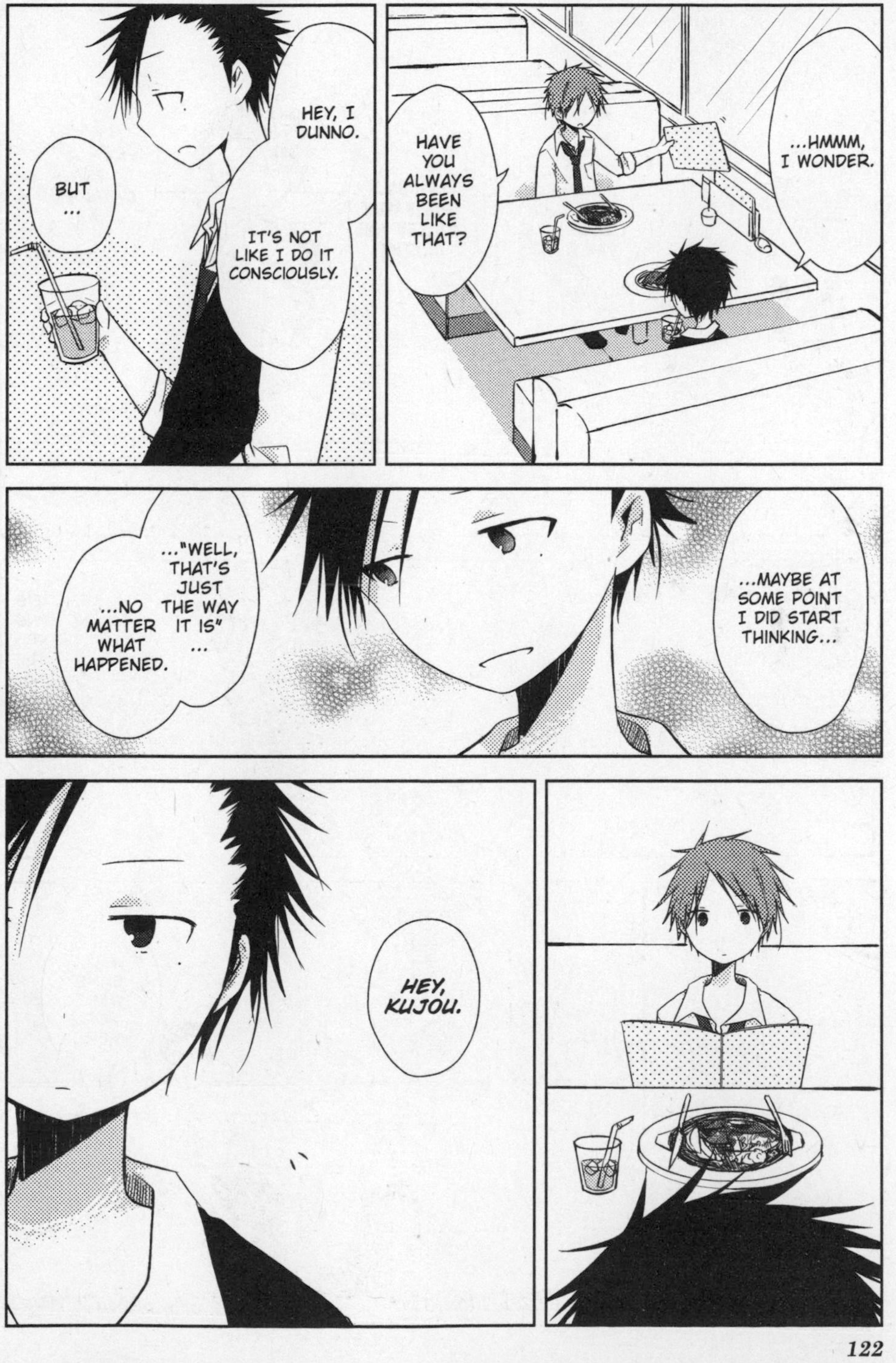
...HMMM, I WONDER.
HAVE YOU ALWAYS BEEN LIKE THAT?
HEY, I DUNNO.
IT'S NOT LIKE I DO IT CONSCIOUSLY.
BUT ...
...MAYBE AT SOME POINT I DID START THINKING...
..."WELL, THAT'S JUST THE WAY IT IS" ...
...NO MATTER WHAT HAPPENED.
HEY, KUJOU.

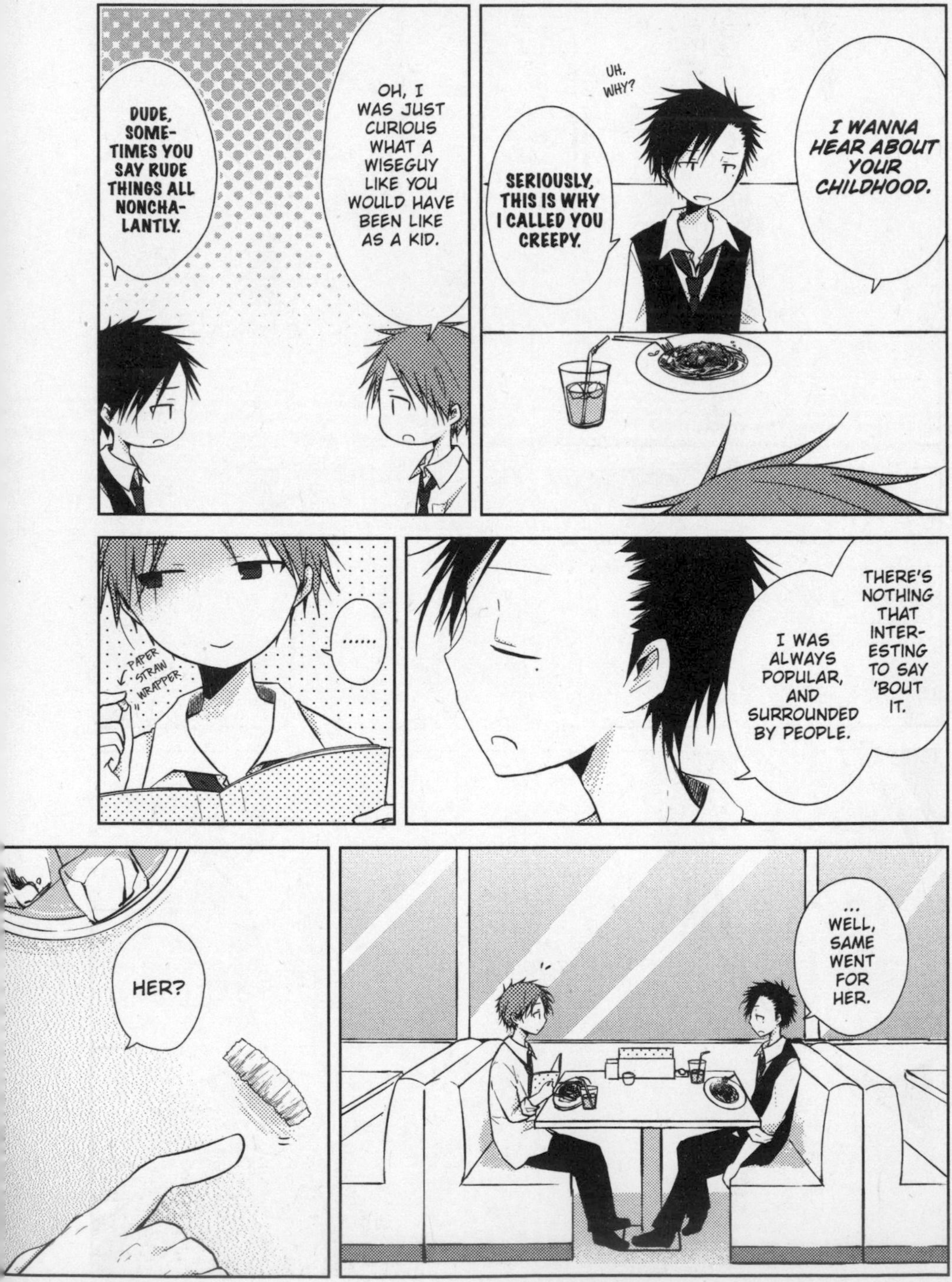
I WANNA HEAR ABOUT YOUR CHILDHOOD.
UH, WHY?
SERIOUSLY, THIS IS WHY I CALLED YOU CREEPY.
OH, I WAS JUST CURIOUS WHAT A WISEGUY LIKE YOU WOULD HAVE BEEN LIKE AS A KID.
DUDE, SOME-TIMES YOU SAY RUDE THINGS ALL NONCHA-LANTLY.
THERE'S NOTHING THAT INTER-ESTING TO SAY 'BOUT IT.
I WAS ALWAYS POPULAR, AND SURROUNDED BY PEOPLE.
......
PAPER STRAW WRAPPER
... WELL, SAME WENT FOR HER.
HER?

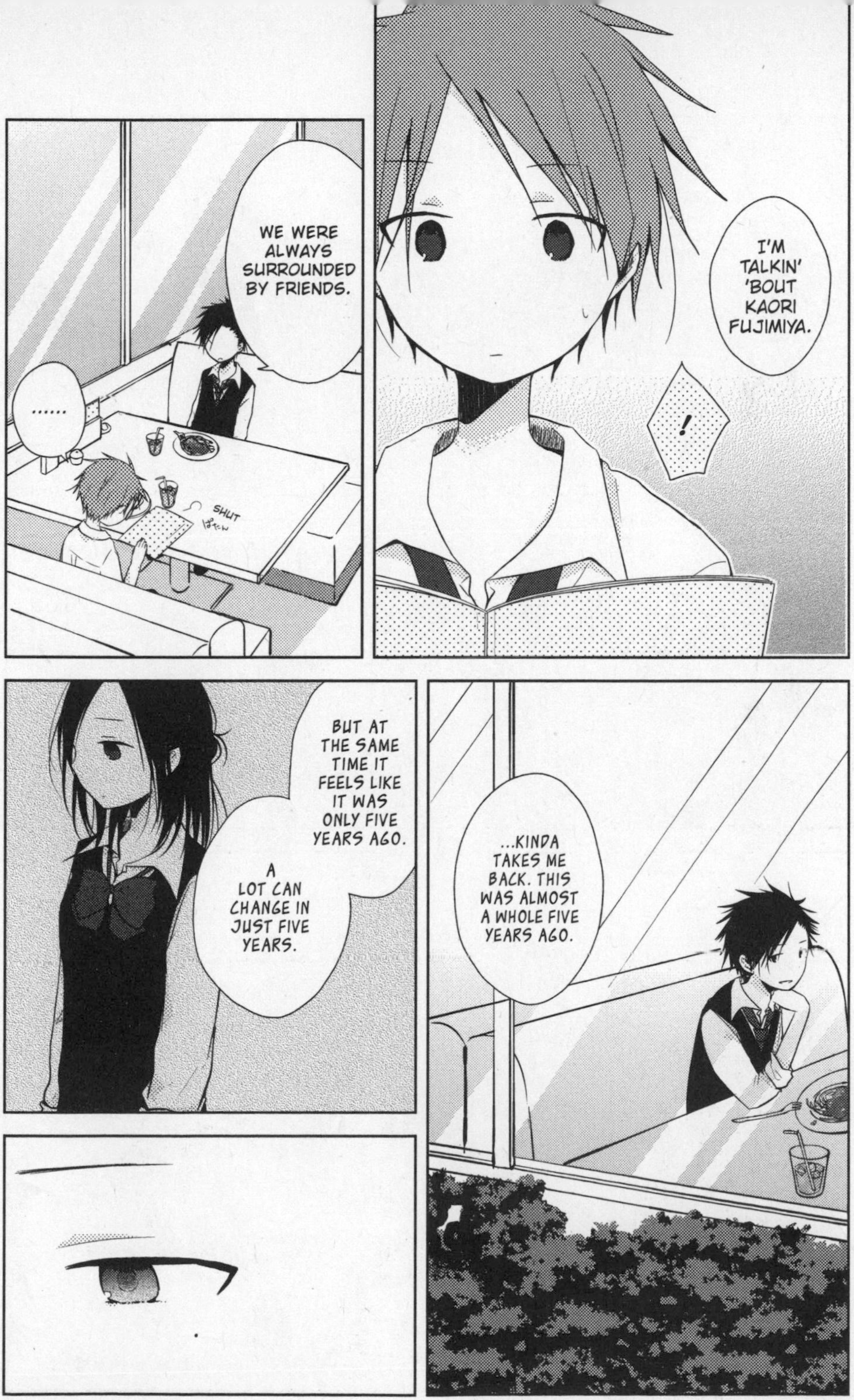
I'M TALKIN' 'BOUT KAORI FUJIMIYA.
!
WE WERE ALWAYS SURROUNDED BY FRIENDS.
......
SHUT
ぱたん
...KINDA TAKES ME BACK. THIS WAS ALMOST A WHOLE FIVE YEARS AGO.
BUT AT THE SAME TIME IT FEELS LIKE IT WAS ONLY FIVE YEARS AGO.
A LOT CAN CHANGE IN JUST FIVE YEARS.

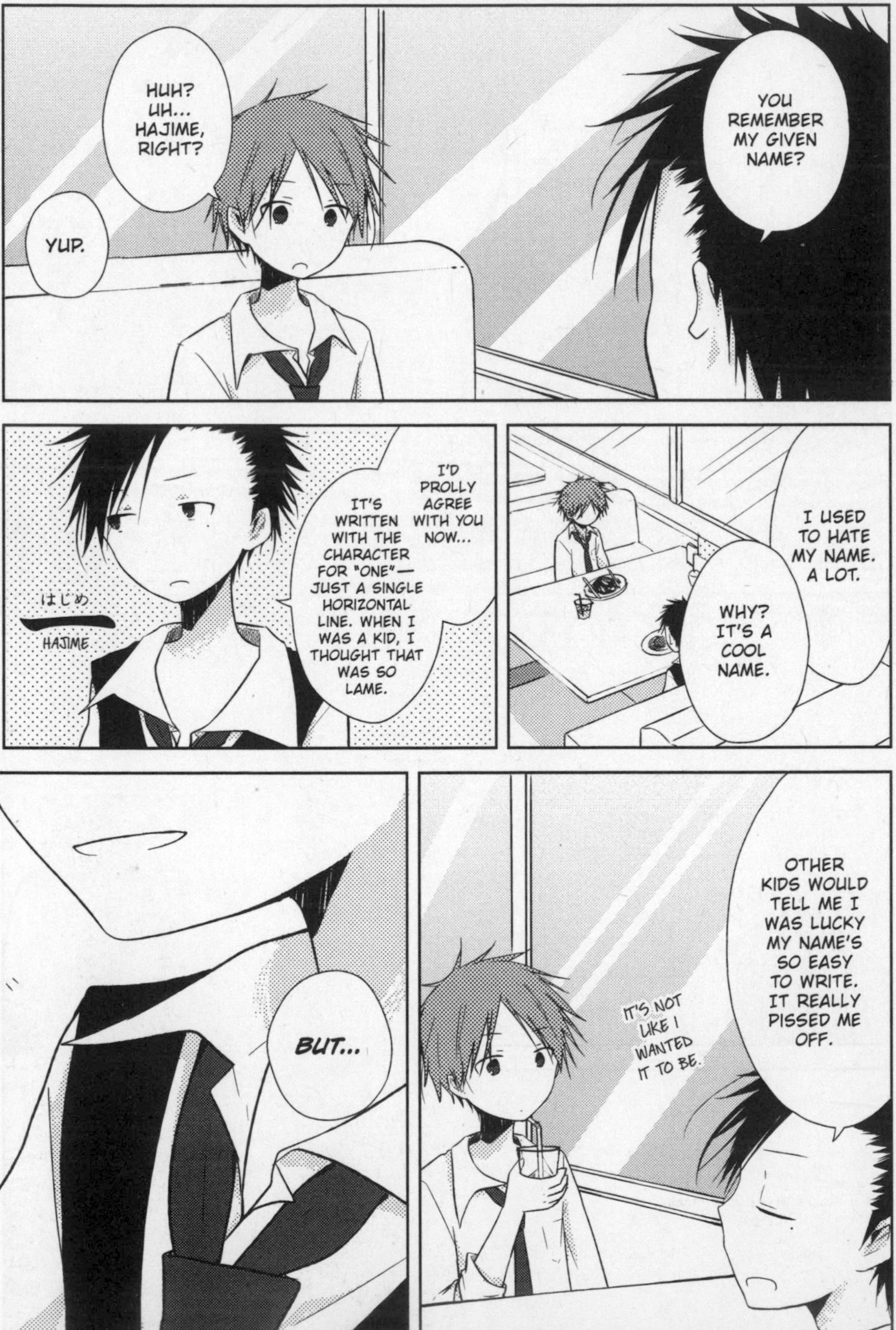
YOU REMEMBER MY GIVEN NAME?
HUH? UH... HAJIME, RIGHT?
YUP.
I USED TO HATE MY NAME. A LOT.
WHY? IT'S A COOL NAME.
I'D PROLLY AGREE WITH YOU NOW...
IT'S WRITTEN WITH THE CHARACTER FOR "ONE"—JUST A SINGLE HORIZONTAL LINE. WHEN I WAS A KID, I THOUGHT THAT WAS SO LAME.
はじめ
HAJIME
OTHER KIDS WOULD TELL ME I WAS LUCKY MY NAME'S SO EASY TO WRITE. IT REALLY PISSED ME OFF.
IT'S NOT LIKE I WANTED IT TO BE.
BUT...

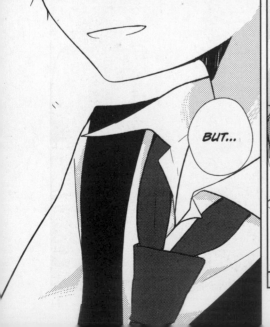

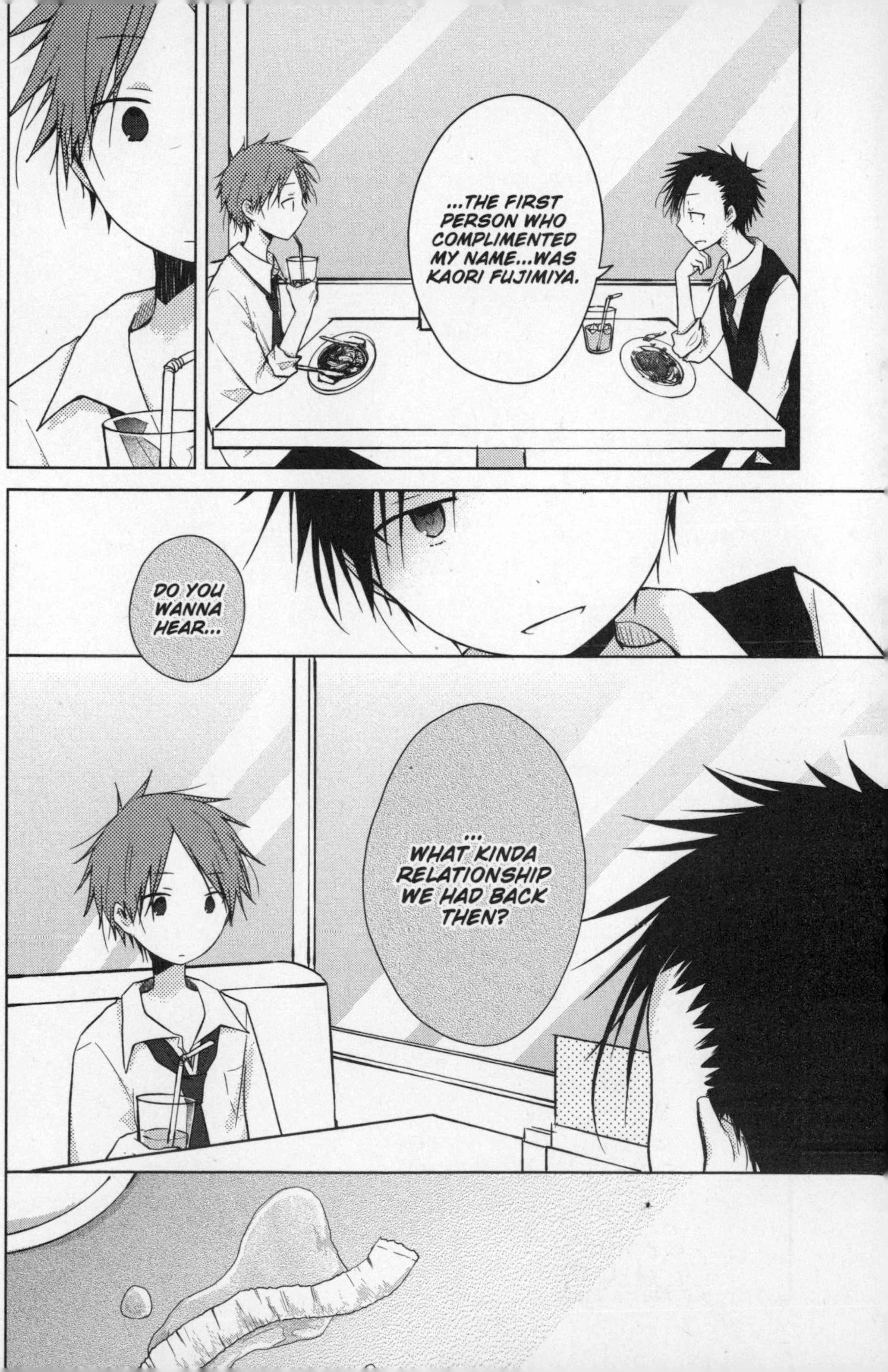
...THE FIRST PERSON WHO COMPLIMENTED MY NAME...WAS KAORI FUJIMIYA.
DO YOU WANNA HEAR...
... WHAT KINDA RELATIONSHIP WE HAD BACK THEN?

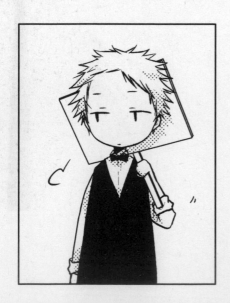

SIDE STORY: ONE WEEK OF *ONE WEEK FRIENDS*

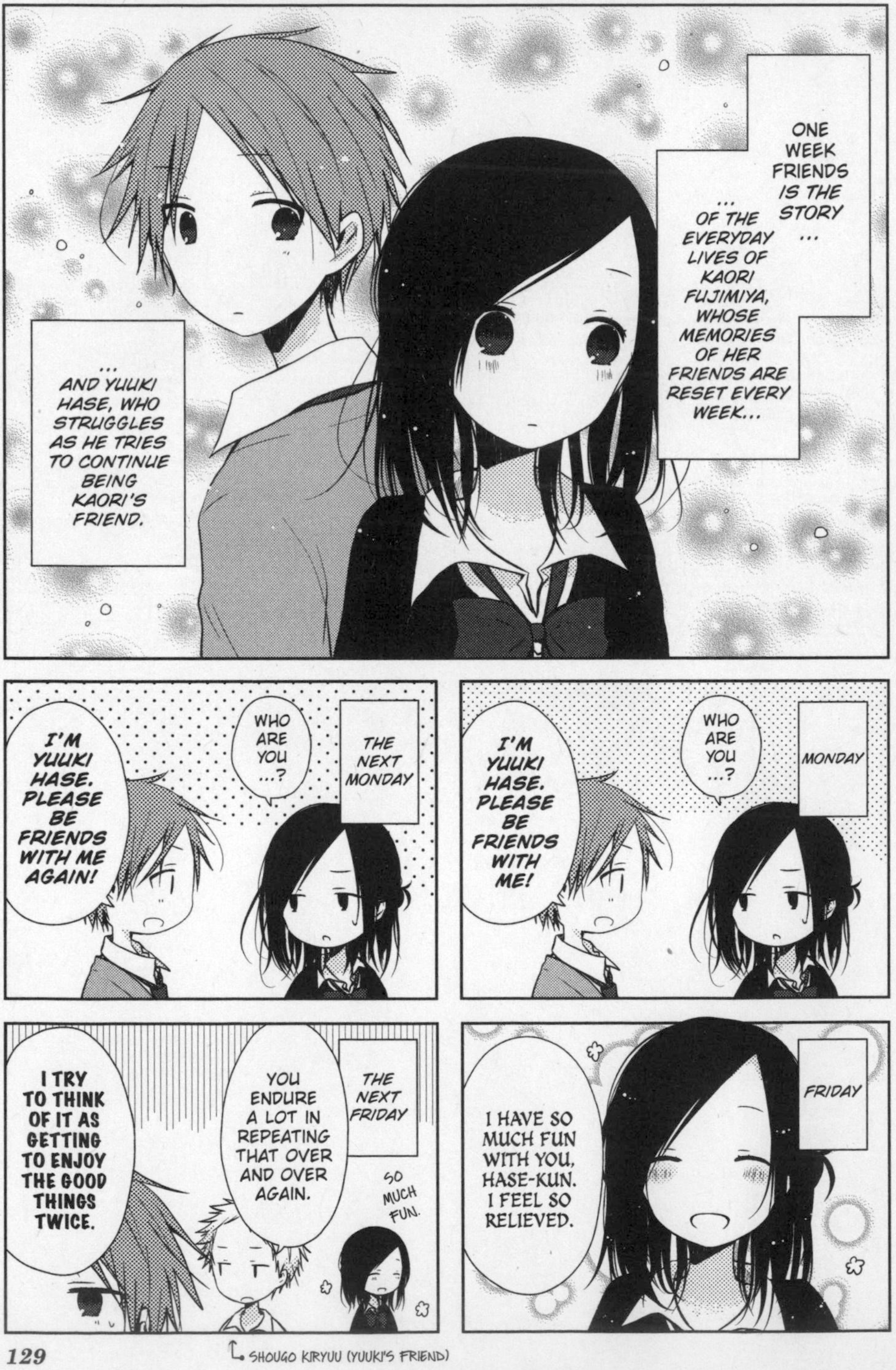

ONE WEEK FRIENDS IS THE STORY ...
... OF THE EVERYDAY LIVES OF KAORI FUJIMIYA, WHOSE MEMORIES OF HER FRIENDS ARE RESET EVERY WEEK...
... AND YUUKI HASE, WHO STRUGGLES AS HE TRIES TO CONTINUE BEING KAORI'S FRIEND.
MONDAY
WHO ARE YOU ...?
I'M YUUKI HASE. PLEASE BE FRIENDS WITH ME!
THE NEXT MONDAY
WHO ARE YOU ...?
I'M YUUKI HASE. PLEASE BE FRIENDS WITH ME AGAIN!
FRIDAY
I HAVE SO MUCH FUN WITH YOU, HASE-KUN. I FEEL SO RELIEVED.
THE NEXT FRIDAY
YOU ENDURE A LOT IN REPEATING THAT OVER AND OVER AGAIN.
SO MUCH FUN.
I TRY TO THINK OF IT AS GETTING TO ENJOY THE GOOD THINGS TWICE.

↳ SHOUGO KIRYUU (YUUKI'S FRIEND)

COLD PERSON

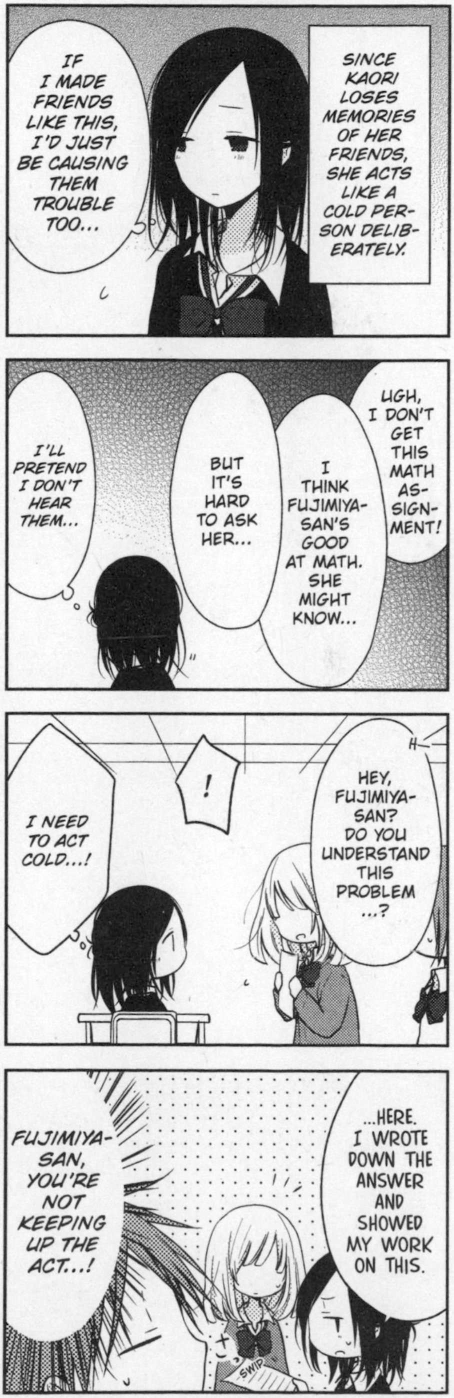
SINCE KAORI LOSES MEMORIES OF HER FRIENDS, SHE ACTS LIKE A COLD PERSON DELIBERATELY.
IF I MADE FRIENDS LIKE THIS, I'D JUST BE CAUSING THEM TROUBLE TOO...
UGH, I DON'T GET THIS MATH ASSIGNMENT!
I THINK FUJIMIYA-SAN'S GOOD AT MATH. SHE MIGHT KNOW...
BUT IT'S HARD TO ASK HER...
I'LL PRETEND I DON'T HEAR THEM...
H—
HEY, FUJIMIYA-SAN? DO YOU UNDERSTAND THIS PROBLEM ...?
!
I NEED TO ACT COLD...!
...HERE. I WROTE DOWN THE ANSWER AND SHOWED MY WORK ON THIS.
FUJIMIYA-SAN, YOU'RE NOT KEEPING UP THE ACT...!
SWIP

SOOTHING

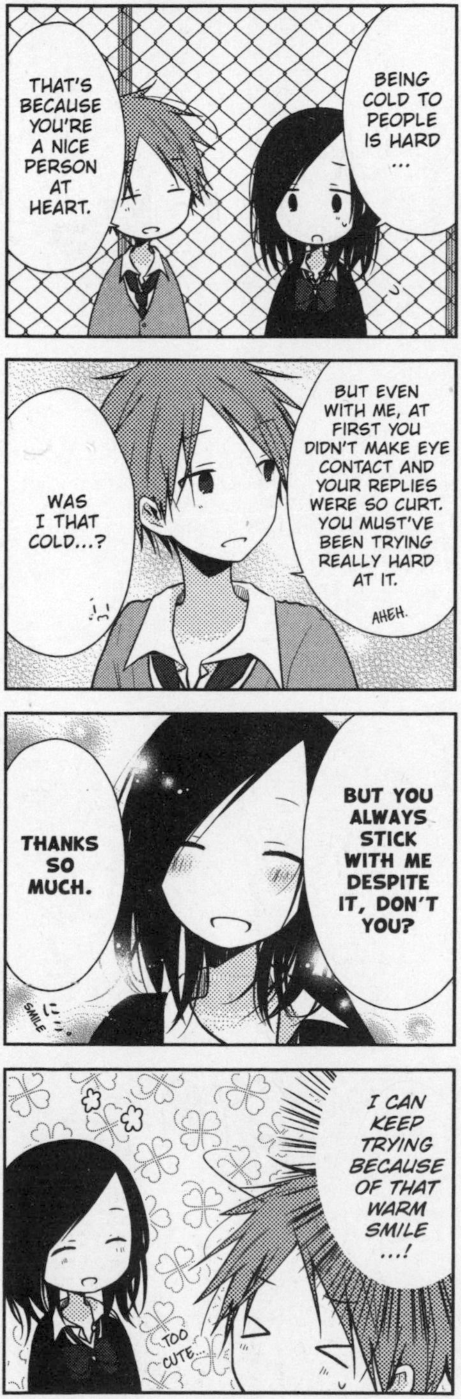
BEING COLD TO PEOPLE IS HARD ...
THAT'S BECAUSE YOU'RE A NICE PERSON AT HEART.
BUT EVEN WITH ME, AT FIRST YOU DIDN'T MAKE EYE CONTACT AND YOUR REPLIES WERE SO CURT. YOU MUST'VE BEEN TRYING REALLY HARD AT IT.
AHEH.
WAS I THAT COLD...?
BUT YOU ALWAYS STICK WITH ME DESPITE IT, DON'T YOU?
THANKS SO MUCH.
SMILE
I CAN KEEP TRYING BECAUSE OF THAT WARM SMILE ...!
TOO CUTE...

MR. OCTOPUS

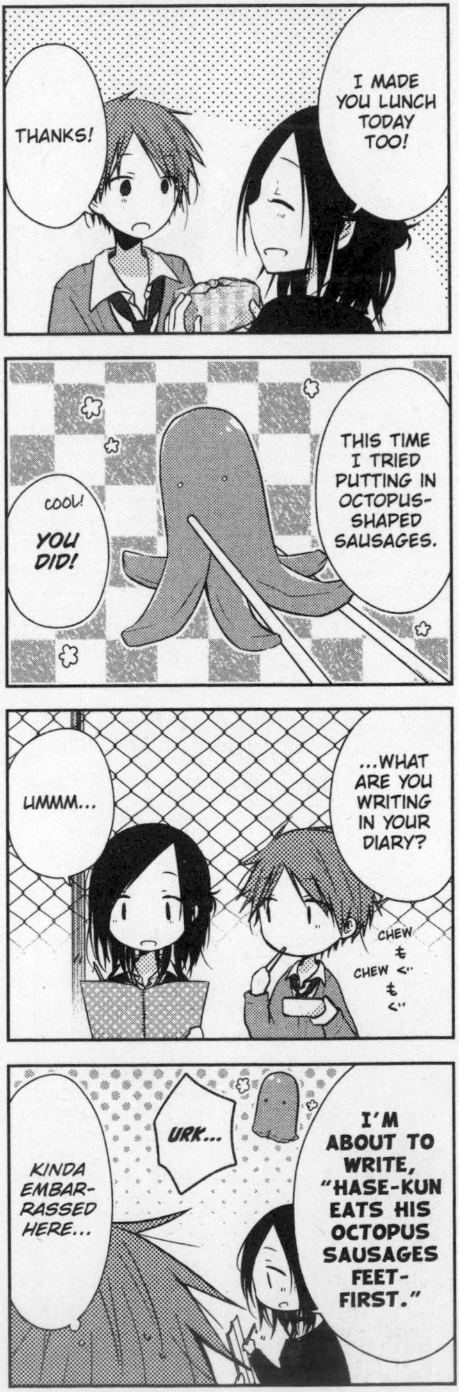
I MADE YOU LUNCH TODAY TOO!
THANKS!
THIS TIME I TRIED PUTTING IN OCTOPUS-SHAPED SAUSAGES.
COOL! YOU DID!
...WHAT ARE YOU WRITING IN YOUR DIARY?
CHEW CHEW
UMMM...
I'M ABOUT TO WRITE, "HASE-KUN EATS HIS OCTOPUS SAUSAGES FEET-FIRST."
URK...
KINDA EMBARRASSED HERE...

AS USUAL

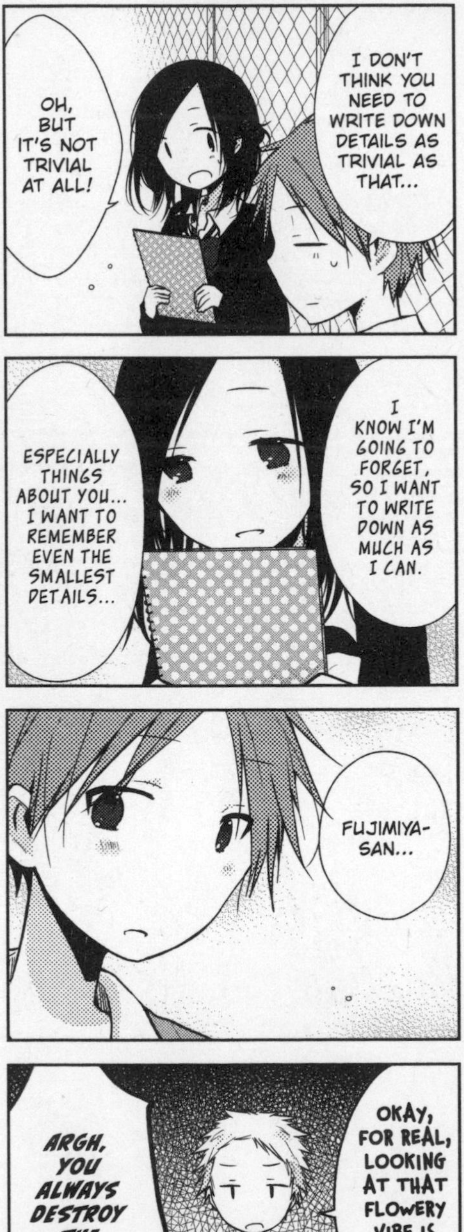
I DON'T THINK YOU NEED TO WRITE DOWN DETAILS AS TRIVIAL AS THAT...
OH, BUT IT'S NOT TRIVIAL AT ALL!
I KNOW I'M GOING TO FORGET, SO I WANT TO WRITE DOWN AS MUCH AS I CAN.
ESPECIALLY THINGS ABOUT YOU... I WANT TO REMEMBER EVEN THE SMALLEST DETAILS...
FUJIMIYA-SAN...
OKAY, FOR REAL, LOOKING AT THAT FLOWERY VIBE IS JUST PAINFUL.
ARGH, YOU ALWAYS DESTROY THE MOOD!
SHOULDN'T HAVE COME UP.

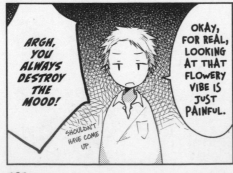

PROGRESS

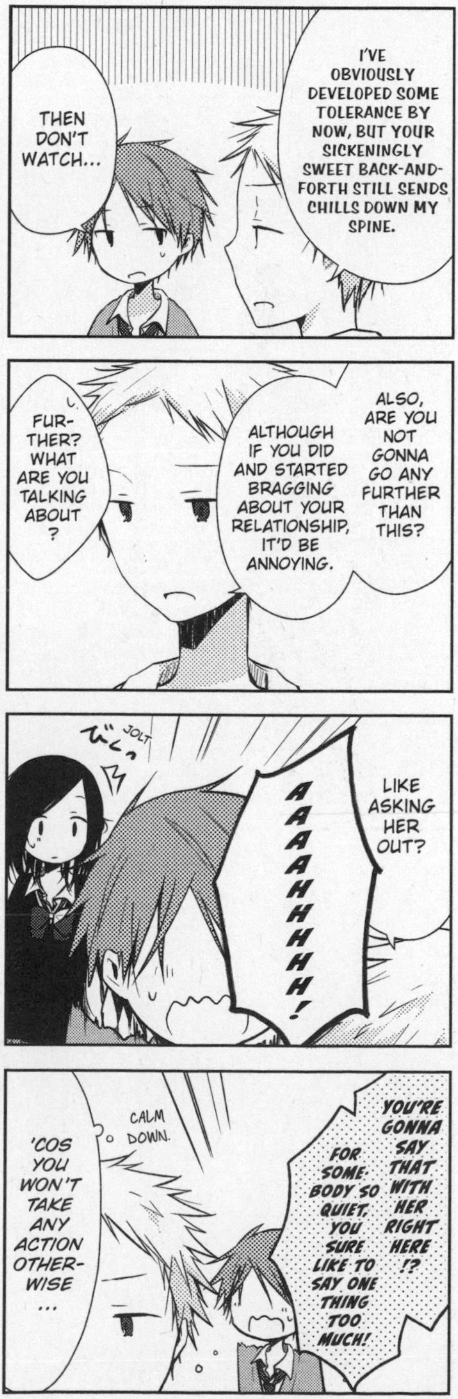
I'VE OBVIOUSLY DEVELOPED SOME TOLERANCE BY NOW, BUT YOUR SICKENINGLY SWEET BACK-AND-FORTH STILL SENDS CHILLS DOWN MY SPINE.
THEN DON'T WATCH...
ALSO, ARE YOU NOT GONNA GO ANY FURTHER THAN THIS?
ALTHOUGH IF YOU DID AND STARTED BRAGGING ABOUT YOUR RELATIONSHIP, IT'D BE ANNOYING.
FURTHER? WHAT ARE YOU TALKING ABOUT?
LIKE ASKING HER OUT?
AAAAHHHHHH!
JOLT
YOU'RE GONNA SAY THAT WITH HER RIGHT HERE!?
FOR SOMEBODY SO QUIET, YOU SURE LIKE TO SAY ONE THING TOO MUCH!
CALM DOWN.
'COS YOU WON'T TAKE ANY ACTION OTHERWISE...

LIKE THAT

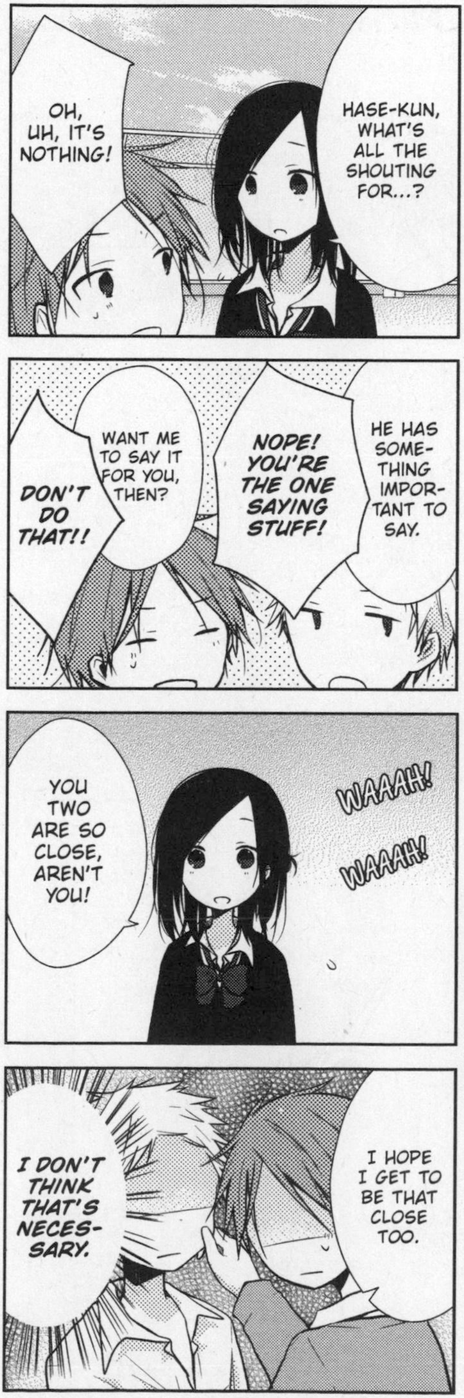
HASE-KUN, WHAT'S ALL THE SHOUTING FOR...?
OH, UH, IT'S NOTHING!
HE HAS SOMETHING IMPORTANT TO SAY.
NOPE! YOU'RE THE ONE SAYING STUFF!
WANT ME TO SAY IT FOR YOU, THEN?
DON'T DO THAT!!
WAAAH!
WAAAH!
YOU TWO ARE SO CLOSE, AREN'T YOU!
I HOPE I GET TO BE THAT CLOSE TOO.
I DON'T THINK THAT'S NECESSARY.

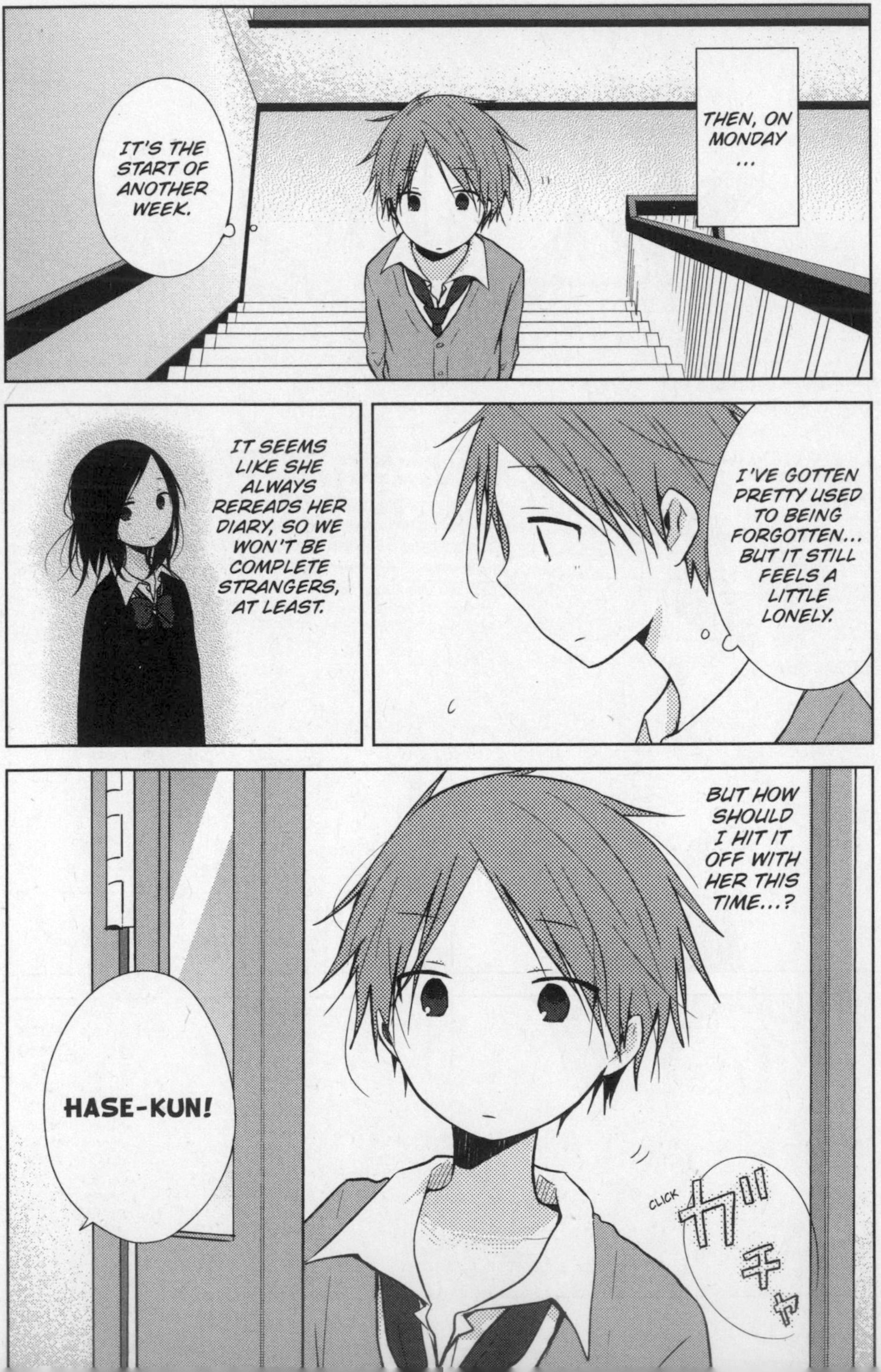
THEN, ON MONDAY ...
IT'S THE START OF ANOTHER WEEK.
I'VE GOTTEN PRETTY USED TO BEING FORGOTTEN... BUT IT STILL FEELS A LITTLE LONELY.
IT SEEMS LIKE SHE ALWAYS REREADS HER DIARY, SO WE WON'T BE COMPLETE STRANGERS, AT LEAST.
BUT HOW SHOULD I HIT IT OFF WITH HER THIS TIME...?
HASE-KUN!
CLICK
ガチャ

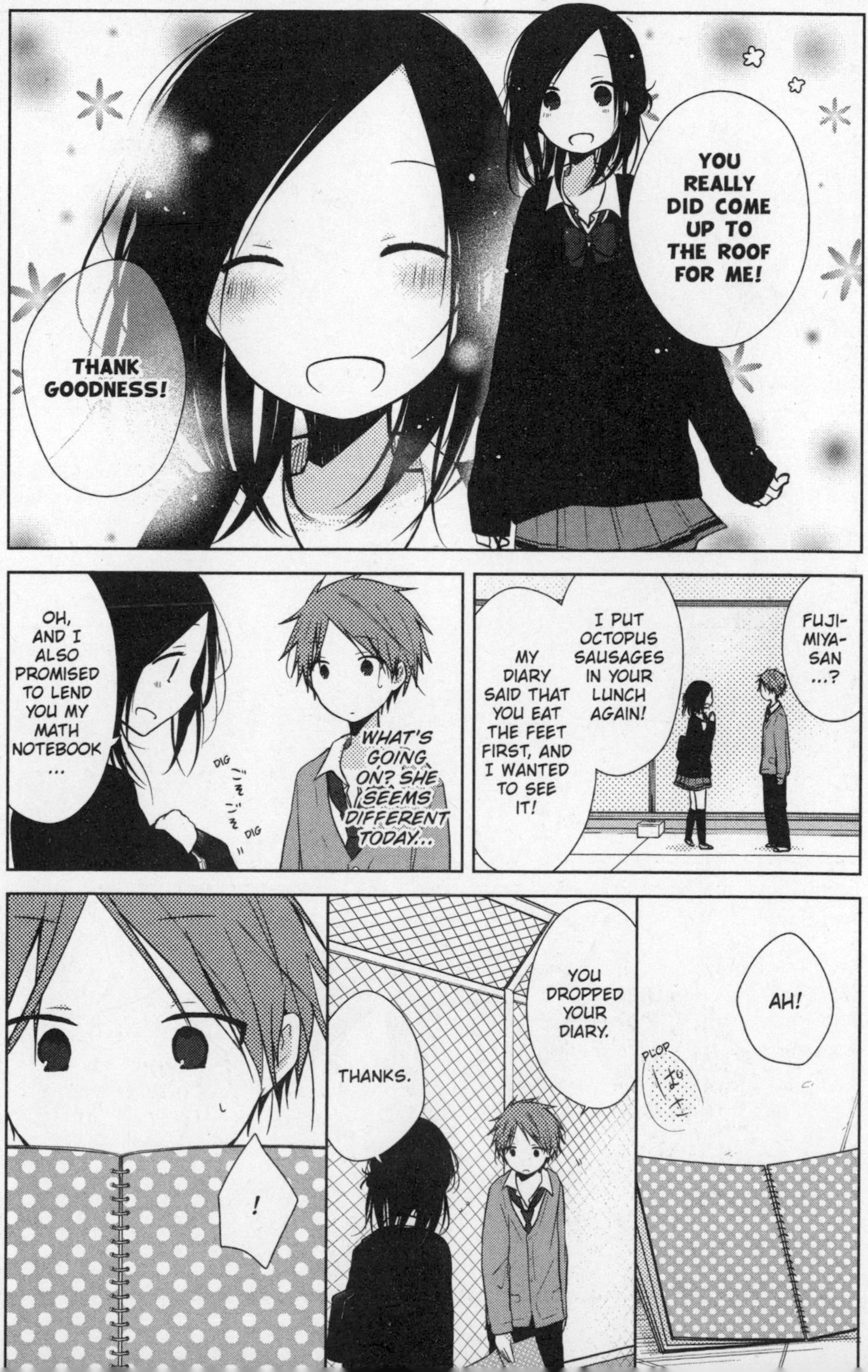
YOU REALLY DID COME UP TO THE ROOF FOR ME!
THANK GOODNESS!
FUJI-MIYA-SAN ...?
I PUT OCTOPUS SAUSAGES IN YOUR LUNCH AGAIN!
MY DIARY SAID THAT YOU EAT THE FEET FIRST, AND I WANTED TO SEE IT!
OH, AND I ALSO PROMISED TO LEND YOU MY MATH NOTEBOOK ...
DIG DIG
WHAT'S GOING ON? SHE SEEMS DIFFERENT TODAY...
AH!
PLOP
YOU DROPPED YOUR DIARY.
THANKS.
!

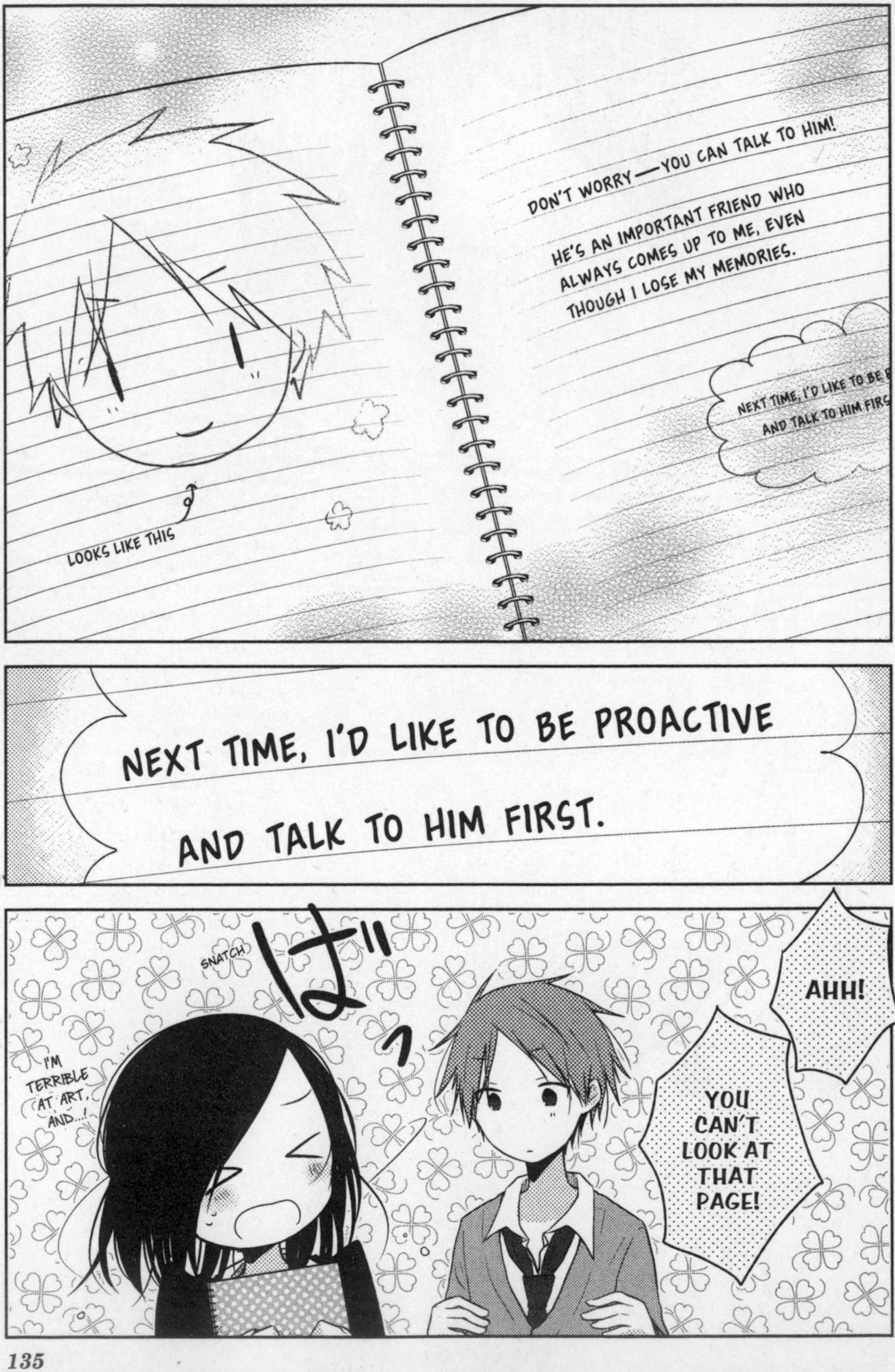
DON'T WORRY—YOU CAN TALK TO HIM!
HE'S AN IMPORTANT FRIEND WHO ALWAYS COMES UP TO ME, EVEN THOUGH I LOSE MY MEMORIES.
NEXT TIME, I'D LIKE TO BE
AND TALK TO HIM
LOOKS LIKE THIS
NEXT TIME, I'D LIKE TO BE PROACTIVE AND TALK TO HIM FIRST.
AHH!
YOU CAN'T LOOK AT THAT PAGE!
ばっ
SNATCH
I'M TERRIBLE AT ART, AND...!

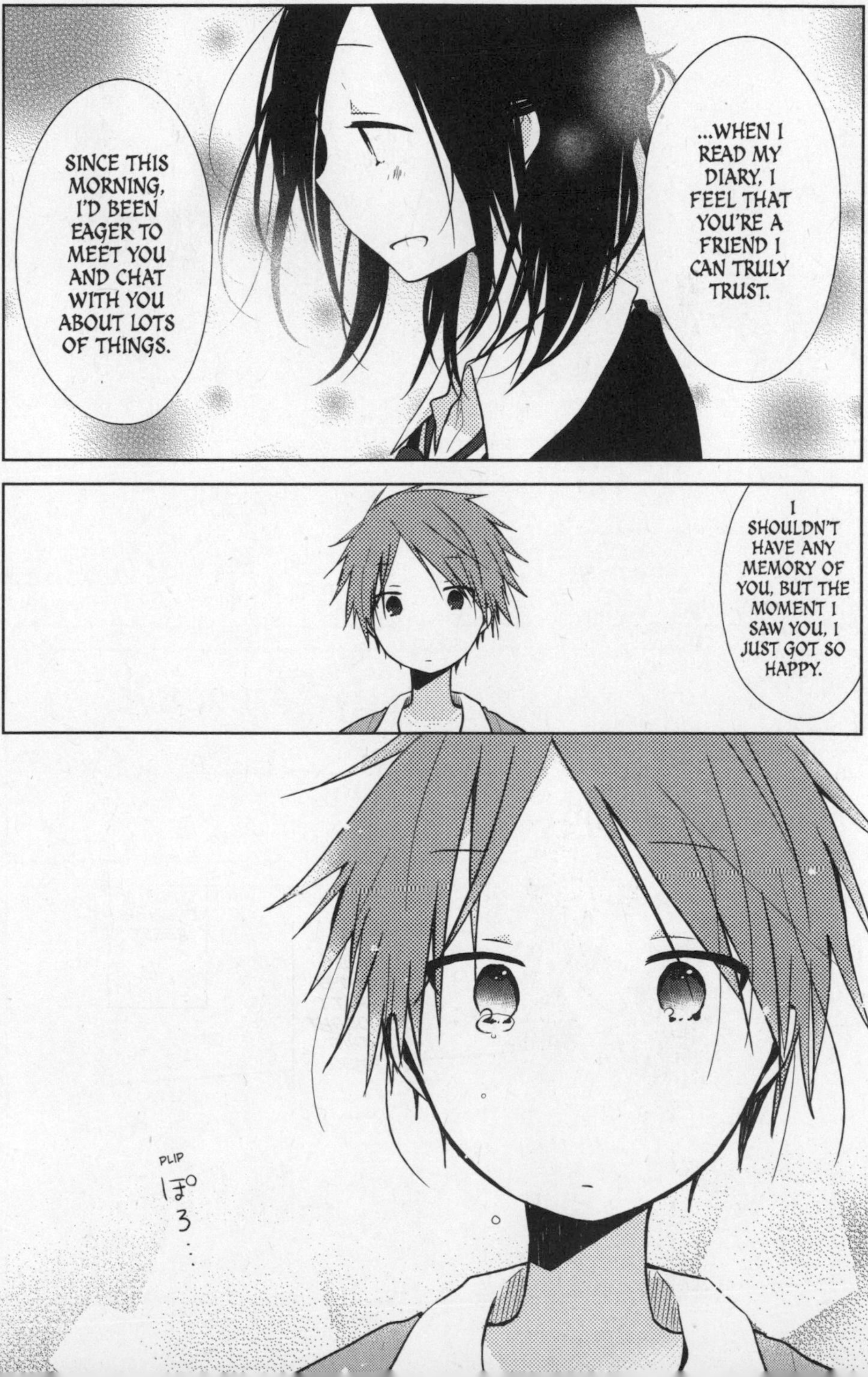
...WHEN I READ MY DIARY, I FEEL THAT YOU'RE A FRIEND I CAN TRULY TRUST.
SINCE THIS MORNING, I'D BEEN EAGER TO MEET YOU AND CHAT WITH YOU ABOUT LOTS OF THINGS.
I SHOULDN'T HAVE ANY MEMORY OF YOU, BUT THE MOMENT I SAW YOU, I JUST GOT SO HAPPY.
PLIP
ぽろ…

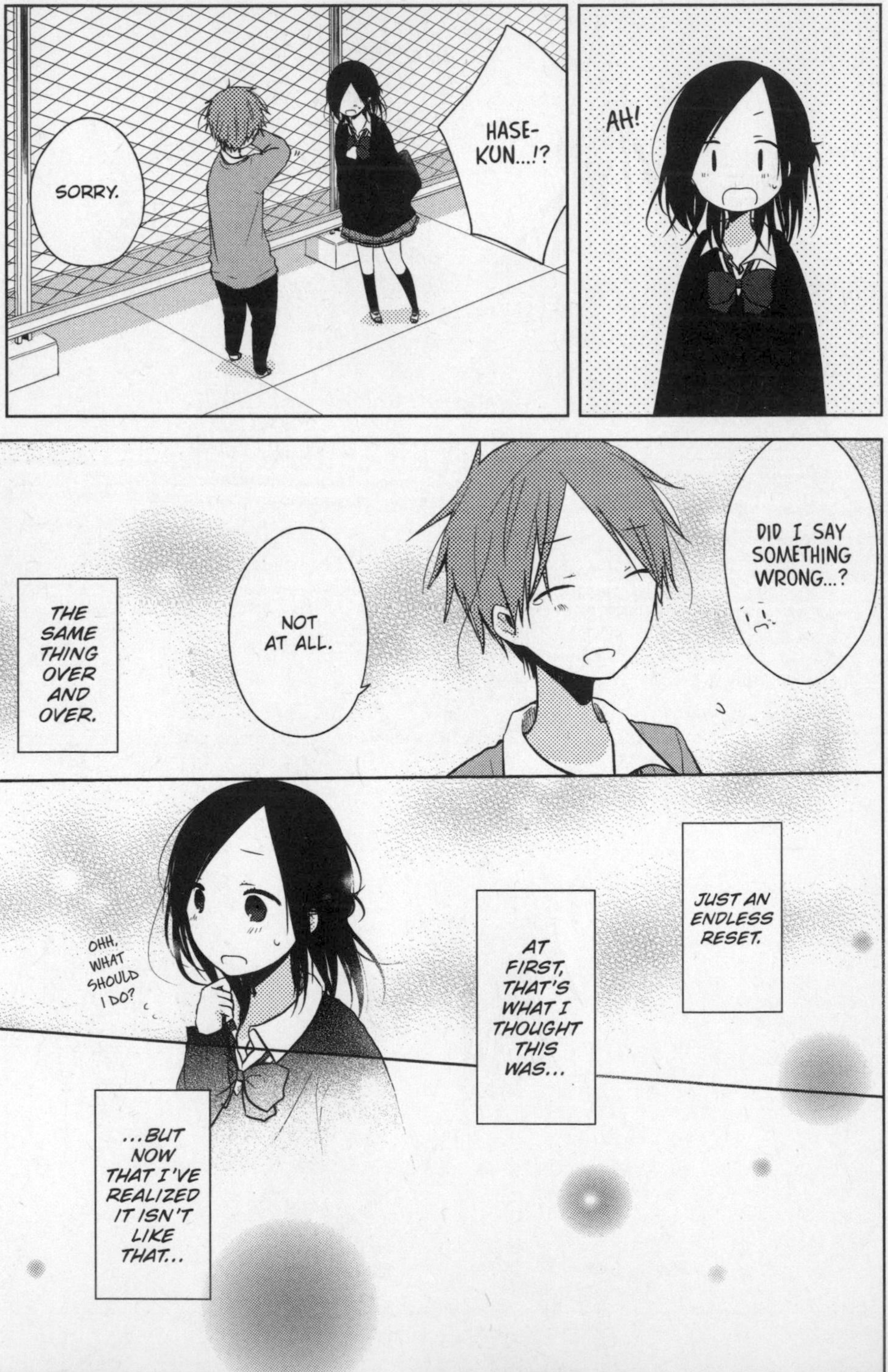
AH!
HASE-KUN...!?
SORRY.
DID I SAY SOMETHING WRONG...?
NOT AT ALL.
THE SAME THING OVER AND OVER.
JUST AN ENDLESS RESET.
AT FIRST, THAT'S WHAT I THOUGHT THIS WAS...
OHH, WHAT SHOULD I DO?
...BUT NOW THAT I'VE REALIZED IT ISN'T LIKE THAT...

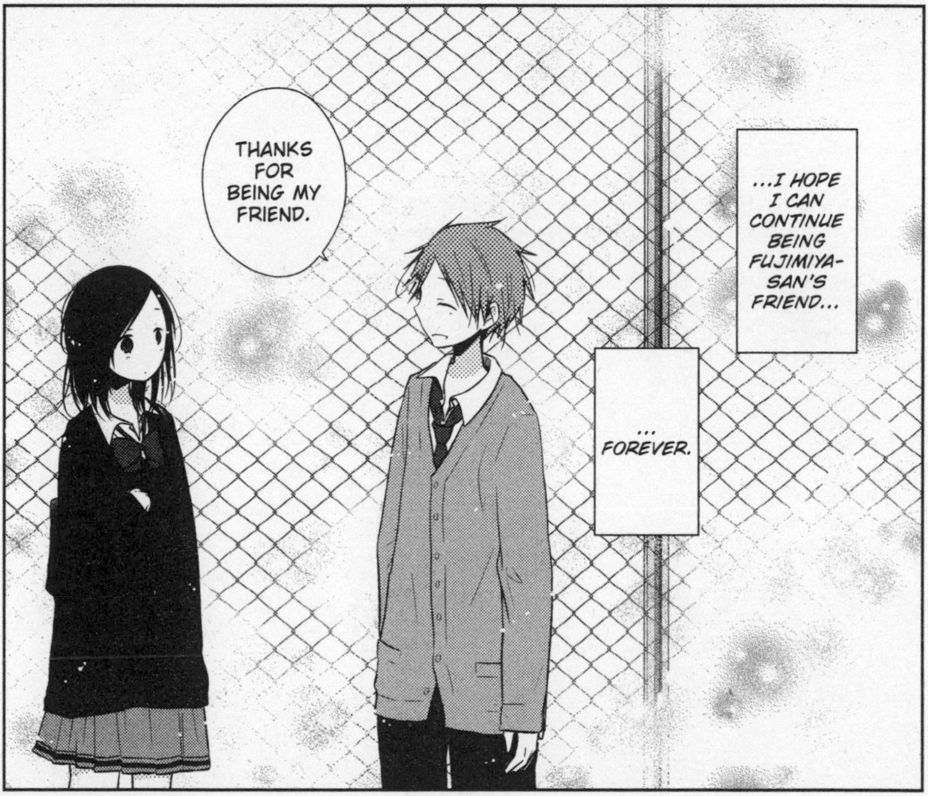
...I HOPE I CAN CONTINUE BEING FUJIMIYA-SAN'S FRIEND...
...FOREVER.
THANKS FOR BEING MY FRIEND.

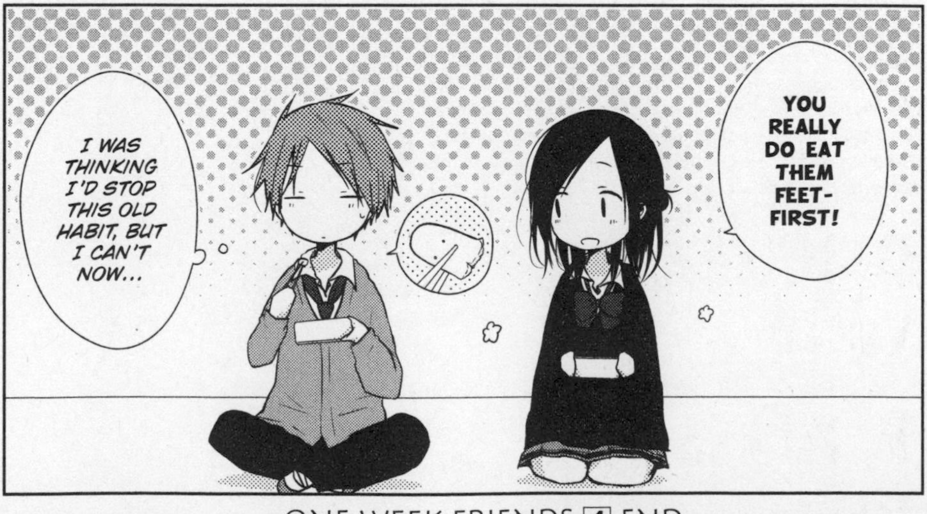
YOU REALLY DO EAT THEM FEET-FIRST!
I WAS THINKING I'D STOP THIS OLD HABIT, BUT I CAN'T NOW...

ONE WEEK FRIENDS 4 END

TRANSLATION NOTES

COMMON HONORIFICS
No honorific: Indicates familiarity or closeness; if used without permission or reason, addressing someone in this manner would constitute an insult.
-san: The Japanese equivalent of Mr./Mrs./Miss. If a situation calls for politeness, this is the fail-safe honorific.
-kun: Used most often when referring to boys, this indicates affection or familiarity. Occasionally used by older men among their peers, but it may also be used by anyone referring to a person of lower standing.
-chan: An affectionate honorific indicating familiarity used mostly in reference to girls; also used in reference to cute persons or animals of either gender.
-sensei: A respectful term for teachers, artists, or high-level professionals.

nee: Japanese equivalent to "older sis."

nii: Japanese equivalent to "older bro."

PAGE 72
Most schools in Japan, from preschool to college, hold annual events called bunkasai, or **culture festivals**. The students of each class decide together on a booth or activity they want to do, with class cafés, haunted houses, and plays being particularly popular choices. The festivals take place on school grounds and are often open to the public.

PAGE 120
In Japan, a **family restaurant**, often referred to as famiresu, is a casual, family-friendly restaurant with reasonably priced food options.

PAGE 125
Japanese names are usually written out with Chinese characters, and the characters represent the name's meaning. Hajime most likely used to think his name was lame and kids would make fun of it because the Chinese character used to write it is the same character as for the number one—a single, horizontal stroke. Not only is this the most simple of all the different Chinese characters that can be used to write Hajime, but it is also the easiest to write overall.

ONE
WEEK
FRIENDS

BONUS ~CULTURE FESTIVAL 1~

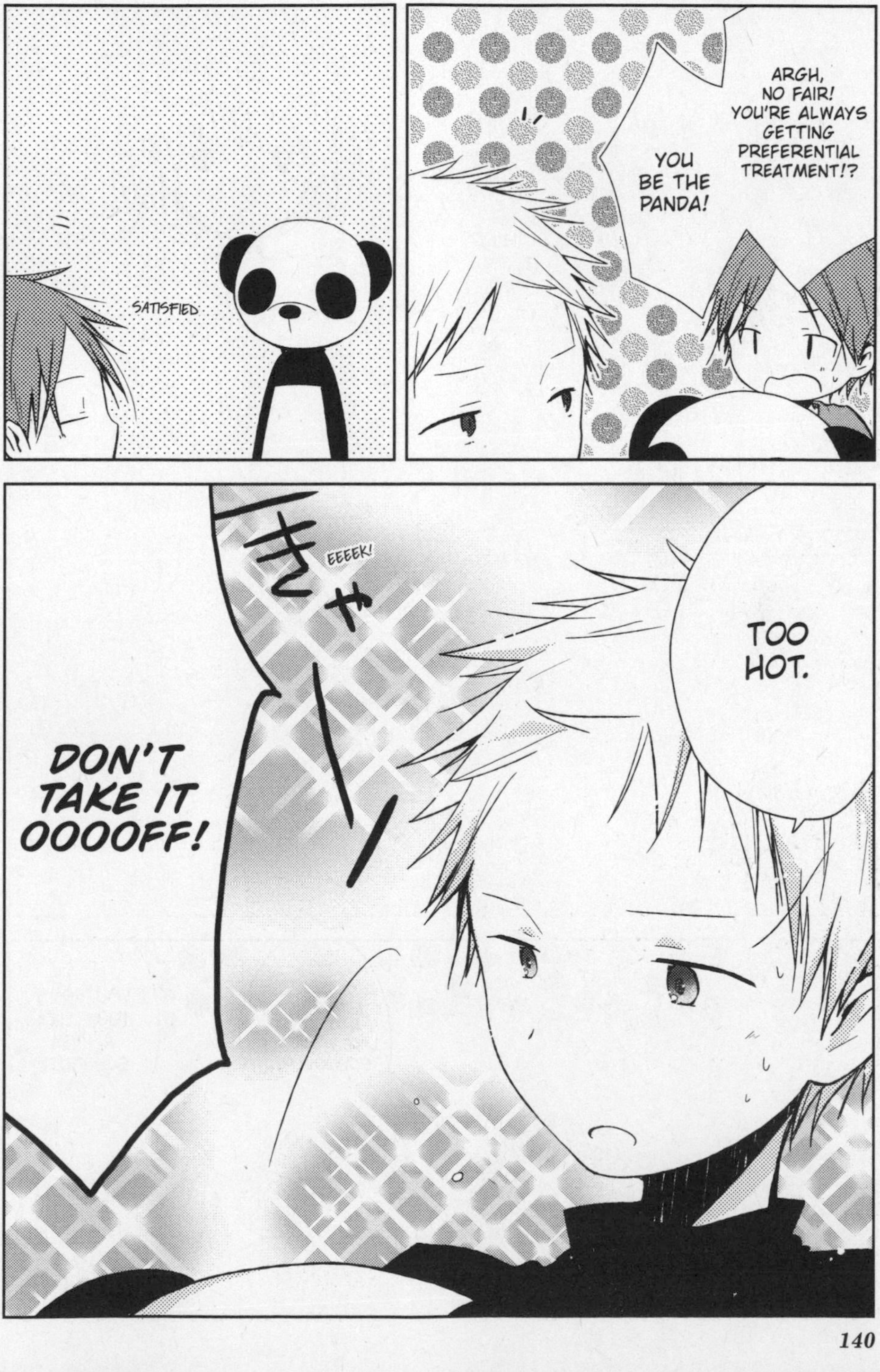

ARGH, NO FAIR! YOU'RE ALWAYS GETTING PREFERENTIAL TREATMENT!?
YOU BE THE PANDA!
SATISFIED
TOO HOT.
きゃー
EEEEK!
DON'T TAKE IT OOOOFF!

BONUS ~CULTURE FESTIVAL 2~

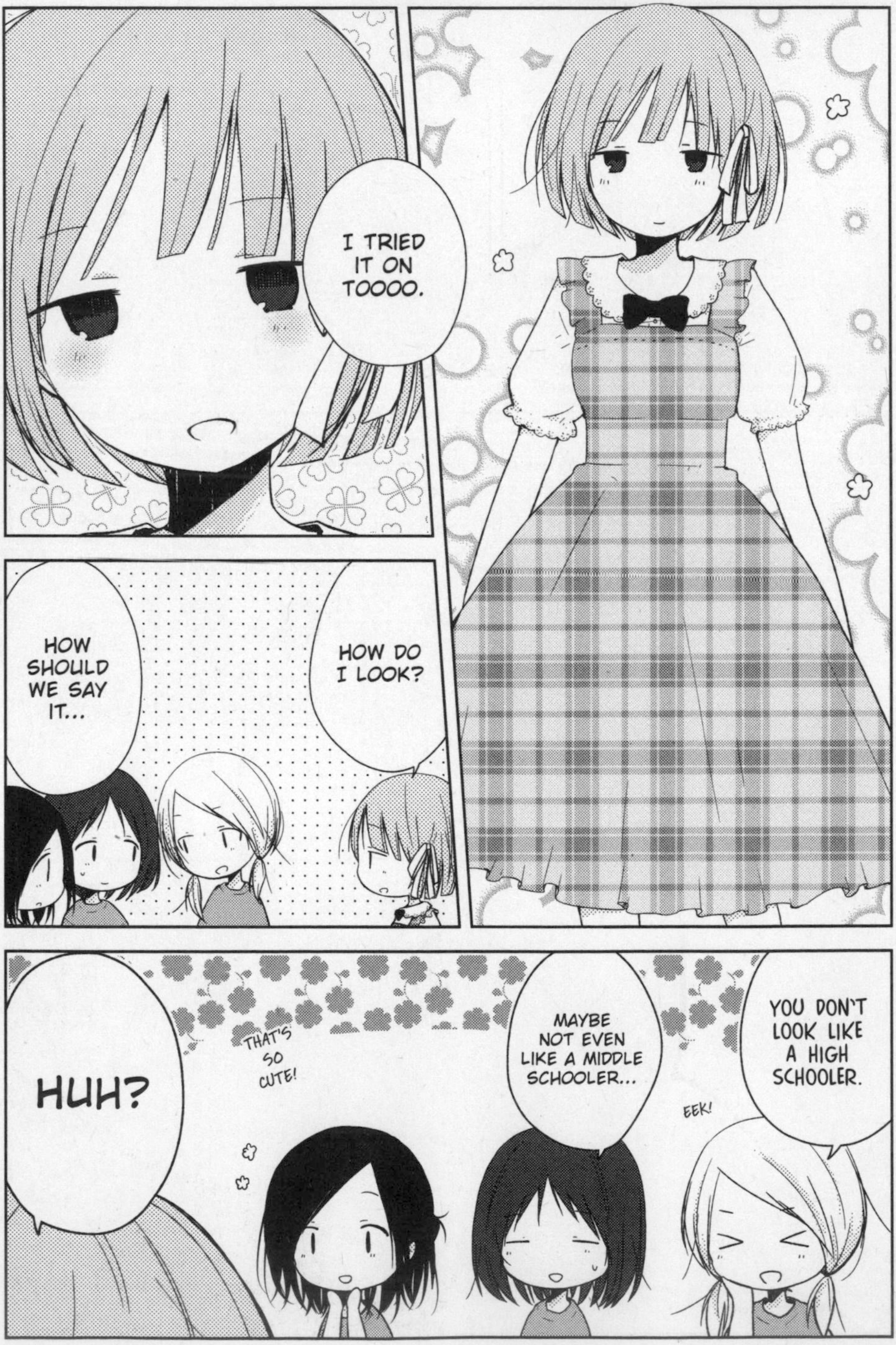
I TRIED IT ON TOOOO.
HOW DO I LOOK?
HOW SHOULD WE SAY IT...
YOU DON'T LOOK LIKE A HIGH SCHOOLER.
EEK!
MAYBE NOT EVEN LIKE A MIDDLE SCHOOLER...
THAT'S SO CUTE!
HUH?

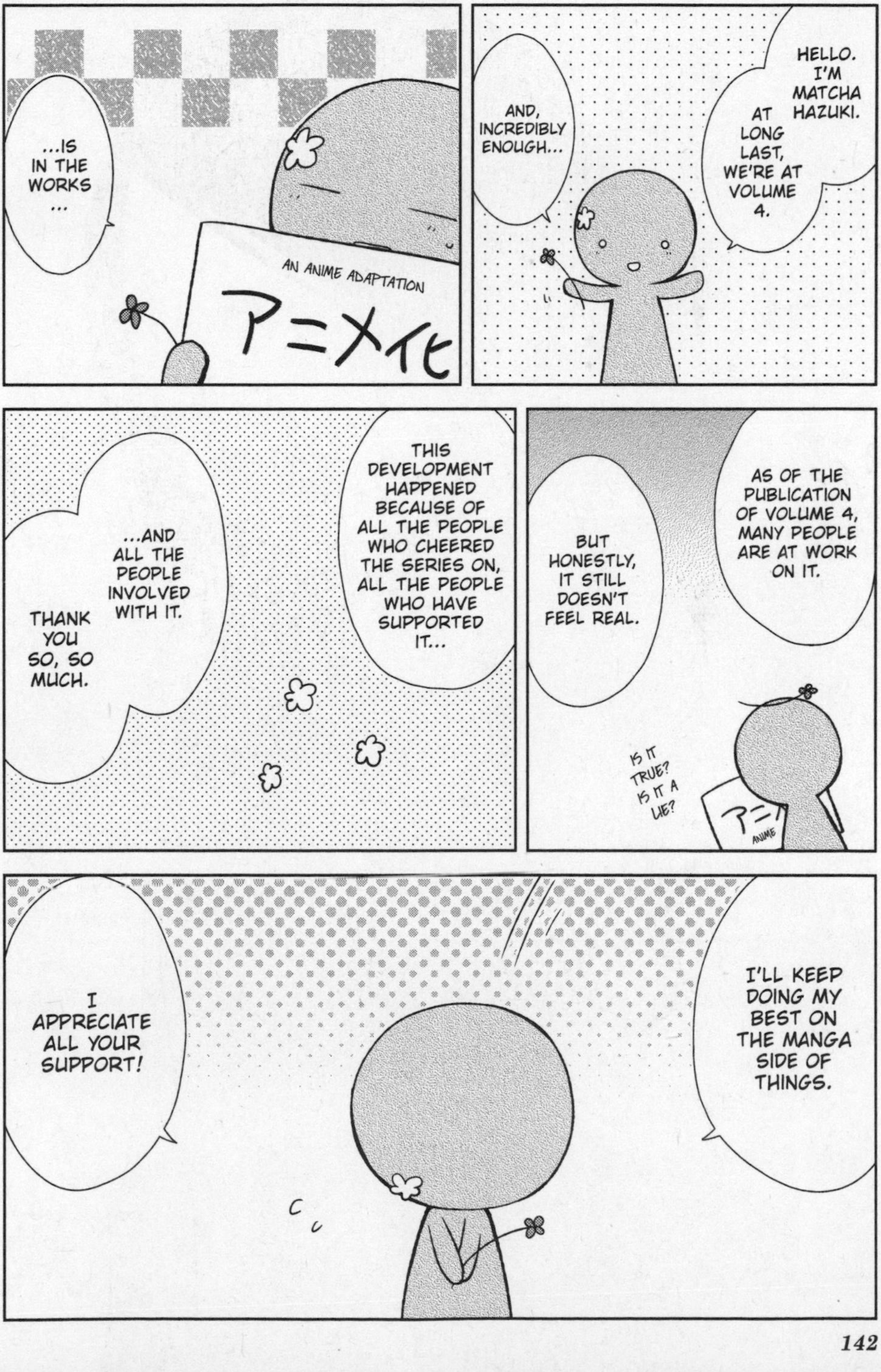
HELLO. I'M MATCHA HAZUKI.
AT LONG LAST, WE'RE AT VOLUME 4.
AND, INCREDIBLY ENOUGH...
AN ANIME ADAPTATION
アニメ化
...IS IN THE WORKS...
AS OF THE PUBLICATION OF VOLUME 4, MANY PEOPLE ARE AT WORK ON IT.
BUT HONESTLY, IT STILL DOESN'T FEEL REAL.
IS IT TRUE? IS IT A LIE?
アニ
ANIME
THIS DEVELOPMENT HAPPENED BECAUSE OF ALL THE PEOPLE WHO CHEERED THE SERIES ON, ALL THE PEOPLE WHO HAVE SUPPORTED IT...
...AND ALL THE PEOPLE INVOLVED WITH IT.
THANK YOU SO, SO MUCH.
I'LL KEEP DOING MY BEST ON THE MANGA SIDE OF THINGS.
I APPRECIATE ALL YOUR SUPPORT!

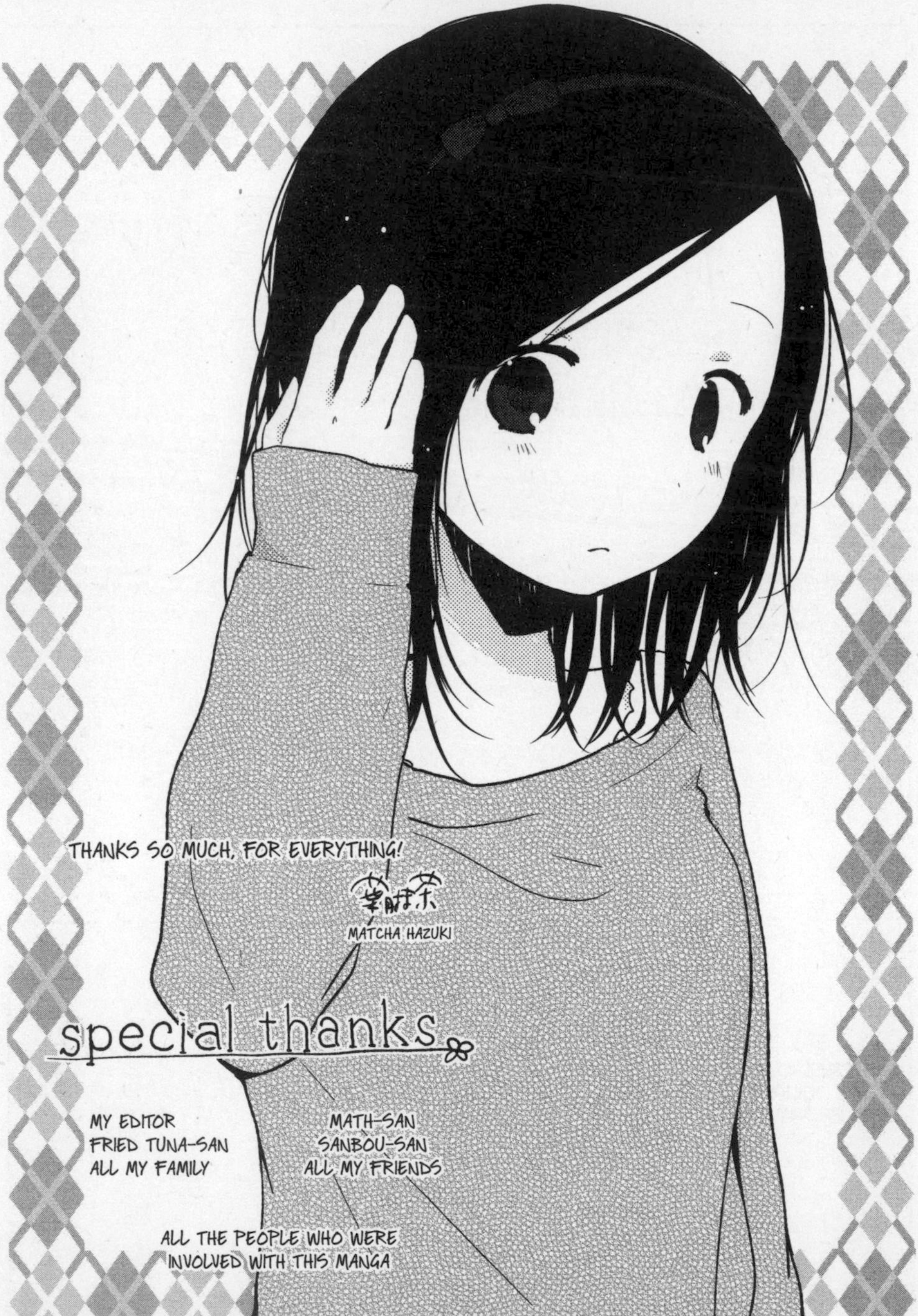

THANKS SO MUCH, FOR EVERYTHING!
MATCHA HAZUKI
special thanks
MY EDITOR
FRIED TUNA-SAN
ALL MY FAMILY
MATH-SAN
SANBOU-SAN
ALL MY FRIENDS
ALL THE PEOPLE WHO WERE INVOLVED WITH THIS MANGA

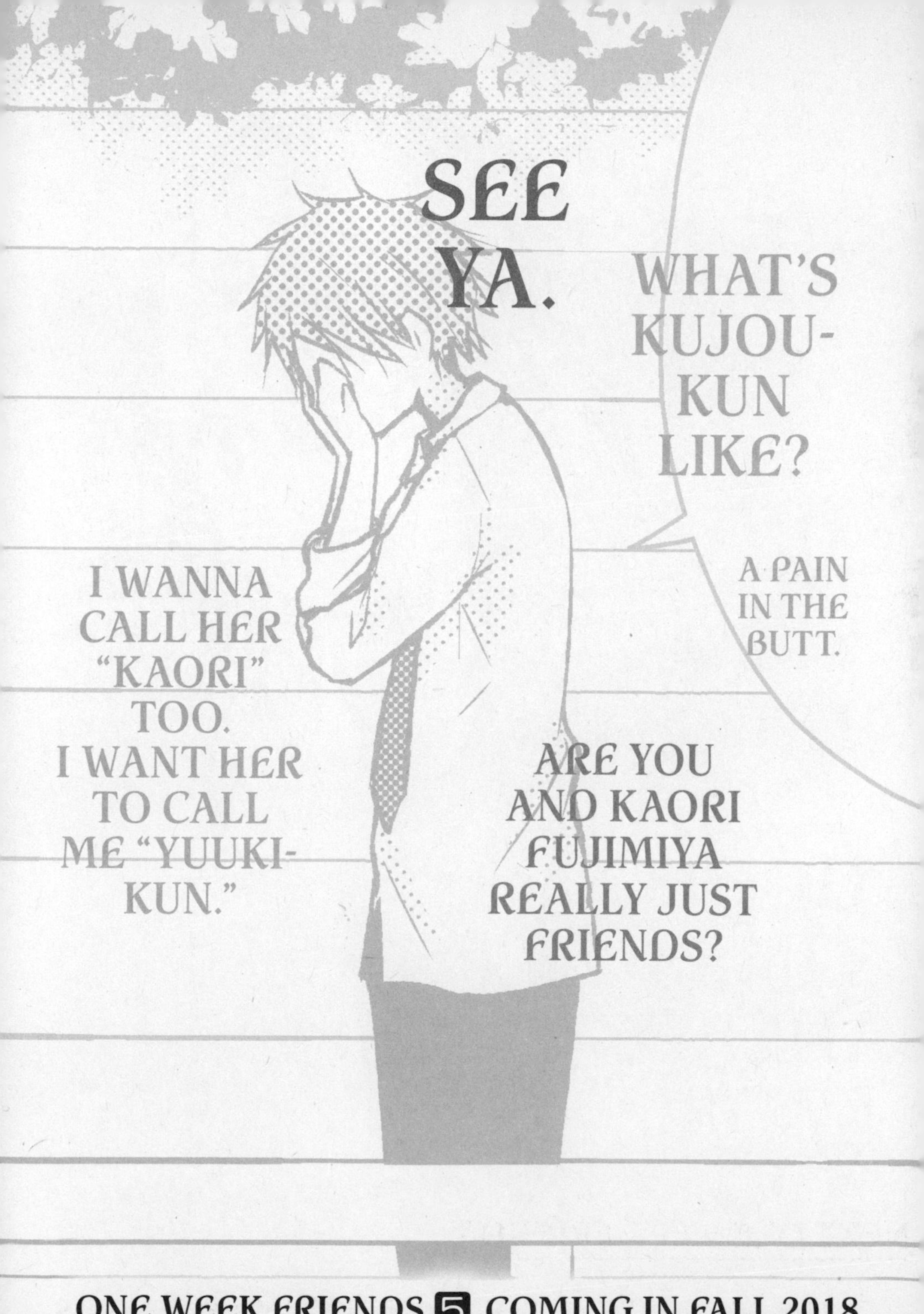
SEE YA.
WHAT'S KUJOU-KUN LIKE?
A PAIN IN THE BUTT.
ARE YOU AND KAORI FUJIMIYA REALLY JUST FRIENDS?
I WANNA CALL HER "KAORI" TOO. I WANT HER TO CALL ME "YUUKI-KUN."

ONE WEEK FRIENDS 5 COMING IN FALL 2018

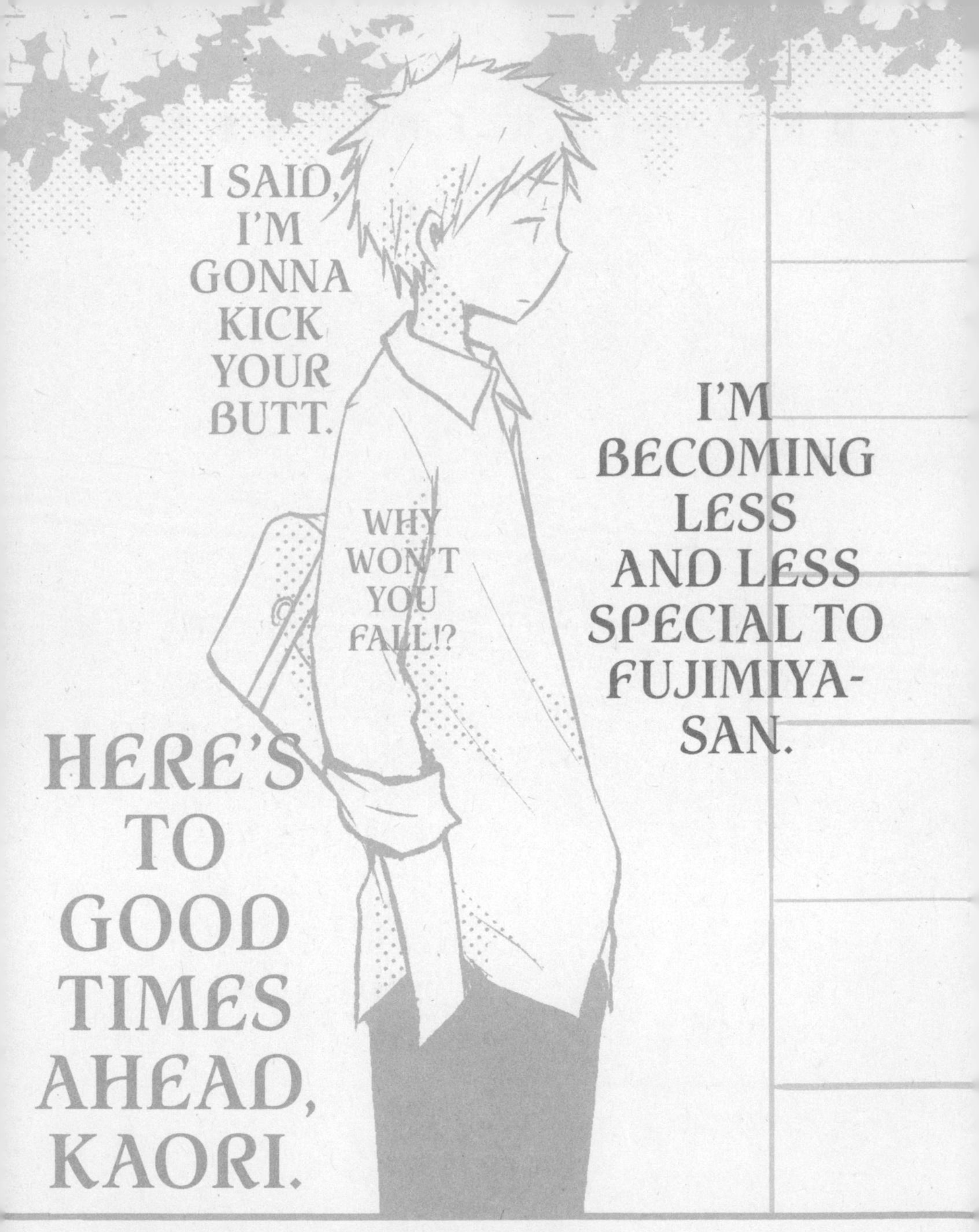
I'M BECOMING LESS AND LESS SPECIAL TO FUJIMIYA-SAN.
WHY WON'T YOU FALL!?
I SAID, I'M GONNA KICK YOUR BUTT.
HERE'S TO GOOD TIMES AHEAD, KAORI.

NEXT ONE WEEK FRIENDS...

THE BOUNDARY BETWEEN FRIENDS AND *FRIENDS* IS...

ONE WEEK FRIENDS 4

MATCHA HAZUKI

Translation/Adaptation: Amanda Haley

Lettering: Bianca Pistillo

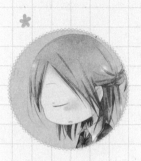

ONE WEEK FRIENDS Volume 4 ©2013 Matcha Hazuki/ SQUARE ENIX CO., LTD. First published in Japan in 2013 by SQUARE ENIX CO., LTD. English translation rights arranged with SQUARE ENIX CO., LTD. and Yen Press, LLC through Tuttle-Mori Agency, Inc.

English translation © 2018 by SQUARE ENIX CO., LTD.

Yen Press
1290 Avenue of the Americas
New York, NY 10104

Visit us at yenpress.com
facebook.com/yenpress
twitter.com/yenpress
yenpress.tumblr.com
instagram.com/yenpress

First Yen Press Edition: September 2018

Yen Press is an imprint of Yen Press, LLC.
The Yen Press name and logo are trademarks of Yen Press, LLC.

Library of Congress Control Number: 2017954140

ISBNs: 978-0-316-44743-0 (paperback)
       978-0-316-44744-7 (ebook)

10 9 8 7 6 5 4 3 2 1

WOR

Printed in the United States of America

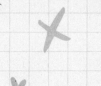
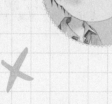

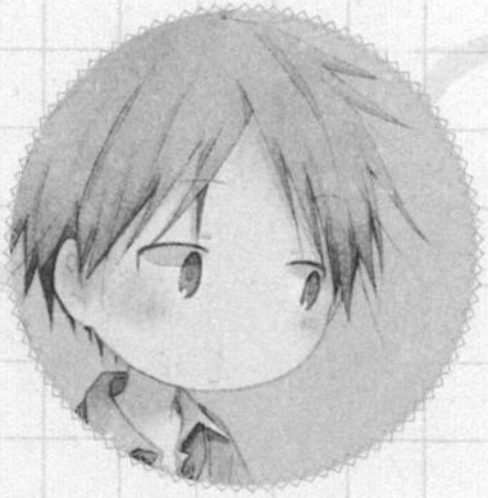